Sentinel

Chad Ballard

This book is a work of fiction. All characters in this novel are fictitious. Any resemblance to actual events or locales or persons, living or dead, is entirely coincidental.

Sentinel: Book One of The Ashen Court
Copyright © 2015 by Chad Ballard

Cover Art by Lindsey Burcar

eISBN: 978-1-943670-26-9
Print ISBN: 978-1-943670-94-9
First Edition: 2015
Printed in the United States of America

To my mom. You taught me to read. You taught me to write. You've been my biggest supporter in everything I've ever done. I can never repay that. I love you. This is for you.

Table of Contents

Chapter 1

"Dead."

For what seemed like the hundredth time that afternoon, Callan's wooden sword clattered to the ground. An instant later, a similar sword slapped into his left knee, and then into his right elbow. The point of the other sword then found itself pressed against the soft flesh of the boy's throat.

With a scowl, Callan turned and grabbed the wooden sword from the red earth and spun to face his opponent. For a moment, he studied the older man. Close-cropped, dark hair. A neatly trimmed beard with flecks of gray beginning to show. There was a shadow of a smile playing at the edges of his mouth as he twirled his blade and opened his arms wide, inviting Callan to advance on him one more time. Callan wanted to say no. He wanted to go back to the bookshelves that lined his room. Instead, he brushed strands of long, dark hair from his eyes and moved toward his uncle once more.

The boy's first blow, a slash at his much taller opponent's knees, was knocked aside with ease. His second, a thrust toward the man's midsection, met the same fate. Callan swung high, aiming for his uncle's shoulder, then lower, at his elbow. Next, he sliced at the other arm in an attempt to unbalance his uncle. With each successive attack, he became more confident and more fluid. The basics of swordsmanship he had been taught since he could hold a weapon began to manifest themselves by instinct rather than through any direct thought on Callan's part. He attacked his uncle's elbows, knees, shoulders, thighs, thrust at his stomach and midsection, with only the briefest of pauses separating each strike.

The group of people who had gathered to watch the training session went largely unnoticed. They were faceless phantoms at the edges of his vision, not people. Their cheers and exclamations of excitement were but background noise, drowning out the sounds of Callan's ragged breathing and muting the solid *thunk* of sword against sword.

"Name the last ten lords of Dragon's Keep, not including your father." Tarryn spoke evenly, as if he were having a conversation over dinner, not staving off attacks by his young nephew.

The names and titles of dozens of long-dead ancestors tumbled their way into Callan's mind, in no particular order. Therring Axehand, Bertrand Iceheart, Revig the Broad. Every relative that had controlled what was now his father's seat flashed through his head.

In that passing moment of thought, Tarryn batted his nephew's sword hard to the left and reached out with his right foot, kicking Callan's legs out from under him. The boy dropped the sword again and sprawled on the hard-packed earth. From his back, he stared up at the blue mountain sky, marred only by a single white imperfection. The voices from the crowd were no longer white noise, but whispered conversations intermingled with some outright chuckles. Frustrated, Callan slammed his fists into the ground and moved to sit up. Instead, he once again found the wooden point of a sword pressed against his throat.

"Dead again, Callan." Tarryn smiled and extended his hand to his nephew. Callan waved him off, though, and stood on his own. The smile sliding off his face, Tarryn continued, "You have to be able to think while you fight. If a stray thought freezes you up like that, you'll get killed every time. How many people were watching us?"

When Callan began to turn his head and make a count, Tarryn grabbed his by the chin and forced his head back around so that they were once again face to face. He scowled still, but his voice was much friendlier when he said, "There were nine. Pay attention to your surroundings at all times. If you can see them and what they're doing, without letting them distract you, your opponent can't use them against you."

Callan lowered his eyes to his boots and took a deep breath, nodding toward the ground. To his laces, he said, "I'm sorry. I'll do better next time, Uncle."

The older man smiled and ruffled Callan's hair, bringing a flush of embarrassment to the boy's face. "I know you will," he said, unbuckling his chest plate and sword belt. "Now, take these up to my quarters. Your father will want to speak with you afterwards, I'm sure."

Tarryn tossed the bundle to Callan and strode off, calling for a horse to be brought to him. Callan supposed that he meant to go hunting in the mountains, or perhaps cliff climbing. His uncle may have even had a woman to find. He had always been a free spirit, more inclined to enjoying himself than ruling over his lands. It was the reason he had abdicated his lordship, and given the position to Callan's father.

He turned and trudged through the pre-noon sunshine, slipping and sliding through the mud left over from the rain of the week past. The crowd had dispersed by this point, leaving him to walk to the castle on his own. Tarryn's sword and armor were heavy, and the long walk up the many flights of stairs to the man's quarters would be tiresome. However, Tarryn assured Callan that hard work built character, so he was forbidden to ask for help in the chore.

He passed guards on his way. The younger, more eager to please soldiers bowed to him. The older, experienced ones nodded or waved, usually with a smile or a few kind words. Just about everyone else ignored him. That was fine with him. Callan wanted nothing more than to get this job done for his uncle and go about the rest of his day.

When he reached the large double doors that housed the living quarters of the castle, one of the passing townspeople was nice enough to hold one door open for him. He thanked the man and stumbled into the torch-lit confines of his father's castle.

The heavy breastplate was the most difficult piece to carry, as far as weight went. It was built for someone of his uncle's height and size. Callan was more than a head shorter and much lighter than the older man. The longsword was problematic as well. The tip of the sword's scabbard dragged and bounced on the stone floor and up the many steps that Callan climbed. He stumbled on occasion, scraping his elbows and knuckles on the walls. Once, he slipped and hit his knee hard on the sharp edges of the stairs. After he realized that none of his uncle's things were damaged, though, he grimaced and stood before continuing his trudge to the top level of the castle.

His task took some time, but eventually Callan reached the floor his uncle's quarters were on. Callan stopped before the simple wooden door of his uncle's bedroom and knocked, just to make sure no servants were cleaning or changing his sheets. No one answered, so he walked in and placed the sword and armor on the small bed that his uncle kept. At that point, he heard raised voices from down the hall. He left the bed chamber quickly, closing the door softly behind him.

There were only a handful of rooms in the same corridor as Tarryn's quarters. His parent's chambers were there, as were the quarters of his father's personal servants and retainers. Callan's own chambers were on the floor directly below, so he was surprised to hear his own name yelled from down the hall. The voices immediately hushed, though, making him believe they were talking about him rather than calling for him.

Confused, he crept down the hall, straining his ears and craning his neck in an attempt to catch more of the conversation. He was only certain of one thing: one of the voices, the one that had yelled his name, was his father. Lord Balen of the Dragon's Keep was obviously taking part in some heated conversation with one of his trusted advisors. It must have been a trusted advisor, for Balen would never have stood for anyone else getting in a shouting match with him.

As Callan snuck toward the voices, he realized the argument came from his father's war room, across the hall from his parents' chambers and directly above Callan's own room. The door was slightly ajar, with a thin beam of torchlight coming through the small crack. Callan moved to his hands and knees and crawled toward the door, peeking through the space between the door and the wall.

He immediately saw the broad back of his father, wearing casual clothing, leading Callan to believe this meeting was impromptu rather than planned. Across from Balen, and facing Callan was, as Callan had guessed, his father's most trusted friend and advisor. General Virgil, one of the most seasoned and renowned soldiers in the entirety of Aelathil, scowled at Balen.

"My Lord, are you telling me you actually want him and his soldiers holed up here?"

Balen answered just as loudly as he had been earlier, "Do you distrust him? Do you distrust his captains and generals?"

Virgil leaned forward, supporting himself on the table with one hand while rubbing at his tired eyes with the other. He responded, "It isn't that I don't trust him. He's young, and I don't know him. I do, however, know most of his generals and captains. I trained some of them. Ask your brother. They aren't made of the same stuff that they used to be. Their men don't respect them."

Balen sighed and cut his general off. "He is your *king*, Virgil. Your trust in him should be implicit."

The general shook his head and tapped his fist on the table, loudly enough to be heard from where Callan was hiding. "We have every reason to be suspicious of him, especially if he's found out about our involvement with Ravitch!"

Balen held up his hand to silence Virgil and spoke quietly. "Murdock and Dastynn should beat the king here by a few days. There isn't any use in making decisions before they show up with more information. You're dismissed, Virgil."

The general nodded and bowed, before sweeping up his cloak and heading toward the door Callan hid behind. Callan stood up quickly, wiping the dust off his knees and scrambling to act as if he were about to knock on the door. Instead, the door flew open and struck him on the forehead, knocking him back to the ground.

A deep laugh sounded above him. Through the veil of stars that danced before his eyes, he saw the bald head of General Virgil. The large man grabbed him under the arms and helped him to his feet, ruffling his hair, just as Tarryn had done earlier. Callan scowled.

Through a wide smile, the general said, "Sorry about the bump, Cal. Your father is waiting for you inside."

Callan nodded and grunted. He walked past the general and into the war room. When he entered, he found himself facing the broad back of his father. Balen turned around at his entry and smiled, his white teeth showing through his beard.

"Good morning, Callan," he said. "I hope that you didn't bloody your uncle too badly this morning."

Callan laughed, causing Balen to chuckle and wrap his large arm around his son's shoulders.

"Don't worry," Balen assured him, "He's had years and years of practice. You'll get there eventually."

Callan shrugged his shoulders "We'll see. He says that I have problems paying attention to my surroundings and thinking on my toes."

Balen smiled and clapped him on the back once more. "I promise you, he had the same problems when he was your age." He waved his hand then, a clear indication he was changing the subject. "Now! I have an errand I need you to run for me."

"Do I have to?" Callan puffed out his cheeks and sighed before continuing, "I was planning on going riding with Kelaya until dark."

Balan shook his head, grinning again. He answered, "Don't worry, you'll enjoy this more, I promise. You can even bring Kelaya along with you."

Callan must have looked as if he was about to pout, because Balen put up a single finger to silence him. "I need you to go to the blacksmith in town and pick up a package for me. Tell him who you are and pay him with this."

Balen produced a leather pouch from his pocket and tossed it to Callan. Cal very plainly heard the jingling of a large sum of gold. Whatever it was his father had him picking up was obviously worth quite a lot.

Callan nodded and pocketed the gold, already excited to find Kelaya and get on his way to the blacksmith. "I'll have it back soon, Father."

The large man smiled and shooed Callan out of the War room, closing the large door with a dull *thud*, which reverberated up and down the stone halls after Callan.

Sentinel

Chapter 2

"So," asked Kelaya, "what exactly are we going to get?"

Callan shrugged and pulled the hood of his cloak tighter over his face to guard it from the driving winds and drizzle that had recently started up. Why his father hadn't sent one of the servants to get this package was a mystery to Callan, but he must have had his reasons. Maybe the package was so valuable he only trusted Callan to retrieve it. If that was the case, though, he would have sent his brother, Tarryn. More than likely, he knew it was going to rain and wanted to make Callan squirm in the inclement weather.

"Father didn't say what it was," Callan answered. "He only said to pay the blacksmith and bring back the package he gives me."

Kelaya nodded as she pursed her lips in thought. She shook her dark hair, wetting Callan with some of the excess water and making him glad he had decided to bring his cloak along with him. His companion had neglected to do the same and had repeatedly declined Callan's offer to let her wear his.

"Are you sure you don't want my cloak," he asked again? "You look like a drowned cat."

She glowered at him and quickened her pace, splashing some of the puddles behind her onto Callan's pants. It was the little things like that, which made Callan realize why the two of them got along so well. Kelaya never treated him like Balen's son, and she certainly never made him feel like the future Lord of the Dragon's Keep. She knew what it was like to have a father with high stature. Kelaya was, after all, the daughter of General Virgil.

"You know," she retorted, "I really don't think your mother would appreciate you talking to a lady like that."

Callan laughed. "Lady? Show me one of those around here, and I'll show you how to treat her."

She playfully shoved him and continued down the cobbled street, doing her best not to laugh. The two of them passed a handful of townspeople walking to and from various shops in the rain. Normally, some of the more formal residents would have recognized him and bowed. Most though, treated him as the scurries in the rain did on this day; they nodded to him when they passed, just like they did to anyone else on the street. Personally, he preferred it that way. His father had tried very hard to make his people feel like he and his family were one of them, and they should treat all of them like they would any other neighbor.

For the most part, it was the older townspeople who treated Callan and his mother and father formally. They were from a time when Balen's father, or even his grandfather, had ruled the keep. Both of them had died before Callan was born, but from what he had heard, the pair of them had been much more formal and expected those they ruled over to treat them as their superiors. Balen had never subscribed to that way of ruling, and for that, Callan was glad.

Kelaya spoke up, her voice rising to project past the increasing amount of rain, "We had better get moving. This storm is looking like it could get out of hand pretty quickly."

Callan agreed, but did not necessarily want to hurry. All that was awaiting him at the keep was an afternoon full of lessons about history and geography. After that, he would more than likely be forced into another sparring match with his uncle. Two in one day was a sure recipe for aching joints and muscles in the morning.

"You're probably right. We should get this errand over with and get dry as quickly as possible."

"Callan," she said, "you should know by now I'm always right."

So, the two of them scurried through the empty streets, doing their best to dodge the falling drops of rain. Callan knew they were close when he heard the rhythmic ringing of the blacksmith's hammer, banging on an anvil. They followed the noise through the soggy streets of the market without passing the slightest signs of life. Not even a stray dog or cat was on the streets this day. Even though night had not yet fallen, the thunderheads rolling in had already blotted out the sun, bringing a premature darkness to the entire mountainside. So, when the blacksmith's shop finally came into view, the fire from the forge shined like a beacon in the night or a lighthouse on the edge of the sea.

Callan and Kelaya ran to the light, arms held in front of their faces. Both were dripping wet already. They ran to the door of the smithy and hammered on it with closed fists, thudding loudly down the empty streets. A voice called from inside, inviting them in, so the pair stopped their knocking and walked inside.

A heavy heat greeted them. The air was saturated with steam and the labored breathing of the aging blacksmith. His bare, sweat-spotted back was facing the young pair, beneath a soaking wet tail of silvery hair. The much older man turned to them and smiled, revealing numerous missing teeth. Callan knew he had been the keep's best blacksmith for a long time, but had never seen the man in person. He was much older than Callan had imagined. Age spots covered his torso, seemingly in spite of the muscles that rippled beneath his skin.

"Can I do something for ye', kids," asked the smith?

Callan stepped forward and lowered his hood, before asking, "Are you Heen?"

The old man nodded, smiling even more widely. "Aye," he said, "Ye' must be Callan. Your father said ye'd be coming by soon."

Nodding again, Callan looked around the shop for the package he was supposed to be picking up. Horseshoes, chains, plow blades, and unfinished swords covered the walls, along with an assortment of tools, nails, and bolts on the tables. He could see nothing remarkable.

Heen continued, "The box is in the house. Gimme a moment, and I'll bring it right out to ye'."

He disappeared inside then, leaving Callan and Kelaya alone. They stood awkwardly, the only sound the pounding of raindrops on the roof of the building. Callan shifted his weight, shuffling from foot to foot. He'd never been one for meaningless talk and had a hard time keeping the flow of a conversation once it had stalled. Luckily for the both of them, Kelaya had no such problems.

"Can I ask you something?"

Callan nodded and turned to face his friend.

"Your birthday is soon," she said. It was not a question. "Are you ready for the big ceremonies?"

Callan shrugged but answered, "I don't think it's as big a deal as it's made out to be. I'm going to be sixteen. It isn't as if much will change." He smiled and slipped his hands into the warm pockets on the outside of his coat. "Father is ecstatic, though. Once I'm a man, I'll be able to inherit the keep from him, and he can make me his legal heir."

Kelaya laughed. "Not to mention, he gets to marry you off to the highest bidder."

"Don't count on it," Callan replied. "I'll marry when I'm good and ready, not a day before."

A voice from the doorway, interrupted them. "Good luck with that, m'boy. I been watching your folk for a long time. Ye' marry who you're told to. Then ye' smile and bear it. Ye' live with it, too. With a big, big ol' smile."

Chuckling to himself, the old man walked to Callan, carrying a rectangular package in his arms. It was wrapped in brown paper and tied with thin rope. He handed it to Callan, who immediately noticed it was much lighter than it looked. He tucked it under his right armpit and bowed graciously to the blacksmith. In exchange for the package, he gave Heen the purse of coins that his father had given him.

"Thank you," he said. "I'll make sure my father gets this as soon as possible."

Heen smiled and ushered the pair out the door, pocketing the gold as he moved. "Aye, I'm sure. Run along, both of ye'. She'll be a big 'un, this storm."

The storm did not disappoint. The winds had increased drastically, and the rain came down harder than ever. Peals of thunder shook both land and sky while Callan and Kelaya ran through the deserted streets. They were alone in their journey. No one else was foolish enough to brave the increasingly inclement weather.

When they reached the keep, Keyala pounded on the oak doors until the guards inside opened the way for them. Once they were safely inside, Callan noticed a tall woman standing in the darkening hallway. Her face was half-shrouded by shadow, but Callan could see the hints of amusement on her features.

"You didn't have to wait for us, Mother. We were fine."

She smiled and grabbed the package from him, tucking it under her own arm. Callan smiled at her, into the face that looked so much like his own. It was very obvious he took after his mother rather than his father. He and Lilliana shared coal-colored hair and a tan complexion. Both were short and then, whereas Balen was tall and had shoulders as large as the mountains he ruled over. Callan even shared his easy-going temperament with his mother.

She answered, "I did have to, and you know it. Your father and I have very different views on appropriate behavior during the biggest storm of the year." She reached out and mussed his wet hair, causing a scowl to come to his face and a smirk to come to Kelaya's. "Besides," she continued, "I told Kelaya's father I would send her to him as soon as you two got back."

Kelaya nodded curtly and bowed to Callan's mother. "Thank you, Lady Lilliana. I'll find him right away." With that, she disappeared down the hall, her wet boots squelching in the relative quiet of the keep.

Callan called after her, "I'll see you tomorrow, right?"

Kelaya yelled back over her shoulder, "You wish!"

Lilliana grabbed Callan by the shoulder and guided him down the same hallway a way, and then into an adjoining staircase to the left. She said nothing until they reached the stairs. "I'm glad that get along so well with Kelaya, Callan. She seems like a very nice girl."

Callan shrugged, still keeping an eye on the package his mother now held. He had no idea what was in it, never mind why he had been sent to retrieve it. "She isn't so bad," he replied.

"How long have you two been spending time together," she asked?

Callan stopped on the stairs, just ahead of his mother and turned to face her, a quizzical frown stamped on his face. "Why the sudden interest in Kelaya?"

"Oh, your father hasn't told you?" She sighed, "Well, I should let him explain it to you."

Callan stood firm and crossed his arms, barring her way up the stairs as she tried to brush past him. "I don't think so. What are you talking about?"

Lilliana tried for a few more moments to wriggle past Callan, but the stone staircase was too narrow, and he was planted above her. After a while, she relented and her shoulders sagged. Her body language screamed defeat, but her eyes showed her true emotion: satisfaction.

"Well," she started, "as you know, when you become a man, you take on the responsibilities of one."

When Callan offered no response, she continued, "This includes raising your own family."

This time, Callan nodded and scowled, drawing his eyebrows to a single point in the middle of his forehead. He knew full well that he was expected to marry after his sixteenth birthday, but he had neglected to give the prospect much thought. The date of his manhood ceremonies had approached too quickly for him to think about. Callan had always assumed his parents would at least let him have some input in choosing his future bride, and he did not like where the conversation was headed.

Lilliana continued without missing a beat. "So, your father and I have decided that, in your best interests, and as a favor to General Virgil, you will be married to Kelaya one week after your birthday."

Callan's jaw dropped. Kelaya was his friend, sure, and she was really the only person of his own age he had spent any serious amount of time with. She was nice enough, but she could also be incredibly obnoxious. She could make him laugh, but she could also make him want to pull his hair out.

He wanted so badly to voice his displeasure to his mother, to tell her how big a mistake she and his father had made. He especially wanted to say he would never, ever marry Kelaya. Instead, he said, "I...wha-what? I don't... Why? I won't!"

His mother scowled, the amusement abandoning her eyes quickly. "You will," she said. "I imagine Virgil is telling her the same thing right now. You have a few weeks to get used to the idea, and I'm sure that in time, you'll come to care for her, and maybe even love her."

Callan started to protest again and more eloquently, but he was interrupted by the voice of a shouting guardsman at the base of the spiral staircase.

"My lady," he shouted, "There's a group of men out here in the storm! They're asking to see either you or Lord Balen. They look serious."

Lilliana turned on her heel and swept down the stairs, Callan hard on her heels. He had heard his father talking about men coming to visit, but they had not been expected for a few days, at least. Either they had made excellent time, or this was a different group entirely. When they reached the doors, Callan's mother motioned to grant the group entry. As the men came into view, Callan got a good idea of what he and Kelaya must have looked like not long ago. The huddled group before him looked as if they had been dropped into a river and dragged along the bottom.

All of them, save one, were unremarkable looking. The other stood out only for his size. He was easily a head taller than the rest of his group, and his shoulders were wider set than even Callan's father. In fact, this man was the only person Callan had ever seen that made Balen seem averagely-sized. However, the big man did not step forward or speak. Instead, the man at the forefront of the group raised his voice.

"Lady Lilliana," he said, "we must speak with your husband. This is urgent."

"Of course," she answered. "Come in and dry yourselves off. Callan, go and get your father. Tell him to meet these men in his war room."

Chapter 3

Over the next few weeks, Callan took an immediate liking to the group. They were, for the most part, soldiers of fortune. Mercenaries who went where the money was and took jobs for the highest bidder. At the moment, the highest bidder was the man who had spoken up the night they had arrived. According to the mercenaries, he was a powerful mage who had known Balen for some time. Callan had not yet spoken to him or seen him perform any magic, but had watched him closely. He had never met a mage before and was incredibly curious.

The man that Callan had spoken to the most was, to the chagrin of his parents, the leader of the mercenary band. His name was Lys, and he reminded Callan in many ways of his uncle. Both were well-travelled, easy going, quick to share a smile, and if the stories were true, expert swordsmen. The two of them sat together at the feast to open Callan's manhood ceremonies. For now, most people were enjoying food, drink, and talk. Lys was currently reaching the bottom of his fourth glass of ale on the day, and was loudly telling Callan what he knew about the mage who had hired him.

"His name's Murdock," said the mercenary. "I haven't seen him do much magic, but rumor has it he's pretty powerful, especially for his age. His kind don't usually come into a lot of power until they're full of wrinkles and bad memories. He's quite a bit younger than I am."

Callan was unsure of how to take that statement. Just looking at Lys, he had no idea how old he was. He had a youthful face, but carried himself as if he shouldered a large burden. The hair on his temples was gray, as well, in contrast with the light brown that covered the rest of his head and cheeks.

"You've seen him do magic then," asked Callan? "He can really do it?"

Lys chuckled into his mug. "Aye, I've seen him. He lit a fire for us one night when it was wet. He cleaned some water for us when we were down to just dirty stuff. He even healed one of the boys' legs after he fell off a horse."

Smiling from ear to ear, Callan looked around the room, trying to find Kelaya. She would have loved talking to Lys, hearing his stories and talking to someone who had been all over Aelathil and the rest of Revaren as he had. He had only seen her sparingly over the last weeks, though, and had not spoken to her at all. According to his mother, she had been told about the marriage and was unhappy about it as Callan was.

Lys continued speaking while Callan looked for Kelaya, so the young man tuned back into the conversation so he did not appear rude.

"And the big guy," Lys said, "in all of the armor. He's a paladin, one of the battle mages out of Immeo. Murdock says his name's Dastynn."

"Murdock says?"

Lys nodded and took another swig of ale. "He doesn't talk. I haven't heard him say a word in the weeks we've been travelling. He points a lot, and grunts. I checked one night while he was asleep, so I know he's got a tongue. I don't think he's dumb or mute, so I'm not sure why he doesn't talk."

Callan's eyes immediately moved to the big man, Dastynn. The hall was crowded with people, but he was an easy man to spot. He was enormous, standing like a giant oak among saplings. His long, red hair was tied back behind his head in a formal knot, and his arms were placed across his chest in a relaxed manner. His bright eyes surveyed the room. Callan had to wonder why he was so alert. No one in their right mind would even consider attacking him. Aside from his great size, he wore ornate blue and white plate armor and carried the most impressive weapon Callan had ever seen. So interesting was it, he had to ask Lys to explain it for him.

"What exactly is that on his hip? It looks almost like a hammer, but not like one I've ever seen."

Lys answered after finishing off his drink and calling for another from one of the servants. "It's a hammer, alright. A heavy one, too. At the Colleges of Magic, the paladins grow their own from some kind of crystal. That's why it looks like a big, blue gem: it is one. The color has something to do with his rank or standing with the Colleges. I'm not sure what exactly."

Nodding, Callan resumed looking at the big paladin. The hammer must have been incredibly heavy for someone, even of Dastynn's size and stature, to wield it. He could only imagine the work it had taken to master such a tool.

As he looked, Dastynn glanced in his direction and caught him staring. Instead of being offended, he smiled broadly and lifted his gauntleted hand to wave. Callan waved back, suddenly at ease. Surely Lys had made some mistake. No war-hardened battle mage would be so friendly to a stranger.

Seeing Callan wave, Balen stood from his seat at the head of their large dining table. The entire hall quieted to allow him to speak. His booming voice carried to every ear in the room. Even those who were intoxicated stopped their drinking to listen to him. "This feast marks the beginning of a very special event for my family! My son, Callan," he said, "will be a man in two days' time!"

A ragged shout came from the throats of many who had taken part too heavily in the free drink. Lys and Callan's Uncle Tarryn were among the loudest. His mother did not cheer but smiled proudly, as did his father. Callan caught sight of Murdock and Dastynn each applauding politely.

"As such," continued Balen, "he will be made my heir to this keep and the surrounding lands!"

More cheers followed. Callan felt uncomfortable as every eye in the hall turned to him. Sweat trickled from his forehead, and his hands trembled. He did his best to bring a smile to his lips, but he imagined it looked more pained than pleased. Lys must have felt the same way, because he reached out and clapped Callan on the back.

"Relax, kid." He spoke quietly, just loud enough for Callan to hear. "This is a party. Have a good time."

Callan did his best to take the sell-sword's advice. He unclenched his hands and relaxed the muscles in his face. He also stretched out his shoulders, trying to relieve some of the tension that had built up in the base of his neck.

In the meantime, Balen cleared his voice to silence the cheers. "So, without further ado, I would like to call my son to the front of the hall so he may perform his first acts as my heir!"

Even though he knew well beforehand that this moment was coming, he still dreaded it. It was tradition among the lineage of the Red Hills that, before his sixteenth birthday, the heir to his father's holdings would preside over the marriage of a couple from the village. Normally, he would have taken part in the marriage with his future bride at his side, but Kelaya was nowhere to be…

There she was.

Through the throngs of people, he spotted her, dressed just as formally as he was. She wore a gown of red and black to match the colors of Callan's family. Her brunette hair flowed down her shoulders and back like a river, practically glowing in the torchlight.

Her clothing matched his own very well. They wore the same colors, but where her dress was predominantly red, his tunic and breeches were mostly black, with trimmings of crimson. She smiled at him with one half of her mouth when they made eye contact and, for the first time, he realized how beautiful she was. The thought made him feel very foolish.

As he approached her, he returned her smile. "You look great, Kelaya. Really."

She rolled her eyes and playfully shoved him on the shoulder. She may have been upset by the marriage proposal, but she was acting just like her old self. She replied, "You don't look so bad yourself, m'lord."

"Oh, don't you even start calling me that."

She smirked as Callan's father approached the two of them. The crowd had become more boisterous in the short interim, so he was forced to raise his hands above his head once more to calm them down.

"Now," he said, "will our engaged couple please come forward?"

They did so, fairly quickly and relatively informally. The groom was a well-dressed townsman whom Callan had never met before. He had been taught their names and occupations beforehand, though, so he knew his name was Ephram and that he was a worker in the lumber mill on the outskirts of the town.

His wife, who was clearly a few years his junior, was dressed in a much more formal manner than her soon-to-be husband. She wore a very fine white dress with an expensive looking veil. Callan was not surprised by this, though. She was the only daughter of one of the wealthiest families around, the owners of the mill that Ephram worked for.

Once they stood before he and Kelaya, Callan spoke up, his voice dripping with uncertainty. "Ephram the woodsman, do you take Serra the miller's daughter to be your wife?"

He nodded and smiled, answering, "I do, my lord."

Callan then turned to the young woman who was to marry Ephram. "And, Serra, do you promise to be a faithful and dutiful wife to Ephram?"

She smiled demurely and, meek as a lamb, nodded toward Callan and Kelaya. "I do, my lord."

Kelaya then stepped forward to do her part in the ceremony. She untied a piece of red satin from around her wrist and held it out to the couple. Ephram extended his left arm while his bride extended her right arm. Kelaya tied their wrists together with the satin before stepping back to stand by Callan's side.

She raised her voice then, sounding surer of herself and more in-charge than Callan had ever heard. "Then may Anashti keep you safe and grant you healthy children. May Chytae keep you well-fed. May Merrick bring you peace and happiness, and may Sabriel leave you be until your time to go."

She smiled and spread her arms wide, presenting the couple to the crowd while Callan spoke up to end the process. "You are now pronounced man and wife!"

A raucous roar went up from the assembled masses as the newlyweds turned and ran down the hall and out the doors. By the time they had made their exit, Balen already stood behind Callan and Kelaya. He clapped the pair on the back, a large smile peeking out from behind his facial hair.

"You both did very well," he said. "Kelaya, your father asked me to send you to him. He'd like to speak with you."

She nodded and thanked him before making her way to her father. Balen then turned to Callan and continued, "I'd like you to meet me in the armory as quickly as possible."

He left without another word, with Callan alone at the front of the hall. With a quick scan of the room, Callan caught a glimpse of his uncle walking out of the hall, followed closely by Murdock and Dastynn. He spied his father's broad shoulders leaving shortly after. Most curious of all, he saw Lys leaving just behind his father, clearly in heated conversation with him.

Callan could not contain himself. He had to know what was so important he leave his own coming-of-age ceremony. He looked across the room to Kelaya and her father, whom had returned to their meals and conversation. When she caught his gaze, Kelaya shot him a questioning, and slightly worried glance. Callan should only shrug his shoulders and make his way to the armory. He exited the hall and made for the stone staircase that led to the arms store beneath the keep. Each step he took, he noticed a slight drop in temperature. The Red Hills were often a chilly place, but the ground beneath it was even more so.

The dungeons were housed near the armory, although they were currently empty. Callan had always questioned the wisdom of keeping a large store of weapons near the convicted criminals, but his parents and uncle always laughed him off.

Since Callan had been old enough to ask about it, Tarryn had replied, "I guess if they're dumb enough to try escaping, they at least deserve a fighting chance."

The memory made Callan smile despite the chill that crept into his hands and feet. By the time he had reached the normally barred doors of the armory, he could see the fine mist that was his breath spreading out in front of his face. The thick doors were hanging wide open, allowing him to enter quickly when he arrived. The male members of his family, along with Dastynn, Murdock, and Lys, all stood, waiting for him.

On the floor before all of them was a large package, wrapped in brown. Callan recognized it immediately as the one he had picked up days earlier. Balen gestured toward it, clearly wanting Callan to pick it up.

"This is for your manhood day," said his father. "Treat it well, and it will do the same for you."

Callan knelt to the ground and began to unwrap the long, rectangular package. Beneath the brown wrapping and twine that held it together was an ornate wooden box. Carved into the box was an intricate mosaic, illustrating the Dragon's Keep and the surrounding lands. Golden clasps held the box shut from the front. Callan unclipped them gently and opened the box, swinging it back on its hinges.

Inside the box, laying atop a bed of red satin, was the most impressive sword Callan had ever seen. It was slightly larger than any he had held before, and definitely too long for him to comfortably wear. His uncle must have known that Callan would notice these things because he spoke up just as Callan's eyes were lighting up with wonder.

"It's going to be a little big for a while," he said. "You'll grow into it eventually. Besides that, it's called a hand-and-a-half sword. It's supposed to look a little bigger than you're used to. You can use it in one hand with a shield or you can hold it with both hands."

Callan could only nod. On some level, he registered what he was being told. Most of his attention, though, was fixed on the shining blade that lay before him. The grip was beautifully made. The handle was a deep black, inlaid with intricate silver designs that were laid flush with each other and the rest of the handle. The silver lining continued to the pommel, where it was wrapped around a blood red, stone jewel. The cross guard was silver as well, but seemed very simple in comparison to the rest of the blade. Arms of silver extended to each side, created a cross shape. At the far end of each arm was another circular red jewel.

The sword shone in the torchlight that lit the armory, its deadly edge gleaming like a beacon in the gloom. He could only imagine being able to spar with this work of —

— A sharp whistling carried through the air near Callan's head. He recognized it clearly, as he'd been hearing it in training with his uncle for years now. On reflex, he grabbed the hilt of his new blade and swung it behind him. With the flat of the sword, he blocked a blow at his head and locked guards with his assailant.

Smiling widely at him from beyond the pair of swords was Lys. Behind him were Callan's father and uncle, smiling just as broadly as Lys was. The immediate fear of being cleaved in two had subsided a bit, allowing Callan to think.

He slowly realized this was all a part of his trials of manhood. The first was his acceptance of the marriage his parents arranged. He didn't do it gracefully, but he'd eventually relented. The second was his performance of the marriage ritual, which he'd done very well. The third, and final, test was that of armed combat. The battle had to be against someone who was not directly related and more than one outside witness was needed. That explained why the three travelers were here.

It did not, however, explain why they were having his test in the bowls of the keep instead of in the court before anyone who wanted to watch. Normally, this sparring match would take place at the end of the feast that was still going on up in the great hall. Callan could not for the life of him figure out why they were being so secluded.

The thought was shoved from his head by another swipe of Lys' sword. Callan batted it away and retreated, circling slowly backward around the dimly lit room. Lys advanced, just as slowly, a smirk planted firmly on his face. He struck out at Callan's midsection, his blade flashing through the air like the sting of a wasp. Callan sidestepped and swung horizontally at his assailant's shoulder. Almost faster than Callan could follow, Lys blocked the attack and stopped Callan's sword dead in its path.

The sheer impact and force of the block jarred Callan through to his bones. He could practically feel his teeth start to shake loose. When he locked eyes with Lys, he noticed that the smirk was gone. Etched there now was the stony, silent face of a man who had taken the lives of many others. He was paid to do this sort of thing. Callan had never even been in a real fight before. How could he even hope to win this battle?

Lys went back on the offensive, taking harder and harder swings at various parts of Callan's body. His face, his chest, his arms, his legs, even his back were the targets of various killing or disarming blows. The first few shots were unsettlingly powerful and strong enough to hurt Callan's hands. The next few caused him to lose all feeling in his outer extremities. As the fight wore on, his arms were so tired he could hardly hold his sword up to defend himself. Still, the mercenary came on, seemingly unfazed by the amount of energy he expended.

Lys' attacks had become nothing more than blurs. His movements seemed wild and without meaning for all the defense that Callan could make against them. They were perfect and indefensible.

Callan grunted and cried out at a sudden pain in his toes. He looked down to see that Lys had planted the heel of his boot firmly on top of Callan's foot. His eyes widened in surprise at the cheap shot, but Callan could do nothing to plan for what came next. Lys lifted his knee and drove it into Callan's groin. The young man's air left his lungs in a *whoosh,* and his new sword clattered to the ground.

Callan's father and uncle nodded to the other three before they turned and walked out together.

Chapter 4

Callan awoke the next morning with a headache that threatened to tear him in half. He could feel his pulse behind his eyes, and he was sure the knot on his temple could be seen from atop the highest of the Red Hills. It took his eyes a moment to adjust to the light in the room, but when they did, he saw the smiling face of Lys staring right back at him. The mercenary gave a friendly wave and walked to Callan's bedside.

Lys clapped him on the shoulder, intensifying the pounding sensations in his head. His smile widened, and he asked, "How are you feeling, kid?"

Callan scowled up at him. "You cheated," he said.

Lys ignored him. "That's a pretty good lump you have on your head there. I hope your lady doesn't get too angry with me."

Callan was having none of his small talk. He glared up at the older man and said, "You cheated. That was the most important test of my life and you cheated me."

Lys shook his head and crossed his arms, looking down at Callan. The smile slipped off his face. "There is no such thing as cheating in battle. You do what you have to do to survive." He reached out with one hand and patted Callan on the shoulder again, this time more gently. "You didn't need to beat me to pass your little test. Your father only told me you had to show you knew the basics of swordplay. You did that, and then some." "So," he finished, "you passed with flying colors."

Callan could hardly believe what he was hearing. All of the stories he had been told since he was little involved winning the final manhood trial. He had planned on facing some knight under his father's command, who would probably let him win in the end. He never expected to get knocked around, exhausted, hit in the groin, and then knocked unconscious by someone he had only known for a few weeks. It had never occurred to him he would be able to lose the fight and still pass the trial. He smiled up at Lys.

"Thank you."

Lys shrugged and turned to make his way out the door. "Don't thank me," he said. "I'm just trying to teach you how to stay alive. I've taken a liking to you, kid. I don't wanna see you get cut up."

He left then, leaving Callan to think about what he had said. Never in his life had he ever dreamed he would meet, let alone befriend, someone like Lys. It was a strange feeling and he was sure his mother would never approve, but Callan was thrilled by the prospect.

The head of the mercenary poked around the doorframe, a playful smile on his face. "Oh! I almost forgot. You should probably hurry and get cleaned up so you can go down to the yard."

"Why," Callan asked?

Lys answered, "The king will be here to wish you a happy birthday in a couple of hours. I'll be leaving before he gets here. Be sure to give him a hug from me."

With that, he was gone for good. Callan's jaw nearly came unhinged at the thought of the king coming to visit not only his father for political reasons, but for the purpose of wishing him a happy sixteenth birthday. So excited was he, that Callan did not register what Lys had said about leaving. He remembered the conversation between Balen and General Virgil, though. Something about this visit had upset the general and Callan had no idea what it was. No matter the reason, he was not going to let it spoil his birthday.

Callan got out of bed and dressed himself quickly, making sure to wear his best outfit, a red tunic and black trousers, worth more than nearly every other article of clothing he owned. He strapped on black boots, shined well enough he could see his face in them. He made to leave, but stopped just short of the door. A smirk came to his face as realization struck him. The young man looked around his room quickly, taking notice of nearly everything in it.

His large, mostly unadorned bed, a dresser with sleeves and pant legs sticking out of too-full drawers, along with some trinkets he had collected over the past few years that lay on top. Miniature carved knights, horses, and lords his uncle had made for him were the most common item. They were arranged carefully in scenes of mock battle. Next to them was a small stick he'd crafted into the general shape of a sword. Kelaya had one to match. Callan smiled when he saw it. Now that he had a real sword, he wouldn't need the fake. He saw the sword next, leaning up against the dresser, still in its scabbard. The wooden box it had been in was on the floor next to it.

He strode proudly and quickly to the dresser, where his sword had been placed after he had been knocked unconscious. He picked the blade up gently, scabbard and all, and belted it around his waist. With a flourish, he spun to face the large mirror that was fastened to his wall, so that he could take in his new image. He had to admit, the sword and fine clothing made him look quite dashing. Callan knew that the blade was a little bit big on him, but that hardly diminished his desire to wear it in front of the king.

Callan's hair, however, was too unkempt to be seen by royalty. He grabbed a bone-handled comb from his bedside table and smoothed it out, doing his best to make it look good, even though it fell halfway down his back. He had taken a large amount of pride in his hair, since he was young. Callan had never once let anyone but his mother cut it, and only then to keep it looking neat. Once he was finished combing it out, he tied it back with a thin piece of twine. He felt that tying his hair back made him look older, and he wanted to look as old as possible, especially on his birthday.

Once he was satisfied with his appearance, he practically strutted out of his room and into the halls of the keep. He passed almost no one on his way outside. The keep was normally much less crowded when there was a festival or party going on, but Callan had very rarely seen it this empty. Every soldier, noble, officer, and member of the staff must have been in the yard, awaiting the arrival of King Ramsey. Callan could understand their excitement. Very few, if any, had actually seen their ruler in person. Callan had never even seen him, and he would be one of Ramsey's Lords when he was older.

Callan took each staircase two steps at a time in his hurry to get to the party that was surely happening outside. He completely forgot decorum in his rush to get out of the keep. After all, there was no one to see him make a fool of himself. His run was made even more awkward by the too-long sword that swung at his hip and knocked against his ankles, feet, and the stone steps he sprinted down.

When he finally reached the doors that led to the yard, he shouldered them open and stepped outside. He was almost bowled off his feet by the staggering amount of stimuli that assaulted his senses the moment he stepped out of the door. People were talking, cheering, singing, and dancing for as far as Callan could see. Everyone was dressed in their absolute finest. Men wore various types and colors of tunics and cloaks. Women were dressed in some of the most brightly colored dresses Callan had ever laid eyes on.

It was immediately apparent that people had come from far away to see the king. Most of those who lived near the Dragon's Keep or served Callan's father wore red and black to formal events, much as Callan was currently doing. Here, though, Callan saw blues, greens, and yellows, the colors of every renowned family within leagues.

Some were even adorned in the white and deep purple of the crown. Normally, dressing in the colors of his majesty was frowned deeply upon. However, when he visited a part of the nation he rarely frequented, exceptions were made. The citizens were, in fact, wearing the clothes as a celebration of Ramsey's arrival, not as a challenge to his authority. As far as Callan had been taught, they would be tolerated for the duration of the king's stay.

He walked through the crowd, doing his best to make his way politely and without stepping on any toes. When needed, he gently shoved aside a shoulder or elbow and added a quiet apology. Callan was rather short, admittedly, and he could hardly fault the party-goers for not always noticing him when he walked by. Besides that, not all of them were local and only very few of them would have known what he looked like. No, today he was not looking for the usual niceties that came with being the son of Balen. He would fully content himself with trying to fit in among the commoners until the king arrived.

It seemed that most of the crowd, both commoners and nobles, gravitated in a single direction. Their curiosity fueled Callan's own, and he fell into step with those around him.

"There's some kind o' wizard over 'ere," said one.

Another answered him, "Arlas said 'e was doin' some kind o' show. Arlas' mouth 'as got 'im in trouble before, though. We'll see."

Callan fell into step behind the two men, his interest piqued. The only *wizard* he knew of was Murdock, the mage who had come looking to speak with his father. He hadn't yet had the chance to speak with him at any length, and Murdock certainly hadn't performed any magic while Callan had been present.

They eventually came upon Murdock, standing atop a stack of wooden crates and surrounded by a large crowd. He wore fine robes, white with a golden trim. The robes were hooded, but the hood was pulled back, revealing all of Murdock's features. The mage's arms were spread wide, and he smiled more widely than Callan had ever seen him smile. As Callan and the rest of the group approached, he spoke to the crowd.

"I don't do this often. Not for a crowd, anyway." He shrugged the robes from his shoulders and handed them to one of the mercenaries who had come with him. The large, bearded man stood off to the side, looking like some kind of assistant. He didn't look pleased to be there. Callan suspected he was being paid.

"From what I understand," continued Murdock, "most of you have never seen any form of magic before. I promise you, nothing I do here will have the potential to harm anyone."

Callan stole a glance at the crowd around him. Most of the nobles and those who had been raised with the advantage of an education knew that magic was real and had heard quite a lot about the good and bad it had done for the Aelathil and the entire continent of Revaren. A lot of the citizens in attendance, however, were not educated. All that they knew of magic was the bedtime stories their parents had told them for generations. They were of the belief that the mages of Immeo were dark sorcerers, capable of corrupting everything they came into contact with.

Murdock seemed to realize they were inherently suspicious of him. Callan crossed his arms and eyed the mage, curious how he was going to answer those suspicions.

The mage gestured to the base of the box he stood on, to a bowl filled with what seemed to be water. He extended his arms and pointed his palms toward the bowl. Even from where he stood, Callan could hear a rushing sound that seemed to come from both Murdock and the bowl. It started faintly, almost too faintly to tell, but Callan was almost sure he could see the bowl begin to quiver and shake.

Then, from the center of the bowl, a tendril of water snaked into the sky. It wavered from side to side as if it had taken on a mind of its own. A handful of onlookers gasped, while others took a step or two back, clearly not sure what to think of what they were seeing. Most, including Callan, stared wide-eyed and open-mouthed. Murdock was clearly amused by the varying reactions. His smile grew, and he seemed to loosen up a bit.

The tendril of water split in two in response to a movement by Murdock. The two halves wrapped themselves around each other, forming a helix shape that rotated and twisted itself above the bowl. Murdock had the water dancing around itself more gracefully than Callan had ever seen a person dance. The audience was silent. There was no applause, and it seemed as if everyone had quit breathing all together. The only sound came from the magically manipulated water that sloshed quietly in the wooden bowl and in the air.

For that few moments, Callan forgot all the stresses of the last few days. He forgot he was officially the heir to the Dragon's Keep, he forgot his parents were forcing him into a betrothal he was completely opposed to, and he forgot the king of Aelathil came to wish him a happy birthday. All that existed for him was the mage and his water, dancing to their own rhythm.

Murdock held the absolute attention of the crowd. Callan completely lost track of time as he watched the performance. Once the initial awe wore off, he tried to get a better look at Murdock. He was much older than Callan, that was to be sure, but he was clearly not of the same age as Balen. He had dark hair, without a single trace of gray. His face smooth, save for his brow. Callan's mother had often said he would end up with a wrinkled brow. He scowled too often when he was thinking or when he was frustrated, she said.

The mage had often been quiet and reserved in his visits. Now, though, he seemed to be genuinely enjoying himself. Callan could not tell if he was acting for the benefit of the audience. Callan would not have been surprised if both were true. Immeo needed to expand awareness of the arcane arts throughout the realm, and they seemed to have chosen a more than willing ambassador.

A loud bugle interrupted Callan's thoughts and obviously distracted Lys from his act. The smile slid from his face, and the water he had formed into an enormous hollow hoop splashed to the ground. Murdock spun his body toward the massive lowered drawbridge that was wide open to allow entry to visitors. More trumpet calls came from that direction, and people began to gravitate in that direction. It was clear what was going on, and Callan immediately broke out into a nervous sweat.

Someone shouted, "King Ramsey! The king is here!"

Why he was becoming so nervous, Callan wasn't entirely sure. He was incredibly excited to meet the king for the first time. Even nobles this far to the east of Aelathil rarely had a chance to see true royalty in person. The things he had heard General Virgil saying worried him, however. He clearly held some level of distrust for King Ramsey and his men, but Callan still did not understand why that was.

Despite his anxiety, he hurried to keep up with the crowd. He would be expected to stand with his family to greet the king. When he scurried to them, breathless and beginning to perspire, his father gestured for Callan to stand at his right side. Callan's mother was on Balen's left, and Tarryn was on the other side of her. Callan was sure the four of them made an inspiring picture.

Tarryn smiled at Callan. "I almost thought you weren't going to make it."

Callan laughed and responded, "Sorry, I lost track of time. Murdock was putting on a magic show."

Balen eyed Callan skeptically, as if he could not believe the quiet mage would perform for a crowd. Before he could say anything, though, the trumpets sounded again, this time much closer. When Callan looked up, he saw a row of soldiers on horseback, framed by a black thunderhead. If the size and speed of the roiling clouds above were anything to judge by, they were in for another storm. King Ramsey had chosen a poor day for a royal visit, it seemed.

One rider broke off from the rest and rode forward. A herald, carrying a flag which bore the colors of King Ramsey the Ninth. He drew up short of Callan and his family and addressed Balen.

He said, "Lord Balen of the Dragon's Keep! I present to you, King Ramsey, the ninth of his name. Sovereign Lord of Aelathil, High Protector of Tal Autem, and future Emperor of the Nassan Flatlands!"

Callan heard his father and uncle sigh simultaneously at the mention of the Flatlands. Callan knew the king had been campaigning there for some time now. It was largely considered futile. The roving tribes to the east were too difficult to stamp out. The effort was most likely a lost cause.

Behind the herald rode a white charger, the only white horse of the bunch. King Ramsey rode atop its back, dressed in some of the most immaculately polished armor Callan had ever seen. It was thin and made of bright silver and gold. The armor was too thin and ornate to be battle-ready, but it made a very striking image.

Ramsey wore no helmet. His white teeth gleamed past his lips as he smiled at Callan and his family. His eyes were hard, though. It was strange. Callan had never seen someone look so pleased and so angry at the same time. He wanted to look away, but that would have been a severe insult. So, he did what he and every other noble-born young man had been taught to do. He knelt on one knee and lowered his head before the king.

"Balen." When King Ramsey spoke, Callan got the distinct feeling he was already displeased with something. Perhaps it was the storm threatening to catch up to them so early in their visit. "You haven't come to visit me in Tal Autem in so long, I've begun to worry about you."

Callan's father smiled and bowed deeply, tapping Callan on the shoulder as he did so. He took it as a sign to stand and moved to his feet as his father straightened his back.

He replied, "I owe you an apology, Your Majesty. Matters here have held my attention for some time."

"Hmm. Do you mean to say you cannot handle ruling both ruling over this province and attending to your duties at court, Balen?"

Ramsey said that with a sneer, drawing an uncertain silence from the assembled crowd. Callan said nothing, but watched his father. His jaw was clenched, and a vein in his neck throbbed in time with his heartbeats. Tarryn had a similar look on his face. The only difference was, his hand had gone to the hilt of his sword. He was gripping the pommel so tightly Callan could see his hand shaking.

Ramsey continued, not allowing Balen any time to respond. "I have sent you many letters over the past few years, Balen. I've asked to give over control your province and allow you and your family to come live in the capitol. You've denied me every time."

With his brows coming together in the middle of his forehead, Balen stepped forward. "You have offered that, Your Majesty. Multiple times. This land was granted to my family by your own ancestors, and I would not see it given away. My son will rule at the Dragon's Keep after I have passed on."

King Ramsey slipped from his ornate saddle and strode directly toward Callan. He stopped a few feet away and eyed Callan with muddy brown eyes. He looked the young man up and down as if he were appraising cattle, then snorted as if he was disgusted with the current stock.

"This *boy*," said the king, "will have rule over no part of *my* kingdom. If his father knows what is good for him, though, he might have a place at court."

Balen stepped forward again, almost coming nose to nose with the king, who was at least a decade his junior. The crowd was holding its collective breath. Balen had always led them, but he was not the king. Standing up to him like this was something most of them would never have dreamed of doing.

Drops of rain began to fall from the darkening sky. Callan felt them on his head and heard them bouncing off Ramsey's armor as he stood mere feet away.

"This *boy* is my son and will claim this land as his birthright, "said Balen, growing ever louder. "That will not be taken away from him by some upstart lordling who isn't worth the oil that shined his father's armor."

The gathered mass gasped outright at that. Callan's mother put a gentle hand on Balen's shoulder, and Tarryn grunted, clearly surprised Balen had mouthed off to Ramsey. The damage had already been done, though. There was no taking it back. Callan could only stand silently at watch.

Ramsey turned to Callan, a fire growing behind his cold eyes. "Your father is a stupid man, boy. I regret you will have to suffer for it. And on your birthday, no less."

He made a *tutting* noise and turned on his heel. King Ramsey made his way back to his huge white horse and unbuckled something from the side of the saddle. After a moment, he produced a bone-white staff topped with a jagged crystal. He looked to Callan and stared at him for a moment, almost curiously. He then swept his gaze to the staff he held, looking upon it like it was some long-lost treasure. He smiled at it like he would to a child.

Then, with ruthless quickness, he shoved the staff toward Balen and the rest of Callan's family. The three of them: Balen, Tarryn, and Lilliana, were lifted into the air and tossed violently into the crowd behind them.

Chapter 5

Peals of thunder shook the keep and the surrounding area as King Ramsey held his staff to the heavens. Both the staff and the king's arm shone with an unearthly glow, bathing the stormy afternoon in a sickly white light. As he gestured, he shouted words that held no meaning to Callan. Wind and rain attacked everyone assembled, each growing in intensity the longer the king shouted. Malicious black clouds converged on the keep, darkening the sky even further.

The staff *thrummed* once, sending a shockwave in all directions. Callan stumbled backward, tripping over the sword and sheath too long for his legs. He crawled back on his elbows like some oversized crab, doing his best to make it to where he had last seen his father and uncle. And his mother. Callan wanted to turn and look for them, but he could not seem to tear his eyes away from the demonic spectacle before him. He had heard of magic for his entire life. Murdock had even shown him some that very morning. This, though, was like nothing he had ever seen. Where Murdock's water-shaping had been fun and innocent, this was different. This brand of magic looked and felt *wrong*.

Another *thrum* emanated from the king and the staff, this time sending out a much more forceful wave of energy. This one struck Callan in the head and shoulders, sending him rolling backward through the red mountain dust. His frantic roll was only stopped when he crashed back first into a pair of armored legs. Looking up, he saw the bulky war hammer and scowling face of the paladin, Dastynn. The much larger man grabbed Callan by the collar and lifted him to his feet like a baby, bracing the young man with his own body. Now that he had a solid foothold, Callan chanced a glance at the king of Aelathil. His eyes had taken on a manic look as if some madness and gripped his heart and mind. He still screamed in his indecipherable language as though trying to tear the world asunder with only his words.

Thrummmmmmm. THRUMMMMMMMMMM. A pair of waves, one right on the heels of the other, came forth from the staff. This time, though, instead of short, concentrated bursts, each proved to be unrelenting and pushed hard against Callan and everyone assembled. If not for the mammoth grip Dastynn had on his collar, Callan thought he would have been blown off the edge of the mountain. Through the wind, rain, and dust, Callan struggled to see any sign of his family. Once, he thought he glimpsed his mother and father, but they were quickly blocked from his view by many bystanders, who had finally broken from their stunned silence and begun to run away from their king's spectacle.

Directly behind Callan, Dastynn let go of the boy's collar and raised his palm toward King Ramsey. His gauntleted hand glowed blue just before a ball of similarly colored energy shot from the paladin and raced for the madness-gripped king. When the ball was within a meter of its target, it changed course, seemingly of its own accord. It veered around the king, striking instead the pike-wielding soldier behind him. The man fell to the ground, dead instantly, and with a smoldering wound in the center of his chest. Twice more, Dastynn aimed his magical attacks at Ramsey, and twice more they diverted from their intended course and missed the king. Through each attack, Ramsey continued his chanting and screaming, taking no notice of the attempts to stop him.

All too suddenly, the king stopped. He stopped yelling, he stopped moving, and from what Callan could tell, he stopped breathing. The brutal waves of power that came from him ceased, as well. Through the stillness, the staff still glowed, casting ghostly shadows across the face of the king and the ground he stood on. Ramsey's mouth twitched into a cruel smirk.

"I told you, Balen, I will have what is mine! You had your chance," he shouted. "Now you and everyone here are going to pay for your mistake."

From the staff, a beam of light shot upward, through the driving rain and into the roiling clouds that blanketed the sky. The clouds split where they were struck by the beam, revealing the blue sky above for the briefest of instants. Through that hole shot two spear-like figures. The clouds closed behind them, obscuring the figures from view for precious seconds. When the diving figures neared the ground, though, it became all too clear what they were.

"Dragons!"

Callan would never know who screamed first, but before long, the air was filled with nothing but terrified cries and prayers to the gods. He and Dastynn stood still as stone statues, watching the monsters unfurl their massive wings and circle toward the keep. The first thing Callan noticed was the immense size of the dragons. One of them, which seemed, from its current distance, to be a sickly shade of green, had a wingspan of what must have been at least thirty feet. The second, whose scales shone a bloody red, was even larger. Its wings spanned a length of nearly fifty feet. As it descended, the red dragon roared, spewing a gout of fire into the black sky.

The green dragon landed on the large stone wall that encircled the keep and the many yards that surrounded it. It stretched out its lithe body like some unholy feline and draped its tail over the wall as it kept a bright green eye on the king who had summoned it. The red, on the other hand, slammed into the southernmost turret of the castle, knocking loose hundreds and hundreds of pounds of torso-sized stones. While it dug its sword-like claws into its perch on the now broken tower, its tail whipped back and forth, knocking even more stones from where they had sat for centuries. The red demon roared again, bathing the top of the tower in crimson flames and melting the crenellations nearest to it.

Callan, along with most of those who were left in the yard, could do nothing but stare in morbid fascination at the spectacle that was unfolding before them. None of them had ever dreamed of catching sight of a dragon in their lifetimes, and now there were two, larger than life and more terrifying than the blackest of nightmares. When Ramsey raised his staff to the sky once more, every head turned to watch him, including those of the two dragons.

When the king spoke, his voice carried much further than it should have, reaching the ears of everyone assembled. His deep voice carried an authority Callan had failed to notice before. *"Karagh, Valiel,"* he said, gesturing to each dragon in turn. *"Kill them."*

Ramsey's words broke the trance that had enveloped the people of the Dragon's Keep. People screamed incoherently as they ran for their lives, some clutching children or spouses to them, others what seemed to be some sort of family heirlooms. Others ran past the king's complacent soldiers to the closed drawbridge behind them. They beat at the heavy wood with their fists and cried in desperation as it refused to yield. Men and women alike clawed at the obstacle, ripping apart their nails and hands in the futile escape attempt.

Dastynn grunted at Callan and tugged on his collar to get his attention. When the young man looked at him, the paladin pointed with his hammer toward a point in the yard not far from where they stood. A group of his father's soldiers had grouped around his Uncle Tarryn, all of them brandishing spears and pikes.

Just as the pair started to move for the group, the red dragon, Valiel, swooped overhead, spewing fire from his gaping jaws. The flames missed Dastynn and Callan, but those behind them did not share the same good fortune. Callan doubled over at the waist and covered his head to avoid the dragon's wrath, but he could hear the anguished screams of those burning as their clothing and skin *popped* and *sizzled* beneath the unnatural heat of the monster's breath. Callan did his best to look away, but he could not help himself. He turned to watch what was happening behind him and was horrified. Men and women alike ran wherever their legs would take them in search of reprieve from the unrelenting fire. Some had already collapsed, their blackened corpses smoldering despite the rain.

Callan doubled over again, this time to vomit. Once he was finished, Dastynn grabbed him again and began to drag him toward his uncle. Tarryn saw the pair approaching and moved to meet them halfway. He embraced Callan with one arm, pulling him close. The older man smelled like soot and sweat, and his arms trembled slightly as he embraced his nephew.

"Balen," he shouted. "I found him! He's here!"

Through the rain, Callan saw his father approach with the mage, Murdock, at his side. Callan's mother, though, was nowhere to be seen. Balen grabbed Murdock roughly, but not unkindly, and shoved the mage toward Callan and Dastynn. He said nothing to Callan, but began to dig through the inner and outer pockets of his coat, clearly searching for something.

Past his father, Callan watched as Karagh, the green dragon, swooped over a storage building filled with hiding villagers. When it cast its deadly breath on the building, Callan expected fire to come forth and burn it and everyone inside to oblivion. Instead, a sickly green mist issued forth from the dragon's throat and spread immediately. At once, Callan smelled rotten meat and other disgusting odors he could not quickly place. The villagers in the storage house broke their cover and ran, some coughing and vomiting blood, others collapsing in the dirt, unable to breathe.

Seconds later, the red monster flew by the same spot and breathed his hellish fire on the choked and gagging victims. The instant the flames touched the creeping, green mist, a massive fireball erupted and decimated the immediate area. If not for Dastynn, the massive explosion would have hurled Callan off his feet. As it was, he kept his footing and was forced to watch innocent villagers be eviscerated and vaporized by the deafening blast. He vomited again, this time on his uncle's boots.

By the time his father found what he was looking for, tears of terror began to stream down Callan's face. He did his best to stop them from flowing, but his shame at crying at such a time only worsened his despair. He was a man now—sixteen years old—there was no reason for him to be sobbing when action was needed. No matter how hard he tried, though, Callan could not stop the tears. Despair had wrapped its black fingers around his heart and mind and crippled him, leaving him virtually useless.

Through the fog of fear that had clouded his mind, Callan was dimly aware of his father speaking to Murdock and Dastynn. He handed the mage a large, brass key and gestured toward the Murdock's chest with one finger, then at Callan. His eyes were sad, but once he finished speaking, he set his mouth in a hard line. Dastynn, silent as ever, nodded twice.

Only then did Balen turn to his son, and clasp him gently on the shoulder. His father's touch broke Callan from his depressed stupor. He opened his mouth to speak, but Balen cut him off with a gentle hand over the bottom half of his face and quick shake of his head.

Grief was apparent in the tone of his voice, but he continued nonetheless. "Callan, I need you to leave with Murdock and Dastynn.

They'll get you out of here and take you to safety." Callan tried to argue, but he was once again cut off. "You'll be fine with these two. They're both good men."

The lord hugged his son tight, and Callan returned the embrace. When they pulled apart, Callan couldn't help but ask, "What about you and Mother? What about Uncle Tarryn, and Keyara, and the general? What about—?"

Balen shook his head, silencing his son once more. "Don't worry about us. We'll be fine. Just get out of here, and be sure to listen to Murdock."

Callan nodded, tears once again threatening to seep out of his eyes. He sucked in a deep breath and nodded again, this time more forcefully, in an attempt to convince himself he was capable of making an escape.

He was briefly embraced by his father once more. "Be safe, Callan. I love you."

"I love you, too."

As soon as the words left his mouth, Callan felt a firm hand grip his wrist. He was pulled through the smoking courtyard by the mute paladin, who was in turn led by Murdock. Screams of the dying and pleas of the desperate were all that Callan could hear as they ran. They passed by burning and ruined buildings, fueled in their flight by the sound of the two dragons wreaking havoc behind them.

Before long, the trio reached their destination, but Callan could not fathom why his father had sent them to this particular spot. Aside from a crumbling storehouse that hadn't been used in ages and the wall that defended the keep, the entire area was dark and empty. A thick layer of dirt and dust coated everything, leaving the place feeling lonely and depressed.

Fortunately, Dastynn and Murdock were much more confident in the escape route than Callan was. The mage held his brass key aloft and muttered a soft incantation, waving his fingers over the key as he spoke. When he finished, a loud rattling sound emanated from a spot in the dirt only ten paces from where they all stood. With his plated boot, Dastynn wiped the grime and dust from the rattling area and uncovered a large, wooden trapdoor. The rattling continued as it seemed that the door attempted to open itself. With a grim, yet satisfied smile, Murdock bent down and inserted the key in the lock, allowing the trap door to swing open.

Through the door in the ground, Callan could just make out the shape of a ladder descending into the mountain. Dastynn went ahead, his hand glowing with blue magic to help provide the barest amount of light. Callan went next, his hands shaking, his breath labored, and his heart threatening to beat through his chest. Tears still stained his quivering cheeks. Murdock was last, pocketing the brass key and closing the trap door behind them. And so, with the roars of Armageddon behind them, the three advanced into the darkness.

Chapter 6

Pyra slipped from the great hall, doing her best to leave politely but without saying more than a word or two to any one person. Had her father not been out on a hunting trip, he would have forced her to stay, citing her duty to the province and to her people. As it was, when her older brother opened his mouth to protest, she waved him off and continued toward the enormous double doors that separated the hall from the rest of the castle. She stole a glance over her shoulder and smirked at Theamere, letting him know he was he was on his own to deal with the various nobles and rich old men who had come to eat at their table.

Ravitch had been gone for nearly two weeks. Had he been around, the bureaucrats would have known better than to come begging for handouts. Instead, like the vultures they were, they came to grovel at Theamere's feet and pick his table clean. For once, Pyra was glad to be the younger of the two and a young woman. She would never have been expected to take over her father's duties in his absence. As it was, those responsibilities fell to Theamere, the one and only son of the Lord of Graveholm. Theamere seemed to enjoy the attention that the rich old men were giving him. All of them wanted handouts and favors and offered very little but praise for Theamere in return.

Pyra had even heard of few marriage proposals passed his way, a majority of the men trying to marry their young daughters off to the Heir of Ice, as Theamere had been often called. Occasionally, some of the more forward nobles had offered up a son to take Pyra off her brother's and father's hands. Theamere declined them all politely. How he did it was a mystery to Pyra. Had some ancient buzzard of a man offered one of his middle-aged sons to her, she might have hit one of her wispy-haired elders.

Rather than resort to violence, she had excused herself. The hall was full of food, talk, and drink. None but Theamere would even notice she had left. The feast was not holding her attention well, anyway. She could practically hear the books in her father's large library calling her name.

Pyra opened the dark wooden doors a crack and slipped outside. Before she had taken a handful of steps down the stone hallway, one of the knights of the keep had fallen into step behind her.

"Gramm, I don't need a guard. I'm only going to the library," she said.

"Of course, you don't, m'lady."

The metal of the knight's boots clicked in time with his even pace, and the netting of chainmail that ran down the back of his thighs jingled like a thousand tiny bells. Pyra had not taken a good look at Gramm today, but she was sure his armor and uniform were each immaculate as always. She sighed.

"I also recall very clearly, telling you to stop calling me that. My name is Pyra."

She heard Gramm chuckle behind her. "You did. However, I'm afraid that I would make a poor excuse for a knight if I couldn't even manage to use the correct title for my betters. M'lady."

Pyra glared back at the young man, offering a killing gaze to the dark-haired, roughly-stubbled knight. She had to crane her neck to see his face, but that was nothing new. Since she had been young, Pyra had been staring up at all of those around her. This was in stark contrast with Gramm. They had known each other for the entirety of their relatively short lives, and since Pyra could remember, her friend had stood a head above the rest of the men his age.

"You won't make much of a knight if you can't follow orders, either," she said with a wink.

Gramm chuckled again, clearly enjoying the torment he put Pyra through. He rested his left arm on the hilt of the sword that swung at his hip and scratched the back of his neck with his right. In the absence of a retort, Pyra smiled haughtily and increased her pace.

"That's a very good point m'lady. Fortunately for me, your father, and in his absence, your brother, are my liege lords. Not you. So, really, I am not required to follow any of your orders."

Pyra's face fell, and she let her breath out in a huff. She increased her pace even further, the stomping of her feet sending echoes through the halls of the keep. She heard Gramm's footsteps fade into the distance but knew he would catch her eventually. He liked to give Pyra a hard time, but the knight was intelligent enough to realize she had not been lying when she had said she was going to the library. After all, nearly everyone in the castle realized she spent most of her time there, poring over historical scrolls and mystical tomes. Many of her father's retainers and friends said she was obsessed. Pyra and Elder Moss preferred to say she was studious.

The door that led to her father's library was innocuous enough. It was made of the same dark wood as every other door in the keep, and more than likely, every door in all of Graveholm. The timber more or less covered the mountainous region. Logging was a powerful industry in the area, and the local craftsmen were incredibly talented.

Behind that door, though, was Pyra's favorite room in the kingdom. Shelves and shelves of books lined the front and right walls of the library, with various colors of covers and bindings. Some of the books were incredibly thin, no more than a sheaf of paper between two bindings. Others were massive tomes, hundreds and hundreds of pages, written in cramped and miniscule script and bound with thick leather covers. Their content covered innumerable topics, from histories of the kingdom and its prominent families, to lineages and trees of Pyra's own family, to poems and stories by some of the most prominent scribes of recent centuries.

The left wall was likewise covered, but with scrolls in lieu of books. Most were of the academic variety. Those were coated in a film of dust as no one in the castle had the time nor, for many, the ability to read such ponderous works. Pyra left them alone because they were boring and written by the very same stuffy old men who were currently boring her brother with their intellectual babble.

No, her attentions were focused on a small pile of scrolls that had been removed from the shelves and piled meticulously on the lone desk in the center of the library. These were scrolls of magic, brought from the great schools of Immeo by Elder Moss. Years ago, upon the elder's retirement, he had brought scrolls written by some of the greatest minds of the age to Graveholm. His own spellcraft, and that of his mentors, was inked on dozens of scrolls, and Pyra had a mind to read them all.

She grabbed the scroll from the top of the pile, unrolled it, and picked up where she had left off the day before, reading aloud so he could better understand the spells that were scribbled on the parchment.

"Fire, for warmth and for destruction," she began. "Magical fire, as natural fire, must begin with a spark. That spark, brought to life in a nurturing environment and given proper fuel, will give rise to flame. Friction is the simplest path by which a spark is formed, more often than not through the snapping of the thumb and middle finger."

Pyra stopped on sighed, rubbing her temples. Spellcrafters had a deep love for making just about anything more complicated than it needed to be. Frustrated by the language, Pyra set down the scroll and readied herself to practice making sparks with magic.

She closed her eyes and began deep breathing, clearing her mind of everything but the current that floated beneath the air, running through everything and everyone. The faintest buzzing reverberated through the library and under Pyra's skin, making her skin crawl and the hairs on the back of her neck stand on end. Her mind, acting as a kind of extra sense, cast out, grabbing at the ethereal river. She gathered the *water* using her mind like she would a bucket, holding as much of the force as she could.

Elder Moss had taught her the steps. Pyra was confident in her abilities. She gripped it, holding the magic tight, forcing it into a spherical shape and snapped her fingers.

Nothing.

She snapped again, this time harder, as if that would make some kind of difference. Again, nothing happened. The young woman focused harder, denying herself any knowledge but that of the condensed magic she held only in her mind. Pyra imagined it held in a tight sphere, rotating swirls of red and yellow, not unlike the sun in the sky, held beneath the translucent surface of the ball.

She snapped again. This time, she felt the temperature in the room increase marginally, and her thumb and middle finger began to tingle uncomfortably. She furrowed her brows and squinted, this time sucking in her breath and holding it. She snapped once more, this time bringing an almost imperceptible light to her hand. Another snap and she heard a faint crackle. One more, the most forceful yet, produced a small ember, like one of those thousands that snapped and danced from the fireplace in the great hall.

Pyra smiled, becoming more excited and all the more focused for it. She snapped more and more frequently, producing a spark with each rubbing together of his fingertips. The heat in the room increased drastically, causing her to breathe more heavily and sweat to drip from her forehead into her eyes. Her fingers had become wet, reducing the friction between them and lessening the sparks that jumped from her fingertips. So, Pyra wiped them on the hem of her dress and snapped once more.

An isolated fire, the size of the flame on a small candle burst into life and hovered above her thumb. The appearance of the fully realized flame startled Pyra so badly that she fell over, knocking down the chair that she sat in. The fire sputtered out of existence just as she yelped loudly and crashed to the ground.

The library door burst open and Gramm entered, looking disheveled and wholly unlike himself.

Pyra looked up at him from the ground, smiling at his worry. "I'm fine, Gramm. I just startled myse—"

The knight shook his head and cut her off, the frantic look in his eyes revealing something else entirely was wrong.

When he spoke, his voice was low and his breathing labored. "It's your father. He's hurt. Run and get Elder Moss. Bring him to the infirmary. Hurry."

With that, he was gone, off and running down the hallway. Only after he'd gone did Pyra notice the trail of blood he had left on the floor behind him. Before she realized it, Pyra was sprinting down the hall, her bare feet smacking on the cold stone. The last she had seen the elder, he had been at the feast, engaged in an argument with some gray-bearded noble.

She slowed her advance when she neared the hall so she didn't hurt herself on the large doors. When she entered, Pyra immediately noticed the noise in the hall had lessened significantly. The food and drink had obviously set in, created a general malaise in the room. Theamere locked eyes with her upon her arrival, and she cast a frightened glance in his direction. He looked confused, but she did not have the time to explain anything to him yet. She had to find the elder.

When she spotted the old man, he was slumped in his chair with his chin on his chest, snoring softly. It appeared the festivities had been too much for him to handle. Pyra could only hope he had not taken part in too much drinking. She needed him awake and sober to help her injured father. She walked to him, quickly but carefully. She did not want to draw any unwanted attention to herself. The last thing her father needed was to have the vultures plucking at him while he was hurt.

Pyra moved to shake the elder's shoulder, but he sat up straight as a rod before she could even touch him. He shook his head to wake himself, while he scratched at the few wispy white hairs on top of his head.

Before Pyra had a chance to explain herself, his gray eyes met with hers. "What happened, child? What's wrong?"

"Father is hurt. Gramm told me to come and get you, but there was blood, and I don't know what happened to him. They're in the infirmary waiting for you, and I don't know how badly he's hurt, and I'm supposed to bring you to him." She panted, out of breath, and stared at him, amazed at how he could stay so calm while she was so upset.

He rose slowly and calmly, nodding his wrinkled and age-spotted head once. "You've done well. Walk with me to see to him, please."

Pyra nodded quickly and offered her arm to the elder. As they walked, he asked her what she knew about her father's injuries. She told him nothing, for she knew nothing but the fact blood was somehow involved. Once she thought about it more, she realized it could have even been Gramm's blood, or someone else's entirely.

So, the pair walked in a hurried silence, moving as fast as Elder Moss's aged joints would allow. As they neared the infirmary, a group of hushed voices could be heard. A group of her father's knights walked toward the pair, blood covering the front of their armor and their capes.

One spoke up, his tone soft, saying, "This isn't a sight for the lady, Elder. I'd send her on her way."

Pyra shouldered past him without a word. The other knights wanted to stop her from going in, she could see it on their faces. None of them were brave enough to physically stop her, though. Gramm might have tried it, but he was in the infirmary still. Pyra could hear him talking to someone.

With the elder just a step behind her, Pyra pushed through the door into the infirmary. She stopped dead in her tracks, her breath catching hard in her chest and forming a twisted knot in the back of her throat. Lord Ravitch of Graveholm, her father, lay on an infirmary bed, covered in dark blood. His face bore the brunt of the damage, with fresh liquid pouring down the left side. His clothes and sheets were all stained a dark red.

Pyra stood in shock. She had never seen her father so fragile, so vulnerable. She wanted to weep for him but could not. She could only stand silently, barely feeling Gramm's on her shoulder and the reassuring pressure he put there.

Chapter 7

Ravitch was hurt badly. He had sustained deep wounds to his back, chest, arms, and neck. The back of his head had been struck with some blunt object, leaving his long hair sticky and warm with drying blood. The left side of his face was in tatters. Claw marks had mangled the flesh there, and torn at his lips. His left eye was gone entirely, leaving him with only a dark, empty socket.

His breathing came in ragged gasps, and the wounds on his chest pulsed with every trembling beat of his heart. Pyra could do nothing but stare at his prone form, wondering firstly how her father had survived such injuries, and secondly, how he was ever going to make a full recovery. Graveholm's medical staff had been working on him for two days now, keeping him tethered to life with herbs and poultices to stem the tide of blood that seeped from him.

Elder Moss had been hard at work as well, not only administering traditional medicines, but casting healing magics on him when the elder's aging body allowed him to expend the energy needed. Still, through the efforts of every available healer, the keep was losing its lord.

Pyra had scarcely left his side since his nearly lifeless form had been dragged in. Ashe had stopped in, as well, but his duties kept him away much of the time. Gramm, Pyra's closest friend, had been kept away by responsibility as well. She had always been able to speak her mind and have conversations with her father. His stillness and silence were at the same time lonely and unsettling.

Word of his injuries had, as worried, spread to much of the castle and the surrounding area. The story of how he had come to be so badly hurt had spread as well, even though Ravitch, the only one to truly know what had happened, had not said a word. Some said he had been attacked by a group of mountain tribesmen and fought them off single-handedly. Others said he had been attacked by a pack of wolves or a bear and had dragged himself back to the castle with only one arm.

The soldiers who had brought him back, along with those that were close to Ravitch, knew a different version of the story. A dead Visani, one of the giant, white-furred feline people who inhabited the forests in the area, had been found dead within feet of Ravitch. It seemed he had killed the beast with his bare hands by choking the life from it. The creature's corpse had been brought back and skinned by those same soldiers. For luck, they had fashioned its fur into a blanket and draped it across their ailing leader.

It made a grisly scene, and Pyra's stomach turned whenever she looked closely at the Visani's head and pelt. It was a scary reminder that her father had come so close to death and was still fighting off the Dark Raven's embrace.

The thought of the goddess of death startled Pyra. Never before had she really thought she could lose her father. Now that she considered it a possibility, she realized she was absolutely not willing to let him slip away. Pyra stood and grabbed Elder Moss gently by the elbow and led him from the room. He seemed startled by the abrupt physical contact but followed willingly enough. When they were alone in the hall, she turned on him with her arms crossed across her chest.

She asked, "What are his chances? I have to know."

The elder shrugged and stole a glance over his shoulder, back toward Ravitch's bed. He responded quietly, "I cannot be sure. He is an incredibly strong man, but he sustained some very severe injuries. Your father could pass on in the next few minutes or he could be awake and talking by tomorrow."

Pyra sagged, her shoulders drooping and her chin falling to her chest. She could handle stress and tragedy. She could handle loss and pain. What she could not handle was the uncertainty and the ache of not knowing. Theamere always seemed so confident he would make it. He had taken on his father's role willingly, but with an unwavering certainty he would be giving the job back sooner rather than later. Pyra, on the other hand, had spent nearly every waking moment at her father's bedside, begging and praying for him to wake up. She had not slept more than an hour or two since he had been brought in. Exhaustion crept in on her and caused her to snap at Elder Moss.

"So, what can we do? I refuse to accept that we are going to leave his life up to fate!"

Moss smiled sadly and said, "My dear, there is nothing that we can do for him. Fate is exactly what we are counting on to—"

"No," she shouted! "I refuse to believe that! You studied for decades at the best magical colleges in the world, did you not? Did they teach you nothing about healing other than fixing cuts and bruises?"

The man's face and bald head turned red and his lips pursed in an obvious attempt to hold his tongue. He stammered for a moment and grasped at straws, doing his best to find an explanation the young woman would understand. Of course, he knew more than that! How dare she insinuate otherwise? But he was aging, and forgetful, and not as strong as he had once been, and he was out of practice, and…

"They did," he stammered, "I do know more, but—"

Pyra interrupted, "Then do something for him! You are, or you used to be, a powerful magician, and you've even told me I'm getting better! Between the two of us, we should be able to help him!"

She dropped her head and chewed on her bottom lip, angry at her father for not being awake, angry at her brother for taking everything so well, and angry at Elder Moss for not being willing or able to bring her father back from the edge of the abyss. The injustice of it all caused her hands to shake and her breath to come in shortened sobs. Pyra turned and pounded her closed fists on the stone walls as tears began to form in the corner of her eyes. The Elder mumbled something under his breath, but she ignored him. He continued to mumble, though, until Pyra was forced to turn and speak with him.

She asked, "What are you trying to say?"

"There is a way," he said. "It is dangerous. It is illegal and forbidden by all civilized nations and the magical colleges. But there is a way."

Pyra spent the next hours sifting through a dusty tome, which was written largely in a hand she could not decipher. The elder, though, had no problem with the reading and translated for her as best he could. The spellhe tried to teach her seemed simple enough. He assured her that the simplicity of it was not what made it illegal. What they would be attempting was known as Blood Magic and would attempt to heal her father through the use of Pyra's own life force.

Since she had not studied magic of this level before, Elder Moss would be performing the healing, using Pyra as a conduit. From what she could understand, he would more or less control her mind and body and channel his knowledge and experience through her so he could utilize her youth and greater magical endurance to heal Ravitch.

"When you say this is illegal," asked Pyra, "what do you mean? What would happen if we were found out?"

Elder Moss looked up from the black-bound book and scratched at the age spots on the back of his head. "It depends on who found us, really," he answered. "If it were the colleges, we would be excommunicated and marked as outcasts or rogue mages. If a more accepting lord discovered us, he would jail us or have us flogged. King Ramsey or another, more conservative lord…"

Pyra was fairly sure she knew exactly what he meant, but she had to hear it from him to be sure. It was as if the risk validated what she was doing for her father, to bring him back to the world and his family. She gulped and asked, "What would they do?"

Moss chewed on his lip, reluctant to answer. The look in Pyra's eyes told him she was in it for the long haul, however, and she had the right to know what they were getting themselves into. "They would kill us," he answered. "More than likely, they would burn us on a public pyre." Over the tip of his crooked nose, he asked her, "Are you willing to put that risk on your shoulders?"

"Absolutely."

The elder nodded, assured of her conviction. "We should hurry to finish the readings, then," he said. "I will not have you going through this without knowing exactly what you have signed up for."

Pyra nodded and leaned forward, as Moss began translating from the book once more. She may have put up a calm and confident façade, but truthfully, she would much rather have discovered another way to help her father. She knew he would never have her flogged or imprisoned. He would certainly never burn her at the stake. Hopefully, Ravitch would never do any of those to Elder Moss, who had practically raised him, either. Still, she was worried his respect for her would dwindle. She would almost certainly be forbidden from practicing further magic if he found out the means through which he had been healed.

The risk of facing his wrath was worth it, though. Graveholm needed Ravitch to be healthy. The weather was becoming colder and colder, and the hints of the first heavy snows were omnipresent. Birds began to fly for warmer areas, and large animals had been gathering their stores to last the cold season. The annual harvests had not been their best in the past months so the settlers and townspeople would surely be restless about their own survival. As much as Pyra loved and believed in her brother, she knew Theamere was not yet ready to lead their people through the end of the year. He would eventually make a great leader for the people of the Northern Provinces, but for now, they needed their father.

A few hours later, Pyra and the elder stood at Ravitch's bedside, looking down at the pale and unconscious form of the Lord. Moss had readied Pyra very well to become a vassal for the healing procedure. All that was required was a grasp on magic, as she had recently proven to herself she could muster with her summoning of fire. Moss had no idea she had experimented with magic without him so he was under the assumption she would be attempting to tap into the mythic power for the first time. Pyra was perfectly content to let him assume such. Her father, should he wake up, would already be furious with her. She did not need Moss to be cross with her as well.

So, the two of them ushered all servants and healers out of the room. Theamere was busy with his duties so they had not even bothered to explain to him what they were going to do. They would be left alone.

"Give me your hand."

Pyra started at the command, lost as she was in her own thoughts. "Excuse me?"

The elder held out a razor-sharp knife and gestured at Pyra's clenched fist. He made a small slicing motion with the knife and said, "I need your hand. The spell requires blood, remember?"

Pyra frowned, unsure of what she had gotten herself into. Thinking of her father, though, she nodded and held out her hand, palm up, and readied herself for the knife. "I remember," she said.

With a steadiness that belied his age, the old man grabbed Pyra by the wrist with one hand and sliced her open palm with the other. So sharp was the knife that she hardly felt the cut. When the warm, red blood began seeping from the wound, though, the pain registered in her brain and began to worry her. She jerked, her hand and arm clenching with pain, causing rivulets of blood to gush down the sides of her hand.

Moss hardly noticed. After cutting Pyra's hand, he immediately removed the Visani's pelt from Ravitch's prone form and with the same knife, cut open his chest at the sternum, toward his stomach.

"Place your wound on his," he ordered. "Be sure to press firmly. Once you find a comfortable position, open your mind to the magic. I will take over from there."

Pyra did so immediately. When her cut touched her father's, she sucked in a breath through her teeth, hissing at the pain the contact brought with it. Her blood spilled onto Ravitch's chest, mixing with his and sliding down onto the sheets that covered his bed. He gave no outward sign he had been cut or that she was touching him. Her hand, resting over his heart as it was, could hardly feel a pulse. They were losing him. They had to work fast.

"Focus," said Moss. "Make sure to breathe."

She closed her eyes and wiped the hair from her face with her free hand.

Breathe.

Breathe.

Breathe.

Pyra felt the wrinkled hands of the elder on her back, placing a constant pressure between her shoulder blades. Within the confines of her mind, she felt for the bubble of magic that had let her create fire days earlier. This time, when she sought it out, Pyra found it much more easily. It was as if it had been waiting for her. She dove into it headlong, losing all sense of self and becoming one with the power that surrounded and permeated everything around them.

She felt a reassuring presence in her mind then. That of Elder Moss. He was encouraging and proud all at once, but he was also worried and frightened. Pyra felt him taking over, her fingers and toes going numb, the pressure on her back intensifying, and the pain in her palm growing exponentially. She tried to scream, to cry out, but could not make her mouth move or her vocal cords react. For a brief moment, she felt panic.

Then nothing.

Chapter 8

Through the inky blackness, the three descended for what seemed like ages. They had been able to hear the sounds of chaos raging above them at first, but now, the only sounds were their own breathing and their boots on the ancient wooden ladder that aided in their escape. Callan did his best to keep his eyes locked on his hands and the rungs they alighted on. Looking toward his feet, the light Dastynn provided only let him see enough to know they were a long way from the bottom of the tunnel. The sight of the blue light fading into nothingness made his stomach turn and his eyes water.

From what he could tell, nothing living had used the passage in a long, long time. The air was dry and filled with dust, which rained down on him from above every time Murdock took a particularly heavy-footed step. Callan was sure, though, he was doing the same thing to Dastynn so he did his best to not complain. It wasn't as if whining would have done him any good at this point. Neither of his companions had said more than a couple of words since they started their long descent. Words would not come easily to Callan, either. His thoughts were of his home and his friends and family.

Had Balen not had some sort of solution for the attacking dragons and the king, he would not have sent Callan away. He had only wanted his heir out of the dangerous area and would call for him as soon as the peril had passed, of that Callan was certain. After all, the lands surrounding the Dragon's Keep belonged to them and had for many generations. They would pass to Callan once his father could no longer rule over them, and then to Callan's own eldest child. Even if Balen could not stop the king and his dragons, surely the other Dragon Lords would see the illegality of Ramsey's attack and do something to restore Callan's birthright.

A loud *crack* and a muffled grunt startled Callan from his thoughts. Below him, Dastynn slid down the ladder, the rung of which his heavy armor had helped to snap in two. The paladin fell to the next rung, breaking it as well, and the one after that. Murdock and Callan could only watch and pray the large man could stop his plummet. As he attempted to save himself, he lost control of his magical light, throwing the three of them into complete darkness.

Another pair of grunts and *cracks* followed, leading Callan to believe that Dastynn would surely end up in pieces on the floor far below. Callan and Murdock would be left to fend for themselves and would be responsible for the burial rites of what would certainly be a broken and battered paladin. The sounds of the plummeting man eventually stopped, though, and Callan listened intently to his surroundings, hoping the paladin had somehow saved himself.

Murdock called out softly into the black pit, "Dastynn? Are you still here?"

An affirmative grunt from below answered his call. Relieved, Callan and the mage continued down, being sure to not stumble over the broken rungs of the ladder. Once Dastynn had safely regained his footing, the blue light began to once again emanate from the palm of his hand. The light was soft enough to allow Callan to see but cast strange shadows on the walls of the tunnel. His own shadow covered Murdock's face, giving his eyes a haunted and intimidating quality. Had Callan not known him to be such a cheerful person, he would have been scared to be so close to him.

None of the three knew exactly how long it took them to move into the bowels of the tunnel. Callan had attempted to count the minutes and hours, but he quickly lost interest. Keeping his hands and feet from slipping was infinitely more important. Regardless of how long their descent lasted, Callan was so relieved when they reached the bottom that he actually let out a chuckle. He was silenced by a hard stare from Murdock. The good cheer the mage had shown over the span of the last few days had vanished completely. The happy, carefree young man had been replaced by a hard-eyed, silently imposing figure. The change in him was almost as worrying to Callan as the destruction that had taken place earlier. Had Murdock been his usual self, at least Callan could have kept some kind of hope. Now, he was left with a sinking feeling in the bottom of his stomach.

Once he had a chance to look around, Callan could see they had entered another tunnel, this one leading horizontally away from the keep. By the light of Dastynn's blue magic, he could see that the tunnel was roughly ten feet tall and just wide enough that the three of them could have walked shoulder to shoulder, albeit uncomfortably. Directly to their left was a stone wall, which provided a place for their distorted shadows to stand. To the right was only darkness. No exit could be seen yet, but Callan could smell fresh air and feel the hint of a breeze on his face. Hopefully, the walk out of the second tunnel would be much shorter than the climb down the first.

"I don't know where this lets out," said Murdock, "and I would rather not get ambushed before the night is out. Any number of people could know about this tunnel so keep your wits about you."

He was undoubtedly speaking for Callan's benefit rather than Dastynn's, and the realization brought an embarrassed flush to the young man's face. As much as he thought he deserved to be treated as an adult, he knew the mage thought differently. It didn't matter to Murdock that Callan was the only son of a Dragon Lord, the mage saw him as only a boy, and a weak one at that. Callan had no armor, no real combat experience, and was armed only with a sword that dangled to the ground and tried to trip him as he walked. He was a liability, and he knew it. He shoved the thought to the side, for the moment. Thinking negatively now would accomplish nothing but frustrating all three men.

So, in an effort to distract himself, Callan asked, "How far down do you think we are? I tried to keep track of rungs, but I lost count after a while."

A thoughtful look came over Murdock's features as he started down the pitch-black tunnel with Dastynn only steps behind him. Callan hurried to keep up, his short legs taking two steps for every one of the paladin's. As they walked, he noticed, rather than causing the noise of their footsteps to rebound around them, the tunnel muted the sound. Even Dastynn's armored footfalls were relatively quiet.

Murdock waited until they had walked for a few moments before he spoke. "If I had to make an estimate, I would say we climbed nearly half a mile down, maybe a bit more. If there were torches or some sunlight down here, I could say for sure."

Callan nodded, pleased Murdock would still speak, at least. The attack by King Ramsey had shaken the mage badly, as it had everyone involved. The man might have seemed angry, but Callan suspected he was more scared than anything. Until today, no one Callan knew had ever seen a dragon in person. They were legends passed down in schools, academies, and bedtime stories for generations. Now, the Dragon's Keep, named for those very legends, had been burned and violated by a pair of the monsters.

Curious, Callan asked, "Have either of you ever seen a dragon? Before today, I mean."

Murdock sighed wearily and rubbed his eyes with his thumb and forefinger, leaving Callan slightly disheartened. His mood changed for the better, though, when Dastynn flashed him a small smile and nodded. It was strange, seeing that look on the big man's face. He looked almost mischievous. The paladin held up a gauntleted hand, his forefinger and middle finger extended.

Callan's mouth gaped in disbelief. "You've seen *two*?"

Dastynn nodded, his smile never wavering. Murdock answered verbally for him, another sigh escaping his lips. "They're more common north of the mountains. We saw a pair of them while we were on a mission there."

As they walked, Murdock added, "Well, Dastynn *says* he saw two of them. I only saw one."

The big man scowled at the mage and shoved him playfully in the back. He turned to Callan again and nodded forcefully, still holding up the same two fingers, an amused smile playing at the edges of his mouth. Callan could only laugh at the big man. From what he could tell, even Murdock managed a little smirk.

Murdock continued, "There haven't been very many reports of them outside of Thryndefst. Seeing them this far south is worrying, to say the least."

"If worrying it's at the least, what is it at the worst?" Callan asked.

Murdock locked eyes with the boy, a grim look etched into his face.

"Terrifying."

After that, the trio walked in relative silence through the tight confines of the stone tunnel. Every few steps, Callan could make out moss growing on the sides of the tunnel by the light of Dastynn's magic. Once, he even though he heard the scraping of tiny claws, which could only mean the presence of rats. In fact, the further they walked, the more signs of life Callan noticed.

On the ladder and in the back of the tunnel, there had been no evidence to suggest that any living being had ever made its way into the stone pathway. Here, though, moss, insects, and the various other indicators of animal life were visible, if not abundant. More than anything else, the moss drew his attention. There was something about it that seemed strange to Callan, but he could not quick place it. Maybe it was the fact that his eyes began to adjust to the darkness that made the moss look strange, or maybe it was the blue glow emanating from the paladin's—

Callan thumped Dastynn on one massive, armored shoulder with the flat of his hand.

"Turn out your light," he said. "I want to see something."

Obviously confused, Dastynn turned to Murdock. The mage looked around for a moment before he came to the same realization Callan had. With a quick nod, he gave his permission for Dastynn to extinguish their light. With a shrug of his broad shoulders, Dastynn snapped his fingers and plunged the three of them into complete darkness.

Except he didn't.

The moss that ran in patches on the ceiling, walls, and floor of the tunnel began to glow luminously, bathing the dark walls and the three people inside with its light. The dark green fluorescence of the moss gave Callan the distinct feeling he was in a forest rather than surrounded by miles and miles of stone. As he walked, he deliberately stuck out his right foot and stepped on the moss, curious as to what would happen.

At Callan's touch, the light from the moss was extinguished and what seemed like millions of glowing spores floated into the air. They floated around his arms, his legs, his body, and those of his protectors like innumerable fireflies. After a few moments of swirling through the air, the lights dimmed and the glowing dust began to settle. Eventually, any evidence of the spores ever having existed disappeared.

Dastynn sneezed violently once, twice, three times. Callan only stared at him for a moment, before breaking out into a fit of immature giggles. The paladin scowled, albeit good-naturedly, and stomped off, taking position at the front of the small group. With a glance, Callan noticed Murdock had managed a small smile. When he saw Callan looking, though, he wiped it away, replacing it once more with a surly and focused look before stalking off after Dastynn.

Callan followed, concerned by the mage's behavior. Now that he had seen what magic was capable of first hand, he was wary of angering Murdock. He didn't think Murdock would hurt him, but after what he had seen a few hours ago, he wasn't sure of much. So, he tread carefully, making sure to never step too closely to the mage, lest he step on the hem of his robes or bump him or do something else that could send him over the edge.

If not for Dastynn's vow of silence, Callan would have had someone to talk to, at least. Instead, he was forced to walk in silence behind two people who more than likely wanted nothing more than to be out of this whole situation. They weren't even from Aelathil. What did they care if dragons had laid waste to the keep? The king who had done it wasn't even their king. Callan thought they must have known his father well, to protect him just because Balen asked them to.

As they walked, Callan noticed a sound he couldn't quite name. It sounded almost like wind, but it was hard to tell, as the tunnel distorted the noise and muffled it. He did, however, notice it was getting louder and louder the further the group walked. So, either something was tearing the tunnel apart around them or they were getting closer to whatever it was making the noise. He had a problem deciding which outcome he preferred. Admittedly, being crushed to death by millions and millions of tons of rocks terrified him, but if the king's magic were making the noise, he would almost rather his end come quickly.

His worries were somewhat alleviated sooner than expected. The tunnel took a sharp right turn, followed soon after by an even sharper left turn. By the time they had taken the first right, the noise grew exponentially in volume. What had been the whisperings of white noise only moments before now turned into a deafening roar that threatened to rattle Callan's teeth from his skull. He clamped his mouth shut and soldiered on, though, aware of the fact neither Murdock nor Dastynn had so much slowed their pace. If they weren't worried, he wasn't either.

Worried or not, all three of them stopped dead in their tracks when they rounded the last corner. The tunnel they had been walking in for an untold amount of time abruptly expanded into a small room, large enough for their trio and perhaps another three large individuals. At the end of that, though, was a cascading wall of water that mercilessly pounded what Callan assumed was supposed to be their exit.

"Oh, gods," said Murdock. "As if this day hasn't been long enough already."

Chapter 9

The roar of the waterfall drowned out all other noise and threatened to deafen Callan to the sound of his own thoughts. His teeth chattered, and his feet shook along with the ground. The relentless, rhythmic drumming of water on stone drove small droplets into the trio's clothes, faces, and hair. Within seconds, Callan's tunic and Murdock's robes were soaked through to the skin. Dastynn's hair was plastered to his head, but the water simply beaded on his plate armor and rolled off, dripping to the floor.

Callan threw his hands in the air and spun to the mage. "What are we supposed to do now? We can't go back the way we came, there are dragons out there! This is just great. We can either drown, starve, or get eaten."

Murdock had no answer for him. He crossed his arms and listened to Callan complain, but said nothing. There was, after all, nothing to say that could get them out of this mess. They were good and well trapped. In fact, an interesting parallel could be made between their current situation and-

BANG!

Callan and Murdock both jumped out of their skin and turned to face the mouth of the cave, where Dastynn now stood. He looked frustrated as if he had made multiple attempts to get their attention before resorting to slamming his crystalline hammer into the gray stone of the tunnel. When the paladin saw he had their undivided attention, he gestured to the lower-left corner of the tunnel's mouth.

Callan hurried over first, being careful to not trip over his sword and stumble through the waterfall to what would surely be a watery grave. When Callan neared him, Dastynn reached out and grabbed the young man by the back of his nearly ruined tunic to prevent that unfortunate fate. When Callan saw what the paladin pointed at, his eyebrows raised into his hairline and a small smile touched the corners of his mouth.

"Murdock, you should look at this."

Confused, the mage walked toward them, raising a sleeve against the splashing droplets of the waterfall. Murdock looked to where Callan and Dastynn gestured. Between the watery mist and the dark of the cave, he was forced to strain his eyes for a moment. When he saw what he was meant to see, though, he couldn't help but smile. Beyond the waterfall and the mouth of the cave, a thin staircase was etched into the side of the mountain. Angled as it was, Callan imagined the staircase would be nearly impossible to see from the ground.

One look at Dastynn said exactly how he felt about the staircase. He looked more pale than normal. His eyes had grown to the size of dinner plates, and he looked as if he was going to be sick. Callan had always quite liked heights, but he was much smaller than the paladin and wearing far less heavy clothing. Callan's tunic and breeches were nothing compared to the massive armor Dastynn wore. Not only would it be much more difficult for him to make it down the stairs, but if he fell, he would fall hard. The shakes in his hands were understandable.

Murdock patted him on the shoulder and shouted over the roar of the waterfall, "Look, I know you don't like heights, but it's a lot better than going back and fighting those dragons!"

Dastynn didn't look so sure. For his part, Callan just wanted to get as far away from the monsters and King Ramsey as he could. Once they had escaped, they could formulate a plan to get his family and the rest of those Ramsey had trapped out of the keep. Dastynn and Murdock were powerful in their own right. They had to have powerful friends. If they didn't, they wouldn't have been able to get in contact with Lys and the mercenaries. They would make sure everything worked out and that Callan's family was saved.

Still shaking, Dastynn moved down the thin staircase. His hammer was strapped across his back, making the descent look even more difficult than it undoubtedly was. Callan went next, careful to stay close enough to Murdock to be caught if needed. The stairs were wet, slick, and eroded from their proximity to the waterfall. The steep escape route was a dangerous one. It was clear this was a route used only in emergencies. Callan wouldn't have been surprised in the least if it hadn't been used in generations.

Once they were far enough beyond the waterfall, on the cliff face that the Dragon's Keep rested on, Callan could see that night had fallen on the mountains. The trio had been walking for much longer than it had seemed. Upon realizing that, Callan felt a sudden weariness. His legs became heavy and unsteady. He wobbled for a moment, teetering on the edge of the stone stair. A hand from above pressing him into the side of the mountain was all that kept him from taking the short route to the bottom of the cliff.

"Keep going. One foot in front of the other. Don't look down."

Callan took a deep breath and nodded, wiping his wet bangs from his eyes. He fixed his stare on Dastynn's back, refusing to look anywhere but at the big man. The moon was just bright enough that he could see beams of light glinting off the plate armor in front of him. A roaring white noise blotted out his other senses. The sound of the waterfall was everywhere. It came from above, dashed against the rocks below, and reverberated off the cliff Callan clung to for his life. He lost track of how long they climbed down the ancient staircase. The dull ache in his arms and legs faded, leaving him numb. The moon's light eventually entranced him, white spots dancing in his vision. By far the worst, though, was the noise of the water. It perverted everything, every thought, every movement. Callan feared he would go deaf or insane if the sound didn't sto—

—Callan stumbled as his foot came into contact with slick grass. The ground was much softer, much muddier, than the stairs, and his knees buckled beneath him. He fell onto his back and stared up at the million bright pinpricks in the sky. He heard a dull *clunk* as Dastynn fell to his backside on the bottom step. Murdock did the same, just a few feet above the paladin.

Lying as he was, Callan could feel mud seeping into his clothes and coating his sweat-soaked skin. It felt strangely comforting, the softness of the mud and grass. After being surrounded by caves and water and moving down stone stairs for hours and hours, he felt as though he was at home in his bed. He chuckled at the thought. The sound of his own laughter, of his own voice, brought such an immense feeling of relief and comfort he could only continue laughing. Callan imagined he looked quite insane, lying in the mud and laughing like a lunatic, but at that moment, he didn't care. They had made it out.

Lost as he was in his own relief, Callan failed to notice Murdock standing over him. Only when the mage knelt and shook his shoulder did Callan stop his laughing and sit up straight. At least Murdock was smiling. Maybe they would be alright after all. Well enough, at least, to get some help for those still trapped by Ramsey and his dragons.

Murdock shook Callan again, this time a little bit more forcefully. "Come on, Cal," he said. "I found a cave behind the waterfall. There's some dry clothes in there for you."

Callan stood with the mage's help and started for the waterfall. He could make out a light, no doubt magically cast by Dastynn again, behind the cascading water. As the two of them got closer, Callan could just make out a path in the moonlight. He and Murdock stepped on it and followed it into one of the largest caverns Callan had ever seen. The roof of the monstrous cave was out of sight, cast into shadow by the paladin's light. The room was at least the size of the great hall at the Dragon's Keep. Instead of housing long tables and chairs and members of the nobility, though, this cavern was almost entirely empty. There was a pair of wardrobes on one wall, with footlockers next to them. A few weapon racks dotted the other side of the room. They held swords, axes, and polearms of various sizes, but nothing approaching the craftsmanship of Callan's sword or Dastynn's crystalline hammer. There were even a few cots and bedrolls up against one wall.

In the middle of it all, was a large table upon which was carved an elaborate map of Aelathil and the surrounding nations. On the floor next to that was a small wooden boat, large enough to fit maybe four or five adults. Murdock moved to the table, which Dastynn had already begun inspecting.

The mage called over his shoulder to Callan, "There are clothes in the wardrobes. Change into something dry."

While the two older men looked over the map, Callan opened what he hoped would be a large selection of clothing. He was disappointed. Inside, there were four identical outfits in varying sizes. All of the outfits contained a tunic in the same shade of light brown. The pants were a few shades darker while the boots were the darkest of the lot. Hanging on the door was a group of matching hooded cloaks. Callan sighed at the poor selection and stripped out of his ruined clothes. It was probably for the best that he changed, anyway. His mother would kill him if she found out he had muddied his favorite set of dress clothes.

Callan dressed as quickly and quietly as he could in the dark cavern. Murdock was speaking to Dastynn in a hushed tone. Callan couldn't understand a word he said, but he sounded frustrated. When he took a glance at the pair of them, Murdock was leaning over the table, looking angrily at the paladin. Dastynn looked angry as well. He, as always, was not speaking, but his eyes and his jaw were set. He gestured firmly at himself and at his hammer, which he had set on the table.

When Callan finished dressing in the drab, mottled browns, he approached the table. Murdock began to raise his voice by the time Callan got near.

"I don't care how much it means to you! We can't have you parading it around out there!"

Dastynn picked up the hammer and held it behind his back as if he tried to keep Murdock and Callan from seeing it.

"No, you can't hide it! Everybody out on the road with half a brain will recognize a hammer like that! And even if they don't, it's more valuable than most homes around here. We'd be robbed by every group of bandits from the Capitol to Graveholm."

Dastynn growled like a dog that had just had its tail stepped on. Callan could practically see his hackles rising. He stared hard at the mage for a moment. Dastynn looked as if he wanted to scream back at Murdock, but opted to instead spit a large glob of saliva at his feet and stomped off.

Murdock rubbed his eyes with his thumb and forefinger. He inhaled deeply and held the breath until he noticed Callan standing there, frozen in place by the anger he'd seen from the mage. He had realized he was intense, but Callan never thought Murdock would think to yell at someone as large as Dastynn. Either they had known each other for a long, long time or Murdock was someone who was not to be argued with.

The mage did his best to smile at Callan. "I'm sorry you had to see that. He can be awfully blockheaded sometimes." Callan could only stare at his feet in response, so Murdock continued, "Him having that fancy armor and hammer along can only get us into trouble. I'll put a spell on the chest so he and I are the only ones that can get to it, though. Don't worry, we've done this kind of thing before. He'll come around."

In fact, when Callan looked, Dastynn was already forcefully removing his armor plates and tossing them into the same wardrobe that Callan had grabbed his new clothes from. His hammer was already buried by the plates. He and Murdock changed quickly into clothes that matched Callan's in every way but size. Murdock's fit him fine, but Dastynn's seemed like it was made for someone a head shorter and a good deal less broad. Once they were dressed, Murdock closed the wardrobe and placed the palms of both hands on the doors. A bright yellow light flashed along the seams of the wood, then disappeared as quickly as it had come. Murdock patted Dastynn reassuringly on the shoulder, and they made their way back to Callan

When the pair arrived, Dastynn tossed a long strip of cloth to the young man.

Murdock spoke for him, saying, "Wrap that around your scabbard. We don't want it attracting attention. Luckily for you, a scabbard is a little easier to hide than a hammer made of blue crystals."

Callan smiled at Dastynn. The paladin didn't look amused.

Instead of returning Callan's smile, he stalked over to the nearest weapon rack and removed a spear. He tied it to his back with another long strip of cloth and moved to the front of the small boat and lifted it by the front. With Callan and Murdock watching, he dragged the boat, scraping it along the stone floor of the cave. Murdock shrugged and followed him with Callan tagging along behind.

The paladin pushed the boat into the water and held it for Callan and Murdock. The two of them climbed in and held on while the small craft rocked and shook under the heavy steps of the big man. He grabbed a pair of massive oars from the bottom of the boat and steered it down the river.

Murdock turned to Callan and gave him a tired smile. "We're headed for Skykirk. It won't take too long, but you should try to sleep."

Callan had drifted into sleep before Murdock had the chance to speak. The three of them drifted into the night, the fires of what used to be the Dragon's Keep roaring in the skies behind them.

Chapter 10

"You let her do what?"

There was a stammering and a shuffling of robes and feet. Pyra couldn't make out the words through the buzzing that weighed heavy on her head. There was more murmuring, and then a loud crash. She strained her heavy eyelids, but they refused to open.

"Listen closely, you old bastard." The voice was unmistakably her father's. He sounded angry. "We had a long talk about that kind of heresy when you got here. You know where I stand on the issue."

She listened more closely, too elated her father was alive to be worried about what had brought about his anger.

"I assure you, m'lord, it was the only way!" Now that she could hear more clearly, Pyra recognized Elder Moss as the second speaker. "You would have died!"

"Then I should have died," roared Ravitch. "I let you waste her time with your magic because it kept her entertained. Now you bring this…this…necromancy into my castle! What's worse, you used my daughter as your vassal!"

Moss made a noise as if he wanted to speak, but Ravitch cut him off. "I swear to you, if she doesn't wake up from this, your wrinkled head will decorate my mantle."

Pyra, still unable to open her iron-plated eyelids, tried to move, to do anything to tell her father she was alright. Everything felt heavy. Useless. She tried to work her throat or her mouth to make some kind of noise. Try as she might, though, her body refused to cooperate. Rather than panic, she focused her thoughts. Her mind worked just fine. Her father was still screaming and ranting at Elder Moss, but Pyra pushed that from her awareness.

She extended herself into the waters of the ether, submerging herself in the cool waters of the magical current. Pyra tried to summon forth some kind of magic. A spark, a flame, any kind of burning sensation.

There was a searing pain in her arm, and she heard a distant scream. Pyra's eyes shot open, and the immense pain in her arm subsided immediately. Once her eyes were open, she saw her father and the elder staring at her, lips sealed tight. The scream she'd heard erupted from her own throat. She clenched her teeth and stole a glance at her left arm, where the pain had originated. It was unmarked and unburned, as if nothing had happened. It tingled still, but whether that was because she had actually burned herself or because she thought she had, Pyra's brain was too muddled to figure that out.

Elder Moss rushed to her side, Ravitch only a few steps behind the older man. Before the elder could even ask Pyra how she felt, Ravitch grabbed him by the collar of his robes and yanked hard. Moss stumbled, unable to keep his balance, and sprawled to the stone floor. Pyra tried to sit up, to ask if he was alright, but fell back to the soft bed in pain. It seemed as if every nerve in her body were on fire.

Ravitch snarled at Elder Moss, "Get out of here so I can talk to my daughter. I'll deal with you later."

"But, m'lord," he stammered, "I really think I should—"

"Go!"

He went quickly. Pyra had seen her father chastise his subjects before but never with so much anger in his voice. Ravitch was a cold man, hardened by the unforgiving winters and vicious creatures of northern Aelathil. Still, she had never seen him order someone from his presence with such violence. Elder Moss, who was one of the most respected mages in Aelathil, and certainly the most powerful in Graveholm, scampered before him like a dog who had just been kicked. She felt bad for the old man, but that feeling was quickly shoved aside by an intense relief at seeing her father up and about.

Ravitch leaned down and hugged her gently without a word. She squeezed him back tightly, not caring about the discomfort in her arms and torso or the thundering behind her eyelids. Pyra felt her father flinch when she hugged him. His discomfort must have been much more than he showed. She shouldn't have been surprised, seeing as his injuries were some of the most horrific she'd ever seen. Ravitch should have been dead

"Father," she began, "I'm sorry, I didn't mean to upset you. I was only trying to help, and Elder Moss said it was okay."

Ravitch shook his head and placed a finger on her lips, quieting her.

"You don't apologize for that or for the old man. I should be thanking you," he said. "I just wish there had been another way to do it. That black magic leaves a bad taste in my mouth."

Pyra smiled a little. It was good to know Ravitch wasn't angry with her. She could see in his eyes…or eye, now, he still had a score to settle with the elder, though. Magic was a confusing subject. It all came from the same place. All of it stemmed from the ethereal plane. She had been told as much by the elder. When she created fire, when Elder Moss healed wounds, when anything was accomplished through magic, the power was drawn from that plane.

"What's the difference between what I've been learning and what the elder and I did to help you? Why was it such a bad thing?"

Ravitch rubbed his remaining eye with the palm of his hand. Seeing him with linen wrapped over the hole in his head was disconcerting, to say the least, but he seemed used to it already. He had always been adaptable. Pyra admired him for that.

He shook his head. "Pyra, I don't dabble in that nonsense. I never have." He sighed and leaned back, putting his hands behind his head, scratching at the wounds that had begun scabbing over already. "My father always told me magic was a trick weak men used to kill strong men. I've tried to be more open-minded than him. I tolerate you learning from Moss, but I won't pretend to understand how magic works. If you want to know about why I was so angry, ask him."

Pyra could only nod. She wasn't sure what to think. Part of her was understanding. Most of Graveholm was superstitious in the extreme. They were so isolated, up in Aelathil's mountains, that it was hard not to be. Religion and personal worries fed into the fear of the supernatural as well.

Another part of her was frustrated with her father, though. He had always been hesitant to let her practice magic, but he had never called it nonsense before. The fact he at least gave credence to the idea that magic was for the weak, and only for men at that, was enough to make her uncharacteristically angry. So what that she was a woman? So what that she wasn't a spear-wielding knight, decked out in her own weight in armor? She wasn't Gramm. She wasn't Theamere. The certainly wasn't her father. Did Ravitch expect her to be ashamed of taking advantage of her strengths?

"I would love to ask him about it, but you just kicked him out, and I'm not sure I'm strong enough to get up and find him yet. You'll have to get him for me and bring him here."

It was hard to tell if Ravitch scowled at her or not. It always had been. His beard and long, black hair gave him a brooding look. The eye wrap and facial wounds made him look downright intimidating. Aside from the fact he had three angry slash marks down the side of his face, the cuts extended to the corner of his mouth, giving it a cruel curl. Looking at him as closely as she now was, Pyra could understand why the elder had left so quickly.

"Gramm." Ravitch called loudly, but there was no anger in his voice. Only indifference. Pyra wasn't sure which she preferred.

The knight stuck his head into the room. He looked tired and disheveled, not at all like his usual self. His eyes were red and bloodshot. The knight looked like he hadn't slept in days.

"Yes, my lord?"

Ravitch stood and walked to the door. "Go find Moss," he said. "Tel him he has an hour to talk to Pyra. I'll be in my study."

He limped out and down the hall, his heavy, uneven footsteps echoing down the hall for a few moments after he was gone. Instead of immediately doing what Pyra's father had told him to, Gramm took a few more steps into the room. They were the only two there, now that Moss and Ravitch had gone.

Gramm moved in nervously, almost sheepishly, wiping his hands on the front of the cloth tabard that decorated his armor. "How are you, um…are you alright?"

Pyra smiled, despite herself. "I feel like I fell off my horse." That got a smile out of him, but she continued, "…four or five times."

"I'm glad," he said. The knight stood still for a moment, wringing his hands together and looking around the room nervously. It seemed like he wanted to say something. Or find a place to sleep. He was most definitely not his usual self. "I umm…I…"

"Gramm," Pyra interrupted, "go and get Elder Moss, please. And then go get some sleep. You look exhausted."

He smiled wearily, but shook his head. "I'll be fine, my lady. I still have rounds to make."

Pyra shook her head forcefully. Too forcefully if the sharp pain that shot up the back of her neck and head were anything to go by. "That's an order, Gramm. Go get some rest."

Gramm nodded again, seeming like it took all of his energy to move just that little bit. "Yes, my lady."

He slipped from the room, much more quietly than Ravitch had. Now, for the first time since she had woken up, Pyra was alone. She could finally relax, if only for a few moments. Now that all was quiet, she could make an assessment of her own body. It hurt, that much was for sure. She was often tired after using magic. She was used to that. Pyra had only summoned fire a couple of times, but each had left her feeling like she could use a good nap. This time, with this new magic, she was a new kind of tired. Her arms felt like they were made of stone, and her head felt like someone hit her with one of the maces her father's knights liked to carry around.

It was a struggle to even keep her eyelids open. Only the thought of talking to Elder Moss about what had happened kept her awake. Hopefully, he hadn't gone too far. Gramm had looked like he was ready to collapse. If the elder had gone managed to make it to his quarters, he might be the one to find the knight, snoring in the middle of a hallway. The thought made Pyra smile. She stopped that quickly. Even her lips felt sore. Really, her entire face hurt. Maybe if she just closed her eyes and relaxed, it wouldn't hurt so badly. Maybe if she only let the muscles in her face and her arms and her legs and her stomach relax, she wouldn't be in so much pain.

What seemed like moments later, she was being gently shaken. Pyra opened her eyes to the sight of the elder, smiling down at her.

"I'm awake," she grumbled.

"Well, you had me fooled," said another voice. "You sure snore an awful lot for an awake girl."

Beyond the elder, with his arms crossed and an impassive look on his face, stood her older brother. Theamere didn't share a lot with Pyra in terms of looks. She was of a small build, with auburn hair and a pale complexion. Theamere was built almost exactly like their father: big. He didn't have the beard Ravitch had, but his face was covered in a dark stubble. Also, where Ravitch let his hair fall wildly about his head and shoulders, Theamere used a short piece of twine to tie his back behind his head.

Pyra sniffed at him. "I do not snore. It's undignified."

Theamere laughed, but he didn't have a chance to respond. Elder Moss interrupted the two of them.

"Pyra, your young knight friend said you wanted to speak with me. Our time is limited, so if you have questions, I suggest you ask them quickly."

He sounded tired, even to Pyra, who had only been awake for a few moments. There was also a shade hiding behind his eyes. The way he kept glancing around the room worried Pyra. The elder looked toward the door over and over again. He tried to keep an eye on Theamere without turning his head, but it didn't seem he was having any luck. Elder Moss was scared.

And Ravitch had sent Theamere to keep an eye on him. Pyra would have been worried, too.

"Okay." She took a deep breath. *Right to the chase, then.* "I want to know why my father was so upset at the way that you…we…helped him."

Moss nodded and sat down in the chair next to her bed. It seemed he had expected the question, or something similar. Still, he looked uncomfortable. Theamere stayed where he was with his arms across his chest.

"I want to be up front with you. There's a lot about magic that you don't know."

Pyra and Theamere shot him identical eye-rolls, but Elder Moss continued speaking as if he hadn't seen.

"You can only control magic you've had some kind of personal experience with." He held up a hand to stop Pyra from interrupting him. "I've only taught you about the most basic of magic. The kind everyone has experienced. That's elemental magic. You've got a very basic control of fire, air, wind, and earth. All mages start there. All of them have experienced those four basic forces of nature."

"Why have you and I focused so much on fire, then," Pyra asked? "And what does any of what you just said have to do with why Father was so angry?"

Moss looked older at this moment than he ever had. His eyes were downcast, and his hands trembled just slightly. He looked like he would rather have been anywhere in the world than in Graveholm right that moment.

Still, he continued, "Well, the people here in Graveholm, you included, seem to have a natural affinity for fire. It permeates your religion, your birth rites, your burial rites. The cold up here helps with that. Without a constant supply of fire, your people would die off. Understand?"

Pyra nodded. Moss sat quietly now, his chin tucked in and his eyes focused on his lap. It was very clear he didn't want to say anything else. Too bad for him. Pyra had to know.

"Elder, tell me. Why was father so upset? You helped him. That can't be a bad thing, can it?"

"Pyra," he looked up and stared at her, tears starting to form in the corners of his eyes. "I don't know that I can—"

"Tell me. That's an order."

Her voice was so stern she surprised even herself. Pyra had never taken to using a commanding tone before. She had always left that to her father and Theamere. This was different, though. The elder kept information from her. He looked over his shoulder to Theamere for support. He didn't find any. Pyra's brother only nodded.

Obviously dejected, Moss looked back at Pyra and continued once more. "To help your father, I didn't just wave my hands and make everything better. I went in and fixed all the damage that had been done to his insides. To do that, I had to have experienced the inside of the human body. I had to know how we, how humans, worked."

"So, you cut open bodies and studied their organs? That's disgusting, but I don't see why Father would be so upset."

Moss shook his head. "I could have done it like that, I suppose, for a basic understanding." His voice sounded hollow, as if he tried to distance himself from the words that came out of his mouth. Pyra could see plain as day that he didn't want to continue, but the elder knew they would make him talk. Besides, Pyra could always go and get the information from her father if she had to. She wanted it from her teacher. She wanted it from Moss.

"I felt like I could get a deeper understanding of the craft by studying the inner workings of the human body while it was still…" Moss coughed, "functioning."

Pyra could only stare at him. Her mind was buzzing in an attempt to wrap itself around what he tried to say. She had to have misunderstood. This was her teacher, her mentor. He couldn't have done anything like that. He couldn't have studied live humans. It was disgusting. It was horrible.

"No," she said. "You didn't."

He didn't respond. He only stared at his hands wrung them to try and stop the tremors going through them.

"You didn't retire from the mages' college, did you?" Theamere spoke up for the first time from his position in the back of the room. "They kicked you out. That's how you ended up all of the way out here."

Moss nodded, but he didn't say anything else. He didn't need to. The three of them could only sit in silence. Pyra was sure Theamere felt the same way as their father did about the issue. All magic, according to them, would have been tainted by acts like Moss'. It was no wonder Ravitch had reacted so savagely to how Moss had healed him. His body had been defiled by knowledge that had come from experiments on humans.

Pyra wasn't sure how she felt about the elder, now. He had taught her so much since she had been very young. What else was he hiding? What other atrocities had he committed to learn his craft? She had a million questions to ask him, but she had to sort them out in her own mind first.

She wouldn't have a chance just yet. There was a knock at the door. A young knight poked his head in and saluted Theamere. She recognized him from around town but couldn't recall his name.

"Theamere," he said, "You have a visitor outside the gates. He wants to speak with your father, but Lord Ravitch said to send you. He says he's in no condition to be climbing up and down staircases."

"Tell this visitor I'll come find him in town tomorrow," said Theamere. "This has been a rough few days for our family."

"Sir," the knight responded, "I can't do that. He's a Visani. A big one. And he seems angry."

Chapter 11

Pyra smiled at her brother's back. She couldn't see much detail beneath the heavy furs he wore, but he was sure that his back was knotted with frustration. He had demanded she stay in bed until she was completely healed. She had responded, in no uncertain terms, that she would never in a hundred lifetimes miss out on the chance to stand face-to-face with a live Visani. They rarely left their caverns in the mountains to venture near Graveholm. One coming to the keep was unheard of. Besides, the closest she had ever come to a Visani was the pelt of the one who had nearly killed her father. She wanted to speak with this one.

The soldier that had come to fetch Theamere was being used as a human walking cane for Pyra. She gripped his arm tightly, refusing to slow her pace despite the dull ache in her entire body.

"What is your name, soldier?"

"My name's Landry, m'lady," he replied.

Pyra smiled at him. "Pyra, Landry. Call me Pyra."

He only nodded. As pale as his face was, she was surprised he'd been able to speak at all. Landry looked like he wanted to get sick. He had seen this Visani. Maybe even spoke to it. Either way, he'd been shaken by the experience. Of course, he probably held onto one of the many superstitions most of Graveholm did.

It was often said that the Visani were snow devils. Creatures of the Pit that had taken the form of a twisted mixture of giant feline and human. Others said they were mutated white lions that had migrated from the grasslands of Nassas generations ago. The truth, as Pyra knew it, was far from either of those. All of her teachers, including Elder Moss and her father, had told her the Visani were a mysterious but intelligent race of creatures. They lived in packs, prides, in the mountains and preferred their own company to that of humans who would more than likely attack them on sight.

As they neared the gates, where the Visani waited, Theamere turned and addressed Pyra. "Sister, you're going to have to let me do the talking. You're still not fully healed, and if you let slip that you're not well…well, any hint of weakness will be seen as an insult."

"Thea," she said, using his childhood nickname, "you sound like Father. I'll be fine."

"No. Do not speak. Stand by my side and stand straight. Do not make eye contact."

Theamere took Pyra's arm gently from Landry and allowed her to wrap it around his elbow for support. "Soldier, return to your post. You look like you're about to cry."

Landry saluted crisply and turned on his heel without a word. Pyra heard his intense sigh of relief as soon as he rounded the nearest corner. Theamere's mouth twitched with the slightest hint of laughter. She would have found it amusing if she weren't so angry at him. The one chance in her life she would get to talk to a Visani, and he was taking it from her. There had to be a way around his order. After all, she couldn't be rude to a guest. If the Visani addressed her, she would be forced to answer. Maybe she would even introduce herself. Maybe the Visani would do the same. Maybe she would be invited back to the village to visit as an ambassador to Graveholm.

And maybe the ice would melt off the mountains. Pyra sighed.

When the pair reached the main gates, the sight of a dozen spear-wielding soldiers greeted them. The armored men had formed a large half-circle around the entryway of the keep. They were completely fixated on what was outside, just beyond Pyra's field of view. The Visani. The soldiers didn't even notice Pyra and Theamere approach.

Theamere shouted, "What's the meaning of this?"

All of the men nearly jumped out of their boots. One of them broke ranks and ran to Theamere, offering a shaky salute.

"Well?"

The soldier sputtered a moment before he found his voice. "If you'll `scuse my language, m'lord, there's a bigass Visani out there."

Theamere took a step forward and glared at the soldier. "He is a *guest*." Theamere snarled. "Take the other men and *get out*."

They cleared out quickly, without even waiting for the man's command. Some of them looked like whipped dogs, with their tails between their legs. Others looked relieved to be able to watch from a safe distance. Pyra noticed with a mixture of pride and worry that her brother reminded her very strongly of their father. Both men were fair with their followers, but could be downright frightening when they wanted to be.

The siblings walked arm in arm to the wide-open doors. Pyra's eyes took a moment to adjust to the bright light of the afternoon sun reflecting off the snow. When they finally did, she gasped aloud, the sound escaping her before she could clamp down on it. She felt Theamere tense when she made the noise.

Standing silhouetted against the white-capped mountains, surrounded by flurries of freshly falling snow, stood the Visani. Pyra struggled to find words to describe him. He was huge. She stood as tall as maybe the middle of his ribcage and could have stood side by side with herself and still not been as wide as he was. The Visani had a mane like a lion. She had seen pictures of them in her books. His, though, was braided and decorated with stones, jewels, and what appeared to be bones. He was covered in fur as white as the snow on the ground. Pyra imagined he would be very difficult to find in the mountains if he wanted to remain hidden. A long tail hung from his back, flicking back and forth in the gentle breeze. There were very few words that could describe him. She settled on intimidating. And beautiful.

Theamere bowed to him. Pyra did as well, but couldn't bow as deeply as her brother. Her back and stomach hurt too badly. She did as she was told, though, and showed no signs of weakness and remained silent. Theamere addressed him.

"I am deeply sorry for the rude welcome my men gave you," he said. "My name is Theamere, heir to the Lordship of Graveholm. My father regrets that his recent injuries prevent him from seeing you himself."

The Visani spoke next, his voice like a deep, throaty purr. "My name is Melhaar son of Gravar, who is the Father of the Clans." He paused and inspected the claws on one hand…paw. "Your men did what they thought was right. I do not blame them for being afraid."

Pyra wanted to laugh. This Visani was arrogant. He was right, though. The soldiers were terrified.

"It is good to meet you, Melhaar," responded Theamere. "Would you like to come in to the keep for some food or drink? Or to get warm?"

Melhaar shook his massive, shaggy head. "No. Your walls are unnatural. Not shaped by the earth. And I am warm. I need no fires like you humans."

He was right, Pyra supposed. His fur was thick, and he wore sparse little. In fact, the only clothing the wore was a few straps of leather that held various pouches and weapons onto his person. There were daggers on his waist, held in very simple sheaths. Melhaar carried no other weapons Pyra could see. Judging from the size of his claws, though, and the two massive teeth that hung from his upper jaw down his chin, he probably didn't need to carry many hand-made weapons. Nature had given him everything he needed to fend for himself

Theamere nodded. "Very well. The offer stands if you change your mind." He crossed his arms around his chest, leaving Pyra to stand on her own. "If I can be blunt for a moment…"

The Visani nodded.

"Why have you come here today, Melhaar? Your people very rarely come near Graveholm, let alone to the front doors of our keep."

Melhaar smiled, showing his gleaming white teeth. "My father went missing some days ago. He has been…ill, of late, and I would like to bring him home." He looked around and inside the front doors, as if expecting to see his father in there. Pyra's heart jumped into her throat. She had a horrible feeling she knew exactly where Melhaar could find his father.

"You see," he continued, "he was injured. My people found his blood in the mountains, and I followed his trail here to Graveholm. To this keep, actually."

Theamere was rigid as a tree trunk. It was obvious he had come to the same conclusion that Pyra had. Gravar, Father of the Clans, was being worn as a cloak by their father. This meeting was going to get tense before things were finished.

"Melhaar," started Theamere, "my people and I—"

The Visani cut him off with a growl. "Where is my father, human?"

For a moment, Theamere didn't move. Pyra was worried he wasn't going to say anything. When he answered, he did it quickly.

"He's dead."

Melhaar became unnaturally still. Even his tail, which had been moving back and forth like a pendulum since they had arrived, went rigid.

When Melhaar said nothing, Theamere continued. "He attacked our father. We brought both of them back here. Father barely survived. Gravar did not."

Melhaar looked sad, then. His ears and the long whiskers on the sides of his face drooped. "I am sorry," he said. "Father had taken on the Blood Fever. It is deadly among my people. Before the disease kills, though, a madness grips the inflicted. I'm sure that my father was not himself when he attacked yours."

Neither Pyra or Gramm knew what to say and Melhaar was silent after that. They stayed like that for a few minutes, each of them lost in their own thoughts. Pyra wanted to break the silence. To apologize to Melhaar for not being able to help his father. She was spared that, though, by the Visani himself.

"May I have his body," he asked? "He must be given to the Goddess if he is to be at peace."

Theamere and Pyra both froze. Pyra wanted to turn and look to her brother for help, to get some advice on what she should do. She wanted to plan a response with him. She wanted to run and hide under her bed. She couldn't move. Her eyes were locked on the massive form of Melhaar. Locked on his cold, black eyes. Theamere, apparently, could not speak either. He shook his head from side to side twice, and then was still again.

"No?" The Visani was incredulous. He had every right to be. "And why not?"

Theamere was still silent. If Ravitch had been there, he would have slapped his son upside the head and commanded him to speak. Pyra wanted to do just that, but she was just as terrified as Theamere was.

Melhaar took a step forward, his voice rising. "Why will you not return my father's body to me?"

Her brother stared at the Visani, at a loss for words. It was very clear he was too scared to say anything that would upset Melhaar. Still, by not saying anything, he was achieving the same end. Melhaar was agitated, clearly. His ears were laid back against his skull and his breaths came much more quickly than they had been earlier. His tail whipped around behind him like it had a mind to jump off his body. She couldn't stand being silent any more. Yes, she had been commanded not to speak, but being silent could very well kill them both if they weren't careful.

She mumbled under her breath, her voice refusing to raise above a whisper. Theamere turned to her, his eyes wide with horror that she had spoken. Melhaar turned to her as well, his face an emotionless mask.

"What did you say, whelp?"

Pyra shook her head. She couldn't repeat it. She couldn't say it louder. He would kill them both

"Tell me what you said!" He was angry now. Shaking. Pyra had no choice.

"The men that brought our father home. They made Gravar into a cloak."

Melhaar froze. He looked as if she had clubbed him in the back of the head. His tail went limp. His lips moved, but no sound came out. For just a moment, he looked like any house cat. Lost and confused. That didn't last long. He steeled himself and drew a bone-handled dagger from a belt at his waist. Theamere's sword was in his hand so quickly that Pyra failed to see him draw it.

Melhaar spoke, his voice emotionless. Cold. "One of your people is *wearing* my father. Gravar, Father of the Clans, is now an article of clothing."

Theamere tried to reason with him. "Melhaar, listen…"

"Silence!" His voice echoed against the walls of the keep. The shout caused Pyra's entire body to tremble. She wanted to work magic against him. Light a fire and hurt him, or scare him away at the least. She couldn't focus on the magic, though. She was too afraid.

"I am Melhaar, son of Gravar who was Father of the Clans. The title is mine now. The blood in my veins runs in the veins of every Visani." He lifted his dagger and pointed it at Theamere. "You are your father's heir, as I am mine. You will die last."

He slashed down with the dagger, but nowhere near enough to hit either of the siblings. Instead, he raised his free hand and cut a deep furrow in the palm. Blood spurted from the wound and soiled the immaculate white of the fresh snow.

"I call for a Blood War, to avenge my father and my people. We will not rest until your line is no more, Theamere, son of Ravitch." Melhaar raised his bleeding palm to his chest and left a crimson streak over his heart. "Tell your father he will die screaming. As will you. You will die as well, whelp." He looked at Pyra then. Her heart sank past her toes.

He threw the dagger in the middle of the three of them, then turned and walked away without another word. Theamere sheathed his sword, his arms shaking so badly that Pyra was surprised he hadn't dropped it.

"Why didn't you kill him," she asked?

"I will. Just not yet."

She watched the Visani walk away, as did most of the villagers. The knights on the walls followed him with their bows drawn, their arrows aimed at his back. None fired. None were ordered to. They all knew it was dishonorable to kill an opponent who had his back turned. Pyra knew that as well. She wouldn't have attacked Melhaar now, even if she had been able to summon magic. She only hoped their honor didn't end up having horrible consequences in the future.

99

Chapter 12

Skykirk really was an amazing town. It was separated into two halves, one on each side of the Havvas River. The two halves were connected by an intricately carved bridge easily wide enough for two or three carriages to cross at once. Callan was on the bridge, standing on his toes to see over the large wall that separated the people of Skykirk from Vaalgur, the waterfall that roared off into oblivion just on the southern side of the town. Murdock had explained Skykirk had gotten its name because of Vaalgur.

"The first people to settle here thought they stared off the edge of the world," he had said. Callan could believe it. The waterfall was so tall, and the mists and the bottom so thick, he couldn't see the ground a few hundred feet below.

"You know, the waterfall was named after a titan."

Callan turned around and saw Murdock smiling at him. He was taller than Callan, so it was easier for him to see over the safety wall. He seemed comfortable staring off into the misty abyss. Callan wasn't so confident.

"A titan?" Callan was incredulous. He knew that giants had roamed Aelathil at one point. He'd never heard of titans outside religious texts, though. Each of the thirteen gods had commanded a legion of titans in their wars with each other, before they had united and created the world as the humans of today knew it. He seriously doubted Murdock was talking about the same titans.

"Mhmm. Vaalgur was a fire titan that lived on this mountain thousands of years ago." Callan couldn't tell if Murdock was pulling his leg yet or not so he stayed quiet and listened. "Titans...real ones...were giant beings made purely from magical energy. So, Vaalgur was made entirely out of magical fire. He took the form of a giant spider. And when I say giant, I mean a few times bigger than your dad's keep."

"What happened to him? Why doesn't he live on the mountain anymore?" Callan couldn't help himself. He was hooked.

Murdock shrugged. "He quit being peaceful. He started burning forests and attacking people. The College sent a war party to take him down. I've never been to the bottom of the waterfall, but I've heard the land still bears a lot of scars from the battle."

"Wow. He really must have been something to see."

Murdock looked like he wanted to reply, but the sound of someone loudly clearing their throat behind them interrupted him. When Callan turned around, he saw Dastynn standing impatiently with the reins of three light brown horses in his massive hands.

"Sorry about that," laughed Murdock. "I was telling a story."

Dastynn rolled his eyes and handed a set of reins to each of them. Then, much to Callan's chagrin, the paladin turned and lifted him into the saddle.

"We had enough to buy three horses and enough supplies for the trip," asked Callan?

Murdock smiled and nudged his horse off to the eastern half of Skykirk.

"Something like that."

Callan decided not to press the issue. He'd find out sooner or later, anyway. His horse followed behind Murdock's and in front of Dastynn's, clearly knowing it was only supposed to follow the leader. It was a good thing he had been trained well. Callan had ridden horses around the keep, but mostly under the supervision of their trainer, and only through the courtyard. He had never ridden a horse through the wilderness before. Gods, he had never even *been* in the wilderness before. He and Keyara had only explored outside of town a few times, and the one time they'd been caught, it was made very clear they were never to do it again.

He hadn't been able to tell Murdock or Dastynn he'd never been outside of his home before. He was too nervous they would laugh at him. It was probably a stupid worry. No, it was definitely a stupid worry, and Callan knew it.

"Murdock. Did you notice that nobody's even looking twice at me? Changing out of my good clothes was a good idea, I think."

The mage nodded and kept his eyes forward. "That's the idea. We've only been away from Ashefall for a few days now so the longer we can go without anyone recognizing you, the better."

They rode in silence, toward the deep forests that made up much of the eastern half of Aelathil. Murdock seemed to be focused on his own thoughts, and Callan was too scared of saying anything stupid to say anything at all. Dastynn was his quiet self. Cal was still unsure if he was actually capable of speaking.

By the time that the sun began to set in the west, Callan was incredibly sore. He had never ridden for so long before. His back ached with every movement, his legs felt as if they had been carrying the horse all day instead of the other way around. And from the constant up-and-down bouncing, he wasn't sure he would ever be able to sit down again. Murdock looked uncomfortable, but not yet ready to stop for the night. Dastynn looked as impassively happy as he always did. When Callan lstole a glance at him, he offered a toothy smile and a wave. Callan laughed, despite himself. For someone who never spoke, Dastynn was awfully funny.

"Murdock, I don't mean to sound whiney, but how far are you planning on taking us tonight?"

He shrugged. "I'm not sure. The horses are in good shape and we've got a creek nearby where they'll be able to eat and drink all they want tonight. As long as the night stays clear, we'll probably go until I can't stay awake anymore."

Murdock turned and smiled at Callan. "Fall asleep if you want. Your horse knows what he's doing. I'll wake you up if I need to, don't worry."

"Okay. Thanks, I'll try."

He didn't have to try very hard. The even footsteps of his mount quickly lulled him into a deep sleep once he let them. Since they had left the keep, had left Ashefall, he had been sleeping very heavily. It was easier to just sleep than to worry about his family. Surely, they hadn't been able to stop the two monstrous dragons. And Balen never would have been foolish enough to fight to the death when he was clearly outmatched. Would Ramsey let them stay once they had surrendered, though? Or would he take Balen and the rest of Callan's family back to the capital, back to Tal Autem as prisoners? Yes, it was much easier to sleep his problems away than face them. There would be a time for figuring out how to get back to his father. Callan was perfectly content to let Murdock decide when that time was

He dreamed, as he had since the night of their escape, of fire and dragons.

Callan stood atop of hill of black stone, surrounded by a ring of flames. Above his head, dragons wheeled in a smoke-filled sky, circling ever lower. Charred bones littered the ground at his feet, and blackened human skulls stared at him, their empty sockets laughing at a hidden joke. Callan had dreamed this same dream before. Until tonight, he had been alone on this hill. Now, though, there was another. A dark figure, cloaked in smoke from the encroaching flames, stared at Callan from the other side of the fires.

"Only one person in living memory has ever slain a dragon."

Callan knew that. Ragnar the Slayer. His ancestor. He tried to reply, but his mouth refused to open. He couldn't move except to look at the burning

horror around him. Although he was free to look away, the shrouded figure held his curiosity and his gaze.

"He and his followers were granted land and make Lords of Aelathil. Kings of their own domains. They have ruled those provinces for hundreds upon hundreds of years."

The voice was clearly male. It was familiar, as well, but Callan couldn't remember where he had heard the voice before.

"Only one person in living memory has ever slain a dragon."

The figure moved to pull down his hood. Still, the smoke obscured his face. Callan couldn't make out any of his features.

He woke with a start.

Night had fallen, and the horses had come to a stop. The night was nearly cloudless, though, and the moon was full. Callan could make out Murdock in front of him and Dastynn behind. Each was awake and alert. Callan was still trying to shake himself from his sleep. They were in a thick forest. He could hear the gurgling of water over rocks not far away. It must have been the stream Murdock had spoken about earlier.

"Murdock, why did we—?"

The mage held up a hand to silence him. Somewhere in the woods, a wolf howled. As if in response, another horse, much closer than the wolf, neighed.

Callan dropped his voice to an almost inaudible whisper. "Someone's out there, aren't they?"

Murdock nodded heavily enough for Callan to see, and then nudged his horse. Callan's and Dastynn's both followed behind.

Once they were moving, the mage spoke in a low voice. "There are a few of them. I'm not sure how many. They've been following us since we left Skykirk."

A chill crept into Callan's skin. Only someone who meant to hurt them would have followed them for so long. He had seen Dastynn fight and was confident the paladin would do his very best to protect him. Murdock had some control over magic as well, but Callan was far from sure of his abilities. As for Callan himself, he was capable with a sword, but he had never been in a real fight for his life. The only time that he had been in any real danger, he had spent the entire time either hiding, vomiting, or running. He was unconfident, to say the least.

"How long did I sleep for?"

Murdock whispered back, over his shoulder, "Only a few hours. It's almost midnight."

A low whistling came to life to Callan's left.

For a split-second, he wondered what could have been making the noise. Then, a dull *thud* nearly jarred him from his seat as an arrow slammed into his horse's neck. The animal screamed in pain, a noise Callan never thought could have come from a living being. It reared onto its hind legs, nearly throwing Callan. How he managed to hold on to his seat, he wasn't sure. Very quickly, though he wished he had just allowed himself to fall.

The horse crashed down on its front legs and immediately forgot all the training it had gone through during its short life. Rather than stick with the others, it neighed again and bolted into the forest, away from the arrows and the screams that followed. Murdock and Dastynn were quickly lost behind them. Callan could hardly make out where they were going and was forced to rely on the horse to put aside its fear enough to not run headlong into a tree. As it was, branches whipped by at breakneck speeds as dirt and mud flew behind them. Branches, leafless, dagger-like fingers came out of the darkness every few seconds and slapped Callan on the face, arms and hands, cutting his clothes and his flesh like tiny daggers.

Every step the horse took pumped think globs of blood from the deep arrow wound. The blood seeped down the horse's neck and soaked Callan's leg. The slick, warm liquid made holding on for his life that much more difficult.

Through all of this, more arrows flew from behind. None hit their mark, but more than one came close enough for Callan to hear the distinctive whistle or feel the rush of air as the missiles flew by his face.

The horse couldn't have been running for long, but it felt like an eternity. Callan's mind was a blank slate of nothing but animalistic fear. He and the horse were similar in that way, at least. It began to slow. From how wet with blood Callan's leg was, the horse had to be in bad shape. It wheezed now, and its pace was anything but even. Before long, arrows came in from the sides, not just from behind.

They'd been caught.

A second arrow slammed into the horse's flank, followed by a third that hit Callan's mount in the chest. The horse fell without a sound, tossing Callan forward through the air. He landed hard with a *crunch* of sticks, dried leaves, and what felt like every bone in his body. He lay still for a few moments, too out of breath and in pain to move. Every intake of breath left him choking.

When he was finally able to move, he rolled his head to one side and saw his horse lying on its side. Callan looked for any signs of life, but the animal's chest was still. He crawled inch by inch across the ground. His head rang from the force of his fall. There was a sharp pain in his chest every time he moved, but Callan was too afraid to look down in case there was some kind of wound there. All he knew was crawling toward the horse. His sword was there. There was shelter there. Whoever it was that tried to kill him would get him for sure without his sword.

They'll probably get me anyway.

Callan made it to the horse and checked it over as best he could. It was dead, there was no questioning that. The first arrow should have killed it. It was a miracle it had carried Callan so far. He made a mental note to bury him properly, if he got the chance.

He found his sword quickly. It was tied to the side of his saddle and, luckily, hadn't fallen underneath the horse. With trembling hands, he unbuckled the cloth-wrapped scabbard so that he could draw the blade. Behind him, he heard laughing.

"You'd best leave that there, boy," came a voice from the forest.

Callan glanced over his shoulder while still trying to get his sword free. Out of the trees moved three men, wrapped in dark cloaks. All three had a bow and quiver strapped to their backs. The man in the middle was tall and bald, but those were the only features Callan could see in the darkness. He had a short sword in one hand.

His hands shaking harder every second, Callan finally managed to get his sword unstrapped. Still quaking, he turned and pointed the tip of the blade in the direction of the three men. He was shaking so hard, though, that the sword wobbled uselessly. He had no leverage, and no way to get to his feet, so he stayed seated. All three of his attackers laughed.

The one with the sword spoke up. "You gave us a nice little chase, kiddo, but game time is over. Get up and come with us."

"M…M…Murdock!" Callan's voice nearly caught in his throat. He hardly managed to make a noise at all, let alone yell. Murdock would have had to been *very* close by to hear him.

The men laughed again. "Murdock? He one of your friends?" Another laugh from the men. "Oh, we left them way behind. Your horse made sure of that. He's…well, he *was* pretty quick, anyway."

Callan made to stand, but the pain in his side kept him down. He gasped and nearly dropped his sword. All the while, the three moved closer. The one with the sword began swinging it around slowly, mocking Callan with every movement of its sharp edges.

"That's a nice sword you got there, too," he said. "Mountain steel looks like to me. One of your daddy's smiths make it for you?"

Callan shook even harder. "You…you know my father?"

This time it was one of the others who spoke up. One of the men with a bow. "Kid, everybody knows your old man. We figger he'll pay a pretty penny to get his runt back."

As they approached, Callan scooted back until he was up against the saddle of the downed horse. They laughed again. He was getting really tired of hearing them laugh. There was no way the last thing he would hear in this life would be the laughing of these three thugs.

Despite the incredible pain in his side, he forced himself into a kneeling position, using the saddle for support. He fixed his grip on the handle of his sword and held it upright, ready to block any attacks from the man with the sword.

Baldy stepped forward, sword in hand. "Put that down. We don't want you hurting yourself, now. Daddy will want you in one piece."

Callan snarled and took a swing at the thug's midsection. With a sneer, the man smacked Callan's sword with the flat of his own and sent it flipping through the air. It landed with a clatter a few arms' lengths away. As far as Callan was concerned, it might as well have been thrown off Vaalgur.

"Now," drawled the bald man, "where were we?"

An arrow sailed from the trees behind Callan and took one of the men behind Baldy in the chest. The force of the impact threw him onto his back, where he landed with a *thud*, then was still.

The dead man's two companions looked in the direction the arrow had come from. For a moment, they didn't move. Then, Callan saw their eyes widen in what was obviously terror. The remaining archer, the one who had spoken earlier, turned on his heel and ran. Baldy stood in place, shaking so hard he dropped his sword, but too terrified to make himself move. Callan could sympathize. He felt the same way, even without seeing what had scared them so badly.

With a roar like thunder, a black streak flew over Callan's head. The bald man stayed frozen as it dashed past him, straight for his companion. The running man screamed, but the yell was quickly cut off by a ripping. Then a gurgling. He fell to the ground with blood flowing freely from his freshly-opened throat.

A monster straight out of Callan's nightmares turned from the corpse and faced the bald man. It was massive. At least two heads taller that Dastynn and just as wide as the paladin when he wore his full armor. It was covered in thick, dark fur and had a head like some kind of massive wolf. Its long arms ended in gleaming claws, one of which dripped the runner's blood. It walked upright, straight at the bald man. He had finally remembered how to use his legs and began to back way, stammering.

"Leave me alone, devil. You got them two, I don't want any part of it."

It advanced more quickly than Baldy could back away and knocked him to the forest floor with a vicious backhanded blow.

It spoke then, with a voice that sounded like gravel rolling down a mountainside. "You broke the contract, Verne." The voice that came out of the monster's throat was unmistakably male. Callan wanted to turn and run, but he feared it would catch him like it had the other man. Terror rooted him in place just as it had Verne precious seconds ago.

Verne scuttled backward, trying to increase the distance between himself and the wolf-beast. "I didn't break no contract. I didn't, I swear!"

The wolfman reached down with one lithe arm and grasped Baldy around the neck. He squeezed until Verne's eyes began to bulge. Even in the darkness, Callan could see his face turning from pale, to red, to blue, to purple. It didn't take long, nor did it take much apparent effort, for Verne's eyes to roll back in his head. As soon as they did, the monster released his hold on the man's neck and let him fall to the ground in a heap.

Without a second glance at the discarded man, the wolf-creature turned and advanced on Callan. A scream wanted to work its way out of his chest, but he was too frightened to make any noise. Instead, he huddled as close to the corpse of the horse as he could and prayed for his life to end more quickly than Verne's had.

The monster got closer and closer, walking with measured steps. He stopped, his clawed feet nearly touching Callan's legs. He bent down, putting his lupine face just inches from Callan's. The smell was overpowering. Callan gagged on it. It was like a cloud surrounding the wolfman that was almost physical. It threatened to force its way down his throat.

"You are Callan?"

Cal jumped when the grating voice addressed him. He tried to back away, to get as far from the monster as he could, but he was stuck between the horse and the wolfman. Where was Murdock? Dastynn? They should have caught him by now.

It spoke up again. "You are Callan, yes?"

How in Sabriel's name did this thing know his name? Callan couldn't find the courage to speak, so he nodded. Maybe if he played along for a while, his head would stay attached to his shoulders. His sword was too far away to get to. Besides, as close as the thing's muzzle was to his face, he wouldn't make it more than a twitch before he was disemboweled. He nodded again.

"Good!"

He sounded almost excited. The wolf-thing stood up to his full imposing height. Callan quirked his head to one side. Good? Was it? He wasn't so sure.

Now that the creature stood tall, Callan got a better look at him. He didn't like what he saw. He was strapped with weapons on his back, his thighs, his shoulders. His hands, claws, were weapons all their own, as were his teeth. His tail wagged like a dog with a toy.

"My name is Torruk Forestshroud," he said. "I've come to take you back to your friends."

"My friends?" Callan's tone was suspicious.

He nodded. "Murdock and Dastynn. And Lys. He knows these men. I know them as well."

"Lys? Why is he here?"

The wolfman shrugged. "I will have to let him explain that."

Callan wrapped his arms around himself and stared past Torruk at the men he had so easily turned into corpses. "You killed those men. All of them."

"No," he said. "Not all of them. The last one, Verne. He lives."

There was no choice, it seemed. Callan could either stay alone in the woods and die for sure, or he could trust Torruk and possibly be eaten. Possibly was better than definitely, though.

"How far are they?"

Callan could have sworn that the wolfman smiled at him. "Not far. Come. I will bring Verne."

Chapter 13

Pyra froze. She hadn't expected to see more than one of the Visani. There were three. All of them eyed her. Blood dripped from their claws and teeth. The old man they had attacked, who had tried to make it to the keep, wasn't moving. Melhaar had said he wanted Ravitch and his line dead. He hadn't said anything about the villagers.

He had come running for the keep, and they hadn't been able to help him. Pyra had tried. She'd run to the main gates to let him in. They had pounced on him before she could save him, though. They saw her now. One of them stalked toward her. Melhaar had carried weapons. These Visani didn't. They had only what nature had given them.

The other two followed the first, toward Pyra. She couldn't fight off all three of them. Not even with magic. She'd never used it to hurt anything before. Still, she was sure she could cause some damage with fire. Not to all three of them, though. There were too many. Where were the soldiers? They were supposed to be coming. She had sent a runner. He should have been back. Unless more of the Visani had somehow gotten in already. They could be in the castle. She had to go warn someone.

Pyra turned on her heel. She smacked head first into a suit of armor. She looked up into the armored knight's face. Behind the steel visor, she could make out Gramm's face, more serious that she'd ever seen it.

"Get behind me."

Pyra moved without saying a word. She stood behind Gramm but stayed close enough that she could watch what was going on. Other soldiers arrived behind him, some still fitting their helmets to their heads or securing swords to their belts. They must have been off duty when the runner found them. Now they formed a half-circle around her, with Gramm nearest the Visani warriors. He was one of the younger knights, but they all knew he was one of the best with a sword. She'd heard some of the older soldiers remarking to her father how good he was. Now, it seemed, she would get to see him in action firsthand.

He drew his sword and detached the shield from his back. The lead Visani, who had stopped stalking forward when the soldiers arrived, began his advance again. Gramm tapped the flat of his sword against his shield and took a few steps forward as well.

One of the soldiers, an older man, whispered in Pyra's ear, "These things don't use armor like we do. They've never had to fight against steel before."

Pyra whispered back, her voice wavering, "Should I be going back to the castle? I don't want to be in the way."

His armor *clinked* when he shook his head. "No, m'lady. Not until these things have been taken care of. Then we're to escort you back to your father."

Pyra's reply was cut off by a savage roar from the lead Visani. He jumped at Gramm, clearing the distance between the two of them in a single bound. Pyra gasped. So did many of the soldiers. Gramm stood his ground, though. He put his right foot behind his left, shoulder-width apart, and held his shield in front of him with his left arm. He moved just quickly enough to knock the Visani aside. The feline's claws squealed across the steel shield as he tried to get at Gramm's throat. He surged forward again but was stopped short by the rectangular shield.

Gramm took a swing at the Visani with his blade, poking at the air, testing his reflexes. He was fast. And his friends closed in slowly. The knight and the warrior from the woods danced around each other, feeling each other out. The Visani was faster and more accurate with his attacks. Most of his attacks landed on Gramm's shield, but some slipped through. His claws couldn't penetrate the steel on his chest or the chainmail that guarded Gramm's extremities.

He was getting frustrated. Pyra was getting worried. Not about the Visani that Gramm was fighting, but about the two that he wasn't. If they were to jump on the knight, it wouldn't be too difficult to get the helm off his head and kill him that way. As distracted as Gramm was with his opponent, they could sneak by him to the group of soldiers guarding Pyra either. The soldiers were no knights. They didn't have the armor Gramm did. Most of them wore leather chest pieces and helms. Some of the ones with richer families, or fathers who had been soldiers as well, had pieces of chainmail or shields. Pyra was sure they would be able to kill the two Visani, but they would pay for it in blood. Pyra had to do something.

She detached herself from the images of Gramm fighting to defend her and the keep and let herself fall into the ether. The magical power washed over her in waves, charging her every fiber, every cell with life and power. She could see nothing but the inside of her eyelids, but she knew so much more. Shafts of magic flowed through everyone and everything in the yard, including the Visani. Different colored lights marked the individuals. Their movements, their breaths, the beating of their hearts. Powerful reverberations came through the Ether whenever the Visani's claws struck Gramm's shield. Pyra had never noticed anything quite like it before. Then again, she had never tried to access magic around so many others before, either.

Without a doubt, it was easier this time. Easier than it had ever been, in fact. She could draw from the various strands that led through the others. Those nearest her, the soldiers, were so fixated on the fight they wouldn't have even noticed if she'd slapped one of them. They certainly wouldn't mind if she siphoned some of the magical energy that flowed through them. She did just that.

Pyra drew energy from the multi-colored strands and focused them in the palm of her right hand. The colors converged there, swimming and dancing into something that resembled a ball. A tiny sun, the size of her fist. The ball never grew in size, but it became denser, almost gaining a physical weight. She could practically feel it in her hand.

Pyra held the ball out in front of her. It bobbed ever so slightly just above her palm. She maneuvered it, pointing the ball at the two Visani who creeped toward Gramm. They were closer than she would have liked. She tensed her arm and released the magic, focusing on sending the ball of energy at the nearest Visani.

Her eyes snapped open immediately. Pyra couldn't *see* the ball, but she could sense it moving toward the two feline-like creatures. It struck the first Visani in the chest. With an unearthly loud *whoosh*, he was blasted to ashes. The concussion of the blast then struck his companion. Pyra heard *cracking* and *popping*, and then watched as he was blown backward and out of the yard. The ashes of his companion lazily wafted after him on the mid-morning breeze.

Pyra dropped to her knees, too stunned to think. How had she done that? How had she come up with so much power so easily? Tears welled behind her eyes. To think, she had just ended two lives.

She didn't have much time to sulk. The Visani that fought Gramm snarled at the realization his compatriots had been killed. He snarled and fixed his black eyes on Pyra and took a step forward. Gramm lunged then, taking advantage of his opponent's distracted state. The Visani had placed himself too close to the knight. A final growl escaped the back of his throat as he was run through with cold steel. He sputtered and fell, blood dripping from the entry wound in his chest and the exit wound in his back. He died quickly, his blood staining the pristine snow.

Everyone turned to look at her then. They had the same questions burning behind their eyes that she did. Most of them hadn't seen magic up close before. Those who had, certainly had never seen someone kill with it in such a brutal fashion. Pyra wanted to be in her bed, beneath her blankets. She wanted Moss, as well, so he could explain how she had managed such a show of force.

Pyra sagged backward. She felt as if she had gone through some serious physical exercise. Those around her caught her, but seemed worn out as well. Had she done that to all of them? She had a lot of questions for the elder.

Behind the steel of his helm, Pyra could see worry etched on Gramm's face. Was he scared of her? Should he have been? A shout from the top of the wall drew his gaze away from her. A lookout.

"There are more of them! They're in the village!"

Gramm gestured at two of the soldiers that guarded Pyra. "Go grab any knights you can find. Anyone that can hold a weapon. Theamere especially. Tell them to meet me in village. We'll be finding refuge for those who need it in the keep."

Though the two men were clearly older than Gramm, his knighthood granted him rank over them. Besides that, he was the only one who seemed willing to take command of the situation. Pyra never would have called any of her father's soldiers cowards, but they were clearly overwhelmed. They needed a driving force and, for the moment, that was Gramm.

"The rest of you," he shouted, "come with me. Pyra, get inside."

She started to argue, but he shouted over her. "I need you to organize medics for anyone who gets injured out here! Now go!"

Pyra listened through the murky fog her mind had become. Gramm and the soldiers ran toward the nearby town, while Pyra turned toward the keep to do what she had been told. She was too tired to argue, too drained to do anything but move. She wanted sleep. She wanted to forget she had blasted two living creatures into nothingness. So, she had to act. Someone had to help usher in those who would be arriving for safety and heal those who were hurt. She could do that.

The next hour was a blur of motion and activity. Healers were summoned, soldiers were dispatched, and refugees from Graveholm were brought into the safety of the keep. Ravitch met with his officers, and Pyra was left to coordinate efforts in the great hall, which had been turned into an impromptu infirmary. Elder Moss had joined the efforts, but Ravitch had forbidden him to heal any wounds with magic. Still, he knew more about natural remedies than most so Pyra was glad to have his help.

The wounded were brought in one or two at a time. Most were, surprisingly, young men. Pyra had expected children and those too old to defend themselves.

Moss explained to her, "You have it backward, girl. The young and the old *aren't* able to defend themselves. That's why they aren't getting hurt. Or if they are, well, there's nothing we can do for them now." He stopped speaking for a moment and tied off a bandage around a man's waist. He had been cut along the bottom of his ribs.

"How did you get hurt, friend?"

The man grimaced and sat up, leaning back on his elbows for support. "Told my wife to take the young ones and run. One of the furry bastards took after them so I tackled him." With a grim smile, he added, "He got me pretty good with some stone knife. I made him pay for it with a cleaver to his neck. Might see if I can find him and get him stuffed."

Moss smiled at the man and clapped him on the shoulder. Pyra only grimaced. She didn't have a family of her own to look after and wasn't sure she ever would. Looking at this man, though, she realized her father would defend her life with his own. Her brother would do the same. Suddenly, those brought in became something more than victims. They were people. They had families. She owed them her best efforts. As did Moss.

She turned to the old mage and whispered, "Moss, I want you using magic to heal anyone you can. But do it discreetly."

"Pyra, your father has forbidden me—"

Pyra shook her head. "You let me deal with father. Help these people."

Moss sighed. He looked like he wanted to say more, but the hard look in Pyra's eyes convinced him otherwise.

Pyra left the magical healing and the really severe injuries to Elder Moss and the healers that took care of people for a living. There were very few of them, though, and Pyra ended up being much busier than she had originally anticipated. She stitched minor cuts, helped stem bleeding wounds, and reset a couple of cleanly broken bones. Sometimes, she would come across an injury that was too much for her.

One man had his knee shattered by a Visani warclub. He was in hysterics and screaming from the pain in his leg. She could do nothing but stand by him and hold his hand while he screamed and squeezed the blood from her fingers. An eternity later, she was relieved by one of the professional healers and sent away.

She went from that man to a small child who had been slashed across the face by one of the Visani. The claws had not cut deep enough to mortally wound the young boy, but he would bear those scars for the rest of his life. Pyra cleaned him up, quieted his tears, and bandaged the wounds on his face. His mother and father were there with him. That was more than some of the injured could say.

A woman who had watched her husband get cut down sat alone in a corner of the hall. She didn't cry, and she didn't seem to be wounded. When Pyra approached her, though, she got no response from the woman. Pyra could only watch as she stared at the wall, a dead look in her eyes. She did her best to initiate conversation, but Pyra was ignored. It was almost as if the woman couldn't hear her. Put off and worried by the situation, Pyra left her alone.

She went straight from the woman to one of the healers, an old man who had been in Graveholm for his entire life. He had always been around, but Pyra had never even thought to speak to him before. She felt almost foolish asking him for advice now. "The woman over there. She isn't hurt, but she isn't speaking either. What can we do for her?"

The healer moved quickly for someone his age, grabbing bandages and other healing supplies. He shrugged in response to Pyra's question. "We can let her grieve. She lost someone she loved. Who she counted on. She'll either get better or she won't. Nothing you and I can do about that."

Then he was gone, leaving Pyra alone in the crowd of tears and blood and sweat. There was chaos going on around her, and she could do nothing to help. It was infuriating to be so helpless. She wished she had learned how to use a weapon or that she was big enough to wear the armor of a knight. Ravitch never would have allowed that, though. As much as he had always looked down on politicians who believed women were good only for birthing babies, he would not go so far as to let his own daughter learn the ways of warfare. In that regard, he had always been supremely protective.

His attitudes had bled off on his children in different ways. Theamere was so much like Ravitch that sometimes Pyra could hardly tell them apart. They walked similarly, talked similarly, and Ravitch looked like she thought Theamere would, eventually. Most importantly, Theamere cared greatly for his family and for those he would eventually rule over. Pyra, on the other hand, could hardly be called rough or imposing. She was protective, but not in the same way as the men in her family. She could help those hurting more directly than her father could. For days now, she had been considering how best to do that. The only solution she could come up with was learning healing magic. She was not willing to experiment on people, though, or use the information Moss had learned doing the same.

There had to be another way. A better way. The act of healing seemed so pure and innocent. Pyra wasn't sure how it had become so foul in her and her father's heads. Someone had clearly taken a radical study of healing and turned the purity of the process on its head. There had to be an ethical method of healing out there. Didn't there?

She thought about the process of healing and magic for the next few hours until the stream of refugees slowed to a trickle, and then stopped altogether. Those with minor injuries had been taken care of and sent on their way. Anyone who had been hurt more severely was still in the hall, being taken care of. Pyra felt out of her element now. She could administer herbs and bandages and kind words, but she had no idea how to care for someone for hours or days after they were injured. That job would have to be left to the professional healers. For now, Pyra needed to find something to do. She could hardly sit around while everyone worked so hard.

The sound of the huge hall doors being flung open gave her something to do immediately, though. A large man in armor was carried in by two other soldiers. He was bleeding profusely, staining the floor red in his wake.

Gramm.

The two soldiers flanking him dragged him through the hall. He was too tall to carry, so they let his feet drag on the ground, disrupting the steady stream of blood he left in his wake. Someone had removed his helmet. There was a cut along his forehead, bleeding into his eyes. It made a grisly picture, especially since his teeth were bared in a genuine smile.

Pyra rushed over to the men and ushered them over to a cot that had been vacated. She cleared the area of dirty bandages and loose medicines. She let them handle putting him on the bed.

Gramm giggled under his breath. "Hi Pyra. Sorry. My lady. Hi."

One of the soldiers groaned and looked at Pyra, his eyebrows knitted together. Concern lined his face, deepening the shadows beneath his eyes and on his gaunt cheeks.

"He got hit in the head pretty hard," he said. "Some Visani whacked him with a big club. His leg is hurt bad, too. That's where the blood's coming from."

Pyra nodded and motioned to the soldier who hadn't spoken yet. "Find a healer," she ordered. "Any of them." She then looked back to the other man as the first ran off to do as he was told. "I need you to get him out of his armor. I have to get at his leg."

The soldier nodded and got to work, unbuckling the greaves and leg plates from Gramm's lower body. He did a much better job of ignoring Gramm's befuddled comments than Pyra would have. She was already shaking badly, and she could hardly hear her friend.

Head injuries were serious. Either they would get better or they wouldn't. There was very little any healer could do for him. A lot of damage to a person's brain was permanent. Pyra couldn't afford to worry about that, though. Not right now. She *could* help his leg and stop him from bleeding out.

When she saw the extent of the damage under his armor, though, she became less sure of that. A huge, winding gash made its way from the inside of his thigh around to the back of his knee. It was deep. Pyra could see muscle and bone beneath the torn skin. She shook more violently and dropped the bandages she had so carefully organized. They scattered over the floor. She moved to pick them up, but a hand on her shoulder stopped her. Pyra looked over her shoulder and saw the old healer she had spoken with earlier.

He smiled grimly, the lines at the corners of his mouth drawing tight. "You should leave, my lady. I can take care of the knight."

"But…but his head," she stammered. "He hit his head and his leg is cut and—"

The healer waved his hand to quiet her. "I know. I'll do my best for him. You've been here a long time, though, and you don't need to see this."

He shooed her away and turned back to Gramm. Pyra hurried away as fast as her exhausted legs would carry her, worried that if she looked back even once, she would be unable to leave.

Before she was out of earshot, she heard, "Where is Pyra…my Pyra Lady. Where is she going?"

Chapter 14

Callan woke from a restless sleep with the smell of burnt meat in his nose. He could hear raised voices, but his head was still too deep in the fog of sleep to make sense of any of the yelling. For a moment, he wondered why his back was so stiff and why he seemed to be lying outside. Had he been sleepwalking? He never had before —

The reality of the situation hit him hard, immediately waking him from his stupor. The events of the previous night came flooding back to his mind. Being chased by men with bows and arrows, his horse dying beneath him, the wolfman tearing two of his pursuers apart and saving him.

The trip back had been long on foot, but uneventful. Verne had cooperated, as if he had a choice in the matter. Torruk had made it very clear that any attempt at escape would end in his death. The three of them had made it to a rather large camp at nearly midnight. Murdock and Dastynn had been there waiting, and so was Lys. Everyone else, the mercenaries who had come with Lys, were asleep when they finally made their way back. Callan had been too tired at the time to remember much, but he remembered the look on Verne's face when Torruk threw him in the dirt at Lys' feet. All kindness and good humor had left his eyes.

Callan could tell he wanted to kill Verne right there. Instead of doing anything rash, though, Lys had ordered the man tied to a tree and put under guard until morning. A bedroll was found for Callan, and he fell almost immediately into an exhausted slumber.

Now that he was fully awake, Callan could hear the voices around him more clearly.

"You idiot! We don't have enough pork for you to be burning our bacon!"

"Hey! I got put in charge of breakfast, and I made the bacon the way I wanted to! I like it crispy!"

"Crispy? Crispy? This is black!"

Callan sat up and rubbed at his eyes. Two of Lys' mercenaries, whose names Callan couldn't recall, were nose to nose with each other over a ceramic pan. The smell of the burning pork had been what woke Callan. The stench was enough to make his eyes water. It really did seem overdone. Not at all like his father's cooks had made it.

Before things between the two could get out of hand, Lys stalked up from behind Callan and stood between the two men. He scowled and smacked each man in the back of the head.

"Sit down, shut up, and eat," he said. "We have more important things to deal with today than how you like your meat." He turned to Torukk, who sat with his back against a large tree, twisting bits of twine around what appeared to be large bird feathers. "Do you want breakfast, Torruk?"

The wolfman shook his huge, shaggy head. "No thank you. I hunted last night." He gestured with the feathers in his hand as if the motion was supposed to mean something. "I cannot eat cooked meat."

"Can't or won't?" When Callan spoke, every head in the company turned to him. It was as if they had forgotten he was along.

Torruk bared his teeth and made a whining noise from the back of his throat. It was one of the strangest things that Callan had ever seen or heard. "I cannot," he said, gesturing once again with the feathers.

Lys walked over to Callan and helped him stand. Cal's legs had fallen asleep as he sat there, and his back still hurt from sleeping on the hard-packed earth. He would have given anything for a bed. Or a pillow.

The mercenary handed Callan a few strips of bacon and a hard biscuit. "It isn't exactly keep food," said the mercenary, "but it's what we've got. If you want something to drink, there are mugs by the fire and a stream in the woods not far from here. One of us can take you there."

Callan accepted the bacon and did his best to eat it. It was indeed burned beyond anything recognizable as pork. The meat fell apart in his mouth and left an ashy taste behind. The biscuit was at least edible. It was hard and salted, but it didn't leave Callan with a bad taste in his mouth. Lys had stood nearby while Callan was eating and called him over when he finished.

"We have to talk about Verne, kid."

Callan looked up at the taller man, worried.

"Verne is a part of my company. He's been with me for a few years, now." Shocked by this, Callan tried to speak, but Lys cut him off. "He and the other two planned on taking you to King Ramsey. They were hoping he'd give them some kind of reward."

They were going to take him to the king? Why? What could he possibly have given them that their contract didn't already cover? Besides, Verne had said they were going to take him back to his father.

"That's not what Verne said. He said that they were going to take me back home and ransom me to Father."

Lys shook his head. "Kid, your father is the one that paid us to meet the three of you here. We're to escort you to Graveholm, way up north." He crossed his arms. "He wanted to sell you, for sure. But not to your father."

Had he really planned on selling Callan to the king? How much money could that possibly have made him? Ramsey had been angry at Balen, sure. Angry enough to torch the Dragon's Keep and attack many of the smallfolk at the festival. His majesty had intended to send a message and did just that. Callan would never forget that day, and he was sure the rest of his family felt the same way.

Lys was speaking again. "…can't be thinking about that right now. We have to talk to Verne. He broke our contract with your father. He has to be punished."

Callan followed the mercenary through the camp and noticed, out of the corner of his eye, when Torruk stood and followed the pair of them. The walk was not a long one. There were a lot of people in the camp, but they were positioned very close to one another. Still, Callan was surprised how close Verne was being kept to the main camp. He could have slipped out and hurt someone in their sleep had he really wanted to.

That idea left Callan's mind as soon as he saw Verne's guard. Dastynn stood next to him, as rigid as one of the massive trees in the forest that surrounded them and nearly as large. His face was impassive as ever, but he smiled at Callan when they locked eyes. Suddenly, Callan felt much safer, knowing that the paladin was protecting him. He couldn't see Murdock, but he knew the mage was close by. He and Dastynn were never far apart.

Verne, for his part, was doing a fine job of not looking intimidated by the huge paladin. He was tied to a relatively thin tree trunk, in a standing position. Thick ropes wound from just above his knees to his shoulders, leaving his legs immobile and his arms pinned to his sides. The only part of him that could move freely was his head.

"You sleep well last night, Verne?" Lys didn't sound as angry as he looked. His voice remained calm, but his eyes had taken on a hard glint.

Verne spit at his feet. "Pit with you."

Lys studied Verne for a moment, chewing on the inside of his lip in thought. He removed the leather glove from his right hand and studied the knuckles for just a moment. Then he struck out with the back of his hand, smacking Verne across the side of his face. A crack formed on his bottom lip and let loose a small trickle of blood.

"Verne, I'm going to make this quick," said Lys. "You broke contract. You killed Callan's horse and tried to kidnap the boy. Do you deny the charges?"

Verne turned and flashed his teeth at Callan. The he was bleeding inside his mouth as well, from the slap. His teeth were stained red. "Sorry 'bout the horse. Seemed like a good animal." He turned to Lys, all laughter gone from his face. "I didn't kidnap nobody. Kid's horse ran off, so I tried to bring him back."

Lys didn't look pleased. "That's funny. Torruk says you, Elvur, and Plick chased him down, shot his horse from under him, and then you came at him with your sword."

Out of the corner of his eye, Callan saw Torruk nod once.

Verne turned his head to stare at the wolfman. "And you're going to believe this filthy animal over one of your own, eh?"

"As of right now, yes."

Verne's eyes widened in obvious horror. "No, no, come on, Lys! You know I didn't mean no harm! You know I'd never break contract!"

Lys ignored him and called out, "Rale! Bring me a sword."

It took a moment, but Rale, one of the few females in the company, arrived with a broadsword.

"Cut him loose please, Rale."

The woman nodded and produced a knife. She moved behind Verne and sawed at the ropes that bound him to the tree. For his part, Verne began screaming loudly. Lys motioned at Dastynn, who tore off a strip of the burlap tunic he wore. The paladin shoved the cloth into Verne's mouth, cutting his screaming off at the source. Rale finished cutting through the ropes more quickly than Callan would have thought and left them to fall in a pile at Verne's feet. The man trembled when he was free as the blood rushed back into his extremities.

He pulled the cloth from his mouth and took a deep breath of forest air. Then turned and ran toward the darkest part of the forest. Dastynn reached out with one massive arm and grabbed the fleeing man by his hair. He spun him back toward the group and let him go. Verne yelped and stumbled right into Lys. The mercenary backhanded Verne again and drove a knee into his stomach, driving him down the all fours.

"No, please. Please, Lys. Don't do it. It won't ever happen again." Verne whimpered. For all of his bravado, it seemed he really wasn't ready for his punishment. Callan wasn't sure he was ready for it, either. It was clear was Lys meant to do with him. Broadswords were good for very few things.

Callan didn't think he was ready to watch someone die for something they had done to him. He turned his head and did his best to inspect the dirt on the path that led back into the camp.

A massive, clawed hand laid itself gently on his shoulder. "You should watch this, child." Torukk's deep growl was kind, but insistent. Perhaps he was right. Whether he had intended it or not, this was happening because of him. The least he could do was watch.

"No, Verne," said Lys, his voice all ice. "It won't happen again."

Verne whimpered some more.

"Now shut up and close your eyes. This will be over quick."

He was right. It didn't take long at all. Lys hefted the broadsword over his head and brought it whistling through the quiet of the early morning. The blade sailed through the air and straight through Verne's neck. A red fountain of blood shot up and out as his head was severed from the rest of his body. Callan looked away then. He had seen people die at the hands of the dragons, and that had been horrible. Seeing what he just had, though, an execution, it was horrible as well, but in a different way. What Ramsey had done through his dragons was impersonal and carelessly violent. When Torukk had killed the two men in the forest, he had done it quickly. Besides that, Callan had been so scared at the time he hardly registered what had happened.

What Lys had just done was personal, though. Verne had broken one of Lys' rules. The contract. Callan felt somehow responsible. If not for his horse running off, Lys might not have had to decapitate one of his men. He backed away from the group, starting to feel like his stomach was going to force its way out of his mouth. The fact he had become directly responsible for someone's death weighed on him like a sickness. He turned to walk back to his mat. Maybe if he could go back to sleep, his stomach would settle down and it would be like this had never happened.

A hand clapped him on the shoulder. "Hold on a second, kid."

Callan turned around and saw Lys staring down at him. "What?" His voice was weak and shaking.

"Is that the first person you've seen die?"

Callan shook his head.

"Well, some people take a little longer to get used to seeing it," said Lys. "I hate to be the bearer of bad news, but that more than likely won't be the last time you see somebody get killed."

"Oh."

"Avoid killing when you can. Don't avoid it when you can't. That's the best advice I can give you."

Callan said nothing. What was there to say? He wasn't a killer. He could hardly stand the thought of someone dying at all. It made him sick.

"Are you okay, kid?"

Callan nodded. "I think so. Is that all?"

"No." He bent down at the knees and squeezed Callan's shoulder. "Don't beat yourself up over things you can't control. It'll eat you up inside."

With that, he walked off, motioning for Torruk and the others to follow him. Murdock and Rale followed without so much as looking in Callan's direction. Rale being indifferent wasn't a surprise. Murdock was. Callan felt like they'd grown close over the last few days, but maybe he had been wrong.

Dastynn nudged Callan with one huge hand and offered him a smile. Cal returned the gesture weakly, and the big man patted him on the back. Dastynn motioned for Callan to follow him and they set off after the rest of the group, toward the sound of running water. Lys had mentioned there was a steam nearby. Callan hadn't seen it yet, but judging the noise it made, the stream was fairly large.

Callan glanced back at the paladin. "If this is some kind of communal bathing time, I'm leaving."

Dastynn smiled and opened his mouth in a soundless laugh. It was strange, Callan thought, to see someone laughing but not hearing any noise. It made him wonder about why Dastynn didn't talk. He clearly had his tongue still, Callan could see that. Maybe he had never learned how. Callan resolved to ask him sometime.

They cleared the trees to find Lys, Murdock, and Rale standing in a semi-circle around Torruk, who was seated cross-legged on the ground. The group looked up as Callan and Dastynn approached, but no one said anything. They were too focused on the wolfman, who seemed to be meditating with his eyes closed and his claws dug into the earth on either side of him. He seemed calm, but the others were clearly waiting for something.

Murdock paced in small circles while Lys leaned against a tree, his jaw muscles working in clear frustration. Rale stood still, her close-cropped hair blowing loosely in the breeze. She watched Torruk but also kept an eye on everyone else in the group.

Torruk's muscles seized, his claws tearing at the mud and dirt around him. He growled as if he was in pain. The wolfman's eyes shot open, nearly bulging from his skull. He shuddered, drawing a deep breath and looking around frantically for Lys. When he found him, he growled again.

"What happened, Torruk? What's wrong?"

Torruk turned to Callan. Even in his inhuman features, Callan could see the sorrow in his eyes. "We have to leave now, Lys. We can't save Balen or the others."

Callan dropped to his knees. Torruk didn't explain what he meant.

He didn't need to.

Chapter 15

"Another one?"

Pyra nodded and stared down at the bloodied body on the ground. It was torn wide open from the middle of the neck to the middle of its chest. She had to think of it as just that: only a body. Over the past days, many of these bodies had started showing up. Pyra had thought of them, the first few, as people. Her heart had broken with each death, with each attack. She had become more and more paranoid as well. This body was the fifth. It was the first she refused to believe had once been a living person.

She looked up at Gramm. "Father hasn't told me much. Are you and the others any closer to finding out how they're getting in?"

He sighed and rubbed his temples. He'd been doing that a lot more lately, especially after the blow he had taken to the head. It happened more when he hadn't been sleeping. At least he had been able to take the wrappings off, finally. Pyra couldn't blame him, though. She hadn't had a good night's sleep in days either.

"Maybe," Gramm said. "Part of the eastern wall is more weathered than the rest of the keep. They could be climbing in through one of the windows there. They cover their tracks well, so…"

"So? So what?"

"So, I don't know," he snapped. "I have no idea! They could be flying in through the top floor for all I know."

Pyra said nothing. Gramm rarely lost his temper with her. If he hadn't been so overworked, he never would have. The other knights were in similar moods. They had taken the attacks personally. Most realized they were working as hard as they possibly could. Ravitch had been among those at first, but he was becoming frustrated. Pyra could hardly blame him. After all, Visani had been sneaking into a now very crowded keep for nearly a week. Ravitch himself had been stuck in his quarters, barely able to walk to his chamber pot without getting sick. He was recovering, but slowly.

"Is there anything that I can do to help?"

Gramm shook his head. "I don't know, Pyra. I wish I did. I wish I had the answers that everyone wants."

Pyra wanted to hug him. To comfort him. As soon as she moved, though, he turned away from her.

"I have to go," he said. "I'm on patrol duty."

He left, leaving Pyra with a body and the healers who had volunteered to clean up the mess. Pyra wanted to scream. Instead, she turned and walked away toward the dungeons. They had been empty until the refugees started coming in. After all, why do something to get yourself thrown in a cell when even the most comfortable places in the region were miserably cold?

The refugees had moved in, though. It was the only part of the keep that had enough room to house them all. The dungeons were crowded and cold, but they provided shelter and some measure of security. It was those who liked to wander at night that ended up dying. The first victims had been refugees. The next two had been soldiers on patrol. Pyra hadn't taken notice who the latest was. She hadn't been able to bring herself to look closely enough.

She descended into the stone underbelly of the keep, the smells and sounds of refugees assailing her from the top of the stairs down. They didn't sound angry, thankfully. Any time so many people were crammed in together, though, they became uncomfortable. Children were running around, quarters were cramped, and the smell was getting worse.

With Theamere running the defense of Graveholm during Ravitch's infirmity, Pyra had taken on the responsibility of trying to take care of the refugees. Elder Moss helped her when he could, along with a handful of healers who had been out of work since the initial attack. Led by Pyra and Moss, the group tried to keep tensions low.

That wouldn't last long if the killings continued. Panic was already starting to set in. If, in another five days, five more had been killed, Pyra was sure the refugees would riot. Pyra hit the bottom of the stairs and was immediately approached by a group of men. She recognized one of them as the refugee that had become the unofficial leader of the rest.

"What can I help you with, Travis?"

Travis and two of his men, whom Pyra didn't recognized, separated from the group and walked to her.

"Who was it, Pyra? Who was killed?"

She shook her head, ignoring the informality with which he addressed her. Gramm wasn't the only one she tried to stop from using her title. "I didn't recognize him. I'm sorry."

Travis' jaw clenched. The men behind him looked scared, but he was angry. That was the difference between Travis and the other refugees: they wanted help while he wanted to stop the attacks from happening. Personally, if he needed to. He came to Pyra often with offers to join up with the soldiers in finding a way to stop the killings. Travis had served with the Royal Army in his youth. He knew his way around a battlefield. However, Pyra needed him down here with the others. They all did. He was kind, yet firm, and had taken well to the role of leader. His life couldn't be risked upstairs.

"We have to do something, Pyra," he said. "We can't just sit here and let them pick us off one by one."

"Travis," she sighed, "you've made this argument before. And I agree with you. But the soldiers are doing everything they can to make sure we're all safe."

He leaned in close and lowered his voice, to block out the group of people who had formed from listening in on their conversation. "You and I both know what they're doing isn't enough. We need to do something else. Something more."

Unfortunately, he was right. The soldiers were doing everything that they could, but without being proactive, they wouldn't be able to stop the killings. "Look, Travis," she said, "there are too many people who can't defend themselves, and they keep leaving the dungeon when they shouldn't be. The soldiers can't follow them around all night."

"I know. I've tried reining them in. Have you ever lived down here, though? Bloody depressing." He stuffed his hands into his armpits and shivered. "We've had some volunteers, ex-military, who want to go out and take the fight to them, you know."

"Absolutely not," said Pyra. "I won't send them out to get killed. I know that the conditions aren't ideal, Travis."

He scoffed at her.

Pyra raised a hand and hardened her eyes. "No. If you and the others with military training want to organize with our soldiers, feel free. I won't allow anyone else to put themselves in harm's way."

He nodded, apparently satisfied. "Okay. That will have to be good enough." Travis took a step back and rejoined the men who had come with him.

"I'll talk to the captain of the guard for you, Travis," she said. "I want to make this work for you and your people."

"I know you do, Lady Pyra. I do. And we all appreciate what you've done." Travis looked over his shoulder into the dark depths of the dungeon. He grimaced. Pyra understood why. The lodgings were anything but comfortable. "I'll do what I can do keep them from getting too frustrated."

"Thank you, Travis."

He nodded again and gave a short bow, then motioned for the others to follow him back into the dungeon. Pyra realized that she had been holding her breath and let it out all at once. She turned on her heel and headed back into the castle proper. She needed to speak to the captain of the guard. He was, for all intents and purposes, the highest ranked civilian in the Graveholm. He reported directly to Ravitch and Theamere on all military matters. He had been working with Ravitch for so long, though, that he was afforded a lot of leniency. The captain acted mostly as his own superior officer. From what Pyra knew of him, he was a good man and very good at his job. Gramm thought very highly of him and Pyra trusted his opinion over anyone else's. So, Pyra trusted him.

The captain normally kept his office outside of the main keep, but the recent attacks had forced him inside along with everyone else. It took some looking, but Pyra eventually found where he had been moved. His new office was in the back of the main floor, attached to the kitchens. Even from outside of the door, Pyra could smell something *off* about his new chambers. She raised a hand and knocked. A rough voice called to her from inside, inviting her in.

She swung the door open and was immediately slapped in the face by a wall of stench. The room was packed with rows and shelves and packages of fresh meat. The captain of the guard sat at a small desk in the middle of it all, with scrolls and ledgers splayed out in front of him. A stack of them was even being held in place with a wrapped meat package. Blood seeped through the wrapping and onto the stack of papers. She was so taken aback by the overwhelming sights and smells of the room, that it took a few moments for Pyra to realize that Gramm stood at attention behind the captain's seat.

Pyra's disgust must have showed on her face because the captain spoke up as soon as he saw her. "It's not so bad once you get used to it, Lady," he said. "Besides, I'm so close to the kitchens that I can send Gramm to grab me a snack whenever I need one. Right, boy?"

Gramm nodded, and the corner of his mouth twitched just slightly. "Yes, sir."

"Now," said the captain, waving his hand toward the door, "go and take a quick lunch break. Give Lady Pyra and I some time to talk."

Pyra interrupted. "Actually, Captain Jordan, I would appreciate it if Gramm could stay. We spoke earlier this morning, and I think that he could have some very important insight."

He nodded. "Alright, then. I'll admit I'm intrigued. What can I help you with?"

"I'm sure that you know about the refugees. They're getting restless. They're scared of being hurt by the Visani."

Another nod.

"Clearly," she said, "something needs to be done about the killings."

The captain nodded again, placed his elbows on the desk, and steepled his fingers in front of his mouth. Gramm looked at Pyra with a curious expression on his face. Pyra couldn't help but enjoy his frustration. She smiled internally. Even in a situation as grim as the one that they were facing, frustrating Gramm was still one of the greater pleasures of her life.

"I assume that Gramm has told you where he believes that the Visani are sneaking in at night?" Another nod. "Well, it's my belief that we should lay a trap for the Visani. We station a group of knights and some of the men from the village in the rooms in the decaying tower. When, and if, the Visani come in, we'll be ready for them."

The captain stared at her for a few moments. She stood still, letting Jordan measure her up. Pyra was almost certain that Gramm was staring at her as well, but she wouldn't let herself look at him. She locked eyes with the older man until he spoke.

"That's an awfully dark thought for a young lady. Surely you would be more helpful down in the healing wards than up here coming up with battle strategy?"

Pyra took a step toward his desk, her eyes wide with disbelief. She was normally not a loud individual, but she raised her voice at the captain, now. "Absolutely not! You know as well as anyone that my father is too unwell to be making these kinds of decisions," she yelled," and that my brother hasn't done enough about the killings." She took a breath and continued, "And if you think that you can talk to me in that manner without any kind of consequence, you have another thing coming. Do *not* forget that I am your superior here, Captain."

By the time she was finished, she was leaning over Captain Jordan's desk, nearly touching noses with the man. She seethed, her breath forced out of her nostrils in short bursts.

Jordan smiled. She almost started to yell at him again, but he spoke first, his voice level and even.

"Apologies, my lady," he said. "I'm sorry if I offended you. I'll accept any punishment that you have in mind."

Pyra blinked and stood straight again. The calmness in his voice as he explained himself was almost unsettling. It was certainly enough to calm Pyra down. As much as her ego smarted from being measured by a man she didn't know on a personal level at all, his argument made sense.

"So," she asked, "what do you think?"

"About what?"

"My plan."

The captain chuckled. "Oh, I think that the plan has merit." He turned to Gramm. "Soldier, go and fetch the men who have taken charge of the refugees. Their leader's name is Travis. He won't be hard to find."

Gramm saluted to his Captain and left. He gave Pyra a smile and a wink on his way out. She did her best to keep a straight face, but she smiled despite herself.

"Now," said the captain, "if you would be so kind as to ask your brother to come find me, we can get the planning started."

"No." Pyra crossed her arms in front of her chest. "Theamere isn't going to be involved in this. I want to be there."

There was a knowing smile on Jordan's face when he responded. "Alright, then." He cleared some space on his desk and started digging around for blueprints of the keep. "Let's get to planning."

#

Hours later, Pyra stood shivering in what had once been a small bedroom in the tower that Gramm had selected as the most likely entry point for the Visani. Ever since the walls began to crumble, people had started moving their living quarters elsewhere. Pyra could sympathize. Wind came through cracks in the walls with gleeful screams, ripping away the warmth from her limbs.

Gramm was stationed in the empty bedroom with Pyra. Besides the two of them, the only decoration was an empty wardrobe and a broken-down bed frame. Pyra didn't know for sure, but she had a feeling that Gramm had requested to be stationed next to her. Theamere may have been her older brother, but the knight had always looked out for her. Gramm rarely let on that he was worried or bothered by anything. That was not the case this night.

He was unusually quiet, even for him. The littlest noises made him reach instinctively for his sword, and he hadn't sat down for the hours that they had been there. Pyra, on the other hand, had tried to find a comfortable seat for herself on the floor. She rubbed her arms and legs to keep away the chill that the wind brought with it.

"I could make a fire for us," she offered for the fifth or sixth time. She hadn't been able to practice her magic as much as she would have liked recently, but she could light a small fire easily enough.

"No fire," Gramm answered again. "They'll be able to smell it burning."

Pyra was bundled up for the cold, wearing layers of furs and coats. She probably could have rolled down a stone staircase and come out no worse for wear. Gramm, on the other hand, had forsaken most of his usual garb. He wore no metal armor, instead, opting for padded leather and a loose, feathered cloak. His explanation was that he could move around more freely without being heard. He must have been freezing, though.

The night drifted on in a similar manner. They spoke less and less as time dragged on. Gramm stood by the door, his hand resting on the hilt of his sword. His shield was at his feet, resting against the door. Pyra had leaned against the bed frame, her eyelids getting heavier and heavier.

"How long do you think it is until dawn?"

Gramm looked over at her and shrugged. She could barely see his outline in the darkness. "I'm not sure," he answered. "Maybe a few hours."

He stopped speaking abruptly and held a finger to his lips. The knight pressed his ear to the door and closed his eyes, listening intently. Pyra strained to hear what he was listening for. At first, there was nothing. Then she heard it.

Tap, tap, tap, tap.

That was it. The signal that they'd agreed to use at the first sighting of Visani climbing the walls. Pyra stood up quickly and silently. She was no longer tired.

Gramm motioned for her to come over to his side. She hurried to do so and grabbed the door's handle tightly with both hands. At the next signal, she would swing the door open wide and Gramm would charge through, along with four other knights and two of the more capable refugees.

She heard them through the door. The sounds were faint, but the scraping of long claws on stone and the heavy breathing of a massive creature were unmistakable. Pyra shivered. A low growl came from the other side of the door and was answered by a similar noise. There was more than one of them out there. Pyra's heart jumped into her throat. There may have been more than two. What if the knights were outnumbered? Her legs nearly buckled behind the fear that had taken over her body.

Then she heard it. The second signal.

Tap. Taptaptap. Tap.

Pyra pulled the door open as quickly as she could and watched wide-eyed as Gramm stormed through, shield first. The silent night was immediately filled with screams and roars and the sounds of weapons smashing into each other in almost total darkness. Pyra counted in her head. Her part was coming up.

Ten, nine, eight, seven…

She stood in the doorway now. The chaos was so complete that she couldn't make out Gramm in the melee.

Six, five, four…

Her hands tingled as the magic moved through her extremities. Pyra held it back for a few seconds. She had to wait until the exact right moment or else she would put her own people in danger. If she waited too long, though…

Three, two, one.

"Now! Duck!"

Pyra threw her hands into the air and loosed a golden light from the center of her palms. The magic was very similar to what she conjured when she created fire but held no heat. There was only bright, unfeeling light. The keep's soldiers had hit the deck and closed their eyes in preparation for the light. The Visani did not. They reeled back on their heels, screeching as their sensitive eyes were nearly burned from their sockets.

The light was extinguished, and the soldiers jumped at their short advantage. There had only been three Visani, and one fell to a sword almost immediately. The other two composed themselves and began fighting back.

Pyra couldn't see the details of the battle. She could only hear screams and groans of pain. Enough moonlight came in through the ruined window that she could catch glimpses of action. She saw blood splatter through the silver light and saw shadows of bodies hit the ground and stop moving. More than one fell. More than two, and still the battle continued. That could only have meant that some of the people of Graveholm were dying.

She nearly jumped out of her skin when a hand landed on her shoulder. She spun to face her attacker, magic welling up beneath her skin.

"Be still, Pyra."

"Father?"

He leaned heavily on a cane and had a raggedness to his breath, but it was indeed Ravitch. Pyra had hardly seen him out of bed since he had been injured, let alone so far from his chambers.

"Theamere came to me when he heard what you had planned," he said with a growl. "You did well, girl."

She started to smile at him, but stopped when she heard an abrupt shift in the battle. She turned to the fight and gasped. There was only one Visani standing illuminated in the moonlight. He was on the window ledge, with Captain Jordan held tight to his body. The giant feline had a dagger made of bone pressed to the captain's throat.

"I will live!" The Visani shouted at everyone who was still standing. "I will live. He will live." He nodded at the captain.

The Visani looked up and locked eyes with Ravitch. "Your family survives this time. Not next time. Next time, more will come."

He moved to shove the captain toward the soldiers. Instead of stepping off the ledge, Captain Jordan roared at the beast and turned into him, driving his shoulder into the abdomen of the much larger creature. They both tumbled out of the window. The Visani's scream cut like a blade through the calm night. It was only interrupted by the ground far below.

Ravitch hobbled from Pyra's side toward the window. The soldiers still on their feet stared at him in awe. Most of them, Pyra knew, still thought that he was on his death bed. He probably should have been.

Ravitch looked out of the window and raised a fist to his chest in salute to the fallen captain.

Chapter 16

Temperatures dropped quickly in the time following the news of Callan's family. He hadn't asked Torruk for details regarding how they had died. He didn't really want to know. A knot had formed in his gut. It was built of a mess of emotions. Deep, heart-wrenching sadness. A sense of loss once he realized that he was now alone in the world. Hiding among those others, smaller, he thought, but still needling at him, was a deep-seated confusion. Where was he going to go?

Callan had no other family. Both his maternal and paternal grandparents had passed away before he was born. His mother had never had siblings. Uncle Tarryn had been his father's only brother. Callan had no older siblings to look to. Even the commoners, those without noble blood, in his father's domain were gone. Torruk had made it very clear that there were few dead from the dragon attacks, but not a living soul remained in the area. Callan wasn't sure what magic he had used to get his information, but Murdock and Lys had both taken him at his word. That was hurt the most: he trusted both of them. They weren't wrong. His world had crumbled.

Travelling with the mercenary group had helped Callan get into his own head. They talked among themselves, sure, but none of them had anything to say to some spoiled brat of a noble. Murdock had offered his condolences, as had Lys and Torukk. Dastynn had consoled Callan in his own way, by placing a firm hand on his shoulder and staring into Callan's eyes. It had been disconcerting, but nice in its own way.

So, Callan rode on the new horse that had been provided for him, wrapped in layers of furs and the warmest leathers that he could find.

He was wrapped in his thoughts as well. He had been for days. Days? Maybe a week. Time had lost its meaning.

"How are you doing, Cal?"

Callan looked to his right. He reached up with one of his fur blankets and wiped at his eyes. The motion was out of habit at this point. The tears had stopped days ago, but he still felt as if he was crying constantly. Maybe he had lost the ability to cry.

"Cal?"

"I'm okay, Lys," Callan replied.

The mercenary rode alongside Callan's. He looked concerned, an emotion that Callan hadn't seen on his face in the time that he had known him. "No, you aren't," he said. "You haven't said hardly a word in days. You aren't eating, you aren't sleeping."

Callan turned his head and stared at Lys. "What do you want from me? What should I be doing? I have *no one*. I have *nothing*."

"I know." Lys nodded. "Which is exactly why you need to get off your *ass* and do something about it. You haven't worked with your sword since we left."

"Why? There's no point."

Lys scowled. "There is a point. A lot of them, actually. Your body needs to stay active, for one. You need to be able to protect yourself. Besides all of that, you need something to take your mind off everything."

Callan shook his head. He just wanted to ride his horse as far away from home as he could. "No, thank you."

"I wasn't giving you an option. Get your sword and follow me."

Lys called the group to a halt for the night. Everyone stopped and started setting up camp. Callan's horse was well-trained enough to stop when all the others did so he was left with a motionless animal beneath him. He wasn't going anywhere. Not that he would want to after the last time that he'd been riding on his own.

He hopped off his horse and snatched the sword and scabbard from his horse's saddle. He'd recovered the blade after Torruk had rescued him. Callan had no intention of ever letting it out of his sight again. He handed the reins off to the nearest mercenary, figuring that they would handle the horse, and stomped off after Lys. He still carried the weapon in both hands, instead of strapping it to his hip. It was too long for that and would have dragged on the ground behind him, tripping him with every step. Ever since he'd nearly lost it when being chased by the *former* mercenaries, he hadn't let it out of his sight.

Lys called from ahead, "You should try strapping that thing to your back. It won't cause you any trouble in case you're trying to walk through a doorway." He looked over his shoulder and cracked a smile. "You just have to learn to walk through sideways."

Callan shrugged. "Maybe."

Lys turned and placed his hands on his hips. "Fine. You don't want to talk? No talk. Draw your sword and come at me." The mercenary drew his own weapon and held it out in front of him with one hand.

They were in the middle of a group of people setting up tents. Murdock and Dastynn were nowhere to be found, but there were plenty of men, a few women, and some horses. Callan had never practiced in any area other than a cleared field.

"Here? It's crowded," he said.

"Yes, here. You think that real battlefields are all one-on-one confrontations with nobody else around? You've got another thing coming, kid. Now draw your sword and attack me."

Callan shrugged and drew his sword out of his scabbard, letting the leather piece fall to the ground at his feet. He gripped the hand-

and-a-half sword in both hands and walked slowly toward Lys. He made sure to not let his feet get tangled in any of the brush or roots that littered the ground of the forest. The trees were few and far between where they were camped out, but hints of nature were constantly underfoot.

Lys never moved as Callan approached. His sword was pointed directly at Callan's throat. It quivered in the slight breeze as Callan got closer and closer.

Thankfully, Callan thought, *there is very little wind.* The temperatures had already dropped enough that adding any substantial breeze would have made him physically miserable as well as an emotional wreck.

A horse whinnied off to Callan's left. He flicked his eyes over for a moment to see where the noise had come from. Lys was on him before his eyes had focused. His smaller sword knocked Callan's to the side with one forceful swipe, then flicked it up and out of Callan's hand. It landed somewhere behind Callan in the dirt. He wasn't sure where. He was too busy staring at the very sharp tip of a very deadly blade that was now pointing into his nose.

"That was sloppy, Cal," said Lys. "I know that you know better than that. Never, ever take your eye off your opponent. Focus."

"I know, I know," he said defensively."

"Then do it. Grab your sword and come at me again."

Callan gritted his teeth and collected his sword. He could practically hear his uncle's voice in the tone that Lys was using with him. Thinking about his uncle made him miserably angry, but he realized that it probably meant that Lys knew what he was doing. Tarryn had been an excellent teacher.

Cal grabbed the sword and spun, rushing Lys in an attempt to catch him off guard. He could see the mercenary's eyes widen in surprise, but he held his ground and his sword level. Callan jumped, raising his sword over his head in a chopping motion.

Lys kicked him in the gut harder than he'd ever been kicked and sent him sprawling, breathless, into the ground. He clutched his stomach as he rolled around, gasping for air that he couldn't seem to find. Lys stood over him.

"Not a bad idea. Fighting anybody inexperienced and you probably would have cut them in half with a move like that." He laughed. "Me, though, or anyone else who knows how to fight, well, you should probably keep your feet on the ground. Don't jump."

He helped Callan to his feet and thrust his sword into his arms. Callan didn't even remember dropping it through the pain in his chest.

"And remember to hold on to that. It's important," Lys continued. "Now, let's go. One more time."

Callan swung his sword at Lys' head before the older man could get his feet set. He didn't even bother blocking with his sword, instead ducking under the swing and taking a jab of his own at Callan's stomach. Cal moved to the side of the thrust and took up a defensive stance, rather than pushing the offensive. Lys did the same and they reset their session.

This time, it was Lys who moved first. Callan deflected a swipe at his ribs, a swipe at his left him, and another at his arm. He had to move more and more quickly as Lys pressed the attack or else he would be outrun and beaten. He had to use the size of his weapon to his advantage. The bastard sword offered more weight and a longer reach. So, Callan took a step back and attacked with an overhead slash.

Lys blocked the attack, but Callan knew that he had hit solidly. He could feel Lys' arm vibrating through the shared contact of the chilled steel. He snarled. Lys grinned.

Cal attacked again, keeping his attacks directed at his opponent's upper body. Elbows, ribs, shoulders, and neck were all targeted. Every time Lys tried to counter, Callan merely stepped back and avoided any harm. He smiled, despite himself. He was winning. He was actually beating back a master swordsman. The fight wasn't going anywhere, though. Callan was slicing and dodging, but never landed a blow. Neither did Lys. Callan had to do something. He didn't have the same kind of stamina that Lys did and would never last as long if the fight continued in the way that it was going.

He drew his sword back and to his side and stepped in, ready to disarm his opponent. Lys moved at the same time he did, stepping into him. The mercenary threw out his elbow and caught a glancing blow across Callan's nose. The younger man wasn't fast enough to move completely out of the way. Water spouted from his eyes. He involuntarily lifted a hand to his face. The brief motion gave Lys enough time to flick the tip of his sword around and again disarm Callan. Again, he was left with the tip of the mercenary's blade touching the end of his nose.

"That," said Lys, who was now breathing heavily and sweating despite the cold, "was impressive. Much better."

Callan rubbed his nose. "Ow."

Lys laughed and dropped his sword to his side. "Sorry about that. You have to remember, though, your entire body is a weapon, not just your sword. If you can punch someone in the nose to win a fight, do it."

Callan nodded and walked to pick up his scabbard from where it had been dropped in the cold grass, wiping sweat from his brow. He picked up his sword from where it had been tossed by Lys' attack. His arms were too leaden to put the sword back in the scabbard so he sat down in the grass.

Lys sat down next to him and gestured at his sword. "You're going to want to sharpen that when you get a chance. Keep that sword in good shape. It'll save your life."

Cal made a mental note to remember that. He found the strength in his arms, though, to slide the blade into the scabbard until all that could be seen was the intricately jeweled hilt. He leaned back on his elbows and got comfortable, hopeful for some time to rest and relax.

"Oh, no," Lys laughed. "We're not done yet."

Callan groaned.

"Have you ever shot a bow?"

Callan shook his head. His father and uncle had always meant to teach him. They never had the chance.

"Well, we're going to have to change that," said Lys. "Everyone who travels with me has to learn how to bring in some food. Come with me."

He groaned again and followed Lys to an outside section of the camp. A tent was set up with various weapons inside. It mostly held swords and daggers and bits of armor. From what Callan could gather, it served as a kind of potluck of weaponry. Anyone who needed anything specific could come and grab it. Nothing was of the highest quality, but all of it was serviceable.

There was a small man whose face was covered in seemingly haphazard patches of facial hair. He looked more like a squirrel or a rabbit than he did a mercenary. Lys called to the man. "Hey! The kid needs a bow. Grab him something small enough for him to use and a quiver."

The man nodded. "Yessir. Yessir, I'll get that for you."

He scurried off into the back of the tent and out of sight for a few moments. When he came back, he had a load of string and wood and ammunition weighing down his mousy frame. He strung up the bow quickly. Callan made a mental note to learn how to do that eventually.

They thanked the little man and carried the equipment out into the woods. They found a nice, secluded spot and Lys set them up to practice. For the next few hours, into the beginning of twilight, Lys showed Callan the basics of archery. After Callan had learned how to use the weapon, they spent the remainder of their time practicing. He nocked the arrow to the string, drew back, and fired.

Nock, draw, fire, nock, draw, fire, nock, draw, fire…

Callan never even had to refill his quiver. Lys made sure that he never ran out of arrows.

"I want you focused," he said. "Don't waste your time trying to find every missed arrow. I'll do that. You just pick a target and shoot."

He was focused on a tree branch. More specifically, where the branch met the larger mass of the tree. None of his arrows ever found the mark. He came close and the more that he shot, the closer he came. The dedication needed to continually fire the bow was therapeutic, though. For a while, he focused on the fact that he was missing and was angry at himself. Then he focused on the burning that the continual motion caused in his upper back, shoulders, and arms. Once that went away, he went fell into a peaceful place in his mind.

For a brief space of time, he knew nothing but the *creak* of the bow, the whistle of the arrow through the trees, the *thud* and *crash* that the arrows made as they landed in the forest.

He only stopped when he felt a hand on his shoulder. It was Lys.

"Come on, kid," he said. "You've had enough for today, I think. You already aren't going to be able to lift your arms tomorrow."

Callan smiled at the older man, his first genuine smile in days. "Alright."

The two of them collected the arrows that they could find. None of them were particularly well made so Lys wasn't too concerned with finding all of them. They were for practice, nothing else.

Once they finished, they walked back toward the camp in almost total darkness. They found a spot for Callan to camp near a giant bonfire that had been started by the mercenaries. They didn't have enough tents for everyone so the fire was a necessity.

"Besides," Lys had said, "we're far enough away from Ramsey and his people that we don't have to worry too much about being sneaky anymore."

Callan fell into his bedroll and wrapped himself up as tightly as he could. Now that the sun was fully down, the forest would get very cold very quickly. Lys made sure that he was settled, and then moved off to his own campsite. He had one of the larger tents, Callan knew.

Before he was gone, Callan called to him. "Lys?"

The mercenary turned around and raised an eyebrow at the young noble.

"Thank you."

Lys offered a small smile and nodded, then walked away into the night.

Chapter 17

"The land is your mightiest ally. Let it help you."

"Torruk, I'm going to be brutally honest with you. I have no idea what you're talking about."

"My people, the Fanir, come from a land far to the south," said the wolfman. "Much of our nation is covered in woodlands and forests, similar to where we are now. The land is our ally." He chuckled deep in his throat. Callan still wasn't sure what to think of the Fanir's sense of humor. "Now, walk me through what happened."

"Again?"

"Again."

Callan crossed his arms in front of his chest. "I shot the deer. A doe. She ran off into the woods, to the northeast. My arrow went all of the way through her."

"Good," said the Fanir. "Now, tell me why you are having troubles. Again." He chuckled.

"I put an arrow through her and she ran away! She should be dead!"

"She is. She might not have known it when you shot her, but she is."

Callan looked at him, perplexed. "Look, I've never hunted anything before. The last I knew, dead things didn't run around. They *died*."

"The body is an amazing organism, is it not?"

Callan could only stare.

"Look at the ground, Callan. What do you see?

He looked. There was a lot of dirt and fallen leaves. There were patches of snow, but the last few days had been rather warm and melted most of it away. That wouldn't last long. Winter would set in fully within the next few weeks.

"I see dirt and roots. Leaves. There's a bug of some kind crawling across my boot. That's it."

Torruk shook his head. "No, no it isn't. Look closer." The Fanir knelt and lifted an individual leaf from the ground. He held it out for Callan to look at. "Now, what do you see?"

"I see a leaf. And…it's wet. Blood. She bled on that leaf. Right?"

The giant, shaggy head bobbed up and down. "Yes. On this one and on many others. As I said, nature is your ally. Use it. Use her blood to find her. She will not have gone far. You made a good shot."

Callan smiled and knelt to where the leaf had been. There were others around it, all covered in a light splatter of gore. He felt stupid for not having noticed it before, but he looked past that. After all, no one had ever taken him hunting before. How was he supposed to know?

Once it had been shown to him, Callan could follow the trail of blood rather easily. Torruk kept his distance but followed Cal into the forest after the deer. The two had been working together all morning. After nearly two weeks of training with a sword and bow whenever he had the chance, he welcomed the change of pace. This was the first time that he had worked closely with a member of the mercenary band besides Lys. It was refreshing to see Torruk in a light other than the one in which they had met. The thought of that night still caused Callan to lose sleep.

The trail became easier to follow the farther that they went along. The blood trail was more prevalent, footprints were left gouged into the soft earth by the panicked animal, and branches and twigs were snapped in its wake. They found it lying in a bramble. It was dead.

"Your first kill," said Torruk. "Congratulations."

Callan smiled up at him, craning his neck to see the Fanir's face. The feeling that he had now really wrapped up how he had been progressing over the past weeks. Lys had made sure that he was always busy. It had kept his mind off the losses that he had suffered. The pain and sorrow were still there, and probably always would be, but they were now shoved to the back of his mind. Misery no longer dominated his every thought. It was a welcome change.

"Thank you. We're going to have to gut it now, right?"

The Fanir was no longer paying attention. He was crouched into a defensive stance, his nose to the air. His knife-like claws were extended from his hands, poised as if for a fight.

"Torruk? What's wrong?"

He sniffed at the air, a low growl escaping from behind bared teeth.

"Torruk?"

"Visani." He practically snarled the word.

Callan stared at him, dumbfounded. "Vis-what?"

Torruk dropped to all fours, looking f like an enormous wolf. If not for the various weapons strapped to him, Callan would have taken him for an ordinary, if giant, animal. Weapons included, he looked like something straight out of a nightmare.

The wolfman glanced over his shoulder. "Grab your sword. Stay behind me."

Callan drew the sword from the scabbard that he now kept slung across his back. He crept through the midmorning forest behind the Fanir, with the still rising sun casting shadows of branches and leaves across the chilled landscape. Callan's breath visibly puffed out of his mouth in white clouds before it dissolved into the air. The overnight dew had left the leaves and the ground soft so the two moved almost entirely silently. Callan made more noise than Torruk, though, who was like a ghost through the morning shadows.

"What about the deer, Torruk?"

The Fanir made a noise in his throat to quiet Callan. "Leave it for now. And be quiet."

He shushed himself again, trusting in his companion to know what he was doing. Callan had never heard of a Visani, but then again, he had never heard of a Fanir until a few weeks ago, either. And he certainly never thought that he would see a dragon. They were myths. And he came to realize very quickly that myths were real.

He was following a myth through a forest. The idea shook him. A year ago, he never would have thought that he would leave his home at all. A few weeks ago, his biggest worry was the fact that he was going to have to marry his best friend. Things had changed, and he didn't like it a bit. He had no greater wish than to be back at home, sleeping in his own warm bed and waking up to his family instead of staring up at a cloudless, starry sky.

Torruk stopped suddenly, nearly causing Callan to walk into him. The Fanir held out one long claw, signaling Callan to stay where he was at. He stopped, but he also held his sword out in front of him and tightened his grip on the hilt. He took a few steps to the nearest tree and leaned onto it, trying to keep as much in view as he possibly could.

Torruk crept forward, toward a thicket that Callan's eyes couldn't penetrate. As thick as the brambles were, it was unlikely that Torukk could see into them either, but his sense of smell had proven itself to be amazing so far. Callan trusted it.

Callan watched as he crept forward slowly at first, but gaining speed with every step. After a few steps, he was running toward the bramble, weapons sheathed and claws extended. He leaped into the air with a snarl and crashed down out of Callan's line of view. There was an initial rustle of movement and thrashing of limbs, but then all was still.

"Torruk, are you okay?" Callan called again, "Torruk?"

There was a moment of nervous silence, then an answer. "Everything is fine, Callan. The Visani was dead before we got here."

Torruk walked out of the bramble, carrying a large, furry creature over his back. The thing was even bigger than Torruk was, and he carried it as if it was nothing. Callan couldn't help but marvel at his strength even though it was mostly terrifying.

He dropped the thing at Callan's feet so that he could get a better look at it. It looked like a giant feline. It looked almost like Torruk, except much more akin to a lion or some other large cat than a wolf like the Fanir. It was covered in white fur that was marred with dirt and blood. It had a large wound in its side that was covered in blood. Callan didn't know much about anatomy, but it seemed like the wound was probably what killed it.

"This is a Visani? It's different, but it looks almost like you."

Torruk snarled, a noise that Callan hadn't heard since the Fanir had cornered Verne and the others that had been chasing Callan. "No. No, not like me. Very different."

"Ok, ok, sorry. Not like you."

Torruk huffed.

Callan inspected the Visani further. It had no weapons on it but was strapped with sheaths, again, much like Torruk. Callan felt that the Fanir was being stubborn. There were similarities between the two that he wasn't talking about.

"What could have killed it?"

Torruk lifted his nose to the air again and sniffed. "Humans. Wait here."

He bounded into the deeper parts of the forest where Callan lost him in the trees. He knew better by now not to ignore when one of the older members of the group told him to stay put. Leaving their side could only lead to getting himself into trouble. So, he stood patiently.

He was rewarded with a short wait. Torruk loped back into sight after only a few minutes. He looked excited. "We're close. I can see Graveholm from the edge of the trees. We can get the others and be there by midday."

"Great! Let's go then! We can pick up my deer on the way back!"

A bugle sounded to the south of them, back in the direction that they had come from. It sounded again, longer the second time.

"What was that?"

Torruk growled under his breath. "Danger. We must hurry. Come."

Callan strapped his sword onto his back again and took off running back to their camp. Torruk stayed ahead of him by virtue of his physique and the fact that he could run on all fours. Callan had the feeling that he could have run much more quickly but kept himself in check for Callan's benefit.

His body had become much more accustomed to exercise over the last few weeks, but he could still feel an ache creep into his legs during the unexpected run. He carried a bow and a quiver full of arrows, which weren't heavy on their own. Adding in his large sword, though, gave his load quite a lot of weight that he wasn't used to lugging around.

The two of them ran until Callan lost track of time and the feeling in his legs. He was gasping for breath by the time that they came into view of the mercenary camp. The clearing was in chaos, with shouts of men and animalistic snarls filling the air. Visani, many of them even bigger than the one that they had found dead, attacked the camp. Most fought two or three mercenaries at once, using their amazing size and speed to their advantage.

Callan skidded to a stop and sucked in deep breaths of the cold mountain air. His eyes locked on Murdock and Dastynn, who fought off a group of the massive felines near the edge of the camp. They seemed to be holding their own fairly well. Murdock held the Visani at bay with short bursts of defensive magic while Dastynn wreaked havoc with his giant hammer. One of the monsters fell to the ground with a crushed skull as Callan watched.

"Torruk," he said, "we have to find Lys. We can't let anything happen to him."

The Fanir nodded. "Stay close to me."

Callan ran after him without a moment's hesitation. For a moment, he wondered when he had decided to do something brave. Normally, he would have hidden in the woods or ran toward the fortress behind him, not away from it. Lys had helped him through an immeasurably difficult time, though. He was going to do everything in his power to return the favor.

A white blur smashed into Torruk's side, just an arm's length in front of Callan. Torruk and the Visani that attacked him both rolled to their feet. The feline had its back to Callan so he acted as quickly as he could. He unsheathed his sword and slashed across the back of the Visani's legs, spurting blood and slicing tendons. It fell with a howl to the ground, where Torruk jumped on it. The wolfman gripped its neck in one clawed hand and squeezed, removing its throat and throwing it behind him. The Visani gurgled away its last breaths. Callan spared him a glance but was too rushed to be horrified by what he had just done.

The two of them didn't wait around for it to die. They ran deeper into the camp, looking for Lys. The young man was unsure how they were supposed to find one man in the melee. He refused to believe that he was already dead, though. They would find him. Lys would know how to get them all out of this. He had gotten them this far.

They didn't run for long. The camp was much smaller and more cramped than it appeared to be from the outside. That fact also gave the illusion that there were more of the giant Visani attacking than there really were. Callan didn't spend the time to stop and count each of them, but he guessed that there were fewer than a dozen. That fact scared him, since he could see the damage that they were doing. The Visani were outnumbered by the mercenaries nearly three to one, but the screams of the humans that were being mauled filled the air.

Callan heard him before he saw him. Lys' voice carried over the screams of the men and the roars of the beasts. He couldn't hear specific words, but Lys had a very distinctive voice. He sounded like a leader. He was someone who could be trusted, and his voice carried that assurance with it.

He found him standing among a group of other mercenaries, calling out orders and directions. They were being attacked by a pair of Visani, the biggest that Callan had seen of the ones attacking. They each stood head and shoulders taller than even Torruk, who was huge by human standards.

Callan looked to the Fanir. "We have to do something!"

He nodded. "Draw your bow. Shoot the one on the right."

Callan hesitated as he was putting his sword back into its sheath. "But if I miss, I'll hit the humans behind them."

"Do not miss."

Hands shaking, he took the bow from his back and removed an arrow from the quiver. He took a deep breath and drew back, letting out his breath slowly. If he missed, there was a good chance he would kill one of the mercenaries. He couldn't miss. He wouldn't.

Callan sighted down his arrow and released, aiming for the middle of the Visani's back. His aim was off, but not by much. He'd wanted the arrow to hit between its shoulder blades, but the arrow dropped, slamming into his back just above his tail. It roared and fell to its knees where Lys dispatched it with both of his swords, driving them into the Visani's chest. It fell to the ground with the mercenary on top of it.

The other turned when it's comrade fell, trying to slice Lys across the back with his stone dagger. It was a dagger in *its* hand, anyway. To Callan, it would have been a full-sized sword made of hard mountain rock. Callan couldn't fire off another arrow in time. He looked to Torruk in desperation.

He knelt on the ground, his claws buried in the earth, as he had been when he discovered the fate of Callan's family. A low, constant rumble came from his chest and vibrated through the ground in the immediate area. Callan could hear the sound and *feel* it through the soles of his boots.

The vibrations moved more quickly than Callan could follow toward the still standing Visani. When they reached it, clumps of earth shot up from the ground and enveloped each of its legs up to the knee. The creature fell forward with a high-pitched, almost terrified, whine. Its legs *snapped* as it fell onto its face. As soon as it hit, another clump of dirt moved from the ground and wrapped itself around the Visani's neck. Its neck *snapped* more loudly than its knees had.

Callan spun on his heel to see if any more of the Visani attacked, but there were none near him. They had finally been driven off by the mercenaries and were running off into the forest. Callan left Torruk's side and ran to Lys.

"Are you okay?" he asked.

Lys stood up and wiped the blood off his swords onto his trousers.

"Fine. Nice shot."

"Thanks." Callan smiled. "We found Graveholm. It's not far."

Torruk nodded growled in the affirmative. "An hour's travel from here. Maybe two."

"Okay then." Lys seemed to be full of energy after the short battle. Callan had no idea how he held himself together so well. Callan's arms and legs were shaking so badly that he could hardly stand.

"Troops!" Lys shouted. "Let's move out. Injured to the middle of the column! We need to make it to Graveholm before the Visani come back."

Lys moved off from where he had slain the Visani and walked toward the forest where Callan and Torruk had been scouting. He clearly meant to move on whether the others were ready or not.

"Lys?" Callan asked. "Aren't we going to bury the ones who didn't make it?"

The mercenary never even looked back. He called over his shoulder, "They knew the risks of this mission, and they died well. Leave them and come with me. We have a lot to talk about before we get you to Graveholm."

"We aren't going to bury them?"

"I said to leave them. Let's go."

Chapter 18

"Gramm, what's going on out there?"

The knight turned, his new ornamental cape, which showed his new position, swishing behind him. "There's a small army outside the gate. A bunch of mercenaries, it looks like."

"Mercenaries? Is father meeting with them?"

Gramm nodded.

"Take me to them."

Gramm nodded and held out his arm for her. She grabbed his elbow and allowed him to escort her to the front gate. Normally, she would have walked down on her own. In the current situation, with an unknown army at the gate, she wanted them to think that she was just like any other woman in the kingdom. She wanted to give the impression that she was unimportant and that she defaulted to her father and brother. Even to Gramm. If they weren't looking at her, she could watch them at her leisure and learn whatever she needed to.

The pair walked out of the front doors into a light snow. They were met by the sight of Ravitch and Theamere, flanked by armored knights, talking with a tall, wiry man who looked as if he hadn't had a good bath in weeks. There was a thin, slightly curved sword strapped to each of his hips, but his hands were clasped behind his back. His position came off as very innocent and non-threatening. That was good as there were plenty of armed men ready to cut him to pieces if he tried anything.

The man was speaking when Pyra and Gramm approached. "I have some men who are hurt. We were attacked by Visani on the way in and managed to drive them off. If you could offer some healing to the ones in the worst shape, they'll be out of your hair as soon as they're able to leave." He paused for a moment when he saw Pyra. The two locked eyes, and he smiled briefly. "The rest of us will leave immediately. After payment, of course."

"Yes, yes," Ravitch growled. "You'll be paid. Besides the boy, who else is planning on staying?"

The man shrugged. "As far as I know, only three. We have a mage and a paladin that travel together. They'll be staying to look after the kid. Our Fanir, Torruk, will be staying as well. He hasn't said why he wants to."

"And the boy? He is in good health?"

Another shrug, this time accompanied by a surprisingly disarming smile. There was more to this man than was apparent. There was something in his eyes that Pyra couldn't place. An intelligence that he hid behind a calm demeanor.

"He's in as good a shape as could be expected. Better, really." Now he looked genuinely sad. Pyra wasn't sure why that fact surprised her so much. "The kid's gone through a lot," he continued, "but I think he's come out stronger for it."

Ravitch nodded thoughtfully and prodded Theamere gently with his walking cane. "Pay the man." Then, while Theamere carefully produced a large sack of gold from a satchel on his side, Pyra's father addressed the mercenary again. "Bring in your wounded. They'll be taken care of and released. I want to meet this child now."

The mercenary nodded and accepted the leather bag from Theamere. He turned around and waved one arm in the air toward a group in the distance that Pyra had failed to notice before. It wasn't so much an army as Gramm has described it. She could make out a large group of mercenaries, but no more than fifty or sixty. Some were on horses, but from so far away, she couldn't tell how many.

A smaller group broke off from the main force and made their way slowly toward Graveholm. Pyra wondered to herself how many they had lost in the attack by the Visani. Judging by the relatively small number of wounded that were now making their way ever closer and the number of those that were still healthy, they must have acquitted themselves very well.

Gramm leaned down to Pyra's level and whispered in her ear. "Do you know anything about the kid that your father is asking about?"

She shook her head. It wouldn't have surprised her if one of Graveholm's old families was bringing in a bastard to take over the estate. Illegitimate children were common when a lawful heir couldn't be brought into the world. Why her father was so concerned about the boy was a mystery, though.

Pyra smiled up at Gramm. "Whoever he is, he must be important. That's a *lot* of gold."

The newly minted captain chuckled. It was good to see that he wasn't taking his position too seriously. He was still Gramm. He was still her best friend.

By the time that the rest of the mercenaries arrived at the gate, Pyra started to get cold. She longed to be inside with her books, either reading stories and histories or studying magic. She couldn't bring herself to do anything for her own pleasure, though. Not with so many sitting idly in the dungeons. Everything she did now was for the good of everyone else.

The group that arrived was eclectic indeed. Most had easily treatable injuries. Cuts that had been too deep to dress in the field, a broken arm, a badly twisted ankle. One of them was the biggest man that Pyra had ever seen, including her own family. His bright red hair stood in stark contrast with the gray weather that seemed to constantly hover over the mountains. He had a long gash in his right leg and could barely support his own weight. A smaller man held him up.

Theamere escorted everyone who needed medical attention inside. Elder Moss and the healers would be assigned to them. Had Pyra been inside still, it probably would have been her job to help. As it was, she got to stay outside where important things were happening.

Once the mercenaries were let inside, only two of their number remained. Their leader, who had spoken earlier, and a young man who was obviously the one that her father had asked about earlier. He appeared to be younger than Pyra, but not by much. His hair was long. Longer even than hers, which looked quite ridiculous on a boy his age. It must have been in style wherever he was from.

"Callan," said the mercenary, "this is Ravitch, Lord of Graveholm and the northern provinces. Lord Ravitch, this is Callan, son of Balen and Lilliana, and the rightful Lord of Ashefall."

The young man, Callan, bowed to Ravitch, one hand clasped over his heart. The other stuffed into his pocket to keep it warm. Pyra had never seen another lord before. The climate in Graveholm was so cold that it had always kept them away. And Ravitch had always kept the family so secluded that they had never travelled to visit any other provinces with him on the rare occasions that he travelled.

Callan spoke much more softly than Pyra imagined a lord would speak. "It is good to meet you, Lord Ravitch. My father always spoke highly of you. I'm sorry that he couldn't be here in my stead."

Ravitch scratched distractedly at the wrapping over his ruined eye. "It's good to meet you too, Callan. I was deeply hurt to hear what happened to your family. I'm very sorry for your loss."

The younger lord looked at his boots. His loss must have been a recent one to draw sorrow to his face so quickly. Pyra's heart went out to him. She had wondered, briefly, why someone so young held such a lofty title. She should have known that he would have had to have lost his family to earn it.

Pyra's father continued, "My son, Theamere is inside. This is my daughter, Pyra." He gestured back to her. She was taken off guard. Pyra hadn't realized that he had seen her arrive. "Her escort is my knight captain, Gramm."

Gramm bowed to the young man, just as low as he did when bowing to Ravitch. Titles meant everything to Gramm, and Pyra knew that he would follow this new lord's orders to the letter. For her part, Pyra curtsied as far as her large coat would allow her.

"Hello, Callan," she said. "It's very good to meet you."

He bowed in return. Pyra couldn't help but think that all the pleasantries were a waste of time. The look on the mercenary's face said that he thought the same.

"It's good to meet you, as well. Thank you for welcoming me into your home."

The mercenary spoke up now, clearly not minding that he was talking over those of much higher station than himself. Pyra had to admire his guts. She tried to do the same as often as possible, if only to annoy her brother and Gramm. There weren't many of higher station than her, of course. But there were enough old, rich men who thought a woman like her should know her place.

"Well, if you don't mind, my lords and lady, I should be going."

Callan looked startled at that. What could he possibly have expected from a mercenary? They were money worshippers, the lot of them. They did their job, usually well, collected their money, and left. Pyra hadn't seen many of their kind, but she had heard stories from her father. They were all the same.

"You're leaving? Just like that?" Callan asked.

The mercenary jingled the bag of coins in both hands, then hefted it over one shoulder. He smiled at Callan in an almost fatherly fashion. "Yeah, kid. Just like that." He frowned thoughtfully. "If I had any wise parting words to give you, I would. But I don't. I never was one for giving good advice. I've taken a liking to you, kid. I don't want to hear about you getting killed. So, take care of yourself, okay?"

"I will. And thank you, Lys. For everything."

"You're welcome. And if you ever need to get in touch with me, ask Ravitch. He knows how to find me."

He ruffled Callan's hair, then turned and walked back toward his own people, leaving the boy looking lost. Pyra's father looked like he wanted to say something to Callan. Ravitch had good intentions, she was sure, but he would undoubtedly make him feel worse about everything. Pyra stepped forward before he could say anything.

"Father, if it's alright, Gramm and I would like to show Callan around. Help him get acclimated to Graveholm." She smiled at her father, then at Callan.

Gramm whispered in her ear, "We would?"

"We would."

Callan caught the exchange and smirked. Good. At least he wasn't completely miserable without his travelling companions. Ravitch missed it, though. His response was as calculated and as expected as ever. It took quite a lot for him to surprise her.

"Very well," he said. "Show him around, let him get a bath. And hurry. We don't want to be outside any longer than we need to."

The Visani had already attacked once today, but that hardly meant that they wouldn't again. Pyra nodded. "Come along then, Callan."

He came after them, and the three made their way into the keep. Ravitch called after them, "And find someone to cut his hair! We need him taken seriously around here. Bring him to my chambers once you're finished."

Pyra watched Callan reach up and self-consciously tug on the end of his hair. As much as he might have been attached to it, for whatever reason, Ravitch was right. Callan was a lord, and the noble families of Graveholm would only take him seriously if he looked like one. She explained as much to him.

"Why do you keep it so long, anyway?" she asked.

Callan shrugged. "My mother liked it."

Oh.

Pyra was at a loss for words. She'd never known her mother. She had taken ill and died when Pyra was too young to remember her. Theamere had always spoken fondly of her, but there had never been any mother-daughter connection. Luckily, Gramm knew what to say. Somehow, he always did.

"You'll remember your mother fondly with it or without it," he said. "And you will have a much easier time getting acclimated here if you get it cut. Some of the nobles really frown on anything different."

Callan smiled up at Gramm. He wasn't tall, by any means, but he wasn't tiny like Pyra either. Still, most people tended to look up to Gramm. Often in more ways than one.

"So," asked Callan, "are you two married?"

A bark of laughter erupted out of Pyra's mouth. Gramm nearly choked. He looked like he wanted to answer, but words were clearly not coming easily to him. His face turned an unnatural shade of red, making Pyra giggle. Callan looked almost as amused as she felt.

"I'll take that as a no?"

She laughed again. "No, no," she said. "We're not. Gramm's been my best friend since we were both very young."

Callan and Gramm shared a look. "What?" asked Pyra.

"Nothing," they both responded at the same time as if on cue.

Pyra chose to ignore it. "Well, what would you like to see first, Callan?"

#

Over the course of the next rest of the morning, Pyra and Gramm showed the young lord everything that Graveholm's keep had to offer. Unfortunately, the threat of the Visani kept them away from the town, but the keep was large enough to keep them occupied.

Pyra showed him the dungeons and explained the refugee situation to him. "We're doing everything that we can for them here. We've a large enough stockpile to keep everyone fed for at least a couple of years. Some of them, families with very young children mostly, are going to be moved to real sleeping quarters as soon as they're available."

"Why not train them as soldiers?" Callan asked. "Then they can help defend against the Visani."

"Some of them have enlisted," Gramm answered. "We aren't going to enlist them against their will, though. We don't need that much manpower at this point. Right now, we're focused on keeping them alive and relatively happy."

After the dungeons, their next stop was the training facility. Gramm showed the two of them, as Pyra rarely visited the area, where the weapon racks and the straw practice dummies were located. The room wasn't in use at the moment, but Gramm assured them that it was often occupied by at least a handful of knights or soldiers.

"Any of them will be happy to spar with you, I'm sure," Gramm said. "I'll do my best to be available for training as well, when I have a spare moment or two."

Pyra considered taking him up to the library and showing off the scrolls that she had been studying. She had no idea what he knew of magic or if he had any interest in the craft at all. She had heard the mercenary leader mention that there had been a paladin travelling with the group. Maybe Callan could tell her about the kind of magic that the paladin was capable of. She had never met one and Elder Moss had never talked in-depth about them.

She didn't know this young man, though. Only a few people got to spend time with her in her library. Gramm knew that he was allowed to come and go as he pleased, but even he left her alone out of respect for her privacy. Moss came in when he felt like she needed a lesson, but other than the two of them, she was mostly left alone.

No, she would keep her books and her scrolls and her magic to herself. If she wanted to learn about the paladin and his magic, she could ask him herself.

"Well, Callan," she said, "how about we go and take care of your hair? Then Father would like some time with you."

Chapter 19

Callan ran his hands along the top of his head, feeling just how bare it had become. He wasn't bald by any meaning of the word, but he couldn't so much as grab a handful of his own hair anymore. He felt naked, standing out in the cold corridor outside of Lord Ravitch's chambers. The pair of guards outside the door paid Callan no attention, but he felt like they stared at him. He was just being stupid. They lived with the imposing figure of the scarred, twisted-faced Lord Ravitch. There was no possibility that Callan was even on their radar.

A voice called from inside, though Callan didn't catch exactly what was said. One of the stone-faced guards opened the door and gestured for Callan to go inside. He did, dropping his hand from the top of his head. He wanted to look comfortable. He had learned that much in court, at least. This, he could handle. He was born for this.

Lord Ravitch sat at a desk, his hands clasped in front of him. "You look almost like a real lord now, boy."

Callan bristled at that. "With all due respect, the way that I look doesn't make me any less of a lord."

Ravitch's brows furrowed. He clearly wasn't used to being contradicted. Before the last few weeks, Callan probably would have just bowed his head and let himself be beaten around verbally. Now, though, he had been through enough that he was no longer going to take abuse from anyone. He'd seen death. He'd *caused* death. He could handle anything. He could handle Ravitch.

"No," Ravitch said, "but it does change how people look at you. There are a lot of very important families here that we need funding from." He stood and walked to the other side of the desk, sizing up Callan with his remaining eye as he walked.

Ravitch continued, "If they don't give us money, we can't buy food. Then we'll have to take it without payment. Then morale goes down. Then we have a revolt on our hands. At that point, we're fighting among ourselves and we're stuck in here because the Visani want to make us into dinner."

He had walked as close to Callan as he possibly could by that point. He was tall, much taller than the younger man, so Callan's nose was nearly pressed into his chest. He could smell the rot and dried blood from his many injuries that had yet to fully heal. Ravitch smelled almost *infected*.

"You might be a *lord*, boy, but you don't know anything about rule." Ravitch was practically growling at that point. "Be pissy with me if you want, but everything that I tell you to do is for the greater good of the people. Your father understood that."

Callan looked up into the scarred face above him. "I'm not my father."

"Oh, that is painfully obvious." He walked back to his desk and sat down gingerly. Callan got the feeling that he was in a lot more pain than he let on. That didn't change the fact that he wasn't endearing himself to Callan at all. "Your father knew the importance of being a good leader. He knew that his people would look to him for guidance. If he looked pampered and privileged, he knew that he would lose credibility with them."

"This is your home," Callan replied. "Not mine. The people here look to you. They have no reason to look to me for anything."

"No reason? You're the first lord other than me that they've seen in *years*, boy. I almost died. They know that I'm not invincible. Just look at me." He paused and stared at Callan, daring him to disagree. The polite thing to do would have been to assure him that he looked every bit a leader. Ravitch was right, though. He looked like he was on his last legs.

"Besides that," he continued, "you haven't met my son. He's a phenomenal warrior. One of the most dangerous men in Aelathil. I'd bet anything on it. But, he isn't a leader. My daughter is a born lady, but the noble families…they won't ever look to a woman to help them."

Callan frowned. "That seems unfair. If she's a good leader, why wouldn't they just follow her? Especially if she's your daughter."

Ravitch leaned across the desk, his voice getting louder as his ire rose. "They're stuck in their ways. Most of this damned nation is the same way. You wouldn't know that because you grew up in the family that you did. Your parents didn't give a *damn* if you were a man or a woman. All that mattered was your ability."

He paused and sat back further in his chair. "That's part of the reason that Ramsey came after your father. That's why your family is dead. They were progressive. The last thing that Ramsey wants is progress. He just wants rule for himself and for whatever heirs he gets some city whore to pop out for him."

That much, they could agree on. Both had reason to hate their king. Ravitch had lost a friend and a conspirator. And equal. Callan had lost his family because of…what? Politics? He wasn't entirely sure what Ramsey had done it. He was going to find out, though.

"Let me get this straight," Callan said. "You want me to look like a leader because you don't think that they'll be following you much longer? You want a successor who isn't your son?"

"Don't get me wrong, Theamere is a good son. He will give me strong grandchildren." He sighed and rubbed at the wrapping over his ruined eye. "Theamere is a warrior, not a leader. I need him to lead my soldiers into battle when Ramsey decides that he's tired of our little rebellion. Which means that the people here need a face to look to for guidance."

Callan nodded. He owed it to the people who could still fight to be good for them. There was a nagging worry in the back of his mind, though. He had never led anyone anywhere. He said as much to Ravitch.

"I know my history. I can hold my own in a fight. I know the basics of politics. I'm not a leader, though. I have no idea how to give your people what you want me to give them. I don't know how to give them what they need."

Ravitch looked satisfied at that. At least he stopped scowling at him. "You'll have help on that front, boy. I don't expect you to become your father alone. Or overnight, for that matter. Murdock will be staying here, as will the paladin. They'll help groom you into a leader. As will any of my other staff who has time."

Callan smiled, relieved that they would be staying in Graveholm with him. He wished that Lys could have stayed, but Callan knew why that wasn't a possibility. There was always another contract. Always more money to be made.

"Will any of the other mercenaries be staying?"

The lord shook his shaggy head. His hair was long. He had a beard that hung down to the top of his chest. The fact that he was so obsessed with Callan's appearance was confusing. Of course, Ravitch had been the Lord of Graveholm for many years. When he was younger, he probably looked a lot like Callan did now. He had gained the respect and the love of his people, though. He no longer had anything to prove to them.

"No. Once they've healed from their injuries, they'll be leaving." His lip curled in an angry snarl. "That Fanir will be staying, though.

As if I don't have enough problems with the Visani already. They'll be chomping at the bit to kill him."

"What did Torruk do to them?"

Ravitch laughed. It was a strange sound. Grating, like metal over rough stone. "Nothing, boy. The Visani and the Fanir have been at each other's throats for thousands of years. If they find out that we're letting him stay with us, they'll come for him."

Callan shrugged. "They're attacking you anyway. They came after us in the forest outside of here for no reason at all. I don't see how Torruk being here changes that fact."

"You wouldn't. You aren't from here. You've spent your entire life locked up in the mountains being pampered by maids and retainers. Balen never taught you about battle, war, or any kind of conflict that wasn't straight out of a history text."

Callan stayed silent. As much as he hated the fact that Ravitch was tearing him down for no apparent reason, everything that he said was true. Callan didn't know anything about real warfare or the world outside of his home. Until recently, he thought the world a kind place. Ramsey had changed that. Verne had done even more to pervert that expectation. After him had come the Visani.

The world wasn't changing, just Callan's view of it.

Ravitch had driven home his point hard enough, though. Callan was done being told that he needed to be better. That he needed to be more like his father. He knew that he would never be Balen. They were too different.

"I won't disappoint you or your people."

A knock sounded at the door. Ravitch called for the guard to come in.

"My lord," he said upon entering, "our scouts are back with information on the Visani camps."

Ravitch nodded. "Send them in." He turned to Callan and said, "You're to meet with Moss, the elder in my employ. Don't ask me why. He wanted to talk to you, and I granted him permission. My guard will escort you."

Callan searched for something to say. How was he supposed to address Ravitch? They were technically of the same rank so was he supposed to use his name? Or would he be expected to call him, "My lord?"

Ravitch scowled with his good eye. "You can leave anytime now."

Callan nodded and walked out without a word.

There was a guard outside, waiting to take Callan to Elder Moss. The young man didn't speak, and Callan didn't ask him to. They didn't have far to walk. Moss held his chambers on the same floor that Ravitch did. The guard stopped outside the open door but didn't wave Callan in. There were elevated voices coming from inside. Callan' recognized Murdock's high baritone.

"If you think I would let him train under you, you've really lost your mind," yelled Murdock. "You've never stuck by anything in your entire career, why would you be faithful here?"

An even-leveled, clearly aged voiced answered, "You turned out just fine. Besides, he might not even have the Gift."

"I turned out the way I did in spite of you, not because of you." There was a *bang*, like something being slammed on a desk. "You haven't heard the last of this, Moss. Neither has Ravitch. You should hope for your sake that he doesn't have it."

Murdock stormed out, then, still in his riding clothes, his robes discarded for now. The mage didn't even glance at Callan. He strode by, a dark shadow on his face. Only when he was gone around the corner did the guard motion for Callan to go into audience with the elder. He peeked his head in, his eyes opening wide at what he saw.

Where he had expected order and cleanliness, he saw chaos and scattered parchment and tools. There were no magical instruments, no spells being cast. There was only an old, hunched man sitting behind a decrepit desk.

He smiled despite the argument that had just taken place. "You must be Callan," he said. "Welcome. Welcome, please, have a seat." He motioned to a chair opposite him.

Callan sat down and scooted his chair as close to the desk as he could get without bumping his knees into the wood. Looking across at the old man, he was reminded of his tutors back in Ashefall. He had the distinct feeling that he was about to be put through a geography test or a history exam.

"Callan, it is very nice to meet you."

Callan wasn't as sure. He liked Murdock and trusted his opinions so far. He didn't think very highly of Elder Moss, obviously, so Callan was guarded. "You too, sir. I'm glad to be here."

"Good, good," said the elder. "I'm not here to waste your time, Callan. I want to test you."

Cal cursed inwardly.

"I want to see if you've got what those of us from Immeo, the mages, call the Gift. It's the ability to access the magical forces that bind our world together. Not many have it. I'd imagine that you haven't met many mages in your life."

Callan shook his head. "No, sir. My father entertained one or two at the Dragon's Keep, but the only one that I had contact with was Murdock." He smiled and added, "And yourself, of course."

The old mage grinned, his yellowed teeth showing past his cracked and wrinkled lips. "Well, as I said, the Gift is rare. This test is quick and painless, I promise. I only need a small prick of your finger. A drop of blood."

Callan's arms tensed. His breath quickened, and he slid his chair back a fraction of an inch. "I don't think so."

The elder waved a hand dismissively. "Really, it will be over in a second. Besides, Lord Ravitch insisted that you be tested."

The young Lord narrowed his eyes. "He said that this was your idea."

"Yes, I'm sure he did."

Again, he cursed internally. There was nothing for it, then. He would have to let this strange man take a blood sample. Murdock didn't trust him, but he also hadn't stopped Callan from coming in. He could have, very easily. With a grimace, he shoved the sleeve of his tunic up past his elbow and stuck his right hand out toward Moss, palm up, fingers splayed. "Get it over with, then."

Elder Moss gripped him by the wrist with his left hand and extended the index finger on his right. He touched the fingernail of that finger to the tip of Callan's middle finger, at the first knuckle. The nail cut through his skin like it was made of steel rather than bits of human flesh.

"Ow!"

Moss ignored him. A slow trickle of blood came from the cut, dripping onto the wood of the table. The initial pain was gone, but the cut still stung. The elder held Callan's hand still and let a few drops of his blood drip onto the table, where it formed a very small pool. Once he was satisfied with the size of the pool, Moss let Callan go. Callan brought his finger to his mouth immediately and sucked on the wound, trying to get the bleeding to stop. He glared at Moss.

Moss ignored him again. He held one ancient, trembling hand over the small puddle of blood. Callan's view of the blood became distorted. He peered harder and harder until he realized that nothing was wrong with his vision. A fine mist had formed beneath the elder's hand, creeping toward Callan's blood. The mist was darker the closer it was to Moss' hand. It paled and became more translucent the closer to Callan's blood it got. Near the blood puddle, there was almost an invisible bubble that the mist couldn't penetrate.

The elder stared at it for a moment, sweat starting to drip from his beaked nose. Without any prompting from Callan, he dropped his hand and let the mist evaporate. The old man sat back in his chair with a sigh. He seemed almost disappointed. Neither of them said anything for a moment. They just sat, Callan staring at Moss while Moss stared at something only he could see, something that he was seeing in the air above Callan's head.

Rather than let the uncomfortable silence drag on, Callan spoke up. "So? Do I have it? Do I have the Gift?"

Moss shook his head slowly from side to side. He seemed much more warn out that he had only a few moments ago. "No, I'm afraid not. You're as normal as they come, my boy."

"Does that change anything? Ravitch's plans for me? Your plans for me?"

Moss smiled weakly. "I have no plans for you, young man. Ravitch might, but I don't. I'm past scheming, past planning. With the Gift, you would have been the fourth mage here. Now we are three, as we were before. An old man past any practical use, a young girl just coming into her power, and one of the most powerful mages I've ever known who refuses to accept his own potential." He sighed and shook his head again and waved Callan away with a flick of his hand. "You can go, my boy. Let Murdock know that he won't have anything to worry about from me."

Chapter 20

Tens of thousands of screams roared from the throats of the populace. Arian smiled. As long as they were distracted, they were happy. The gladiatorial games made him happy as well. He enjoyed the combat, even if it was less than militarily sound. The crowd gasped. Arian leaned back in his plush seat and folded his hands behind his head.

The blacksmith swung wildly with his stone hammers, trying to break past the butcher's guard. The broadsword made that fact much easier said than done. Arian scoffed at them. They'd been allowed to choose their own weapons. Why they hadn't picked a sword and shield, he could not understand. Then again, they didn't have a phalanx of brothers surrounding them. There was no cavalry here, no spearmen. No armor.

"What are you thinking about?"

Arian smiled. "Tactics, my emperor. Only tactics."

Cestus smiled back, his immaculate teeth showing past his salt and pepper beard. "There is more to it than that, I think."

"You're correct, of course. I want battle. I want to lead my men into the savage wastes and bring the inhuman tribes into the warm bosom of the empire." Arian paused and cast his glance back to the combat in the arena. Blacksmith had managed to pick up a few deep cuts on his arms and chest. He needed to land a heavy blow or two. Break some bones. Or he was going to die. "I want to be written into history. I want the poems, the songs, the glory."

The emperor nodded, keeping one eye on the fight and one eye on Arian. "You always have." He took a sip of his wine, the mid-afternoon sun shining off his crystal goblet. "Fortunately for you, I have a campaign in mind."

Arian reached for his drink, a glass of water, and took a long drink. "I'm intrigued, of course. But I don't have the faintest idea where you could send me. Your armies have rid Orthielle of bandits and rebels. The Nassans have kept to themselves."

"I'm sending you farther away than just our borders, Arian. What do you know of the kingdom of Aelathil?"

He shrugged. "Enough. Their king inherited the throne from his father nearly fifteen years ago. He has been trying to expand into Nassas without much success."

"He's also made some very powerful enemies recently," said Cestus, keeping his attention on the battle.

"The tribes? They are not so strong as they could storm Aelathil's walls or overcome her soldiers."

Cestus shook his head, snorting with derision. "No. Not the tribes."

In the arena, Blacksmith landed a heavy blow to the wrist of the butcher. He had finally broken inside the huge reach of the broadsword. The wrist snapped and the steel dropped to the sand. The butcher's screams were drowned out by the roar of the crowd. Cestus and those in his personal, shaded box clapped politely. Arian was among them.

Blacksmith kicked the other gladiator, who was now unarmed, in the stomach. Butcher was driven to his knees with the air knocked from his lungs. He lay in the sand, clutching his broken wrist to his body. His good hand clawed at the dirt, seeking reprieve from what he knew was coming quickly. The hammer-wielder dropped one of his weapons and used his free hand to grab the butcher by his scraggly, dirty hair. Blacksmith wrenched his head around, forcing him to look to Cestus, to his emperor.

The bearded emperor of men raised one hand, drawing a hush from the huddled thousands. He was still for only a moment. Then he clenched his hand into a fist. The crowd roared.

Barbarians. Arian took a sip of his water. He watched as the blacksmith crushed the butcher's skull with his remaining hammer. He hit him once, twice, three times, until his head was nothing but splintered pulp, bleeding into the sands of the arena.

Barbarians.

"The tribes are of no consequence to even a small nation such as Aelathil," continued Cestus as if nothing had happened. "No, he has angered those who his ancestors put into power in the first place. His own governors. The lords of the provinces. They planned rebellion in secret."

The emperor shrugged and drank at his goblet of wine as the slaves removed the butcher's corpse. There would be another bout soon enough. The blacksmith had survived to fight another day.

"He found out, of course. There are few such things that can be kept from a powerful king. King Ramsey had the rebel killed. Brutally from what our spies have gathered."

"Oh?" Arian had seen many brutal deaths. "He hanged him? Drew him and quartered him?"

"The king set dragons on him and burned his holdings and his family to ash."

Arian set his goblet down. Dragons? The thought brought the tales of his youth to mind. Great, burning beasts that were rulers of land, sea, and sky. They destroyed everything that they came across, whether it was village or town or fields of grain. The fact that this king was controlling them, these creatures out of a myth, was frightening.

"Dragons? That's impossible."

"With the teachers you've had, and the expeditions you've been on, I would have imagined that you would know by now…there's no such thing as impossible."

Cestus put down his wine and secured his wrap around himself. He said his goodbyes and exchanged a few pleasantries with those around him, then motioned to Arian. "Come with me."

He followed, past throngs of people and out of the packed arena. The pair of them, general and emperor, walked through the capital of the empire. Dominion was a quiet city. Nearly everyone watched the fights. Rich and poor, it brought them all together. Cestus had been wise to reinstate the weekly battles. His predecessors had dismissed them as barbaric and beyond civilized people. Cestus had seen it differently. It provided the populace with a distraction, as well as providing the justice system a way to punish the more egregious criminals. Like the butcher and the blacksmith.

A happy people were an easy to control people. There had been much less work for Arian and the other soldiers to do in the city since the fights had returned. The decreased military presence in the major cities, those outside of Dominion included, gave way to exploratory outings. Much to the disappointment of the empire's enemies, it also meant that conquering was much more frequent. In recent years, Orthielle had expanded her borders to the northern and southern seas.

"I came from simple stock, Arian."

Arian listened out of respect, but didn't pay close attention. He had heard this story before, and the emperor always started it out the same way. He enjoyed his life lessons, did Cestus.

"My father was a farmer, like his father and grandfather and great-grandfather before him. I wanted to avoid that life so I studied, and studied hard. I was a scholar who learned under the best tutors in the empire…small as it was back then."

As they walked, and Cestus described his rise through the political and military ranks, Arian admired the art that lined the streets. Giant statues of past kings and revered generals stared down on the normally crowded streets. Scattered amongst them were representations of the gods. The same thirteen that most humans worshipped. The ones that all of them would, eventually, if Cestus had his way. It wasn't that he was particularly religious, Arian had noticed. He cared more about unifying the people than any particular set of beliefs.

"Orthielle is growing my boy, but she isn't big enough. Empires need to be expansive and, so far, this one is only tall. She stretches as far as she can to the north and south, but there are plenty of other lands to conquer, to bring into the fold."

Arian looked at Cestus out of the corner of one eye. The comment surprised him. He had always spoken of stopping his expansion, at least for a while, once they could touch both seas. That had been achieved mere months ago, and he was already talking about spreading even further.

"Where will you conquer next? We have the Nassan Plains to our west and the Wild Marshes to the east. There is very little to be gained in either direction."

Cestus smiled and clapped Arian on the shoulder. "The plain is to bypass Nassas entirely. I want Aelathil."

"Did you not tell me *very* recently that their king has dragons at his disposal," Arian asked? "What threat could we post to him?"

"Alone? Over this great distance? Not much of one," Cestus answered. "If we join forces with these rebels, though, our combined numbers should be able to wear down even a king with dragons at his back."

Arian considered it for a moment. Orthielle was home to the most powerful infantry in the known world. Still, fighting that kind of war, over hundreds, even thousands of leagues, would be nearly impossible.

"Our armies are great, my emperor, but we cannot possibly feed all of our forces over such a distance."

"I know, I know," said Cestus. "Be patient. I have no intention of sending the entire army. Only the Firebrands."

Only one legion. The most powerful in the empire, possibly the most powerful of all time, but still…only one.

"And I want you to lead them," he finished.

Arian stopped in his tracks. Why would he send Arian all the way to Aelathil in charge of such a prestigious unit? Surely, one of the elder, more experienced generals would have been a better choice. In fact, by not choosing one of them, Cestus would surely make a few enemies in his court. It was not the general's place to question his emperor, though.

"You honor me, Highness."

"Yes. I do. I expect nothing less than complete domination of the west from you. After you've seized control of Aelathil, we can pinch the tribes in and drive them out. Nassas will be ours as well."

"If I may ask, Highness, how is this to be done with only one legion?"

"Easy, my boy," answered Cestus. "We ally ourselves with the rebels. From what I can gather, they have much support in Aelathil and plenty of financial backing. Our Firebrands should be enough to tip the balance in their favor."

"After we've taken out Ramsey, what then," asked Arian?" Who is to be the new king?"

Cestus answered with an imperious smile. "After King Ramsey is dead, your forces will betray the rebels. You will be the new king." He laughed at the stunned expression on Arian's face. "Then, as king, you will coordinate with my forces here and we will crush Nassas. The entire process could triple the size of our empire."

The two walked in silence for a while. Cestus took his turn at admiring the beauty of the city while Arian studied his boots. The black, shined leather nearly reflected his face. The bronze buckles would have had he been close enough to them. They were dirtying up around the edges. The sands of the arena were to blame for that, no doubt. He would have to clean them. After all, a general could not be respected if he was not dressed immaculately. Arian had dealt with disrespect enough in the early years of his career. He had been the youngest ever to reach the rank of general in Orthielle's legions. He was just over thirty-five now, and if he were to take the position on this very day, he would *still* be one of the youngest ever. It was a fact that he was extremely proud of. But to be king?

"Arian, you haven't answered me. What do you think of the plan?"

He hesitated. "You want my opinion, Majesty?"

"I do, yes."

"In truth, I think it brilliant. But risky. The Firebrands are your best defense against attack at home."

"They are. However, they are also the best offensive force that this empire has ever known. I would trust to other legion to bring you your kingship," said Cestus. "Now, I believe you have an excursion to plan and a legion to ready." The emperor stopped and turned briskly, saluting with his right fist on his left shoulder.

Arian returned the salute. "Yes, Father."

Chapter 21

"I know you've been training a long time for this," said Murdock, "but I would be remiss if I didn't tell you to be careful."

Callan strode ahead of him, a confident smile playing at the edges of his lips. He felt readier for this than he had for anything in years. After all the training, all the hard work, all the study, Ravitch was finally sending him on an important mission. Alone. Sure, he had been taken along on raids and supply delivery. He had even been allowed to guard caravans on their way into Graveholm. This time, though, he would have no superior. He was in command. The task was daunting, but he was ready for the responsibility.

The pair walked out into the yard, which had been walled off against the increasing Visani attacks. Callan had not been training alone, either. Those who had lived in the villages surrounding Graveholm had been made into fine soldiers. Most of them were archers, good ones, and had been defending the walls for months now. The Visani couldn't get near the keep during the day anymore. The walls had been fortified well enough that they had given up trying to sneak in at night, as well.

"We're doing well here, Murdock. *I'm* doing well here. You worry too much."

"Someone has to."

"Let Ravitch worry like a mother hen. It's his job, after all."

Murdock frowned. "You're a lord as well, you know. You should take some of the responsibility yourself."

Callan turned to face the mage and walked backward. He opened his arms, gesturing to his clothing and weapons. "Look at me. I'm about to lead a unit against Herken at Garrad. I call that responsibility." He rolled his eyes. "Besides, Ravitch has made it very clear that his lordship takes precedence here. And I'm okay with that. I've never wanted to rule anyone. You know that."

He turned around and placed his hands behind his head as he sauntered to the gate, Murdock trailing wordlessly behind. They were met by a small group, just over a dozen in number, at the wall. Dastynn was among them, standing out by sheer force of size. He had found another war hammer to replace the one that he had left behind, this one made of a large slab of stone. It was more banal than the crystal hammer, but likely just as effective.

Gramm was there, as well, with Pyra standing in his shadow. The two always seemed to be together. They had since Callan had arrived, at least. He wasn't the only one who wondered why they weren't married. They seemed perfect for each other. People had said that about he and Kelaya, though. He had disagreed. Theamere stood at the front, his arms crossed and a scowl on his face. He looked exactly like Ravitch when he made that face. Especially when he directed it at Callan.

"Do you have any idea how long you've kept us all waiting," asked the lord's heir? "Do you?"

Callan smiled at him. "Not nearly as long as I could have, believe me. Looking this good takes effort, Theamere. I'm not surprised that you haven't figured that out yet."

Pyra snickered into her hand behind her brother's back. The look on Dastynn's face said that he had very nearly laughed out loud. Luckily for Theamere and his pride, the paladin had a sense of decorum that Callan lacked.

Theamere's eyes softened. As much as he gave Callan a hard time, he knew that he really did care. The young lord and the heir approached each other and grasped each grasped the others' forearm.

It was the closest that either of them had ever come to embracing the other, and that would likely never change.

"Remember," said Theamere, "don't drag your right foot when you attack. It'll throw you off balance."

"Giving advice now, Theamere? I'd watch what you say. He's been beating you soundly for almost three years now." Smiling, as he had been doing more and more often around Callan, Gramm approached the pair of them. Theamere took a step back, his ears turning red. Gramm gripped Callan in an awkward, one-armed hug.

"He's right, though. You drag your foot."

"I know, I know. And I swing with just my arms too often. Sometimes I take too long to lace my boots up, too." Gramm looked like he wanted to smack Callan in the back of the head, so he half-ducked. "I'll be careful," he said, serious now. "I promise."

Pyra stepped forward next. They hugged quickly. They'd become close in the years that Callan had lived in Graveholm. She'd looked after him for the first months until he'd become acclimated. Callan was an only child and had grown up without many children his own age. After Kelaya, who had been his only real friend, knowing Pyra was as close to having a sister as he had ever known.

She was with him, in the back of his mind, always. Even before they were old enough to be married, Callan and Kelaya had been inseperable. He missed her dearly, even as the years passed. He would avenge her and everyone else eventually. He only need an opportunity.

"Don't do anything stupid out there," she said.

"Me? Something stupid? Never."

"Please?"

"Okay, okay," he said, "I'll avoid doing anything really dumb. Just for you."

She smiled up at him. He wasn't as small as he had been when he arrived. A growth spurt after the first year had seen to that, and now she had to tilt her head to look him in the face. "Thank you."

Dastynn approached as Pyra slipped back to Gramm's side. The paladin knelt so that he was eye to eye with Callan. The smile that was usually plastered to his face was gone now, replaced by a stern look. He stuck out his forefinger and prodded Callan in the center of the forehead with it.

Use your head.

He moved his hand down to the center of Callan's chest and made a gripping motion, as if he tried to remove something

Take your heart out of it. No emotion.

Dastynn then reached behind Callan's shoulder and gripped the hilt of his sword. He yanked on it hard, shaking it from side to side, trying to get it out of the sheath. He nodded, obviously satisfied, then pointed at it Callan's head again.

Don't lose that.

They had a good system for communicating. Callan wasn't on the same level as Murdock yet. The mage always seemed to know exactly what Dastynn wanted to say. The two of them had been travelling together the majority of their adult lives. But Callan and Dastynn had a system that worked for the two of them. The big man still hadn't elaborated on why he didn't talk, and Murdock still said that it was nobody's business but Datynn's. Callan was content with that.

"I'll be fine, big guy," he said. "Don't worry about me."

Dastynn ruffled his hair.

I know. I won't.

"Enough goodbyes." Theamere stepped forward. "It's time for you to get going. Torruk is waiting for you in the forest."

A stable boy walked forward, leading a horse by the reins. He handed the lead to Callan, who then hopped deftly onto the back of the animal. The saddle was comfortable enough but built for riding quickly. It only held enough food and fresh water for a few days of travel. After that, they would be hunting for every bite.

Theamere was right. Callan had spent enough time saying goodbyes. He spurred the horse into a canter and rode her through the front gate. It was still early morning so the risk of a Visani attack was much lower than it would be at night. Still, there were archers posted on the wall around the keep, ready to cover Callan should any attack come.

None did. Callan saw no Visani. All that he passed were the rotting remains of a caravan that had met an unfortunate end on its way to the keep. Snow drifts had covered most of it by now. Still, some wood paneling and supplies that had been deemed unsalvageable were left outside. There were a few bodies buried there as well. Callan rode on into the forest.

He reined in his horse just inside the tree line. "No Visani, Torruk?"

The wolfman emerged from the shadows. "They have been unusually quiet. Nursing their wounds, I think. Or preparing something. We had better hurry back. Gaveholm might need us sooner than later."

"Let's get going, then," Callan said. "I would hate to miss out on any excitement."

Callan rode quickly with Torruk keeping pace by running on all fours. He had better endurance than any horse that Callan had ever seen and could run just as quickly. The Visani were similar. He would have hated to fight them out here in the forest, in their own element. He had never fought one up close, save for his first encounter with the monstrous felines. His only experience with them had been from atop a wall, firing arrows into groups of them. There was no certainty that he had even hit any of them.

"They sent just the two of us to storm a keep," asked Torruk? "I admit, I have much to learn of humans still, but this does not seem like good strategy." He spoke as if he were not running through rough terrain, without gasping for breath. Callan could not help but be impressed.

"We aren't exactly supposed to be storming them," Callan explained. "They have documents that we need. Troop movements, shipping routes, that kind of thing. Your job is to distract whatever watch forces they have while I sneak in and take what we need."

"You would think," said the Fanir, "that Lord Ravitch would have shared this information with me."

"He isn't very trusting of outsiders. Don't take it personally."

"I do not."

Ravitch's mistrust of others bordered on xenophobia. He had been battling barbarians from the northern mountains for his entire life. He had always known that the Visani to be dangerous but had never known that firsthand until one had nearly taken his life. Now that they were at war, he saw every non-human as a threat. Unfortunately, that included Torruk, who had devoted himself more entirely to their cause than many of those from Graveholm. Ravitch would let the Fanir do some of the more unpleasant of the rebels' jobs, but he would not trust him. He wouldn't even let Torruk live within the walls of Graveholm. If Callan were being honest with himself, Torruk probably preferred it that way. He had a natural affinity for nature.

Callan couldn't worry about how Torruk was being treated now, though. He had a very important mission to accomplish. Nira was a relatively small city. It was south of Graveholm but a relatively easy trip. All that Callan and Torruk would have to do was follow the Frostcloak River for roughly a week. If the weather stayed on their side, they could even shave a few days off the mission.

The two travelled quickly that first day, and made good time. Better than Callan had anticipated. Still, his horse needed rest and Torruk couldn't run indefinitely. They made camp just out of sight of the Frostcloak. It was the widest and deepest river in the region, feeding off snow that melted in the mountains and ran south. Callan started a small fire so that he could cook some of the provisions that he had brought with them. He hadn't brought much so he was in for a light dinner. The heat from the fire would help as well. The wind and snow had stayed away, but the cold was still bitter and biting.

"Torruk?"

"Yes?"

Callan leaned back on one arm, stirring his pot of stew with the other. He angled his feet toward the fire, keeping them warm. Torruk didn't stay as close to it as Callan did. His fur was perfect insulation against the cold.

"Could you tell me about yourself," he asked? "I feel like I don't know anything about you."

"My people feel that our pasts are our own. Our memories are really all that we have to ourselves."

Callan cast his eyes down. "Oh. I'm sorry."

Torruk barked out a laugh. At least, Callan assumed it to be a laugh. It sounded like the rumbling of rocks falling down a hill. "Do not be. I will not tell you my own past, but if you would like, I will tell you one of the stories that my people tell our young ones."

"I would like that." Normally, being compared to a child would have upset Callan's pride. Coming from Torruk, though, he couldn't bring himself to be hurt. The Fanir was too genuine to insult someone.

"Long ago," he began, "before my people and your people ever came into contact, there was a great war. Packs fought against packs, brother fought against brother, and pups fought against their parents. Our shamans, the wisest of us all, lobbied for peace for years. They were unsuccessful and were forced to use their magic for war rather than for peace and healing."

The wolfman scratched into the dirt with one claw, drawing something as he talked. Callan removed his stew from the fire and set it aside so that it could cool.

Torruk continued. "The shamans were not meant for war. The spirits that they communed with were for healing. Guidance. Not destruction. They went to a darker place and spoke with more terrible spirits. They became corrupted by these new powers. The former leaders of our packs became warmongers."

Callan ate his stew quietly, soaking in every word that the Fanir said. He was quite the story teller. His voice carried weight, as if he had actually been there. The night's shadows and the flickering firelight gave the small camp a ghostly ambiance. Callan shivered, but not because of the cold. The pain in Torruk's words put a chill in Callan's bones.

"The strongest of the Shamans, and the most corrupt, was named Aganavar. His soul had been lost to the deepest pits of the spirit worlds. He was more demon than anything else. Aganavar turned on his allies, using his newfound power to kill and maim anyone he thought to be out of line." Torruk was still carving something into the ground. Callan tried to get a look at it, but the Fanir brushed it into nothingness with a sweep of his paw.

"The packs banded together for a single cause: to kill Aganavar and the other corrupted shamans. Weeks passed and the battle moved to our most holy forest. It had no name in any language. Not back then. The mightiest warriors of the combined packs cornered Aganavar there. In a final attempt to escape, he set fire to the forest."

Their own fire danced in Torruk's eyes. The remnants of Callan's stew remained to one side, completely forgotten.

"His ploy was unsuccessful. Aganavar was killed and took many of the finest warriors that the Fanir had seen in generations with him. Try as they might, even though the darkest of the Shamans was killed, the fire would not go out. Spurred on by darkness, it burned for months. Years, even, until there was nothing left for it to consume. The holy forest was gone. We have a name for it now, even in your language."

"What is it?"

"The Bone Wastes."

"Well," said Callan, "that's cheerful."

Torruk chuckled. "It is named for the way that the fallen, burned out trees look like bones in the moonlight. The spirits that were released when Aganavar was killed are said to still be dwelling there, haunting the wastes."

Callan asked, "Is there supposed to be a lesson to that story? You said that you told it to your young ones."

Another chuckle. "It would be a poor lesson if I had to spell it out for you. Go to sleep. We will travel far tomorrow."

Sentinel

Chapter 22

A thousand swords rang off each other in the mists of the early morning. Spearmen marched in time, thrusting at invisible foes at regular intervals. Captains and sergeants shouted orders at their charges, but they were too far away for Pyra to hear exactly what they were saying. From her chamber window, she could see the entire training field filled with soldiers of all callings. Infantrymen, cavalry, spear-holders, tacticians, engineers, and officers all scurried around beneath Pyra's gaze.

As much as she wished that she had some form of command over any of them, she didn't. Her brother stood on a platform where everyone could see him, shouting orders to anyone he felt was out of their place or doing something incorrectly. Ravitch, having finally been left alone by the medics, was limping around the yard, leaning on an elkhorn cane, a double-headed axe strapped to his side. Years of injuries stacked atop each other seemed to have finally taken their toll on the Lord. Ravitch wasn't moving as well as he had when he was a younger man.

He was doing much the same as Theamere, except on a more personal level. Whenever *he* saw someone doing something wrong, he let them know with a swing of the wooden cane, usually to the back of the thigh or the shoulder blades. Pyra didn't envy them.

Ravitch wanted Theamere to be more visible than himself. He was grooming him to take over the lordship once Ravitch was unable to rule, and needed to make sure that the soldiers grew to respect his son. He wanted the same thing for Pyra. At least, she thought that he did. Ravitch needed the support of local rich families, though. He needed their money. If he put Pyra in charge of them, many of them would laugh in his face and close their coin purses. She slammed the window and turned away.

A startled servant stood in the doorway. She was young and obviously hadn't been serving very long. Otherwise, Pyra would have recognized her. She was probably one of the villagers, taking on work to earn extra food for her family.

Pyra calmed herself and smoothed out her dress. "Can I help you?"

The girl didn't compose herself quite as quickly. "Yes. I mean, I think so, my lady. I have a list for eating. I mean for the feast. I—"

"Slow down," Pyra interrupted. "We're not in any rush. Take a deep breath and tell me what I can help you with."

She took a moment and breathed deep a couple of times. After a few seconds, the girl was ready to speak again. Pyra motioned for her to do so.

"I have seating arrangements for the feast here," she said. "I was told to bring them to you for your approval."

Ah, the feast. Pyra had been trying very hard to put it out of her mind. Before the army marched out of Graveholm, an enormous party would be thrown in their honor. They would rip through their food and drink stores at an incredible rate and throw off all the calculations that had been done to feed everyone in the coming months. Pyra had protested it to no avail. Ravitch and Theamere both thought that giving the soldiers a good time would make the march and the battles easier on them. Nothing prepared a man for war like a full stomach, she supposed.

"Yes, thank you. Bring them here."

Pyra grabbed the papers from the servant and walked to her desk. She sat down on her comfortable, cushioned chair and grabbed her charcoal stick to begin making notes. Whoever had put together the dining arrangements had obviously done so randomly. Rival woodcutting families and carpenters that absolutely detested each other were seated at the same table or close enough to cause problems. She began scratching out names and replacing them with more suitable substitutes, talking to herself as she worked.

"Wratt's and Dillit's children are courting. They should be sitting next to each other." She scribbled some more. "Holin and Provan hate each other, though, so I need to find a replacement. Couran and Holin should get along fine. Their wives gossip together. Provan can move next to Jisold. They'll argue all night, but it should be good natured. Branx can share war stories with anyone so it doesn't matter where he sits—"

The servant spoke up. "My lady, if you don't mind me asking…"

"Yes?" Pyra didn't look up from her work.

"What exactly are you moving everyone around for?"

Pyra smiled, but continued working. "I'm trying to prevent a bunch of patriarchs and businessmen from ruining the feast. If I put them next to people that they like, there is a much smaller chance of any fighting or yelling breaking out. Father wouldn't want any drama on the night of his big dinner."

"You know every one of them well enough to do that?"

She shrugged. "I make it my business to know everyone. I'm not my father or my brother. I can't order them around. If I know what they want, though, what they need, then I can help them." She smiled again. "I don't know you, though. What's your name?"

The servant girl stammered. "Me? You want to know my name, my lady?"

"I do, yes."

"I-I...my name...I'm Valerie, my lady."

"That's a very pretty name." Pyra stood and shook the excess charcoal from the parchment. "Now, if you would, please follow me. I need to speak with our cooks about the feast's menu."

"Yes, my lady, of course."

Pyra sighed to herself. "And please, Valerie. Call me Pyra."

The young girl smiled and bounced on her toes. "Okay," she answered with a toothy smile.

They walked through the keep, from the uppermost towers where Pyra's quarters were located, down through hallways that had been left mostly empty by the soldiers outside. Some of their families were housed in the upper levels, but most lived on the bottom floors and in the dungeons, having transformed the lower levels of Graveholm into a kind small, indoor town. The upper floors were reserved for Ravitch's family and the servants. Valerie followed closely on Pyra's heels. It was obvious that she didn't know her way around the castle very well yet.

Pyra led her to the kitchens, where they were immediately accosted by the smells of the coming night's dinner. It smelled delicious, but all too similar to recent dinners. The scent of venison and various steamed vegetables was nearly overpowering. A huge vat of stew was being stirred in the center of the kitchen. Had Pyra not been eating the same type of stew for nearly a year now, she would have found the scent appetizing. As it was, with the current state of the siege, there wasn't a lot of variety available. Before the Visani had become aggressive, regular caravans came from all over Aelathil and Cheryr. Now, merchants were afraid to send their wares to the far north. Pyra couldn't blame them. There was a good chance that any goods sent up would be taken and their escorts would be dismembered.

"Lady Pyra, may I be of some assistance?"

The head chef. Just the man Pyra had been looking for.

"Actually," she said, "you can." The portly man smiled, his jowls rumbling with the motion. He'd always had a soft spot for Pyra and her brother. When they were younger and their father was busy, they would sneak to the kitchens, and he would find some snack for them. On occasion, he had even left out a plate out when he had been too busy to feed them himself. He was getting older now, but he was still just as jolly.

"Valerie, wait by the door, please." The girl bowed and left Pyra to speak with the chef. "Sir, I need your help."

He smiled again, grabbing a ladle out of a nearby pot and bringing it to his lips. He winced. "It needs work. This isn't nearly good enough to feed to your father and the rest of the city's nobility! It needs more. Something from the private stocks, I think."

"Actually, sir, that's what I came to talk to you about."

"My lady?"

Pyra crossed her arms in front of her chest. "Orow, you know as well as I do that this feast is a waste of resources that we simply cannot afford to lose. This siege has been going on for three years now. Who knows how much longer it could last."

Orow sighed and placed his ladle on the table next to him. "My lady, have you thought that maybe this feast will be good for morale? That maybe what these people need is a bit of good food and fun rather than fearing for their lives as they do every other day?"

"Yes," she said. "I have thought of that. I've also thought that more and more time is coming between each caravan. I've thought that less and less of the ones that do come are making it through the Visani."

"Pyra, listen." He pulled up a stool and put his considerable girth on it. "Sometimes, a little excess can be exactly what people need.

Some fine food, a good time. Strong drink. These things can cure man an ailment."

"I agree with you." She smiled. Orow smiled back at her. "But," the smile dropped off his face, "we simply can't afford as much excess as you have planned. Make good food. Serve good drinks. Budget accordingly. Cut corners where you can."

"You cannot put a price on comfort or happiness, Pyra."

Pyra stepped forward, her eyes alight. "My father, your lord, put me in charge of this feast. So, yes, Orow, I can put a price on it if it pleases me." She prodded him in his wide chest with a slender finger. "My interests are not in the comfort or happiness of those who live here. I care only for keeping them alive. So, you will do as I say."

She turned, whipping her skirts along behind her. Her shoes clicked on the stone floor. Cooks and kitchen attendants did their best to keep from staring at her.

Valerie met her at the door with a smile and a curtsy. Pyra turned and faced Orow, who was still sitting, staring curiously after her. "And *you*, Orow. You will call refer to me as 'My Lady.' Nothing else."

The two women rounded the corner, Pyra scowling and Valerie trying her best to not laugh. She was angry at herself, probably more than she was at Orow. He had argued with her, yes. She was unaccustomed to being directly disobeyed. Pyra may not have had the respect that her brother commanded implicitly, but she had at least expected her direct orders to be followed without question. She didn't like raising her voice or getting angry. Anger was a loss of control. If nothing else, Pyra had control of her life. Usually.

She was so focused on her own inner turmoil that she had failed to hear the soldiers coming back in for their afternoon meal. Valerie called out to her, to stop her from walking right out in front of them, but she didn't hear. Pyra collided face first into the chest of one of the men who had been standing just outside the kitchens. She looked up and saw only a grizzled beard hiding a ruined face.

"Father! My apologies. I was not watching where I was going."

He patted her on the shoulder, his face contorting itself into some aberration that tried its best to resemble a smile. The scarring on his cheeks and his mouth contorted the gesture. The wrappings around where his eye used to be made it something else entirely. Something animalistic and aggressive. Valerie squeaked. Pyra smiled back.

"It's okay, girl," said Ravitch. He left his hand on her shoulder and steered her down the hallway. He cast a look at Valerie that sent her squeaking and curtsying and scrambling down the hall back to her other duties. Pyra grimaced as well.

"I heard you dealing with Orow. You did well."

Pyra did her best to keep her expression flat and political, but she couldn't help but smile to herself. Ravitch wasn't one to dish out compliments regularly. She brushed her hair behind her ear and said, "Thank you, Father. I've been trying to be more of a leader. I've been trying to be more like you."

He removed his hand and put in into the pocket of his coat. The other was wrapped around the head of his walking cane. It thudded along with every other step that he took. The corridor was teaming with soldiers, all of whom were exhausted from their daily training drills. Most were too weary to even notice their lord and his daughter walking among them. Ravitch excused them. He never had enjoyed standing on ceremony. Still, those who did recognize the two of them offered small bows or nods in their direction. Ravitch returned every one.

"I've decided, against the advice of everyone around me," he said, "to leave you in charge of Graveholm while the army is away."

Pyra stopped walking. She stared at her father and opened her mouth to ask why. To ask what had made him change his mind. He held up a hand to interrupt her.

"No matter what those old men say, no matter what the traditions say, I know that you would better serve our people than any of them would. I know that you will do absolutely anything to make sure that our people survive. Even defy me." He smiled again and gestured toward the kitchens. "You just proved it in there."

Pyra didn't know what to say. She had always wanted to be taken seriously. She was smart and she knew it. She was capable of running Graveholm. All her life, she had only ever wanted a chance. Now that one was being handed to her, she was dumbstruck. Luckily for her, her father continued talking so that she didn't have to.

"I'll be leaving Gramm and some handpicked troops behind to make sure that you're protected. You won't have to worry about the Visani while we're gone."

Pyra frowned. She was thrilled to have Gramm staying with her, but she still had nagging worries. "Don't you want Gramm with you? I don't know anyone better than him with a sword."

"Me either," replied Ravitch. "That's why I want him here. Losing him will be a blow, but I wouldn't trust anyone else with keeping you safe."

"Neither would I." She smiled, despite her worries.

"Good! Now," he said, "keep this to yourself for a while. I'll be officially announcing it at the feast. I'd like to take the nobles by surprise when they can't make a big fuss about it."

Ravitch winked with his remaining eye and kissed her on top of the head, the same way that he'd done when she was small. It was the most affection he'd shown her in years. He was gone before she could say anything. She was left standing alone among a steady stream of soldiers, with a heavy but welcome weight forming on her shoulders.

Chapter 23

A trickle of blood ran down Callan's palm and the front of his arm. He grimaced in the darkness, biting his tongue and choking on a groan. He glanced up. There was a flickering light not far above him. In the almost total darkness of the night, it lit up his destination like a beacon. After what seemed like an eternity of climbing, he was closer now to the top of the tower than he was to the bottom. It was a relief, nearly being at his destination, but it also caused him no small bit of anxiety. There was a lot of open air between his current position and the hard ground below.

He sucked in the cool night air and shifted his weight. Luckily, he'd been able to find a block of stone that stood out a few finger-widths further than those around it. It gave him a minute to catch his breath and rest his aching limbs. It also gave him time to think, which unfortunately allowed unwelcome fears to creep into his mind.

There were guards on the top of the tower that he was perched on. If he was going to get inside and take the reports of troop movements that he needed, those men would need to die. The idea of taking a life made Callan's stomach churn. He had injured a Visani to save Lys, he had fought more of them in defense of supply caravans, and he had even helped raid a royal weapon cache. Still, he had never directly taken a life. Gramm and Murdock had been preparing him for it for years now, but the idea of it still made him cringe. Like it or not, he had a job to do.

An animalistic noise ripped through the silent night. It was somewhere between a roar and a howl, and it was absolutely blood-curdling. Torruk. The sound was followed up almost immediately by very human screams. It was the distraction that Callan had been waiting for.

Cal gritted his teeth and resumed his climb, feeling above him for handholds wide enough to grip. The task wasn't as difficult as he'd thought it would be. The tower was old and hadn't been maintained well. Finding a place to put his feet was more difficult, but he managed. He had only slipped once so far. The throbbing in his hand reminded him of that. He had no intentions of repeating his mistake.

More shouts and screams and snarls disrupted the quiet behind him. Torruk hadn't told Callan what he had planned on doing to distract the soldiers. Truth be told, Callan was glad for that. He didn't particularly want to know what the Fanir was doing. He tuned out the grisly noise and continued his climb, hand over hand, moving toward the flickering torchlight that marked his destination.

He found plenty of hand and foot holds and made good time to the top. Poking his head just high enough over to the crenellation to see, he glanced around the tower's ledge. One man walked toward him, patrolling along the perimeter. His attention was clearly on the noises coming from below: the screams, roars, and shouts. There was another guard walking the opposite way. Callan couldn't follow his eyes in the darkness. Each man carried a torch, casting shadows across the stones and their faces.

Callan waited and watched for as long as he dared. He had to make sure that no one was on the tower he hadn't seen. There wasn't. Only the two guards. Sweat dripped down his face and arms despite the chill, and his extremities were starting to shake from supporting his weight. Besides, he had no intention of hanging off the side of this tower for any longer than he had to. The guards were circling. As soon as the nearest one had his back to Callan, he would move.

It didn't take long.

He took a breath. Two. One more. He heaved himself up onto the top of the tower. It was more of a walkway, really. There would be a door that led to the interior of the castle. Callan just couldn't see it yet. The walkway was three or four arm-lengths long. It wasn't a lot of room to maneuver. He'd have to keep his sword sheathed on his back.

He took that all in with a glance. As soon as he had taken stock of the situation, he moved. One foot in front of the other. He moved toward the nearest guard.

One step. He drew his knife.

One step. He reached toward the neck of the guard's tunic.

One step. He grabbed the man's shirt and yanked.

One last step. The guard let out a yelp as Callan's knife sank into his neck. He clamped a hand over the man's mouth, cutting off his yell before it could carry through the air. He gurgled, blood leaking from the gash in his neck and from his mouth. Callan pulled back the knife, then drove it into the guard's chest. Then he drove it in again. He let the man down easily so that his body hitting the ground wouldn't alert the other guard.

His *body*. Callan had just killed a man. The guard had just been doing his job, and Callan killed him for it. He could feel his stomach trying to revolt. He shoved the vomit down. This was not the right time for remorse or regret. He had a job to do.

He turned on his heel and ran silent as snowfall toward the other guard, using the light of the man's torch to hunt him down. He turned along the rounded edge of the tower as he ran. Callan came face to face with the other guard. He had turned around. He opened his mouth to shout. Callan couldn't let that happen. There was no backup. No one could know that he was here.

Callan threw his knife. It hit the guard in the shoulder, handle first. The man wasn't hurt at all, but the action was enough to make him flinch and cut off his call for help. Callan rushed him, diving at his midsection. The guard swung his torch. It came close enough to

Callan's head that he felt it singe the hairs on the back of his neck. He tackled the man to the ground. Callan shoved his forearm against the guard's throat, cutting off any chance that he had to cry out. With his free hand, he grabbed the man by the scalp. Callan bounced his head off the stones once, twice, three times, until his eyes rolled into the back of his head, and he stopped moving. And breathing.

Two men.

Callan moved on. He found the door and shouldered his way in. Luckily, it was unlocked. He really didn't relish the idea of digging around the corpses that he'd just created to find a key. He slipped inside and found himself in a spiral stairwell. As far as he could tell, that's all that the tower was. A stone case for a giant stairwell, with a watchtower on the top.

Callan was on the eastern end of the castle. He had to get to the main level, across to the northernmost staircase, then up to the third level where Lord Delaney kept his quarters. He would have the documents that Callan was after. If he didn't, he would know where they were.

He made it down the stairs quickly and quietly, then out into the dark interior of the castle. Really, it was more of a mansion house. Generations ago, Oakheart was the capital of Aelathil. It was near the middle of the nation, had easy access to rivers, and a large farming community to support it. The expansion of the shipping industry across the entire continent of Revaren had changed that. To move good from nation to nation, and to bring them in, massive ships had to be built. Ports were needed for the ships. A coast was needed for the ports.

So, Tal Autem was built on the biggest port where the money came in. It quickly became the capital of the small, but growing, nation. Oakheart was left to rot. The massive city that had once surrounded the castle dwindled and was overgrown. Retaken by the land. Some of the farms were left to this day. Small villages were scattered through the area. The castle had become Delaney's personal living quarters. He'd even named it after himself. Delaney. Graveholm. Ashefall. Those were proper names for keeps in the realm of Aelathil. By all rights, his keep should have been named for the town surrounding it: Oakheart. The only reason that Balen's keep had been called the Dragon's Keep was that Ragnar the Slayer himself had been the first to rule there.

Callan moved on. The inside of the mansion was much more open than the walkway on the tower so he drew his sword from his back. It was the same weapon that his father had given him for his birthday years ago. It had hardly left his side since. He held the weapon in both hands and shuffled forward. Small lanterns lit his way through the opulent corridors. It was surprising that there were so few guards about, until he really thought about it. Most of them would be out dealing with Torruk's distraction. The others would either be out on watch duty or guarding Delaney himself. Or dead.

Still, there would be servants who would need to be avoided. With his sword out front, Callan slid through the hallway into what seemed to be a waiting room where guests could chat before dinner. The door to his right would be the dining room. So, he continued forward, through the white double doors on the other side of the room. He eased them open, peering into the hallway beyond.

There was one man there, wearing chainmail armor that glinted dully in the light of the small lanterns. He was leaning on his sword, sticking the point into the rug at his feet. There was a wooden shield on his back. No helmet. This was the main entryway. There were two massive doors, which the guard faced, and a grand wooden staircase, dressed in red-gold carpet. Those were the stairs that Callan had to climb. He had to get past the guard.

Quickly. Get his attention. Get him in here. Kill him. Move on.

Leaving the door cracked, Callan coughed twice. The guard snapped his head up.

"That you, Arv," he asked?

Callan coughed again, harder this time, like he was choking.

"Arv?"

Through the thin slit between the doors, Callan saw him sheathe his sword and walk toward the waiting room. This was going to be too easy. He coughed one more time and gripped the hilt of his sword tightly in both hands. The door swung open.

"Hey," asked the guard, "are you alright?"

Callan lunged forward, sword extended, and drove the blade into the guard's stomach. His eyes shot open with surprise, his pupils dilating, then shrinking as life fled him.

Callan shook his head. He couldn't speak. In this moment, he hated himself.

He fell with a grunt, as good as dead before he hit the ground. Callan stepped over him and opened the door again.

"Gods, what in the hells happened?"

Oh no, the dining room. I should have checked the dining room.

"Lott? Lott? What did you do? Who are you? What did you do to Lott?"

Callan turned slowly, drawing his sword up into the ready position.

"You're Arv, I take it?"

"You killed him!"

Arv wasn't very smart. Or he was in shock at finding one of the other guards, a friend maybe, dead. Callan rushed at him without another word. He swung at his midsection from beneath, trying to cripple him before he could muster any kind of defense. Arv managed to draw his sword and deflect the attack. It was more of a lucky swing than anything else. From the way he held himself, to the way he still hadn't pulled himself together, Callan gathered that he wasn't a seasoned fighter of any sort. There was no reason to torture the poor man. He would end this quickly.

Callan swung his sword horizontally this time. The steel sang through the quiet night until it collided with Arv's own sword. The guard's angle was poor and his grip was worse. The sword flew out of his hand and clattered to the ground near the dining room door. Callan reversed his grip and swung again in the opposite direction. Without his weapon, Arv could only throw up his arm to defend himself. His hand thudded to the ground, followed immediately by his head. Both began pooling blood, soaking the fine carpet in crimson.

Four men.

His stomach turned. He had to move on. There was no time for dwelling on the killings yet. He had plenty of time to hate himself on the ride back to Graveholm. Callan wiped the blood from his blade on Arv's trouser leg and moved into the next room.

Up the staircase he went. The walls were covered in a deep red carpeting. Callan guessed that most would find it warm and welcoming. He found it claustrophobic. It muffled sound in a way that was very helpful in his current mission but made him feel as if the walls were closing in on him. Sound couldn't echo in a tiny, enclosed space, and it didn't echo here. Callan moved faster, wanting to end this and get back on the road as soon as possible.

Delaney Castle's innards were silent. Its thick walls had even blocked out the sounds of men trying to deal with Torruk. Callan's trip to the third floor went unimpeded. The lord's chambers were in the center of the hall in the largest room on the floor. As soon as he rounded the final steps on the stairwell, Callan could see the room, a flicker of firelight illuminating the doorway like a beacon. There were no guards posted outside of the room or anywhere in the hall.

Strange.

Callan sheathed his sword on his back, silent as a whisper. Any kind of swordplay at this point would be sure to wake the entire castle. Callan couldn't risk that, so he drew a thin dagger from his belt instead. It was weighted well, but not perfectly. The smiths in Graveholm weren't as skilled as those in Ashefall. The dagger wasn't meant for throwing, though. The weight wouldn't matter nearly as much as the sharpness, and it had plenty of that.

He slid along the wall, keepings his head and shoulders low enough to avoid the copious decorations that decorated it. A scream ripped through the hall, shattering the stifling silence. It came from Delaney's room.

"I told you not to yell, girl. You're not making it any easier on yourself."

The nasally voice had to belong to Delaney. Callan cleared the rest of the hall in three strides and peeked his head around the corner into the room. A young girl, probably a servant, was on the ground clutching her hand to her head. Bright red blood streamed from beneath her fingers. Delaney stood over her, a bulbous mound of flesh. He was easily the fattest man Callan had ever seen. A few wisps of hair clung to his skull, with wisps and clumps of facial hard sticking to his neck. Ravitch and Balen, and Callan by extension, were all lordly in their own ways. Each of them were vastly different, but all looked the part.

Not this man.

"Now, get up on the bed like I told you," said Delaney.

She whimpered and Delaney made to kick her while she was on the ground. Callan stepped into the room.

"Lord Delaney?"

The obese man turned around, a look of unrepentant contempt on his piggish features. His beady eyes looked Callan up and down, not lingering for even a second the dagger he held at his side or the hilt protruding from over his shoulder.

He answered, "Do I know you, boy? I didn't order anything from the kitchens. You'll get out of here, if you know what's good for you."

Callan stepped forward, his knuckles white on the leather-wrapped hilt of his weapon. He hadn't yet decided if Delaney was as stupid as he was fat, or if he was brave in the face of danger. The young lord stopped just in front of the older man.

"Do you have a son, my lord?"

Delaney's brow furrowed. Not bravery then.

"An heir? Anyone to carry on in your name after you die?"

Broken and yellowed teeth peeked out from Delaney's lips in a horrible facsimile of a smile. "I've got a few," he crooned. "Most of 'em not by my wife, but she squirted out at least a couple. I was getting ready to make me another one before you interrupted."

The girl whimpered again. Delaney laughed.

Callan jammed the dagger as hard as he could into the bottom of Delaney's jaw and into his mouth. The obese lord dropped to the ground gurgling while his lifeblood leaked out of him in frenzied spurts.

Five.

Callan asked the serving girl, "Are you alright?"

She only nodded and hugged her knees to her chest. Cal nodded in return. He walked to the bedside table and opened the single drawer. It was full of papers, as Callan had expected. He leafed through the pile until he found what he had been looking for. Shipping records. Troop movements. Travel routes. He emptied the entire contents of the drawer into a pack on his side and turned to leave. He nodded once more to the girl and left the room, ignoring the quivering mass of the corpse on the ground.

He hadn't taken more than a single step out the door when he caught a flash of movement out of the corner of his eye and a blinding pain erupted in the side of his head. Stars filled his vision. He stumbled back. The blow hadn't been enough to knock him unconscious. A voice rang in his ears, but he was too dazed to understand what it had said. It spoke again, this time almost clearly. The third time, he understood it all too well.

"Callan?"

Chapter 24

All that he could see was a white light, searing into the back of his brain. The voice called his name again, but he couldn't see anything. He couldn't orient himself. He staggered.

"No, it can't be. You died. You died!"

There was a sharp smack across his face. Whoever it was had hit him again. He stumbled, but the stinging pain cleared his head some. He backed into a wall, his hands fumbling for the dagger at his side. The dagger that was still lodged in the former Lord Delaney's bottom jaw. Callan grimaced and sagged to the ground. Fumbling hands grabbed at his sword, but it was no use. His head was still swimming. His fingers refused to obey. Both arms fell to his side. He'd failed.

Callan looked up into his assailant's face. She was tall, almost his own height. Dark blonde hair framed her face and ran down her back. She was in servants' garb. A servant, just like the one he had saved a few seconds ago, had beaten him.

"You bastard, you died. How could you?"

He rubbed his eyes. The blur faded, leaving a perfect view of a face that he'd never thought to see again.

"Kelaya?"

She kicked him. She kicked him in the side, in the legs, in the feet, and everywhere else she could reach. Callan was too weak and still too dizzy to do anything but curl up and let her take out whatever frustrations she was feeling. She yelled and cursed and said things that he'd never heard come out of her mouth or any other lady's mouth for that matter. For all that, the surprise was nothing next to the fact that she was alive and he was seeing her again. He'd given up that hope a long time ago.

Eventually, she tired herself out or hurt her foot. Either way, she stopped kicking him and collapsed in a heap on the ground next to him. She sobbed. He felt like doing the same, but he had to get out of this place and back to Graveholm. He'd be damned if he was going to lose Kelaya again. She was coming, too.

"Kelaya…"

"You didn't die. You left us. You left us, you left me." She shook. "Why? Where did you go?"

He sighed and rubbed his temples, most of his faculties coming back to him. He could think straight, and the world had just about stopped spinning in circles. He reached out a hand and placed his on her shoulder, just as he had when they were younger and she was upset. She jerked but didn't brush him off.

"I'm sure you have a lot of questions. I do, too. But we have to get out of here and there isn't a whole lot of time to do it. Once we're on the road, I'll explain anything you want."

He stood, using the wall for support. He was still dizzy. Callan held out his right hand for her. Kelaya hesitated, but she took it and stood. The sounds of frenzy were still muffled by the walls of the castle, but Callan knew that Torruk couldn't keep his distraction up forever. They walked out the way that Callan came in. The halls were still silent, still claustrophobic. The stain on his soul was still there. He would atone for the deaths later. He had to. All of that took a back seat, though. Kelaya was back. He had her. His past wasn't entirely gone.

They didn't take the tower out. Callan wouldn't risk securing her to a rope, even if it sacrificed some of their secrecy. Kelaya led him through a side door, and they escaped the castle without any molestation. Callan was glad for it. He didn't want any more blood on his hands on this night, or ever again.

"Where are we going, Callan?" Saying his name seemed to make her feel better. Every time she said it, she seemed more certain, like she was convincing herself that he was really alive. If it worked for her, maybe it could work for him, too.

He smiled and tugged her toward the forest. "We'll wait just inside the tree line, Kelaya." It worked. "Torruk should be finishing up soon. Then he'll join us." He smiled wider. "Don't let his appearance put you off. He can be intimidating."

They didn't have to wait long. The shouts and screams from Oakheart died down, and for the first time since he'd been hanging by his fingertips on the tower, Callan got nervous. Had they quieted because they killed Torruk? He doubted it. The Fanir was dangerous. It wasn't long before Callan heard a rustling in the forest close by. They hadn't lit a fire for fear of being found by Oakheart's soldiers.

A throaty voice called out, "Callan? Are you out here?"

It was Torruk. Callan called back, "I'm here. There's someone with me."

The Fanir came through the underbrush. He seemed unharmed, which brought an unwilling sigh of relief from Callan. Kelaya gasped but caught herself and regained her composure. Torruk looked first at Kelaya, sizing her up. Then he looked to Callan, his eyes asking if he was sure about bringing someone else to Graveholm.

"She's from Ashefall," he said. "She's a friend from home."

Torruk nodded. Nothing seemed to surprise him. He nodded, then inspected Callan. He asked, "Are you hurt?"

For the first time, Callan looked down at himself. He cringed. The blood of five men stained his tunic and the skin of his hands. There was almost certainly more dried red on his face and back as well.

"I'm alright."

They found Callan's horse where they had left her, still grazing and enjoying the quiet of the late night. She'd been conditioned to be around Torruk so the wolf-like Fanir didn't upset her. The same couldn't be said for most humans. They were on no strict timetable, now that the mission was completed, so taking their time was no problem. Callan and Kelaya climbed onto the horse together. They would walk her most of the way so that they didn't exhaust her. Neither of them wanted to walk back to Graveholm. Torruk didn't seem to mind.

Once they were back on the road, Torruk leading the way, Callan turned back to Kelaya, who was seated behind him, her arms wrapped around his midsection. "I promised you answers. You can ask me whatever you want."

She was quiet for a moment. For a time, he thought that she was still too angry at him to ask anything. He was shaken by her anger, almost as much as he was by the lives he had taken. Was she angry that he was alive? Did Kelaya wish that he had stayed dead and gone?

"How did you do it," she asked, finally? "How did you make it out?"

He found himself not wanting to revisit that day. He'd tried very hard to forget about it, to push the thoughts of the fire and death from his mind. Still, he answered her. "There was a tunnel that led under the mountain," he said. "Murdock and Dastynn got me out of there. You remember the mercenary company that showed up a few days before everything happened?"

He felt her nod against the hollow between his shoulder blades.

"We met up with them, and they took me to Graveholm. That's where I've been for the last three years."

"Graveholm? Is that where the rebellion is? You're a part of it, aren't you?"

He grunted in the affirmative. "How much do you know about the rebellion?"

"Delaney talked about it a lot with his son, but not often around the *servants*." She practically spit the last word into the back of Callan's head. "I didn't hear much. Mostly that it was centered somewhere up north. I don't think they ever expected that one of the lords were directly involved."

Callan smiled over his shoulder. "Two of them."

"Did you kill Delaney?"

He tensed for a moment, the question taking him off guard. She obviously hadn't glanced into his chambers after she had smashed him with...whatever she had hit him with. "I did. He tried to take advantage of the girl in there with him." He grimaced. "The original plan was to leave him alive, but I couldn't when I saw that."

Kelaya laughed for the first time since they had rediscovered each other. It was a dark laugh, not light and happy like the laugh that he remembered. "I heard her screaming so I grabbed a torch bracket off the wall. When I saw a man coming out of Delaney's chambers, well, I thought you had hurt her. So, I hit you."

"Well, you hit me hard enough. I'll have a knot on the back of my head for a week." He rubbed the swollen spot on his skull gingerly. He was still a little fuzzy from the blow.

They rode in silence for a few leagues. Callan knew that Kelaya had more questions to ask, but she was obviously hesitant to ask them for some reason or another. He couldn't blame her. Still, he wanted information as well.

"How did *you* make it out of there? I thought everyone had died. I thought I was the only one who made it."

He felt her shake her head. "Almost all of us made it. The initial attack didn't last long. The dragons did their burning, but once he had us all corralled, Ramsey called them off." She paused and took a shaky breath. "He questioned your parents, your uncle, and my father. None of them would talk to him, so he hung them all above the gates to the keep."

Callan kept his composure, but only barely. He had known that they were dead ever since Torruk had found out. He hadn't needed to ask. He hadn't wanted to know how they'd died. Now that he did, he felt that he was ready to start grieving again. There was no time for that. Not anymore.

Kelaya continued. "By the end of that day, Ramsey had us all in chains. He marched us straight here and let Delaney have his choice of servants. He took me and a few others. Mostly men to work the fields. I don't know what happened to them or to the ones who went with Ramsey. We weren't treated particularly badly on the road, but I don't know how long that continued for."

"And how did Delaney treat you?"

She didn't answer, and he didn't press her. Something told him that he didn't really want to know the answer to that particular question. After all, Kelaya hadn't seemed disappointed that he'd taken the lord out as violently as he had.

"So, is this what you do now?" She sounded bitter. "You kill because someone else tells you to?"

Did he? Why had he killed those men? Why had he killed Delaney, beside the fact that he was going to hurt that servant girl? Ravitch hadn't told him to. In fact, he'd been advised against it. Not forbidden, of course, but he'd been told that he probably shouldn't unless it became necessary. He had, though, and he would catch hell for it, as well as the other four that he had killed.

"Nobody told me to kill him. I was just there for the troop information."

"You kill because you want to then? I don't see how that's any better. At all."

"No," he said. "I killed Delaney because he was going to hurt that girl if I didn't. She couldn't defend herself so someone else had to step in. At that moment, I was the someone else."

Kelaya scoffed. "You're a protector then? Here to save the day?"

He thought for a few beats. Is that what he was there for? There were going to be plenty of people who would need help soon. War was on the horizon and it created need wherever it went.

"Maybe, yeah" he said. "Maybe that is why I'm here."

The days flew by now that Kelaya was around. She didn't talk much, and most of what she did say was critical of Callan. She'd had a hard few years, and he didn't blame her for being so down. Still, he wanted her to be happy. He had always cared about her and still did. When they were within sight of Graveholm, he brought up the feast.

"The soldiers are going to be leaving soon," he said. "In the next day or two, there will be a feast. A sendoff for them. You're more than welcome to come. It will give you an excuse to dress up, have a few drinks, let loose for a night. What do you think?"

He glanced back over his shoulder and smiled. She returned it, which only spread his smile further across his face. "That sounds like a lot of fun. I would love to."

Chapter 25

The feast was still more extravagant than she would have liked, but Pyra was happy with how everything had turned out. The music was loud, but enjoyable. She'd been able to find a family from the city who played and upgraded their food allotment for their services. A group of hunters had managed to sneak out of Graveholm and bring back a few mountain boar and an elk. Those would be served as the main course. The rest of the food was being provided from the stores. Pyra didn't like it, but she had to make some concessions.

She watched from the doorway as Ravitch drank and caroused with his guests. It was part of the reason that his people love him so much. He was gruff, angry, and mean, but he was one of them. Ravitch had never been a faceless leader who ruled from an enclosed castle. He went among those who lived under his protection. He knew them, even many of those who weren't noblemen or owners of the carpentry businesses.

"I'm almost glad that I'm not the captain of the guard anymore. I wouldn't want to deal with any of these people once they've had too much to drink."

Gramm had been standing so silently that Pyra had almost forgotten that he was there. Almost.

She laughed. "Are you sure you aren't just happy because you're allowed to have a few drinks of your own if you're guarding me?"

He shrugged and took another sip. Seeing him drinking was rare in itself, but he actually seemed to be enjoying himself, which was rarer still. "I don't mind having a drink every now and then. You look tense, though. Maybe you could use one."

"There's nothing wrong with being a little tense. I put a lot of work into making this feast a success."

Gramm took another drink and smiled, looking more happy and relaxed than he had since he'd become a knight. "Still, it couldn't hurt you to lighten up a little bit."

"Me? Lighten up?" Pyra laughed. If *Gramm* thought that she seemed too uptight, something must have been seriously wrong. "You know…fine. Maybe I should go get a drink."

He clapped her on the shoulder and moved off toward the drink table. "Don't worry, m'lady, I'll get it."

Pyra glowered at him, but she couldn't help a smile coming to her face. She watched his broad shoulders weave through the crowd until he disappeared from view, then turned her gaze back to the rest of the party-goers. Callan was there, sitting with his mage friend and the paladin who never spoke. The girl that he had brought back from Oakheart, Kelaya, was with them as well. The two young women had met briefly, but as busy as Pyra had been, she had not gotten to know her as well as she'd have liked.

Callan seemed different since he'd come back. He was less lost in thought. Less single-minded about everything that he did. That wasn't to say that he had started slacking in his training or in his responsibilities…he hadn't. However, he seemed more interested in what was going on around him. Pyra couldn't tell if he had been brought to attention by having his old friend back in his life, or if he was putting on a show for her benefit. Either way, he was a lot more fun to be around.

Gramm came back quickly, shouldering his way through the crowd, but not impolitely. The red tint in his cheeks showed that he'd had more than just a single drink or even two. He was a big man. It took a lot of alcohol to affect him. He had a second drink in his hand. It was much smaller than the mug he'd been drinking from. When he got closer, he offered it up to Pyra.

"I'm sorry that I took so long," he said. "The new guard captain wanted my opinion on patrols and how often he should switch out shifts."

"Did you give him good advice?"

A smile touched one edge of his mouth. "I told him that my job was to look after you. His job was to put together the watch."

She managed a very unladylike snort. "No, you didn't."

"No, I didn't."

"Well? Then what did you tell him?"

He sipped again. "I told him what I would have wanted to know in his situation. I told him where he was in the right and gave him some advice on areas where he needed help."

Pyra eyed her drink. It was dark and heavy looking like most of the alcohol served in the northern reaches of Aelathil. She'd always preferred imported wine to the rums and whiskeys and other hard liquors that everyone else seemed to enjoy so much. Truth be told, the smell had always been enough to turn her off from them. She'd never taken a drink. With Gramm standing there, though, she felt compelled to at least make an attempt at it.

She tilted her head back and drank, sucking down a much larger gulp than she'd meant to. It filled her mouth and clogged up every one of her senses. It overpowered her nostrils until she felt like she was suffocating. Her throat closed, rather than let her swallow the huge amount that she'd tried to take in. The entire time, she was acutely aware of Gramm staring at her, an amused smile on his stupid face.

Although it burned her throat, Pyra jammed her eyes shut and forced herself to swallow. The alcohol burned all the way down her throat into her stomach. Not at all a pleasant experience.

She managed to gasp out, "What are you laughing at?"

"Only your infinite grace, my lady," Gramm said.

"Ass."

His smile only broadened, the dimples on his cheeks pushing nearly into his ears. She'd always loved his smile and the way that his eyes reflected his mood. Too often, men at her father's court wore blank faces to hide the lies behind their words. Gramm either didn't or couldn't. He was genuine to the core, and she admired him for it.

"So even-tempered, as well," he said.

Pyra couldn't decide if she wanted to slap him or kiss him. But that could have been the liquor talking. So, she looked back to where Callan sat with Kelaya. He was keeping her entertained to the best of his ability. Callan was so different from the others at Graveholm. He was quick with a smile and always easy to talk to. He liked to joke around, but was never mean or insulting. From what she had seen of him, he was great at what he did, as well. He was deadly with most kinds of swords and daggers and more accurate with a bow than she could ever be. She attributed that to his absolute single-mindedness when he set himself to something.

More than once, she had seen him work himself to exhaustion. Soldiers or knights, sometimes even Gramm, had carried him from the training grounds when his legs refused to obey him. Pyra couldn't blame him. He'd lost absolutely everything. Neither could she emulate him. She lacked the focus to demand that much of her mind and body. It was probably why she had never really mastered magic. She was knowledgeable and competent, but that was where her skill ended.

Seeing Callan with Kelaya, she thought that he looked truly happy. The girl was still on edge in the unfamiliar place, but she seemed to be enjoying herself at least somewhat. Whether what they had was an incredibly friendship, romantic love, or some combination of both, she couldn't tell.

She asked Gramm, "Do you ever wish that you had what they have?"

He quirked an eyebrow at her. "Who?"

She waved a hand at the two of them. Callan waved back. "Callan and Kelaya."

"I think about it a lot, actually. How I want to spend my life beyond knighthood, I mean."

"Really," she asked? "Do you have some special lady in mind? There are plenty of pretty ones walking around."

"Maybe," he shrugged.

"Maybe? Come on, tell me!"

He shook his head.

"Tell me! I won't laugh at you!"

"Promise?" The booze had made his cheeks red, but the crimson deepened even further then.

"I promise," she said, placing a hand over her heart.

"Okay," he said. "It's you."

"What?"

"It's you. You're the special girl."

Pyra struggled for words. Her? "Me? Gramm, I don't know…how…me? I'm flattered, but…me?"

He shook his hand at her dismissively. "It's okay, you don't have to say anything. I guess it had to come out sometime."

Gramm threw back the rest of his drink, finishing it in a single gulp, and walked away into the crowd, leaving Pyra to face the feast with only her booze for company.

#

"Do you remember the man I pointed out earlier? Tobben?"

Kelaya nodded. "The one with more beard than face, right?"

Callan pointed down the table to where Tobben had been earlier seen chugging more rum than any man's stomach should be able to contain. The cobbler had no family in Graveholm so there was no one to be embarrassed that he was unconscious in a cooling pile of cooked venison, drunk out of his mind.

Kelaya laughed into her own plate of food, nearly choking on the same venison that Tobben had buried his face in. "Does he do that often?"

"If Tobben isn't carried to bed at the end of the night, he considers it a night wasted."

"And you," she asked? "Has anyone ever had to carry you to bed after you've had too much to drink?"

He shook his head, making his stomach tumble and his world pitch around him.

"No, not me," he said. "They've never had to babysit me."

Not yet, anyway.

He'd always preferred to have his head about him, whether at a feast or a more regular dinner. Callan had let himself go on this particular occasion, though. Far too much rum and other various drinks had landed in his stomach. He wasn't as drunk as Tobben, but he was certainly not in his normal mindset.

Kelaya looked to be in the same position. Her cheeks were flushed red and she laughed with more intensity and regularity than Callan had seen since he'd brought her back with him. She had also slid closer and closer to him as the night had worn on. Normally, he had a fairly large space bubble that he didn't want anyone to break. Kelaya was different. Or maybe it was the liquor. He found himself leaning in to talk to her and leaning even closer when she had something to say. When their shoulders brushed, he let the touch linger, rather than pulling away out of reflex.

"Do you want to dance," she asked?

Callan started. "What?"

She pointed to the middle of the hall, where tables were being pulled out of the way to form a makeshift dance floor. The musicians had started playing a slower tune, and the husbands and wives had started making their way out to the floor.

"Usually, the old married couples go first. If you want to wait until it's more appropriate, I would love to."

"More appropriate?" She sounded incredulous. "We were engaged. Are engaged. We have been for years now. Or had you forgotten?"

He shook his head and stared into the depths of his cup, where the remains of his drink were sloshing around. "No, I hadn't forgotten."

"Then what's the problem?"

Callan looked up at her. She didn't look as upset as her voice suggested. She'd always been good at pulling his strings. Not much had changed over the years, apparently. "Neither of us was too happy about the idea of marrying the other, if you remember correctly. I guess I didn't know where we stand now."

She grabbed his hand and stood, pulling him up with her. She led him to the dance floor, each of them on slightly unsteady feet. Once they were there, she grabbed his right hand in her left and put her other on his shoulder. He put his free hand on the small of her back. Neither of them could dance particularly well, but they swayed in time with the music.

"I don't know where we stand either, Cal." She smiled at him. "I missed you, though. I thought that everything I had known was gone. Then you showed up out of nowhere and, well, I missed you."

He laughed. "You have a funny way of showing it. My head still hurts from when you hit me." He paused while she stared guiltily at the ground

They danced to the beat as well as they could. For as much as he trained his body to be well-balanced and intense, he was an awful dancer. Something about the mix of alcohol in his system and the closeness of Kelaya made him stumble all over himself. He'd often heard swordplay compared to dance, but he'd never felt that way. Swordplay was about finding the most efficient way to put a piece of steel into a soft part of the opponent's anatomy. Dancing was flowery and without real purpose. Nobody had ever been killed dancing.

Throughout the night, they got the hang of the dance. Everyone else around them changed their movements subtly with every song that played. Not them. They danced to their own rhythm, keeping to themselves and ignoring the others around them. Callan found himself wishing that the two of them had done more of that when they were younger.

Both of them always had duties. Kelaya to her father and Callan to his parents. The loss of his parents had left a hole in him that he doubted could ever be filled. Still, the freedom that he had now, in Graveholm, was like a breath of spring. He had duties here as well, but they were of his own choosing. No one was forcing Callan to fight back. Now that Kelaya had found her way back to him, or him to her, he was more determined than ever to finish what they had started.

Eventually, after hours had passed and Callan's legs were numb from dancing, and most everyone had retired to bed, the two of them were left to their private dance. They were doing little more than swaying now, with Kelaya hugged tight to Callan's chest, her head resting on his shoulder. He absentmindedly played with the ends of her hair, rolling the light brown locks between his fingers.

"You know," he said, "I…"

She looked up at him, her green eyes staring into his blue ones, for just a second. She leaned in and pressed her lips to his. His eyes widened for a moment as his breath caught in his throat. He tried to finish his thought, finish his sentence. She wouldn't let him, she was insistent. So, he folded into the kiss. Callan closed his eyes and relaxed into Kelaya. He wrapped his arms around the small of her back, and he gripped his shoulders. For a few moments, at least, they acted like they were the only ones in the room.

Chapter 26

He found himself again in a dream.

Shackles bound Callan to a stone wall, metal bands cutting into his wrists. His legs dangled uselessly below him. Beyond his feet, far below, flames tore apart a forest. Smoke, thick and black, drifted from beneath and assaulted his eyes, his nose, and his mouth. Uneven edges of stone dug into his shoulders and lower back. Not a wall, then. A mountainside.

Callan coughed and turned his head as far as he could to keep the smoke and ash from his eyes. To his left, he could see almost nothing. Beyond the smoke, the skies were red. The view to his right was similar, save for a small outcropping of rock that jutted out only a few arms lengths away. A cloaked figure, the same from the other dreams, sat on it with his arms crossed.

"You'll have a job to do soon."

Callan coughed out, "A job? What do you want from me? What do you need? Who are you?"

The figure waved his hand dismissively. "It doesn't matter what I want. It doesn't matter what I need. It doesn't matter who I am."

"Then why do you keep coming to me? Does that matter?"

"More than anything," he whispered.

The figure stood and uncrossed his arms. He drew down the hood on his cloak and looked at Callan. For the first time, he got a good look at him. Dark brown hair, flecked with spots of gold framed his face. He had large, observant eyes and pointed, angular features. At first glance, he seemed too young to be giving anyone instruction, but there was a quiet intensity about him that Callan trusted.

"You're going to have to protect them, you know."

Callan screwed his eyes shut against the smoke. "Them? Who?"

"All of them."

Callan's eyes snapped open. He was breathing heavily, sweat pouring off him. The dreams were coming more and more often now, but they were rarely that clear. Even more rare were the ones that he could remember with any detail in the morning. Those pale eyes stared into him even now. He could feel the intensity that hovered beneath the surface of the cloaked man's pale visage like a current through the room.

"Are you alright? You started tossing and turning. I didn't know if I should wake you."

He rolled over and squinted in the relative darkness of the predawn. It had only been a few days since the feast, but Callan was already growing accustomed to Kelaya's face being the first thing that he saw every morning.

"I'm alright," he said. "Just another dream."

Smiling, Kelaya leaned in and pressed his lips into his. "About me this time?"

"I wish."

She kissed him again. "Stay with me today. I can distract you from those dreams."

This time, he kissed her back. "You know, I just might."

A knock sounded at the chamber door. Callan sighed and rubbed at his temples. He looked apologetically at Kelaya, but she was already smiling and shooing him out of bed.

"Go. They need you. I'll be here later."

After one last kiss, Callan stood and dressed quickly in the dark. He would have to leave Kelaya alone for a while, but she had acclimated to Graveholm well. She would be fine for a few hours while he took care of whatever was needed of him.

Once he was dressed in a simple white tunic and trousers, he opened the door to the man who had come calling. Calling him a man was generous. He was a young boy, dressed in the chain vest and cap of a guardsman.

"Lord Callan," he said, "Something has happened. Lord Ravitch needs you immediately."

He saluted, left fist to his right shoulder.

Callan smiled at him. "Alright. Take me."

He followed the boy through Graveholm castle. It was more crowded than normal, this early in the morning. Men were moving about, throwing on armor and gathering up weapons as they moved. Were they being attacked? He couldn't hear the sounds of a battle. Why else, though, would the men be dressing for a fight? He gently nudged the messenger boy in the back, and the two of them hurried along.

They found Ravitch in front of the great hall, he and his men blocking the doorway. All of them were outfitted for war. For the first time since he had come to Graveholm, Callan saw Ravitch dressed in full armor and armed to the teeth. Ravitch wore his Visani-skin cloak, the white fur rippling down his shoulders and back. The beast's head encompassed, Ravitch's own. His face glared out at the world from behind the dagger-sharp teeth.

"What's happening," Callan asked?

"We're moving out."

Callan lit up. This wasn't just some exercise to get the troops used to getting up and moving quickly. They were going to pack up and go, presumably to battle.

"Where to?"

"Oakheart. When you killed Lord Delaney, his oldest son became Lord Davin. The idiot decided to publicly declare his support for our cause. Apparently, he's got more backbone than sense."

"Why is that a bad thing," Callan asked? "We can use all the help we can get."

"Because," Ravitch answered, "King Ramsey decided that he was going to use Davin as an example. Kind of like he did to your family. He's dispatched soldiers to take care of the Oakheart problem."

Callan's heart sank into his stomach. He had put the knife in Delaney. Now the rest of his family was in danger. Would Ramsey kill Davin's subjects? Would he bring the dragons? The same dragons that haunted the skies of Callan's nightmares were forcing themselves back into his waking life. He wasn't ready for them.

Ravitch spoke again, breaking Callan out of his terror for the moment. "You're riding at the front of the column with me. Go to the kitchens and get enough rations for two weeks. Meet me back here, ready to go, in half an hour."

Callan saluted and left. It didn't take long to get everything that he needed. He brought a single change of clothes—the road didn't offer much in the way of opportunities for cleanliness—and grabbed the food that he'd been told to. Now all that was left to do was say goodbye to Kelaya.

He sighed and moved back to his quarters.

When he opened the door, she sat on the edge of the bed, glaring at him.

"You're leaving." She didn't ask. Someone had gotten here before he had. Callan suspected Murdock.

"Only for a couple of weeks," he said. "Lord Delaney's son has gotten himself into trouble with the king. We have to pull him out of the fire."

"Which son?"

"Davin," he said. "Do you know him?"

She shook her head. "Not well. He didn't live in the castle. He's always had a good reputation, though. He's not much of a warrior, from what I know. If anybody needs protecting, it's probably him."

If anybody in Graveholm knew about Davin, it was Kelaya. He trusted her opinion more than he trusted nearly anyone else.

"I won't let anything happen to him. Or the rest of the family."

Her face was impassive. "And what about me? You're just leaving me here?"

He rubbed his eyes, sagging internally. "I don't have a choice. No women are coming. Just the soldiers. Even Lady Pyra is staying here."

"Sure, she's staying. She's ruling the entire region. I'll be sitting in my room by myself."

"There's a lot you could do around here," he said. "Nobody is expecting you to work yet, but Pyra would be more than happy to find something to keep you entertained."

She nodded and fiddled with the bed sheets. He bent down and kissed her.

"I'll be back before you know it. Take care of yourself," he said.

#

Pyra's legs shook uncontrollably beneath the hem of her dress. On the battlements of Graveholm's keep, she watched the only family she'd ever known, her brother and father, march off to war. The city sprawled out before her, with soldiers, horses, caravans, and banners flapping in the wind, weaving through the streets, homes, and small yards.

From her position on the roof, she could see the destruction laid out by the Visani. Mills and other businesses were in ruin. Homes had been completely torn apart. Still, in some places, dried blood stained the pavement. No one had been allowed to move back and start rebuilding yet. Raiding parties still combed the city on occasion, searching out anyone who dared defy their terror to retake their old lives.

They were hers now, her huddled masses. She didn't think that she was ready for the responsibility. She knew she wasn't ready. The nobles were already upset that she had been left in charge. Some had proclaimed that they would have nothing to do with her as their lady. Others whispered behind her back that Gramm was really in charge and that Pyra was a figurehead for her father's progressive agenda.

Still, she was determined to get them through the next few weeks. She would prove to everyone that a woman could lead just as well, if not better, than a man. Beyond that, she would prove that *she* was a leader.

A gauntleted hand alighted gently on her shoulder. Gramm.

"You're ready for this," he said.

Pyra shook her head. "I don't know. There's so much that I don't know about how this is supposed to work."

"Good. Don't lead like your father would. Don't lead like *they* would expect you to. Be yourself. Lead as yourself. Make them respect you."

The shaking in her legs slowed. She could do this. She believed in herself. Gramm believed in her. That was all she needed.

She could do this.

Chapter 27

There are so many of them. I can't deal with all of this. I can't even get their attention.

"Gramm, can you do something about this," she asked?

There were hundreds of people here. All of them had turned out for her first time holding court. Gramm stood by her side, but it seemed that everyone else had decided to turn her into work into a circus. Most of the townspeople had shown up, she imagined, out of sheer boredom. The dungeons in the depths of the keep had been cleaned up to the best of their ability and made livable, if not comfortable, but entertainment was at a premium lately. Watching Pyra hold court as a group would likely be the only interaction they would have with each other for a few days.

Gramm, who stood stoically, as always, behind her massive oaken chair, raised a hand to the teeming masses. A few glanced his way, but even those continued in their conversations. Everyone else pointedly ignored the knight. Gramm smiled nervously, a question hiding behind his eyes. Pyra knew him well enough to guess at what that question was.

"Go ahead. I need their attention."

He glanced around for a moment and grabbed a child-sized ceramic vase, filled with a potted evergreen. Most men couldn't have lifted the potted tree at all. Gramm did it with ease. He hefted it over his head. Still, no one even looked his way. An instant later, the entire pot and tree crashed into the floor, practically shaking the entire hall.

Dead silence followed.

"Thank you, Gramm," said Pyra, loudly enough that her voice carried across to everyone in attendance.

She stood, folding her hands in front of her. "Thank you all for coming," she said. "I would like to get proceedings running as smoothly as possible. So, if the first in line could come forward, I would appreciate it."

"Also," she added, "if you would like to continue any conversation, feel free to do so *outside* of the hall."

You're in charge, Pyra. They'll listen to you. Be firm with them.

She took her seat once more and waited for her first charge to come forward. It was a townsman, a young man in faded clothing. He was clearly one of the poorer men who had been fortunate enough to make it into Graveholm. Staggering behind him, wearing a plain green dress and carrying a young child, was his *very* pregnant wife.

"My lady," he said, keeping his eyes on the ground and wringing a woolen cap in his hands, "my wife will be having our second child soon. My mother helped in delivering the first, but…"

He stopped and took a shaky breath. Pyra smiled at him, in what she hoped was an encouraging manner. She felt as nervous as he looked. "Go on."

"My mother delivered our first, but she died a little over a year ago. She was old and we'd all expected it, but now there's no one to deliver the baby."

"What's your name, friend," Pyra asked?

"Erin, my lady."

"Relax, Erin," she said. "We can find a midwife for you. Go talk to Elder Moss. He'll know more about the process than I would. Tell him that I sent you, and he'll be more than happy to help."

"Thank you, my lady. Thank you." He bowed on his way out, and his wife made an attempt at a curtsy, but her belly made that difficult for her.

She called for the next petitioner and relaxed into her high-backed chair. One down. A small boy and girl walked down the aisle. The girl was openly crying, and her brother obviously had been until recently. His eyes were red and swollen, and he still sniffled and rubbed at his nose with the back of his sleeve. Pyra's heart broke before either of them said anything.

"What can I help the two of you with?"

The boy sniffled again. "Our father is sick, m'lady. He can't work. We're all really hungry."

"What of your mother?"

Another sniffle. "I don't remember Mum much. She died when we was little, m'lady."

Pyra could relate. All that she knew of her own mother had been learned from stories that Theamere had told her. Ravitch never talked about her. Ever. He had never been overly emotional about anything, but she had seen the pain in his face whenever his wife was mentioned. She couldn't think about that, though. Not at the moment.

"Are you going without food since he can't work?"

The boy nodded and the girl let out a soft sob. "We're hungry, m'lady. Really hungry."

This was an easy fix. "Go to the kitchens and tell the head cook that you're going to be given a week's worth of rations."

The boy brightened. "Thank you, m'lady, thank you."

"You're welcome," she said, "but this food is a loan. Once your father is healthy, you'll both work in the kitchens until Orow decides that the debt has been paid off."

"Yes, ma'am!" Both scurried off.

Pyra looked back at Gramm. He gave her a reassuring smile, his eyes and mouth telling her that she was doing well. That was all the validation that she needed.

A man from one of the noble families came next. He sauntered to the fore of the group, looking back at a small group of other nobles behind him. They snickered, and he smiled back, as if Pyra wasn't watching their every move.

He began without being prompted. "Pyra,"

"Excuse me," she interrupted.

"My lady, my lady, of course." She immediately disliked his tone. He looked very pleased with himself as he stroked his drooping mustache. "If I may continue, my lady?"

"You may."

"My name is Hollace. I am the head of the carpenters' guild in Graveholm." She knew that, of course, just as she knew the names of every other prominent member of that particular guild. Most of them were in this room, watching the proceedings as if they were a circus show.

Hollace continued, "I've decided that my family is hungry as well, my lady." He put a mocking intonation on her title. Hollace was a bachelor with plenty of money. Everyone was on rations but that didn't stop some of the wealthier members of society from buying rations from the poorer families. He wasn't hungry in the least. "I would like a weeks' worth of rations ahead of time as well."

"Hollace, I've seen no evidence of you needing extra rations."

"You saw no proof from those children, either. They have just as much need as me. I am hungry so I would like more food."

"You can have nothing if you insist on wasting my time."

He crossed his arms and scowled. Pyra couldn't help but think he looked like a spoiled child. "I have no family, so I need less food. I receive less than a family of more than one would. I expect, no, I demand a weeks' worth of rations."

"You presume to make demands of me, Hollace?"

"I do."

Pyra found herself in an unsteady situation. If she was too firm with Hollace she would seem a tyrant. That would be in poor form, considering that she had never held court before and hadn't watched her father's proceedings nearly as often as she would have liked to. If she was too lenient, though, this would become a regular demand. That could not happen.

"You will be on half rations for the next two weeks," she said. Hollace's face immediately turned a bright shade of crimson, and he worked his mouth in an attempt to form some obviously furious retort. Pyra continued before he could speak, "I'll be joining you in this fast, just to prove to you that it isn't some huge burden."

Hollace took a haughty step forward, raising an angry finger in Pyra's direction. She heard Gramm suck in a breath. His armor rattled as he tensed inside of it. Pyra held out her arm and stopped him from doing anything that the both of them would regret.

"Hollace, if you take one more step toward me, you'll be hung off the battlements by your ankles for the rest of the day." He stopped. "You *will* eat half rations for the next two weeks, as will I. Gramm will see to it for the both of us."

"But—" he started.

"Leave. Now."

He stood still for a moment, trembling just enough that Pyra thought he would say something else. He had too much sense of self-preservation to do that, though. Instead, he stomped off, back through the crowd, ignoring his group of compatriots altogether. They followed after him, like ducklings chasing after their mother.

A guard pushed his way past the men on their way out and made his way directly to Pyra's seat. He looked terrified. Pyra motioned him to come closer before he spoke. If he had bad news, she didn't want to worry everyone else immediately.

"What's happened," she whispered?

"Two Visani, my lady. A mother and young child. They just showed up to the gate. The mother is demanding, no, that's the wrong word…she's begging to see you, m'lady."

Her heart caught in her chest. The last time she had been close to a Visani, Captain Jordan had tackled him out a window.

She asked, "Did she say why she needed to speak with me?"

The guard shook his head. She felt guilty for not recognizing him. She was sure that Gramm knew exactly who he was and most of his life's story. "No. She seems scared. It's hard to tell with them. They're so…different."

"And the child. How young is it?"

"Young. Didn't say a word. I think it's a boy the way she talked about it."

Over the guard's shoulder, Pyra could see the crowd expectantly staring at her. She made her decision quickly. That, she found, was going to become very important in the coming weeks. She'd always been a quick thinker, but it had never been necessary for the wellbeing of others. Now that it was, she almost wished that Theamere was here, ruling instead of her.

"Gramm, go to the two of them. Bring them here. I'll see them."

He looked at her, concern in his eyes. "Are you sure, Pyra?"

"No," she said, "but I don't see that I have much choice."

Chapter 28

Callan stared into the crackling flames, thinking back to his dreams. He could see the burning forest as if he was still asleep. When he'd first started having the dreams, he'd forgotten them almost immediately after waking. They had plagued him for years now, though, ever since he'd left home. They didn't come every night, but near enough that he often dreaded sleeping. The other night with Kelaya was the only time that the figure had shown himself, though. Callan was sure that they meant something. They had to. He couldn't live with the consequences in his own mind if they didn't.

He wasn't crazy. There was a purpose to these night visions, he was sure of it. This figure, whoever he was, needed Callan for something. Else he would leave him alone.

"Callan?"

He looked away from the popping embers. Murdock sat on his haunches next to the fire, looking concerned at Callan. "Hmm?"

"You've been staring into that fire for nearly an hour," he said. "You haven't eaten anything all day, either."

"I'll be alright, don't worry about me."

"I do worry about you. So do all of the soldiers who are looking to you to lead them." He liked to consult Callan whenever he felt that he wasn't being a good enough leader. They'd often argued about the same topic. The mage meant well, but it grated on occasion.

"They don't need me to tell them when they need to eat. These are grown men we're talking about," he said. "They're soldiers."

Murdock scowled. "Oh, you think so?" He leaned back onto his hands, relaxing his position but not his facial expression. "How old were you when you came to Graveholm? Sixteen?"

Callan nodded.

"Most of them are that old. Some younger. Even the ones that are a little older have never been in any serious battle." He sounded like a teacher, now. Callan didn't know much about the mages order, but he thought that Murdock would make an excellent mentor to an apprentice someday.

He continued, "Do you think, at that age, you wouldn't have looked to someone to do absolutely anything?"

"To feed myself? I don't think so."

Murdock barked a laugh, startling one of the soldiers that walked by. Callan got a good look at his face, behind his helmet. He really was young. Had Callan looked like that when he had come to Graveholm? Sure, he had been a man by the laws of the land, and this soldier was either sixteen or nearly so, but looked like a scared little boy.

"That's funny," said Murdock, "I remember a child that wouldn't even wake up in the morning without Lys' approval. And that was only three years ago."

Callan recoiled internally. That stung. He hadn't thought about Lys in quite some time. He owed his life to the mercenary, in more ways than one. Not only had he and his merry band taken Callan away from Ashefall, he had taught him how to fight. How to survive. Without the skills that he had picked up on the way to Graveholm, Callan would have either died in the wilderness or have been completely unprepared for the training that Gramm, Theamere, and the others had planned for him.

Mollified, he asked, "So you want me to be their Lys?"

Murdock shrugged, glancing back over his shoulder at the throngs of soldiers that milled about behind him. "I don't think they need Lys, no. If they needed Lys, we'd have tracked him down and hired him."

"What do they need, then? What can I do for them?"

"You've got a lot of unique life experiences, Callan," he said. "They need you to be you. They need to know that their entire world isn't going up in flames. They know that Orthielle hasn't come yet, just as well as you do."

Callan hadn't thought that Orthielle would have worried the soldiers as much as it did Ravitch. They hadn't heard anything from Emperor Cestus regarding their pleas for help. The success of the strategies that Ravitch has planned out hinged on their military aid. Of course, the men would be worried about that. It was their lives that were being spent. Callan felt instantly stupid.

They lapsed into silence after that. Murdock sat with his own thoughts, while Callan stared back into the flickering flames, trying to find some answers in the orange and yellow. They weren't forthcoming, and Murdock seemed to be done talking. Callan didn't need to be Lys. They were different people, no matter how much Callan was indebted to him. Callan wasn't in this war for the money. He had involved himself because it was the right thing to do. And for revenge. No matter how many times he told himself that he was involving himself for purely selfless reasons, he would always in the back of his mind and in his heart want to hurt Ramsey for what the king had done to his family.

He stood up after a while and looked over the camp. Most of the men had their tents set up and were preparing dinner for themselves. Ravitch and Theamere had their own tent at the middle of the encampment, which stood out with flags and banners so that messengers and runners could find it easily. Callan didn't want to speak to a group near there. Any that he chose close to the command tent would be of higher rank than those on the edges. Instead, he chose one at random and walked over.

There were five men sitting around a poorly built fire, slowly turning a hunk of rationed venison on a spit. He tossed his pack down on the ground between two of them and sat down with a groan. His knees were killing him and his back hurt from riding. These men, if they could really be called that, had been marching all day. They would be feeling sorer than he would, especially if they weren't used to marching over uneven ground.

Only one of them even glanced at him when he sat down. The others were either staring at their food, their feet, or the ground, trying not to fall asleep.

The man said, "You can use our fire, but we don't have any extra rations."

Callan grinned at him and nodded. "Not a problem. I brought my own." He gestured to his pack.

Recognition slowly dawned on the man's face. His eyes widened in horror, and he scrambled to his feet, throwing a fist to his chest in salute. The others started and their eyes darted to Callan. They jumped to their feet as well, saluting as fast as they possibly could.

Callan smiled at them and waved a hand dismissively. "Sit down, sit down. I'm here to eat not to give you a hard time."

One of them spoke up, "Apologies, my lord. We're all just worn out. We didn't notice you."

Again, he waved his hand. "It's fine, really. And call me Callan, please. Ravitch is the lord. Here. I'm just a soldier."

"Not like us, though. Not quite." The youngest looking of them spoke up, a smile on his face. "You get to ride that big horse at the front of the column all day."

"Oh, I *get* to?" Callan laughed. "You try bouncing around on one of those monsters for six or seven hours and let me know how your ass feels after."

The tension in the air practically melted away. Callan hadn't had a lot of time to make friends in the last few years. He had dedicated himself so fully to becoming a better archer and better swordsman that his only real friends had been Murdock, Dastynn and, to an extent, Pyra. He'd never been the most social person, anyway. Kelaya had been his only real friend growing up. There had been other children around, of course, but he had enjoyed his relative solitude and his studies to spending time with children of his own age.

Callan and the soldiers ate their dinner and laughed until full darkness fell over the camp. Curfew wasn't until an hour after sunset so they had plenty of time to drink and dice and tell war stories. The extreme lack of the latter worried Callan. He was the only one who had been in any kind of real combat, and that had been only weeks ago, when he had assassinated Lord Delaney. These particular soldiers didn't know that he had been the one to kill the lord. He wasn't particularly proud of the fact.

In the midst of the men teaching Callan how to play a dice game, one of them cast a terrified glance over Callan's shoulder. His eyes widened and his hand went to the hilt of his sword. The others did the same. Without any of them saying anything, Callan knew who was coming up behind them.

"Hello, Torruk. Would you like some dinner? We have plenty."

The Fanir's soft padding stopped. "No, thank you." He growled. "You humans cook your meat. It takes away the flavor."

Callan smiled and laughed softly. The tension in the group lessened visibly. Torruk was different and nearly beast-like. But he wasn't a terrible monster. If these soldiers were going to work and fight alongside him, they would have to realize that he was not their enemy. He was not a Visani, although Callan imagined that the two peoples were more similar than Torruk would admit.

Torruk spoke up again. "May I speak with you, Callan? In private, please."

The two of them walked from the group to a more secluded area of camp. Callan crossed his arms against the cold and looked up into the Fanir's gold and black eyes.

Torruk didn't waste any time. "There is a camp beyond the hill to the north. Four men are camped there. They are wearing King Ramsey's colors."

Oh no. "Do they know that we're here?" He knew the answer, but he had to ask. He had to have confirmation of his fears.

Torruk nodded. "Yes. Every few minutes, one of them crawls to the top of the hill and watches the camp for a time."

Callan rubbed his temples with the palms of his hand. "Are you sure? Absolutely positive?"

"I am."

He would have to deal with them. "Alright. You stay here in camp. Tell Murdock if you find anyone else spying on us."

He moved off without another word, back to the campfire and the other men. He couldn't risk any of the spies, whether they were actually spying for Ramsey or not, make it back to their master. This wasn't Castle Delaney. This time, he had backup.

The others were still gambling. Hopefully none of them had drunk too much to be useful. He would find out in a moment.

"Everybody stand up. Follow me. Be quiet and discreet. Alright?"

They did as they were told, and none of them shakily. They were sober. At the moment, that was all that he had to go off of. He didn't know if they could be quiet, if they would follow orders quickly, or how talented they were. He could ask them each, but there was really no way of knowing if they were even capable of taking a life. Not until the moment was upon them. Callan hadn't known that he was capable of killing a man until he had done it.

He walked directly to his tent and sat down in the back, near his cot. The soldiers followed quickly and crammed themselves into the standard-sized sleeping space. Callan had been given a tent meant for only one person. The six of them barely fit. They didn't have to for long, though. Callan explained the situation to them and told them that they were going to be the ones to solve the problem.

"We're going to walk out of this tent in three minutes. We're going to walk to the east and round the hill through the woods. When I give the word, we attack." He paused and took a look at the group. No objections. "If you can't kill them, stop them by any means necessary. Any questions?"

No one raised any. He waved the men out of his tent and watched as they filed out, one by one. Only one stayed behind. The young man who had joked about Callan's riding a horse earlier.

"Yes?"

"I've never killed anyone before."

Callan stood and walked to his side. "It isn't easy. It will stay with you for a long time. You'll lose sleep over it." The boy, for that's what he really was, didn't look encouraged. "But when it comes down to you or them, the choice gets made for you. Either you kill or you die. It might not be an easy choice to live with, but it's an easy one to make."

The boy nodded, reassuring himself that what Callan had said was good advice. Callan could only hope that it was.

Chapter 29

With Callan in the lead, the group wound their way through the forest, quiet as shadows. These men were good at moving quietly. At least, they were good enough. The forest was not completely silent. Owls, ravens, and other birds of the night sang and cawed enough to hide the quiet rustle of their footsteps in the underbrush. Wolves howled in the distance, but they were far enough away that Callan wasn't worried. Still, the calls were eerie.

"I heard that there are daggercrests in these woods." Callan couldn't tell which man had said it. "Twice the size of bears and smarter than wolves."

"It's a good thing you're as dumb as you are then." A second man. "I hear daggercrests can't stand the taste of stupid. Messes with their digestion."

The others snickered and Callan couldn't help but join in. Still, he stopped and motioned for them to be quiet. They were getting close, and he didn't want the king's spies to have any idea that the soldiers knew where they were, let alone that they were coming for them.

Under his breath, he whispered his plan to the others. "I'm going to climb up into the treetops and move in from above. When you run into their camp, stop and wait. They won't have a fire burning so don't walk right into them. When I come out of the trees, you attack. Got it?"

They all nodded.

Callan turned and made his way to the nearest tree with low-hanging branches. He didn't glance back at the soldiers as he began his hand over hand climb. He couldn't afford to show any lack of confidence in them. They needed to know that he trusted them fully, even if he didn't necessarily even trust himself to do the job perfectly.

There were too many variables at play, the least of which was the inexperience of his men.

Luckily, the trees grew close together here, with huge branches that wove together in interlocking patterns high above the heads of everyone who walked beneath them. This was an old forest with a lot of history in its roots. Normally, he imagined that just about anyone could appreciate the inherent beauty in the greens and browns. For the last few days, though, Graveholm's army had been trudging around, stumbling over roots in the undergrowth and rocks hidden in moss. Besides that, Callan's soldier was right. There were plenty of signs that a pack of daggercrests were in the area. Tree trunks had been scraped away, small saplings had been dug up and chewed on. They were only active during the early hours of the morning, though. He just hoped that none of his men stumbled through their bedding.

Callan made it into the lowest hanging weave of branches. They had some give and bounce to them, without making him think that they would snap and send him tumbling thirty feet to the ground below. Unfortunately, he couldn't see his men anymore. The foliage was too thick. He would just have to trust them to do what they needed to do, just as they were trusting him to do his own job.

The going was easier than he had expected it to be. Easier than it should have been. Callan had been expecting something to go horribly wrong. Someone to spot him, one of the soldiers to trip and make a loud noise, or one of those daggerspines to come roaring out of the underbrush and eat the six of them.

He shoved his doubts from his mind and crept along. Night had fallen completely by this point, and the only light came in the form of slivers of moonlight flitting through the leaves that blew in the wind overhead. The moon wasn't full, but it was bright enough that Callan could see at least a few yards in front of him.

There was a scrambling to his left. Callan nearly jumped out of his skin. One hand went to a small knife at his side, while his other went to the base of the branch so that he could balance himself out. In the darkness, he couldn't see what had made the noise. He stood statue still, with only his eyes moving back and forth, searching for the culprit. A pair of yellow eyes blinked back at him from the next tree over. His eyes froze.

The eyes blinked. A squirrel scrambled forward from the darkness, staring sleepily at Callan. He let out a sigh of relief. Mentally, he apologized for waking the squirrel. Maybe its family. He resolved to leave some extra food in the area before the army moved on in the morning.

He continued forward. The men would have gained some ground on him, partially because they had the luxury of walking on solid ground and partially because he'd paused for a stare-down with a rodent. Still, he was glad he'd done it. Better to be careful than in the stomach of some carnivore or lying on the ground with every bone in his body shattered to pieces.

"Gods, I can't wait to get out of here."

Callan froze again. The voice had come from directly below him. He was practically standing on them.

"We can leave at dawn," said another voice. "We'll check them one more time once daylight hits, just to make sure that they're still going the same direction."

"Oh, come on." The first voice again. "It's bright enough tonight. We can at least get a good start. It's not like we don't know where they're going."

What?

"No. We've got our orders."

The first voice sighed. "I know, I know. I could just really go for some real food. This bread is stale and if I have to go one more day on dried meat, I'll go insane."

Callan slid down through the branches at his feet, to the next level of the weave. This level offered a better view of the forest floor. They had a lean-to set up against one of the larger trees. Embers glowed faintly from a smokeless fire. By the little light available, Callan could see the two men who had been speaking. One was directly below Callan, his back to the tree that Callan was in. The other was, unfortunately, facing the base of that tree. The most direct way down was to land practically on top of the man directly below Callan. Unfortunately, that would leave him in full view of the other man.

He hadn't forgotten about the other two, though. They were more than likely asleep. The fact that more than one man was on watch duty said a lot for the fact that they were worried about being so close to the army. Having all four awake at this hour would have been a waste of energy, though. The other two were probably light enough sleepers that it would only take a single shout to wake them up. Sleeping like a bear didn't lead to a long life.

I've been waiting up here for too long.

The others would be getting anxious. He had to act and, again, trust that they would cover for him.

So, he acted.

Callan dropped down through to the next level of branches with a crash and cursed under his breath. He could have been much more silent in his approach.

"What in the hells was that?"

He jumped again, this time all the way to the ground. He fell in a crouch, bending his knees to prevent any damage to his legs. The landing hurt badly, but he didn't break any bones. At least, not that he felt immediately. He found himself immediately behind the man who had been sitting near the base of the tree. The dagger that he'd threatened the squirrel with was still in his left hand. He steadied himself as soon as he'd landed and drove the dagger down and to the side, into the man's neck. A yell shattered the relative silence of the night.

Damn.

Callan wrenched the knife around the man's throat and dropped him to gurgle out his last breaths on the ground. His soldiers ran in from his right. The youngest one, the one who had told Callan he wasn't sure that he could take another person's life, led the charge, his sword raised over his head as he was rushing headlong at the lean-to where the sleeping soldiers were lying.

"No!"

He'd been right. They were light sleepers. Before the boy was even close, they were both awake and throwing off their heavy, woolen blankets. Like all the other seasoned soldiers Callan had spoken to, they apparently subscribed to the idea that sleeping with a blade at their side was the safest way to sleep. The boy had a shortsword in his gut before the others had caught up to him. He dropped to the ground without another sound, his animal yell dying in the air around them.

Two other soldiers, it was too dark to tell which two at this distance, closed in on the lean-to and clashed with the two sleepers. That left the man directly across from Callan. When Callan glanced back at him, he was running toward a group of horses that were picketed away from the camp. Callan cursed himself for not having noticed them before. He had to stop the spy from getting back to whoever his superiors were. It was impossible to know what information he had that he was taking back. None of it could make it. Besides that, they obviously already knew some of the plans for the army's movements. If Callan could stop some of those ideas from becoming confirmed facts for Ramsey's army, he would.

He had to.

Callan charged after the man, trusting the soldiers to take care of the other two. There were four of them and only two spies. He had to believe that the numbers game would play out in their advantage, as well as the element of surprise. Callan had his own job to do. His feet squished into the soft loam of the forest floor with ever step, but he got no closer to the other. He was just not fast enough to beat him in a foot race.

A different tactic then.

He drew the bow from his back and nocked an arrow to it. He dropped to one knee and drew back, aiming at the middle of the runner's back. Callan released, losing his arrow almost immediately in the darkness. A shout of pain rang through the air, but the spy didn't fall. He'd been hit obviously, from the way that his body jerked, but he continued running for the horses. Callan managed to fire off another arrow, but heard no yell or gasp. As far as he could tell, he'd missed. In the meantime, the spy jumped into the saddle of one of the horses and sliced the rope tying it to the tree with his sword. Then he galloped into the forest and was lost to sight.

Callan looked back to his men. They had dispatched both of the spies and were huddled around a small figure on the ground. The boy. Callan cursed under his breath that he couldn't take the time to mourn. His chest ached with anger at himself for bringing the young man into this situation, but he couldn't let himself be slowed down by his emotions.

He yelled to the men, "Take him back to the camp. Find Murdock and tell him that I gave the order for him to be the acting Lord of Ashefall until I get back."

"Where are you going?"

"One of them got away," he answered. "I have to go after him."

"We're going after you!"

"No, you're not," he ordered. "I can go faster on my own."

And no one else will get hurt on my account.

Ignoring the protests of the soldiers, he went to one of the remaining horses and untied the tether that kept him from roaming around. He swung a leg over the saddle and into the stirrup, then looked in the direction that the spy had taken his horse. Even in the relatively dim moonlight, the trail was easy to spot. He hadn't been particularly careful about hiding where he'd been going. More likely, he was too worried about the arrow that was sticking somewhere in his body to be picky about covering his tracks.

From what Callan could tell, he was running straight southeast. That would put him more or less in a direct line to Oakheart. The spy would have to be stopped before he could make his report. Not only did he now have an unknown amount of information about what made up the entirety of the rebellion's army, he now knew that his spying had been exposed. He knew that someone was more than likely chasing him. If he made it back to his superiors and told them that someone had caught on to the spies, they would undoubtedly speed up their plans for attack. If the king's forces killed innocent members of Oakheart's population before the rebellion could arrive to stop them, the blame would now rest squarely on Callan's shoulders.

"Come on. Take me home. Follow the leader."

The horse jolted forward into a trot, into the dark of the forest and after a man who Callan couldn't allow to do his duty.

Chapter 30

By morning, he was no closer to finding the spy than he had been when he left. The trail was still clear, but the other man had gotten a good head start on him. Besides that, he had been more than willing to run his horse at a gallop through the forest all night. Callan was too concerned about his own wellbeing to risk his horse breaking a leg over some covered root or rock.

He stopped on occasion to make sure that he was still following the right trail, but it was so easy to follow that he almost hadn't bothered. Still, he had to be sure that he was moving in the right direction.

The forest was left behind by noon of the first day, giving way to what, during most of the year, was rolling green hills. Snow covered the ground during the winter months, though. There was none to be seen now, however. Recent warm days had melted the snow into the dirt beneath, making the trip a muddy slog. The spy's horse left deep ruts in the mud, giving Callan an easy path to follow. When Callan had been tracking the man through the forest, there had been a bit of a blood trail to follow, from the arrow that he'd stuck the spy with. It was hard to tell now, though, if the blood flow had stopped or if the red was simply blending in with the dark brown of the thick mud.

By nightfall, Callan's horse needed to sleep. He would have loved to continue going on, but he couldn't afford to work his horse to death. He had to get back somehow. Hopefully, the spy would be feeling the same way. If he was willing to run his horse into the grave, there was a chance that Callan would never catch up to him.

He slept lightly that night and watered his horse at a nearby stream. The closer to Oakheart that they travelled, the easier it was to find water. That was why the city had been founded, after all. A huge amount of people could make a living when an abundance of fresh water was around. Graveholm's own supply was nearly permanent with snow runoff from the mountains. The climate was too cold for most outsiders, which was why Graveholm had never been as large as many of the southern cities.

Near noon of the second day, the trail changed course. From Callan' last mission in Oakheart, he knew that they were getting close. The way that the trail was taking would lead right around the city without coming in direct sight of it. Going around made sense, from the spy's perspective. He wouldn't want to give the new Lord Davin any idea that there were soldiers coming. King Ramsey wouldn't have known that Ravitch sent a warning. Hopefully. Apparently, he already knew that there was an army coming to stop him. They could only pray that he didn't also know that Oakheart would be ready to defend itself. Again, hopefully. If Oakheart wasn't ready, the coming battle would be incredibly one-sided. Graveholm and the rebellion would be crushed in a straight-up fight.

The mud eventually gave way to more solid ground and to a completely dissimilar forest from the one that he had left behind. The trees here were thin and sick looking, and everywhere Callan walked his horse, there was a clear view of the sky. Luckily, the ground was now covered in green grass rather than thick mud. Every handful of yards, a red splotch dotted the ground. The spy was still bleeding, meaning he hadn't died in the saddle.

Callan reined his horse in. He could see the other man's horse up ahead, with no rider. Was he sleeping? Dying? Relieving himself? Callan slid out of the saddle and tied a robe from the horse's bridle to a nearby tree. He crept forward, keeping an eye on the horse for any sign that it might give of where the spy might be. It wasn't forthcoming with any helpful information.

Dumb animal.

As he got closer, he could hear something in the distance. A low rumble that he couldn't quite recognize. Then he heard something closer. A groan. The horse hadn't made the noise. It was too human sounding for that. Again, the groan. He moved closer, moving as silently as a gentle breeze, toward the clearing that the horse was in.

There. There he was.

The spy had propped himself up against a tree, where he sat moaning and groaning, his face a mask of unhidden pain. Half of Callan's arrow was sticking out of his right shoulder, below the collar bone. Blood had seeped through his tunic and ruined the shirt. His right arm dangled uselessly at his side while his left applied pressure to the area around the puncture. It must have hurt badly. And if he had been bleeding this heavily for nearly two days now, he was almost certainly dying.

The man looked up and saw Callan. He didn't move, but his eyes hardened and his lips locked into a thin line.

"You killed me," he said. "I made it all this way with an arrow in me, and I'm still not going to make it. Am I?"

Callan nodded and walked closer, drawing the bastard sword from his back as he did. He looked the man in the eyes and answered, "It looks that way. You've lost a lot of blood."

"Gods damn you, boy, why were you even chasing me? Could have let me die in peace."

Boy? The man was mocking him. Callan knew that he was young, but he was still in the prime of his life. He was young, but still a man. This soldier was older. A graying beard covered his face and neck. He clearly hadn't had much time to shave recently, or hadn't cared. Still, a man's death bed was no time to be condescending. Especially to the one holding the sword.

"You did your job, spying on the army. I had to stop you from bring that information back to Ramsey."

The man tried to laugh, but bent over coughing in pain instead. When he raised his head, Callan saw that blood had dribbled onto his chin. He was not long for the world. "You think he doesn't know, already? He has resources you can't even," he broke into another coughing fit. This time he didn't even bother bringing his hand to his mouth. Blood shot forth like spittle before he finished, "fathom."

Callan got closer. "So why lead me all of the way out here? Why run? Why not fight when you had the chance?"

He laughed that sick, dying laugh again. "You killed my brother when you jumped out of that tree. I wanted to be able see you get yours. With my own eyes."

Someone chuckled behind Callan.

Oh no. Stupid. Stupid, stupid, stupid.

He spun around slowly, tightening his grip on his sword. Three men had entered the clearing behind him. He'd been so focused on the spy that he hadn't noticed that anything was wrong. The one in the middle was still laughing, his hands toying with the hilt of a pair of nasty looking daggers at his sides.

"You killed my brother. You killed me. But I'm going to watch you pay for it before I go to the other side."

The three advanced at the same time, fanning out so that they could flank Callan. He moved away from them until his back was against one of the trees nearest him. The two flankers each wielded swords while the man in the middle had drawn both of his daggers. He looked competent with them, but Callan was confident that he wouldn't have an issue with him since his bastard sword offered such a sizeable reach advantage.

Callan angled his body to the side, making himself as small a target as possible and held his sword in a defensive position. The three closed the gap between them quickly. One took an adventurous jab at Callan's midsection. He batted the attack away easily. As soon as he did, the man on the other end stabbed quickly at his leg. He sidestepped, rather than swinging his sword around again. Instead, he took an offensive swing at the dagger-wielder.

The man *caught* Callan's sword with his blades, a notch in each grabbing the sharp edges of his sword with the two daggers. He twisted sharply, wrenching Callan's sword from his hand and tossing it backward over his shoulder. Callan was left weaponless and cornered by three men who wanted to not only kill him, but embarrass him. Hurt him.

The man on the left had attacked tentatively. He was worried. He was weak. Callan kicked out at his leg, buckling it at the knee. The limb didn't break, but the man collapsed on it. Callan followed up with a knee to the face, forcing his way out of the trap that he had put himself in.

A whisper of wind touched the back of his neck as a sharp edge swung within a hairsbreadth of taking off his head. He spotted his sword lying not far away and dove for it. His hand found the hilt, and he came up swinging. The soldier that he had kicked stood closer than he should have been. Callan opened a deep cut on his attacker's chest. The soldier fell to the ground, screaming and bleeding.

The other two stalked toward him more slowly now. The one that had been chuckling scowled now, all laughter gone from his eyes. He walked toward Callan, those notched daggers gleaming. They were strange and effective, but they wouldn't surprise Callan again. He couldn't afford to let that happen.

"You can turn around now," Callan said. "You don't want what he got." He gestured at the man whom he had cut, who was writhing on the ground, clutching the wound on his chest.

"He isn't dead."

"No, but if you think any of you are making it back to your king, you're mistaken."

"*Our* king," said Daggers. "*The* king."

Callan took a few quick, shuffling steps toward the pair of them. He swung his sword in an arc over his head and brought it down toward the remaining swordman. When the man moved to block, Callan stopped his attack and spun, ducking low to avoid the daggers that came at his neck. Using the momentum from his spin, he swung at the swordman's legs. His sword slowed as it sliced through the skin and muscle of the man's thigh. He screamed as well.

Callan finished his spin and stood tall once more. He drew back his blade and shoved it straight through the injured man's chest. A second scream stopped in his throat, and he fell to the ground in a quiet groan.

"You don't have to die," Callan said to the remaining man, Daggers. "You can walk away from this."

Daggers advanced silently. He swung once at Callan's face and once at his stomach. Callan leaned out of the way of each strike. He swung high twice more and again, Callan dipped his body out of the way, trying to create as much distance between the two of him as he could manage. They continued that dance with Callan leading them in a slow circle around the clearing. He could see the frustration building on Daggers' face while sweat beaded down his forehead and into his eyes. He was getting angry. Callan kept calm and collected, as he'd been taught. Getting excited in a fight was a good way to get killed.

Tired of their game, Daggers reared his hand back and threw one of his blades at Callan's face. Callan leaned back and to the side, and watched as the long piece of serrated steel flew close enough to his nose that he could practically smell it. A relieved breath hissed out from between his teeth.

Daggers threw the other weapon into the meat of Callan's thigh before he could right himself.

Callan's vision flashed red, and he collapsed to the ground. Someone had branded him on the leg. Someone had stuck him with a white-hot poker. That was the only thing that could possibly have hurt that badly. Someone yelled in pain. It must have been him, but it sounded so far away that it couldn't have been. Besides, he had never made a sound like that in his life.

"Not so quick now." Close. Almost on top of him.

A cough. A wheeze. "Should have done that before he arrowed me, I guess."

"You want me to bring you over here so you can finish him?" Close, again.

Cough. Cough. Cough. "No, no." Cough. "You earned it."

Callan opened his eyes. He hadn't realized that he'd clamped them shut to push away the pain. Daggers. Daggers sauntered toward him, a smirk on his face. Callan blinked and Daggers was there, knelt over him and grasping the handle of the dagger that was lodged in Callan's thigh. He twisted it, just a little. Callan whimpered. Daggers found that amusing. He did it again.

He could still feel the hilt of his own sword in his palm, but it seemed too heavy to lift. His arms wouldn't obey him. Why?

Daggers *yanked* on the blade and pulled it out of Callan's leg. He yelled again, this time loudly and harshly enough to hurt his throat.

The hard knuckles of the back of a hand struck him across the mouth. He tasted blood.

"Shut up. We don't want anybody coming looking. Besides, this'll be over soon. Maybe." He chuckled.

Callan stared up at the man's silhouette, the sun shining brightly behind him. He was a pure-black figure now rather than a man. The figure raised one hand, dagger gleaming in the light, and brought it down toward Callan's stomach.

He found his grip on his sword. It felt lighter, suddenly. Everything did. The world was clearer. His own blade whistled up to meet that of the figure. He overextended. Instead of meeting steel, his blade met flesh. It sheared through the skin and muscle, then the bone, then the muscle and the skin. The hand holding the dagger landed next to Callan's head with a *thump*.

Daggers doubled over in pain, staring in horror at the bleeding stump where his hand had been. His eyes flashed from the arm to Callan and back. Callan forced his sword up and through his neck, then twisted and pulled, almost completely severing the head from the body. Daggers fell to the ground in a silent heap.

Callan pried the dagger out of the dead fingers near his head. He scooted over to the man whom he had injured first, and whom was still struggling into the afterlife. Callan drove the dagger into his chest and finished his journey for him. He cut the jacket off the corpse, then, and cut it into large strips. He tied the dark fabric around his leg, putting pressure on it to stem the bleeding. He had enough sense to do that before the high of battle left him.

He stood and tried to put weight on the leg. It quivered and shot a line of fire up his entire body. He grunted, but the leg held. Callan hobbled toward his horse.

The noise, though. That dull roar. He could hear it again, now that the clearing was quiet. He had to figure out what it was. He limped forward, past the spy who had led him on this chase in the first place. Back into the trees he moved, until he lost sight of the bodies. He crested a hill and stopped dead.

Below him was an army. A huge army. Bigger than the one that Graveholm had brought. He had to get back. Fast. He spun and stumbled, his head suddenly light. Callan knew that he would have to move more slowly than he tried to do, or he was never going to make it.

He stumbled, half falling back toward the clearing and his horse. Toward the sound of the wracking coughs of a dying man.

Chapter 31

Four soldiers escorted the two Visani into the hall. Pyra had ordered the room emptied of anyone without military training. She wanted to see what they needed of her, but she wasn't stupid. Gramm and his men would be close at hand. She had one of them, one of the few that could read and write, keeping notes on the meeting so that anyone curious could later read what had happened.

The Visani were similar to those that Pyra had seen before. This was the closest she had been to one of them since Melhaar had declared a blood war on her family, though. These two were much smaller. The female was taller than Gramm, and wider, but seemed almost tiny when she remembered their clan-head. She looked sick, and her child looked no better. If Pyra had been standing, he would have been only slightly taller than her.

Both had their hands bound behind their backs with thick rope. Pyra ordered the ropes cut. "I won't have my guests bound in my hall," she said.

The soldiers looked at her incredulously. None moved until Gramm gave an approving nod. Pyra might have been their lady, and in command of the goings on at Graveholm, but Gramm was their commander. He had their respect. The men did at they were told, then retreated a few steps. Every soldier in the hall had their hands on their swords. Even Gramm.

The Visani both rubbed feeling back into their wrists once the ropes were cut. Pyra waited for them to finish before speaking.

"I would know your names before we speak. I am Pyra, acting lady of Graveholm."

The female inclined her head, showing Pyra her throat. The young one did not. He stared at the ground, his tail limp and his ears flat. "My name is Ramat. My son," she gestured to the youngling, "is Jeraal."

At the sound of his name, Jeraal cast a fearful glance at his mother, then at Pyra. He looked as scared as Pyra felt. The first time she had met a Visani, he had promised to kill her entire family. The next time, a group of them had killed nearly everyone in Graveholm's town. After that, they had invaded the keep itself. Still, she did not think that they were as barbaric as some of the others did. That was the only reason she had allowed this audience. Her father would have had them killed on sight.

"Ramat. I like that," she said. "What can I do for you."

The Visani stood straight and showed her neck again. Pyra found the gesture amusing. She had seen dogs at play, or fighting over a bone, do the same in surrender of a bigger opponent. Maybe the Visani gesture had similar meaning.

Ramat spoke with a thick accent. Her teeth seemed to get in the way of her words, but she spoke slowly enough that Pyra had little difficulty understanding her. "We are hungry, *Ferash*. The winter has been long. Warriors eat most of the best food. Clan Chief Melhaar eats better than anyone."

She paused, waiting for a response from Pyra. "What did you call me, Ramat?"

The mother cast her glance down. She looked almost embarrassed. "*Ferash.* In our tongue, it means Fire-Starter. You earned the title after the first battle."

Pyra remembered very clearly. She had incinerated one of them and nearly done the same to a second. Her own soldiers had avoided speaking of the event near her. Still, she knew that it was spoken of even after more than three years. Clearly, the Visani had not forgotten either.

"You honor me, Ramat," she said. At least, Pyra thought that it was an honor. Maybe the Visani used the term as a curse on her. The question of hunger still had to be addressed. Her title could wait. "You honor me, but do you mean to say that Melhaar would like me to feed his troops while he lays siege to this keep?"

"No," said Ramat, "no, forgive me. I was not sent by Melhaar. My child, my Jeraal is sick. Melhaar told me to leave him in the forest for the wolves when he was born. I could not. But I can no longer feed him. The winter was too long. Too harsh."

Pyra looked again to the smaller Visani. It had been a sick Visani that nearly killed her father. Gravar, their former Chieftain had contracted what they called the Blood Sickness. It had caused him to go insane and attack Ravitch while he had been out hunting. What Jeraal had must have been different, though. Melhaar had told Pyra and Theamere that the Blood Sickness was deadly.

"If your child is so sick," Pyra asked, "why are you not sick as well? Did he not infect you?"

Ramat shook her head again. "He eats normally. He runs, he hunts, he bathes. His body is not sick. Jeraal is brain-sick. Damaged."

Again, Jeraal looked to his mother. Hearing his name seemed to be all that could get a reaction out of him. Pyra's heart went out to the small Visani.

"What of Jeraal's father?"

"Dead."

Pyra didn't ask how he had died. More than likely, one of her soldiers had done the deed. Gods, maybe *she* had done it. Could one of the two Visani that she had killed have been Jeraal's father? She could not think of that. She could not let some unsubstantiated blame cause her to lose focus or lose sleep. She could not think of these Visani as human. To humanize them was to befriend them, and they had slaughtered too many soldiers, knights, and innocents for her to let that happen. Maybe she was her father's daughter, after all.

"Give us a moment, Ramat."

The Visani nodded and placed a clawed hand on her son's shoulder. Pyra turned to Gramm, who knelt by her side. "What do you think, Gramm?"

He grunted. "I know you feel for them. I almost do, too. You can't afford to be a humanitarian, though. You saw the reactions of some of the nobles when you offered food to those starving children. Do you have any idea what would happen if you fed these two?"

Pyra nodded. "They would revolt." She had known the answer before Gramm had opened his mouth. Still, she trusted him more than anyone else. Hearing his opinion validated her own.

She stood and folded her hands in front of her. Ramat turned to her, on full alert. The Visani's eyes were wide, and her ears stood at attention. Her tail quivered in what Pyra could only think was anticipation.

She said, "I'm sorry, Ramat, but we can scarcely feed our own. I have no choice but to deny your request."

"But, *Ferash*—"

"Furthermore," Pyra cut her off. "tell anyone else who thinks to come begging, that is not Melhaar coming to surrender to us, will be killed on sight."

Saying the words twisted Pyra's gut. She wanted to help them. She wanted to two sides to be able to get along. But she also had to please her own people and keep them alive. They were her priority. Her nobles may have been despicable human beings, but they were still humans. The Visani were not.

Ramat's jaw slackened. She knew as well as Pyra did that she and her son had both, more than likely, been sentenced to death. "You would see us starve, *Ferash*."

Again, her stomach tightened. "No, Ramat. I would not see it. You may leave now."

The Visani snarled and lowered her head. She went from stunned mother to furious predator in the space between two heartbeats. The soldiers around her moved, but they were not fast enough. Ramat took a pair of running steps and threw herself at Pyra. Her eyes bulged with fury, and for a split second, Pyra took note of the beauty of a huntress in action. Her brain reacted before she did. Calling magic had always cost her a lot of concentration and effort. This time, the river came without the slightest manipulation on Pyra's part. The energy flowed to her fingertips and poured forth.

A bolt of lightning shot from Pyra's fingers with a *crack* and struck Ramat across the chest. She fell in a heap on the stone floor with a smoldering wound across her chest and shoulders. She did not move.

Pyra spoke, her voice as cold as the mountain air. She was too frightened to feel anything but sharp fury. "Take the child outside the gates and point him to the forest. He may take his mother with him."

Jeraal looked at her, then. His yellow eyes were uncomprehending of what had happened. Did he even realize that his mother was dead? That Pyra was to blame? Pyra knew in her heart that sending him back would kill him as surely as the lightning that had struck down Ramat. She was not a murderer, though. Killing the attacking huntress was one thing, but she would not slaughter a helpless child.

"Take him now."

Her shoulders shook as soldiers ushered the child out of the chamber. It took two of them to carry Ramat's corpse. Pyra would not cry. She could not. She expected her soldiers to kill Visani for her, she could not pity them. She could not allow her fear to dominate her. She was not a murderer, but nor was she a coward. Pyra was a leader and would prove to those around her that she deserved to be followed.

Still, she welcomed the gentle hand that Gramm placed on the back of her neck.

Chapter 32

"You really made a mess of that."

A dark shack this time. It was the first dream that Callan could remember where he couldn't feel the heat of flames licking at his face and arms. Out the window, though, he could see a red-orange glow on the horizon. The sharp-nosed young man from the other dreams was there, as well. This time, he wore no hood. He rested his arms on an old, rotting table, his golden eyes boring into Callan's green ones.

"It could have been worse," Callan answered. "I got all four of them. I even made sure that the spy died quickly. I didn't make him suffer."

"Congratulations," said the man, dryly. "You killed four men. Do you know how many that is in the grand scheme of things?"

Callan didn't.

"Zero. Nothing."

Callan pushed his chair out and stood up. He walked to the window and stared out at an ashen expanse. The fire had already done its work here. Embers still smoldered in some places, but nearly everything had been petrified by the heat of the flames. The horizon, though, burned bright.

"Is this what you want me to prevent? Is this what I'm supposed to be protecting people from?"

"Yes."

Callan turned on him, throwing up his hands in exasperation.

"How am I supposed to stop this?"

The man smiled. "You aren't if you do something stupid and get yourself killed."

The man sat relaxed at the table. Callan stood on the other end of it with his elbows on the table and his head in his hands. "So, is this what would have happened if I had died?"

The man looked confused. "No. This has already happened."

The shack was gone, but Callan could smell fire. He could only think that he had somehow been moved to the fire on the horizon. He wasn't hot. He was actually as comfortable as he could have expected. He tried to gather his legs under himself and stand up.

A flash of pain shot through his leg and the rest of his entire body. His eyes opened wide and a yelp escaped his throat. He screwed his eyes shut and gritted his teeth to do his best to block out the awful hurt. It was only a marginally successful endeavor.

Someone moved off to Callan's side. "You proud idiot."

Callan groaned.

More movement. "Do you have any idea how badly you jeopardized everything that we've been working on for the last three years? What about everything that has been going on without you for a *decade*?"

Murdock.

Murdock?

"You're selfish. Selfish and ignorant and unfit to be making decisions in regard to this army. If I were in charge, I'd send you home. You're lucky I'm not."

Callan tried to speak but all that his dry throat could manage was a croak.

"What?"

"Eleven," he whispered. "I've killed eleven people."

He heard Murdock sit down next to him. He was lying on a bed, he realized. How had he gotten there? He didn't remember much after he had put the spy out of his misery. He'd left the clearing after that and headed back toward the army. Where they had been when he left, anyway. He remembered being thirsty and dizzy, then…nothing.

"You did what you had to do, Callan," Murdock replied.

"What happened to me?" He didn't want to talk about the dead bodies that he had piling up around him.

"Torruk found you in the forest a couple of days ago," Murdock said. "You had fallen off a horse. You'd lost a lot of blood. The healers and I did what we could to heal your leg, but the damage was pretty severe."

Callan winced and opened his eyes. Murdock looked exhausted. "How severe?"

"Nothing permanent, thankfully. But you won't be walking again for a day or two. You're lucky that I was here. Any non-magical healer wouldn't have been able to heal the muscle damage." He paused. "Ravitch has called a halt to the march until you're better."

"No. We can't stop." Callan propped himself up his elbows. "They'll beat us there if we stop. They know that we're coming."

"Wait," Murdock sat up, suddenly more alert. "You didn't stop the spy?"

Callan shook his head. "I did. I stopped him. They already knew. I have to talk to Ravitch."

Murdock looked worried at that. He looked like he was thinking over the ramifications of that fact, like Callan had done when he'd learned of it. There were very few sources that could have given that information away. A traitor in the midst of the rebellion was the first that came to Callan's mind. He knew that it was likely that Ramsey had placed spies of his own in the rebellion, or near it. Any soldier would have been able to sell that information. How they'd have gotten it to the king was what had Callan baffled. Then again, he was no mage.

Callan asked, "Is there any magical way to send information from Graveholm to Tal Autem?"

Murdock shook his head. "Not that doesn't give off a large signature."

"A what?"

"A signature. It's like a magical tremor. A footprint that other mages can pick up on," he answered. "If anyone used any kind of magic near this camp, I would know about it. If they used a spell like the one you're talking about, Datynn and I would *both* have felt it. Neither of us did."

"Could it be some spell that you don't know about."

"Yes," he said. "Possible, but not likely. Unless it was developed very recently."

Callan frowned. "And all of our messenger birds have been accounted for?"

"Every one of them."

He cursed under his breath. "I still need to talk to Ravitch. He needs to know."

"I can tell him," Murdock said. "You're in no condition to be walking around."

"Fine. But tell him that we need to move faster if we're going to beat them to Oakheart. They've got a head start on us."

Murdock opened his mouth to protest, but Callan interrupted. "I can't be responsible for this army being held up any longer. Put me in a supply wagon and I'll ride the rest of the way. Unless you want to carry me." He laughed, sending a sharp pain through his leg again. "Not exactly dignified, but it's what we would do for any other wounded soldier. Right?"

He knew that he was, and so did Murdock.

Callan must have nodded off after that. A side effect of the healing that Murdock had done on him. He woke up later to an unbalanced bouncing. If the jostling wasn't hurting his leg so badly, he might have felt satisfied with himself for convincing Murdock to see things his way. Instead, everything hurt. He might have been riding along in a wagon, but he still had an incredibly painful, partially healed knife wound in his leg.

"Your leg hurting you?"

Callan looked up. Ravitch rode next to his wagon on a giant gray stallion. His one good eye had a look of what almost seemed to be amusement. That couldn't be right, though. From what Callan had learned over the last few years, Ravitch ran only on two emotions: angry and disappointed.

"It doesn't feel great," Callan answered.

Ravitch tossed a small package, wrapped in thick brown paper and tied with twine. "That," he said, "is Anashti's Balm. Take out a leaf and chew on it. It'll dull the pain. More than one leaf and it'll put you to sleep."

"Thank you." He wasn't sure why Ravitch was being so kind all of the sudden, but he wasn't going to complain.

The Lord tossed him another wrapped package, this one cylindrical. "And *this* is a map of Oakheart." As Ravitch spoke, Callan unwrapped the Balm. The leaves were roughly the same size as his little finger.

Ravitch continued, "I need you to look through it and familiarize yourself with the city. You're going to be leading a strike team against Ramsey's officers."

Callan popped one of the brown-streaked leaves into his mouth and chewed. The plant was sickly sweet, and as soon as he bit into it, he felt a bit lightheaded. He made a face.

"It doesn't taste great," Ramsey laughed, "but it will help the pain. I've picked up my fair share of battle wounds in my time, and I've found that nothing helps quite like Anashti's Balm."

He was right. Already, the stabbing pain in Callan's leg had receded to a dull throbbing. "Who else is going to be on this strike team?"

"You'll have three archers, five seasoned footmen, and Dastynn."

"What about Murdock," Callan asked?

"He's in charge of keeping Lord Davin alive. He'll lead a group of knights into the castle and make sure that nothing happens to our new *friend*." He practically spat the last word out.

"Not a fan of Davin's, I take it?"

Ravitch sneered. "His father was foul, but at least he knew how to govern. Davin's soft. More of a philosopher than a soldier."

"So, you'd rather his father be on our side? I can't imagine you and Delaney being great friends."

"No," said Ravitch, "I'm glad that Delaney is dead. But he was a known commodity. His son is not. I don't like unknowns."

Callan was glad to have this conversation with Ravitch. He had spent the last few years living in the place that he ruled over, the place that he called home, and yet he hardly knew him. Ravitch had always been a distant figure, letting Pyra and Theamere act as his public face. He wondered what he had been like before he'd had his face mangled by that Visani. Callan doubted that he'd been much of a social creature but just maybe he had been more personable. Just maybe.

"You did a good thing, you know."

Callan frowned. "What do you mean?"

"When you killed Delaney. When you killed those spies. It may not seem like it now. The first few kills always grate at your soul. It gets easier. You just have to let yourself know that you're doing the right thing."

He wasn't totally convinced. "How did you do that? How did you get past it?"

"I told myself that every time I took a life, every time I killed someone, that I was doing it for my family. I love my family. I would do absolutely anything to keep them safe. If that means putting people in the ground, so be it."

"My family is gone," said Callan flatly. "I can't protect them."

"No." Ravitch looked sad, maybe regretful. It was the first time that Callan had ever seen him show that particular side of himself. "But you can avenge them. You can make sure that Ramsey never takes another family away from another child. Is that worth killing for?"

"I don't know," Callan said. "I guess we'll find out soon."

"I guess we will."

A horn blasted in the distance. Three times. Ravitch wheeled his horse around, looking for the source of the sound. Callan propped himself up as far as he could but couldn't see over the edge of the wagon.

"It can't be them," Ravitch said. "We're still two days from Oakheart. They can't be here this fast!"

"No," Callan replied, "they can't be. Respond to the call. See who came to visit."

"You don't think—"

"I do."

Ravitch waved his arms to his horn blower. The man raised the ivory to his lips and blew three blasts in answer. Another call, acknowledging the response sounded from the east, over a hill. A group of men on horses crested the hill, banners snapping in the wind behind them.

"Besides the fact that I'm not as young as I used to be, I'm also missing my good eye." Ravitch almost seemed like he was joking. Callan couldn't believe it. "What do those banners have on them?"

Callan shielded his eyes against the sun and squinted.

"A sword. It's on fire. On a gray banner. Maybe white."

Ravitch grinned like a small child. "Have you ever heard of the Firebrands, Callan?"

"No."

"Well, I have a feeling that you'll never forget them."

Chapter 33

Gramm sat next to her for the next hour without saying a word. He didn't need to. Neither of them had anything to say. Besides, any consoling or pity on his part probably just would have made Pyra feel worse. She had flat out refused aid to a starving mother and child. Not only that, she had threatened their lives if they thought to ask again. The move was sure to win her favor with some of the nobles and those among her people who were going hungry. The soldiers would like it because it showed that she was willing to make the hard choices against the enemy. Just about everyone else would undoubtedly believe that anything she could do to hurt any Visani would be the right decision. All-in-all, it was an excellent political maneuver. Why, then, did it make her so sick to her stomach?

Gods, this hadn't even been the first Visani that she had killed. Seeing that young child, though, looking so empty and lost. Knowing in her heart that she had condemned him to starve to death made Pyra want to cry. That was why she had ordered the hall cleared of everyone but her and Gramm. Not because she was too exhausted to answer any more appeals, after her attack, like she had told her petitioners. No, she was more worried that she would burst into tears at any moment and didn't want them to think her emotionally unstable.

Just like a woman, they would say, *to fall to pieces after killing someone that tried to tear her head off.*

Just like a woman to break down and cry at the first sign of real danger.

It's a good thing she keeps Gramm around, in case she needs a man to handle any real problem.

She could practically hear them talking about her. It made her blood boil, but that was why she had sent them away. If she could just have some time with her thoughts, she would come out on top of the situation.

"Gramm," she asked, suddenly curious, "do you think that I'm a bad person?"

"Of course, I don't." He didn't even hesitate.

"Even after what I did," she asked?

Gramm sighed and spoke slowly. "I think that you made the only choice you could have in that situation. That doesn't change the fact that you're a good person."

"You can't tell me that sending that child out alone was something that a good person would have done, Gramm."

"I get it," he said. "You want me to pity you. I won't."

Her face reddened, but she couldn't bring herself to say that he was wrong.

"Besides, what were you going to do? Kill him? Make me kill him? I don't think so. At least this way, he's got a chance."

He was right, of course. She never would have executed Jeraal, and she certainly wouldn't have ordered someone else to do it for her. Besides, she doubted that Gramm would have even if she had given the order. He was loyal to her, but he also held her to a higher standard than she often held herself, especially morally.

She looked at him, for the first time since they'd been left alone. His eyes were locked on hers. He didn't look away. Pyra was almost unnerved, but she held his gaze. Her pulse quickened. He may not have been the most handsome man in Graveholm, but he wasn't the ugliest either. He wasn't rich, either, but he cared for her. He had said as much himself. They had always been close. Since they were children, they had been friends. Deep down, she cared for him in the same way that he cared for her. Romantic feelings were hiding beneath the surface, but she had never been able to make herself give voice to them. After how she had reacted when he'd confessed his feelings for her, would he still reciprocate those feelings, even?

Something in her face must have given her away. "What is it?"

"I don't know," she said. She couldn't bring herself to admit the way she felt. It was better that way. Nothing could be done until her father returned, anyway. Perhaps when Ravitch was back to his own duties, she would be left alone to pursue her own life. She could do a better job of letting Gramm into her life.

"If you say so," he said. He didn't sound convinced.

Someone knocked loudly on the doors leading to the interior of the keep.

"Come in," Pyra called.

It was Travis, the man who'd been unofficially leading the refugees. Pyra hadn't had much contact with him recently as he'd taken up training to be a knight. He was older, much older, than most who took up the position, but they had both agreed that if he was going to be leading the townspeople, he should have a position that carried some official weight. So, he'd signed up under Gramm.

"What is it, Travis," he asked?

He bowed, once to each of them in turn, and addressed Pyra. "Visani, my lady. They're coming out of the forest, moving through the town. They'll have us surrounded soon."

Pyra stood, forgetting her self-pity for the moment. "Have they made it clear what they want? Are they waving peace banners? Have they sent a messenger?"

Travis shook his head. "None of that, m'lady. They're armed to the teeth, every one of them. They look like they mean business."

Gramm cut in, "Travis, they've attacked before. Shoot some arrows at them, drive them off."

"If you'll forgive my saying so, sir, I don't think they'll be scared off by a few arrows. There's too many of them for that."

"How many," Pyra asked?"

"It's hard to say," he replied. "All of them, I'd wager."

"Gramm, we had better get up to the wall."

Travis couldn't have been far off with his guess. Pyra had never dreamed that there could have been so many Visani hiding in the forest. With their white fur, they blended in almost seamlessly with the snow. The powder hid their exact movements, making everything that they did a blur, rather than a distinct action. Gramm gripped the edge of the wall so hard that she feared the stone would crumble. He had never been one to show much emotion, but the look in his eyes said that he was scared. If this was enough to make Gramm visibly frightened… Pyra shuddered.

"What do we do," she asked?

He took a deep breath and surveyed the town and the surrounding forest that continued to pour forth the enormous Visani. She could tell that he wanted to lead his men out and fight them until they were pushed back into the woods. There would have been untold glory for him had he been able to do it. As humble as he was, and always had been, Pyra knew that saying no to honor of that magnitude was difficult for anyone. Gramm knew better, though.

"We hold them off. I'll get as many archers up here as we have available." He seemed sure of himself. She had always admired that about him. When he made a decision, he stuck to it. In his own mind, he was right. "They'll try to get into the keep. They have no other reason to attack with these numbers. I'll have my most senior knights on the walls with rocks and boiling water to keep them off."

"What about you? What will you do?"

He smiled at her. "I'm going to be with you, in case something goes wrong. If any of them get over the walls, they'll have to go through me. I won't let that happen."

Gramm gave out his orders and soldiers came running to do his bidding. Archers lined nearly every open space on the battlements, raining arrows down on any Visani who got within range. Pyra could only wonder why they had chosen this moment to attack. It couldn't have been because she had killed Ramat and sent Jeraal away. That had only happened a few hours past. They had been planning this attack for some time, that much was obvious. Had the mother's pleas been a distraction from the attack? Perhaps. She had seemed so earnest, though...

It mattered little now. They attacked. She could look into their reasoning later, once they'd been repelled.

She ran water to the archers and refilled the quivers for them when they ran low. Those tasks were normally left for young men or those too old to fight any longer. Some of the nobles would surely look down their noses at her for helping in such a manner, but she couldn't bring herself to sit in the hall or in her quarters while men fought to defend her. Gramm never left her side, even for an instant. For his part, he offered encouragement where it was needed and pointed some of the younger archers at the best targets. Having him near made them visibly more confident. Pyra was sure that he had the same effect on her. Yes, when Ravitch came back, she would make more time for Gramm.

Noon was long past when a messenger came to Gramm and Pyra in the keep's yard. They were between water runs and had stopped to take a drink themselves. The runner bowed stiffly to Pyra and saluted Gramm. He didn't wait for Gramm to address him before he spoke, his words spilling into each other in his haste.

"You need to see this, sir. Top of the wall. Follow me."

He rushed away without waiting for an answer. Pyra hurried after him, Gramm coming quickly behind her. They met the soldier again once they were on the battlements. He pointed out beyond the abandoned homes and shops of Graveholm at the dark forest beyond. Pyra squinted, shading her eyes from the afternoon sun with one hand, but could barely make out small figures running through the trees. Her vision had never been the best. Gramm cursed loudly beside her, drawing startled glances from the closest soldiers.

"What is it? I can't see, they're too small."

Realization hit her like a fist as soon as the words left her mouth. Gramm saw the knowledge on her face, but said nothing. His jaw was clenched tightly enough that he might have ground his teeth down to nothing.

"Those aren't Visani," she said.

"No. Those are men."

"What are they doing out there? They aren't fighting, they aren't rushing the keep."

Gramm shook his head. He didn't know any better than she did.

They didn't have to wonder for long, though. Soon, men on horseback rode slowly out of the trees. Four of them rode side by side with another four in a row behind them. Ropes were attached to each horse, pulling something out of the forest. A great shadow moved through the trees where the foliage was thinnest. Smaller trees were flattened or uprooted by the massive structure as it rolled behind the horses. It cleared the trees quickly, revealing men pulling behind the horses and more pushing from behind.

A catapult. A massive catapult.

The soldiers on the near side of the keep had noticed it by now. Whether she noticed that men were working alongside the Visani, she did not know. She hoped that they hadn't. If they were as confused as she and Gramm were, their aim could be impaired. At this moment, they needed to be killing machines not thinkers or worriers.

The wooden monstrosity was set back and ready to fire. A black boulder, large enough to see from even the large distance that separated them, rested in the firing bowl. Someone in the forest lit a torch. The tiny speck of light moved to the boulder, which erupted in flames.

Pyra heard the creak of the giant weapon's arm. She heard the crash as its arm collided with the base. She even imagined that she could hear the whistle of the projectile as it sailed through the air, closing the distance to the keep walls with alarming speed.

The boulder hit the center of the wall with a cacophonous *crash*, breaking the boulder into smaller fragments of burning rubble. Neither wall nor man stood a chance. The wall was obliterated down the ground level. Those who weren't thrown backward or upward by the boulder's strike fell to their deaths when the wall beneath them disintegrated.

It seemed as though an earthquake had hit the keep. The force of the shockwave knocked both Pyra and Gramm from their feet. Screams of pain and fear filled her head. Gramm tried to talk to her, to make sure that she was alright. She was vaguely aware of the fact that she waved him off, telling her that she was fine. He couldn't hold her attention any better than the hurt and dying men around her could.

She only had eyes for the Visani that came through the wound in the wall, crawling and climbing over broken stones and bodies.

Chapter 34

General Arian Morningblade was an imposing figure, even standing next to Theamere and Ravitch. He was nearly as tall as they were, but not anywhere near as rough. He looked like a prince out of some storybook. He had bright blond hair, the likes of which was incredibly rare in Aelathil. It was tied back behind his head. He was not burly, but he radiated strength. Where beards were common in the west, especially Graveholm, where it was miserably cold most of the year, Arian was clean shaven.

He wore burgundy armor with gold trimming and pauldrons shaped like wings. His cape looked as if it were burning. Red, orange, yellow, and purple swam together on his back, reminding Callan of the dreams that he had been having so often. His helm covered most of his face. Only his eyes and mouth could be seen as there was an arrow-shaped protrusion that guarded his nose.

In the two days that they had been riding together, he had hardly said a word. He'd insisted that the emperor had sent him to lead the Firebrands, but that all of them were there to help in the rebellion. The legion was under the direct command of Arian, but he would be taking his orders from Ravitch, Theamere, and even Callan.

The Firebrands were said to excel at the very skills that Graveholm's army lacked. Callan had never heard of them in his studies growing up, but Ravitch clearly knew all about them. Whenever Arian was out of earshot, he would rave to Callan and Theamere about their martial legend. Their skill in the field, whether they were used as footmen or cavalry, could potentially turn the tide of the war.

"Why do you think that Orthielle came to help us," Callan asked Murdock? The two of them were riding in the rear of the column with Dastynn, away from Lord Ravitch and the general.

Murdock shrugged. He and Dastynn didn't seem to share Callan's level of concern over the issue. "Money, probably. That and Aelathil has been growing in military and political strength in recent years. If Orthielle allies themselves with us, they gain friends and connections."

Callan was still skeptical. "They're an established military force. They're bigger than we are and they have more resources. Why would they need us as allies?"

"There's a lot that goes into something like this, Callan," he said. "You'll have to learn something about politics sooner or later if you're going to be a lord."

"Well, I don't have time for a lesson at the moment, so if you would just explain it, that would be great."

The mage glowered at him. "They want to keep an eye on us. You had better believe that Arian will be reporting back to his emperor about our money, or fortifications, and our other allies. All of that. Beyond that, they want to know the military capabilities of whatever side ends up winning this war."

"You think that they'll want to invade us." He wasn't asking anymore.

Murdock nodded. "I think it's a matter of time."

Callan resolved to keep an eye on the general. He seemed amiable enough, and willing to take commands from the rebels, but there was no telling how long that would last. The Firebrands weren't numerous enough to take out Graveholm's army, but they could do some serious damage if they decided to turn against them. One legion, no matter how skilled, could win a war of any particular scale. Besides, Ramsey's armies would be in their way even if they could defeat the rebels. For now, at least, Callan would have to trust that they would do their jobs and help to win this war. After that, he could go back to being suspicious.

The column marched through the morning and afternoon, pausing only briefly to eat and take the occasional rest. Graveholm's soldiers took the breaks with enthusiasm, but the Firebrands seemed more annoyed to be stopping than glad for the respite. They seemed like they had the capability to march indefinitely without being tired. Callan was curious about how they had been trained and how they had grown up, but he didn't want to seem like he was prying information out of them. If he still wanted the information after the battle, he would have plenty of time to ask those still alive.

As noon stretched into the late stages of the day and on toward twilight, rainclouds formed over the heads of the marchers. A light drizzle started as the sun began to set. Callan made his way to the front of the column to get his directions for the night from Ravitch. He saw the lord conversing with Arian at the head of the army. With them was a soldier that Callan didn't recognize. Both the soldier and the horse that he had rode in on were clearly exhausted. Both were breathing heavily, their chests pumping in and out in a desperate search for oxygen. Before Callan could get close enough to hear what the man said, he rode off, presumably to get something to eat and drink.

He rode to Ravitch and asked, "What was that all about? What's happening?"

"They're attacking the damned city," he growled. "They beat us there and they're breaking down the gates."

"At night? That's suicide."

Arian spoke up then, his voice even and calm. "Not with the rain coming in. Oakheart won't have access to any torches or pitch to defend themselves. The royals could break in and take control of the city with minimal resistance."

Ravitch cursed under his breath. "We can't move fast enough to stop them. We just don't have enough horses."

Callan looked between the two older men. "What about the Firebrands? They've all got horses and there are few enough of them that they could make good time."

"No," said Ravitch. "No offense to you, General, but I don't think that Lord Davin would be too receptive to an army with strange banners showing up at his gates, even to save him."

"None taken."

Callan cut in, "Send our banners with them then. Send Murdock, Dastynn, and I as well."

"Right, sending the man who killed his father is a sure way to win his trust." Ravitch sneered.

"He doesn't know who killed his father. I didn't exactly stick around to introduce myself."

Ravitch tugged on his beard, his eyes hard as stone.

"We don't have a choice anymore," Callan said. "If we're going to save Oakheart, we have to go now."

"General," Ravitch asked," what do you think?"

"My Firebrands can move faster than the bulk of your army and cause significant damage in a hit-and-run assault," said Arian. "If we leave now, we have a chance at running the royals off until morning. By then, the rest of your army will have time to join us."

"Fine. Go, but be careful. No unneeded risks, understood?"

Both Callan and Arian nodded and kicked their horses into action. Arian went to gather his men, and Callan went to tell Murdock and Dastynn the plan. Murdock wasn't happy about going in without support from the main body of the army, but he understood the dire situation that they had found themselves in. Dastynn, on the other hand, seemed excited just to be going into action. He was a happy person and very friendly despite his complete lack of speech, but Callan had always sensed a silent intensity beneath the surface. The paladin's hand gripped the handle of his stone maul, fidgeting with his gloves at the prospect of a fight. Callan was confident in what they were going to do and knew that his friends were as well.

The Firebrands were ready by the time that the three of them arrived. Arian had them all horsed and ready to travel. Their efficiency was almost inhuman.

As Callan had never commanded a group of men before, he allowed Arian to lead the attack. The general was more than willing to take over. The legion set off at a brisk pace. Luckily, they had less than a mile to travel before the city would come into view. The royals had just barely beaten them. That frustrated Callan to no end, especially after the efforts that he had gone through to stay healthy and travel. His leg was healing as well as could be expected. He would be able to make a difference in the coming battle, despite the constant pain that he felt.

As they neared Oakheart, the sounds of soldiers screaming became less of a distant roar and more of a reality. Oakheart's front gates came into sight before dark had fully fallen. Had Callan not been in the middle of a charging group of cavalry, he would have stopped to take in the morbid vision of the royal army smashing away at the wooden gates with a massive battering ram. Their sheer numbers brought Callan's heart into his throat. They couldn't win this. They would be crushed. The rebels had a total of just under thirty thousand soldiers, including the Firebrands. The royals had at least double that. He shivered.

Still, the five thousand Firebrands moved forward as one. Those on the edges brought about their shields, forming them into an arrowhead. Callan, and the others in the middle of the group, carried on as they had been. With Arian in the lead, the spearhead rushed the soldiers guarding the back of the battering ram. The shields, in combination with the armor that covered the necks and chests of the horses, slammed into the royals with a cacophonous *crunch*.

They had seen the Firebrands coming. They had raised their shields and spears and readied themselves for the charge.

They weren't ready.

The speed and force of the attack shattered the royal line. Wooden shields, spears, swords, and bones shattered to splinters and dust. Men and horses screamed. Royal soldiers were tossed into the air and to the sides, trampled under the weight of five thousand horses.

Then they were through. They wheeled their formation around, not even bothering to dodge stray footmen or archers. If they were in the way, they were trampled. The only exceptions were those who dove out of the way.

Arian led the Firebrands around for a second attack. This time, the royals were less prepared than they had been for the first attack. Again, the charge decimated the line of men attacking Oakheart. A heavy scent of iron filled the air. Blood. It clogged Callan's nostrils and made him want to vomit. He hadn't seen this much death since the last time that he'd been present for a royal assault. He had been different then. He'd been a child. And weak. Now Callan was prepared. At least more so than he had been all those years ago.

The Firebrands ran around for a third charge. Again, they decimated the royals. There was a hint of pity for them in Callan's heart. They were doing what they were told by the man who ruled them. Ramsey controlled their lives and the lives of their families. But this was war and Callan shoved all his pity that he felt to the back of his mind and out of his heart. He couldn't afford to feel bad for them.

The third attack broke the royals. They sounded their retreat horn, dropped the battering ram in the mud and made a hasty, disorganized run to the main force of their army. Arian's forces had not lost a single man or horse. Callan couldn't believe it. Some of them had picked up minor wounds and were bleeding from various cuts and scrapes that they'd taken, but none of the injuries seemed remotely life-threatening.

Callan leapt from his horse and approached the gates of Oakheart. One of the Firebrands rode behind him, carrying the banner of Graveholm. The glint of a metal helmet peeking up over the battlements alerted Callan to at least one archer watching the proceedings. He called to the men above him, "I need to speak with Lord Davin. Immediately, please."

A smooth voice called back, "Who's calling on him?"

"Lord Callan, son of Balen, the Lord of Ashefall and envoy to Lord Ravitch."

He'd done it. He had finally announced to the world that he was alive. It struck him at that point that this archer was now the first person outside of Graveholm to know that Ramsey had failed in his complete destruction of Ashefall's ruling family.

"Your father was Balen? If you're who you say you are, I served with your uncle. Tell me his name and I'll tell my lord that you need to speak with him."

"His name was Tarryn," Callan shouted back.

The archer stood up, revealing a man in plated armor and a green cape over one shoulder. Not an archer after all.

Lord Davin, Callan presumed.

Davin called down to his gatehouse, "Let them in! I'll meet them in the courtyard."

He met them quickly with a retinue of guards. All of them looked exhausted. They weren't trained soldiers, even less so than Graveholm's men. The Firebrands picketed their horses in the stables that Davin's men pointed them toward. Again, even after the attack, they didn't appear remotely tired. Callan, on the other hand, stood on quivering legs. Murdock and Dastynn stood on either side of them. He would have to rely on the two of them to prop him up if his knees gave out.

"Lord Callan," said Davin as he approached, "it really is you. I hope you don't mind me saying, but you look just like your father."

Davin, however, looked nothing like his father, but Callan kept that thought to himself. He was graying, but younger looking than his years. He must have taken after his mother because Callan could see none of the cruelty in his eyes that his father's were full of. "Not at all, Lord Davin. Thank you."

"You won't remember, but we've met before. You were weeks old, if that, and my family visited yours for a feast. Your mother let me hold you for a time. She was a great woman."

"Again," Callan said, "thank you. But we have more pressing things to talk about than my mother and father. You seem to have a problem with the king. I've got General Arian Morningblade here with me. Lord Ravitch and his son, Theamere, are on their way with the bulk of our army."

"With all of you here, we should be able to repel them easily."

Arian interrupted. "If you'll pardon my saying, my lord, nothing about this will be easy. King Ramsey's army outnumbers us at least two-to-one. We need to discuss strategy before Ravitch arrives."

Davin pursed his lips. He was obviously more confident than he had any reason to be. Callan was cautiously optimistic after watching the Firebrands do their work, but he was a realist. He knew that this was going to be incredibly difficult.

The rain began to fall in earnest.

Arian continued, "Besides that, my lord, take a look at your men. They're exhausted."

Davin looked over his shoulder, as did Callan. The Firebrands seemed fine, but the others, the ones who had been holding off the siege, were breathing hard, standing on shaking legs.

"Your people are terrified."

Beyond the soldiers, Callan could see the city folk they were supposed to be defending. They peeked out from behind windows and doors. Children hid behind their mothers and watched as their fathers prepared to defend them. The force from Greaveholm would need time to recover from its long march. They wouldn't have any time, of course, but they would need it.

"You need a plan, Lord Davin," said Callan. "If you'll listen to General Arian and do exactly as he says, we might just have a chance."

Sentinel

Chapter 35

Callan stared out of the window, into the rain-soaked dark before the dawn. His throat was dry but not because he was afraid of what was to come. He'd had problems falling asleep, even for a few meager hours, and had taken some of the medicine that Ravitch had given him. He had fallen asleep quickly, but now his tongue felt heavy and cracked. Others, down in the streets, perched on rooftops, and hiding in alleyways, were likely afraid. But Callan couldn't find it in himself to be scared. The rain came down in sheets and making enough noise as it hit the stone streets and buildings that Callan could focus on it rather than the coming battle.

Murdock and Dastynn were with him, for now. As dawn approached, Murdock would leave to defend Davin, while Dastynn would stay with Callan to do their part. They would, as Ravitch had explained earlier, be responsible for hunting down royal officers to disrupt their lines of leadership. For now, though, the three of them sat together in the cold and damp bedroom of an uninhabited house.

"Dastynn," Murdock spoke quietly, "I've been working on a gift for you."

The paladin looked up from his hammer. He had been smoothing down the stone with a small chisel. Callan wasn't sure why, and Dastynn wasn't talking. He looked inquisitively at Murdock and waited for the mage to continue.

"I created a new spell. It's taken most of my energy over the last few days, but I think that it will work." He fished around in his pocket and pulled out a silver ring, inlaid with a small red stone. Then, from a different pocket, he pulled out a silver amulet on a thin chain. It also had a red gem in the center of it. He tossed both to Dastynn.

The big man picked up the amulet and let it dangle from his huge hands. He squinted at Murdock in the darkness, then looked over to Callan, a question hiding just behind a curious frown. He seemed intrigued by the prospect of whatever it was that Murdock had done.

"Don't ask me," Callan said. "He never told me about any of this."

Callan hadn't even known that spells could be invented. He thought that it didn't seem too far-fetched, though. After all, someone had to have come up with the spells that were used by mages on a regular basis. It stood to reason that there were others out there that hadn't been discovered.

Murdock smiled. "I'm not getting excited yet. It might not work."

"But it should. Right," Callan asked?

He smiled. "It should. Dastynn, I need you to smash the amulet first."

Dastynn started. Murdock repeated himself, "Smash the amulet. It's okay. If the spell works, it works. If it doesn't, I'm just out a broken amulet. Go ahead."

Callan watched with interest as Dastynn placed the amulet on the ground and stood up, grasping his stone maul in both hands. He looked to Murdock for reassurance once and received only a small nod in response. He shrugged, then lifted the hammer over his head and brought it crashing down onto the piece of jewelry.

There was a sharp, initial crack at the amulet was crushed between the stone floor and the maul. Then a second, louder noise, that sounded as if thunder had exploded in the center of the room. A bright light flashed, staggering Callan back into the window sill. When it faded, the amulet was gone and had been replaced by a large bundle. A grin split Murdock's face in half.

"Now the ring," he said.

He swung the hammer again and one more temporarily deafened Callan. He had the sense to shield his eyes this time, though. When he lowered his hand from his face, the light had faded. Where the ring had been was an even bigger hammer than the one that Dastynn was swinging. Instead of stone, the head was made of bright blue crystal.

They had left that hammer and Dastynn's armor, which Callan assumed to be in the package, back in Ashefall, locked away in a chest.

"That's not possible," Callan said.

Murdock's smile broadened. "It wasn't, until recently. Moving people and objects through space on their own can't be done. I had to connect two pairs of objects, Dastynn's things with the ring and the amulet, and then swap them. I had been storing most of my spare energy in the gems at the center of them for over a week. When Dastynn broke them, the energy made the transfer possible."

Dastynn stood up and hugged Murdock, lifting his feet off the ground. Callan had been hugged by the paladin before. Murdock's ribs probably felt like they were going to disintegrate. The mage hugged him back, though.

"I won't be there to fight with you, but I'll be damned if I'm not going to do everything I can to keep you safe. If that means getting you your hammer and your armor, then so be it."

Someone knocked on their door. Dastynn let Murdock down and answered it. Lord Davin stood on the other side, dripping wet with rain and looking scared out of his mind.

Callan jumped to his feet. "What's wrong?"

The Lord of Oakheart wrung his hands together and stammered, "Murdock, it will be dawn soon. If you would be so kind as to…to wait for me at the castle, I'll…I'll be there shortly."

He sucked in a deep breath and cast frightened eyes toward Callan. "A group, a mob really, a big one…they've said that they're leaving. They won't fight. They said that they wouldn't have died for my father and they won't die for me. We can't lose them."

Murdock gasped quietly. A sinister growl emanated from Dastynn's throat. He didn't need words to share how he felt. Callan felt much the same way. He had an obligation to remain level-headed. So did Davin, but he obviously didn't have his emotions together.

"Don't worry. We won't lose them," Callan said. "Murdock, go to the castle and wait for Lord Davin. Dastynn, you come with me."

Lord Davin asked, "Where are you going?"

"I'm going to remind them what we're fighting for."

He had to wait for Dastynn to don his armor. First came the chainmail vest, then a dark blue, plated one to go over it. Then a similar setup on his legs. Next came the plated gauntlets and graves. He topped it off with a midnight-blue coat that covered his arms to the wrists and nearly brushed the ground when he walked. The paladin hefted his hammer and followed Callan out into the rain.

Callan sunk nearly ankle-deep into the mud. He grimaced and pulled his foot out with a sucking sound and walked toward the sound of the crowd that was obvious now that they were outside. He moved as quickly as he could, until they came into view. There were hundreds of them. Thousands. A writhing mob, screaming in the streets when they should have been resting. There were only a few hours left until dawn, when the royals would undoubtedly be attacking.

He caught sight of Theamere, milling around amongst them, shoving and yelling, trying to get them to settle down. If anything, he made things worse. Callan shook his head. Ravitch's son had a good heart, and he meant well, but he didn't understand people. He didn't know how to calm down a single person, let alone an entire group of worked up soldiers and peasants, all against fighting for a man they didn't respect. That was the root cause of the problem, after all. They didn't respect Davin. Callan didn't even know him, had hardly met him, and he had a hard time seeing him as anything more than a nice man. These people knew Davin better than Callan did. If he really was an incompetent leader, they would know. From what Callan had seen of the man's father, the entire family was more than likely looked on in a poor light.

"Come on, Dastynn. We need to get to higher ground."

Callan followed behind the paladin, as he shouldered his way through the teeming mass of people. Those that saw him coming had the sense to move out of the big man's way. Those who didn't see him felt him when he shoved them out of the way.

Callan caught bits and pieces of the screaming.

"We won't die for you!"

"I can't leave my family!"

"Ramsey is our king!"

Callan and Dastynn found a raised statue in the middle of the square where the mob had gathered. It depicted a man, dressed for farming, that stood over twice Callan's height. Rather, it had before age, weather, and other abuses had removed its head and neck. The top of its shovel was weathered away as well. The two of them climbed the steps onto the platform that the statue stood on. They now stood almost entirely above the crowd.

Callan shouted, "Hey! Listen"

Not one person turned to him.

"You can't give up on this fight!"

Again, none of them.

"If you think that they'll spare you, you're wrong!"

Dastynn placed his hand on Callan's shoulder. He stopped shouting. None of them were paying him the slightest bit of attention. They were too busy screaming at their officers and at Theamere.

Dastynn held up his hammer. Callan could have sworn that the massive gem that made up the hammer's head was glowing from within.

It was. The glow grew, blue first, then so bright that it seemed almost white. It turned the blackness of the square to day. Callan threw his arm up in front of his face to shield his eyes. So did the soldiers. The light stunned them into silence. As it faded, Callan brought down his arm. Dastynn lowered the hammer, and with it, the light. They all stared at him now. He had their undivided attention.

Callan nodded his thanks to Dastynn, and then spoke to the crowd, "I know that this doesn't look good."

They started screaming again. Callan cringed. Dastynn raised his hammer, but before he could bring the light to blind them again, the crowd got the message and quieted down.

"I know that this doesn't look good," he repeated. "These soldiers have come to your home, your city, to burn you out of it, all because your lord spoke in favor of the rebellion."

The crowd shifted as one. It had almost taken on a life of its own, a giant, swarming beast.

"It isn't fair, but it's happening. You *are* in danger. Your homes, your families, your lives are all in danger." He raised his voice, becoming more and more confident in himself as he spoke. "Ramsey has done this before! Three years ago, he came to Ashefall and killed everyone I ever loved. His soldiers cut down people I had known for my entire life. They got my friends and my family. Ramsey's dragons burned my home to the ground."

They had heard the rumors of dragons by now. Callan wasn't sure how they had started. This was the first that he had openly talked about the dragons since that awful night three years ago. Maybe some scouting patrol, sent to assess the damage to Ashefall. Maybe

Murdock, or Theamere, or even Ravitch. It didn't matter. The people of Oakheart knew about them, and they were terrified.

"You all know the stories of Ragnar the Slayer. The man that killed a dragon."

Some nodded. Others only watched.

"He was one man. One man, who brought down one of those monsters with his own hands. What makes any of you different? You have your friends, your families, and your homes at your back. No, you don't have the training or the armor. You don't have masterfully made weapons. You don't fight for a living…no one is paying you to be here."

"You have something that they don't, though."

He paused, letting his message sink in. He wanted them to think about it. Wanted them to squirm, wondering what they could possibly have that the royal army didn't.

"You have desperation. They have made you desperate, and in doing so, they have made you dangerous."

The crowd roared back at him, but this time, their anger wasn't directed at him or at their officers. It was directed at the army that waited for them to come out of their city. The army that waited to force them from their homes.

"Tell me that you're ready to give up your homes! Tell me that you are ready to watch your wives and your children die so that Ramsey can prove a point!"

No one said a word.

"No? Then tell Ramsey that if he wants a *thing* from you, then he's going to have to pry it from your dead hands!"

They screamed back at him.

And over the horizon, dawn broke.

Chapter 36

The gates fell quickly. They splintered and collapsed under the might of two battering rams. Callan heard it happen from his position in the city. As soon as the gates fell, soldiers would be pouring into the city like ants over a hill. This was where the rebels had the advantage. They would use the streets, the alleys, the buildings, and everything else in Oakheart to their advantage.

Callan's small force was grouped in a leather shop, which had been abandoned by the family that owned it when the armies had arrived.

"The gates are down," Callan said to the men. "We wait a quarter of an hour, then we move. The first officer we see dies. Got it?"

They all nodded. Callan was no expert in war. He'd never led men into battle before. However, he had proven that he had some skill at selecting a target and neutralizing it. Hopefully, by killing the leaders of the royal army, they could create enough disruption in the ranks to give themselves a significant advantage. The goal of this battle was not to kill every royal in the field. That just wasn't realistic. There were too many of them for that. Instead, they had to make taking Oakheart not worth the loss of men that the royals would suffer. They had to make sure that the prize was not worth the price of winning.

Callan looked to Dastynn. "Are you ready?"

In answer, the paladin lifted the hood on his coat. A thick mist formed in front of his face and coalesced into a black mask, trimmed in the same deep blue as his coat. There were no eye slits of any kind.

"You can see out of that?"

Dastynn nodded.

"Okay then," Callan said. "Let's move out. Dastynn, we'll follow your lead."

The paladin hefted his war hammer and walked out into the street with Callan and the rest close behind. The street that they were on was empty so they took a left turn and headed toward the gates and the sounds of battle.

The closer they got, the more Callan could make out the differences in the sounds that he was hearing. At first, it was just white noise. A far-off rumbling. The group of them rounded a corner and came into an alley. Empty. Now he could hear the distinct sound of metal on metal. Men screaming. Callan's heart began to race. He hadn't seen a real battle in his lifetime. Not really. The attack on Ashefall had been a slaughter, not a real battle. His assassination of Lord Delaney had been just that. An assassination. His chase of the spies had ended up being more of a brawl than anything else.

Now, he followed behind one of his only friends in the world into a real fight. Men on both sides would die. Already had died. He would be responsible for some of those deaths, either by sticking his sword into them or giving the order for someone else to do it.

Remember why you're doing this.

His family was dead because of Ramsey. As much as he hated that soldiers had to die for him to get at the king, he was willing to do what was necessary. Beyond that, beyond revenge, he had to make sure that Ramsey thought twice before sending his army after anyone who spoke out against him.

The group came out of the alley and ran right into a group of royals. Callan's sword was out of the sheath on his back and in the stomach of the nearest royal before any of them had time to react. He ducked a swipe at his head and jumped backward, out of the way of a return swing. Dastynn's crystalline hammer struck Callan's assailant in the chest and sent him tumbling. A pair of arrows sprouted from the chest of another royal. Two more went down under the weight of Callan's footmen.

Callan spun around to assess his men with blood still pounding in his ears. They hadn't lost a man. None of them were even injured, it seemed. They were lucky.

"Everyone ready?" They all nodded back at him. "Okay, keep going. After you, Dastynn."

They hurried along the city streets toward what sounded like the edge of the battle. It was quieter there, anyway, and Callan hoped to get a good vantage point. They were in a wealthy part of the city. The buildings were all connected with no way to see between them. The group ran down the wide avenue without seeing another soul but surrounded by the sound of warfare.

They rounded the corner and caught what they had been looking for, a line of royal soldiers. Among them was a man on a tall horse, wearing purple and yellow feathers in his helm. The mark of one of Ramsey's field officers. Unfortunately for them, he saw them at the same time that they saw him. The officer rallied the men nearest him, and they advanced toward the group of ten in an organized march.

Callan grouped his men quickly and haphazardly but as well as he could with the time that he had. He and Dastynn were in front with the five swordsmen lined up behind them in a loose clump. The three archers flanked them.

They had all seen Dastynn fight by now. They knew that the best course of action was to let him initiate any kind of fighting. He knew that as well. Dastynn held his hammer to one side and lifted his hand to the incoming soldiers, palm forward in a way that Callan had only seen once before. When the paladin had been defending him from a different group of soldiers. The ones that he had focused in on then hadn't fared well.

Neither did these.

A white-blue ball of magic sprung from his palm and slammed into one of the approaching men and blasted him backward into his comrades. They got up and continued their slow advance. He did not. One more man fell in the same way before the royals changed their tactic. With a shout from their commander, they charged.

Two arrows flew from Callan's left and one from his right. Only one of them struck its target, leaving a bleeding hole in the front shoulder of the officer's horse. The animal screamed, but its rider forced it forward with the rest of his men.

Then the forces collided.

Callan's entire world became flashes of steel. He could make out no details on anyone. He didn't see faces or expressions or body language or men with lives. He saw suits of armor with weak points in the joins and neck. He stabbed, parried, shifted his weight around, stabbed again, slashed, dodged, ducked, slashed, and swung his sword until everyone who came in front of him was dead.

He took stock of the fight, ignoring the blood dripping from the end of his sword and pooling on the ground. Ignoring the blood that had splashed onto his face from the wounds he'd inflicted on others. They had lost one of the archers. Callan wanted to bury him but knew that now wasn't the time. There were a lot of men who wouldn't be getting a proper burial or a funeral pyre today. The royal officer was dead and lying in a broken heap on the cobblestones. His horse was nowhere to be found. It must have thrown him.

Callan signaled for his remaining men to carry on. They didn't have the luxury of rest. As they resumed their trek through the city, a line of men turned from the main battle and faced them. Another officer led them. He had many more men with him than the first did.

As they charged, Callan lifted his sword in preparation. There was a job to do, and he meant to see it done.

Dastynn stepped in front, again taking the point. Callan had never asked the paladin to put his own safety before Callan's own. He meant to make it up to him after this was all over. Dastynn turned his armored shoulder to the rushing soldiers. When they were within feet of him, a pulse, the same color as the magic that he had been throwing earlier, sizzled the air in front of the rebels. The royals leading the charge were thrown into the sky, to the sides, straight back. Those who collided with buildings did so with wet *thumps*. The men who were shot into more open areas skidded and bounced until their momentum died, leaving them in still heaps. Those that went airborne crashed down, splattering the cobbles with their remains.

The survivors hesitated, mouths agape and eyes wide. Their legs shook and weapons trembled in suddenly weak hands. Dastynn struck out, slamming the top of his hammer into the chest of the nearest enemy combatant. The man's chest shattered with a *crunch* that Callan felt throughout his entire body. The attack acted as a signal for the rest of their little band to jump to action.

Again, a steel blur clouded Callan's vision. He saw nothing but steel and blood but vaguely remembered the techniques that he'd been taught. The ones that he'd trained for the past years to master. A slice along his left forearm brought the battle into stark clarity. He was staring down an officer, now off his horse. The rest of the royals were dead behind their commander. Callan didn't risk looking over his own back to see how many men he'd lost.

The officer sneered and advanced. Callan moved to parry, but a bolt of pain shot through his injured arm. He didn't move fast enough to block his opponent's feint. He earned another small slice, this time on the front of his leg.

The light armor that he had chosen because of the freedom of movement that it offered did almost nothing against good steel. He would be cut to ribbons if he didn't do something soon. The officer danced around him, favoring Callan's injured side. Both of his injuries were on the left side of his body, leaving a gaping hole in both his offense and defense. The man moved in and out like a snake, trying to land more small strikes on Callan's body. Nothing pierced his thin armor, though. Callan landed blows that were just as ineffective and bounced off chainmail and plated armor.

He was getting dizzy.

The officer broke through Callan's guard and struck out with the pommel of his sword. The blade's handle *clunked* into Callan's forehead. He stumbled back, the world fading to gray around him.

Screams saved him from falling to the dark. His face was hot. He tasted blood. The pommel had opened a gash on his head and it was bleeding into his mouth. He spat. Why was there so much screaming? Why was it different? The officer advanced, swinging his sword at Callan's head. He ducked, and the force of the attack left the royal off balance. Callan lunged forward and drove the point of his sword into the man's armpit, in the weakest area of his armor. He collapsed, dead before he hit the ground.

Still, he could hear screaming. He looked around, trying to catch his bearings. Blood loss still had him dizzy, as did the blow to his head. Callan staggered in a circle as realization came upon him. Those weren't the screams of battle or of men fighting men. Those were scared screams. Terrified.

An armored group rounded a corner, sprinting toward Callan's position. He could see purple, gold, red, blue, black, and green among them, marking them as both rebels and royals. They ran past Callan, ignoring him and the others near him. They were yelling, some crying, others making incoherent noises. He caught only one word.

Dragon.

The force of that one word nearly floored Callan.

Suddenly, he was back home. Back at Ashefall. Fires were burning along the ramparts and the grounds while people Callan had known his entire life choked to death on poisonous fumes. He tasted bile and felt sick again as Dastynn dragged him through the crowd to his family. The screams were the same.

"Dragon!"

Through his daze, Callan hurried in the opposite direction of the now steady stream of soldiers trying to escape, toward the source of their fear. They ignored him, and he let them run. The rebels might have been deserting their duties, but he could hardly blame them if there was a dragon. Ravitch could deal with them later.

He rounded the last corner on the street. There it was. The dragon perched on the side of a tall building, its vivid green scales and leathery wings shining in the sunlight. Atop its back, wielding a familiar staff, was bald man with a shaggy beard. Not King Ramsey. The dragon roared, spewing forth the same fumes that had strangled the life from the citizens of Ashefall. It fell heavy on the streets of Oakheart, coating the street like a fine mist. The red dragon, the fire-starter, was nowhere to be seen.

A heavy hand touched Callan's shoulder. Dastynn. Sometime during the fighting, he had removed his mask, showing his face to the world. The paladin's eyes were set, his jaw clenched. His other hand gripped the handle of his hammer at his side. Together, they watched rebel and royal alike collapse into writhing, gagging heaps on the ground.

"Dastynn," said Callan, "we have to do something."

With another earsplitting roar, the dragon leapt from the building's facade and crashed to the street below. Its massive claws tore cobbles from their place and threw rubble high into the air. It rained back down like gray ashes, coating everything near the dragon in a thin film of dust. The man atop its back waved his staff once, and the dragon snapped out its neck, grabbing a retreating rebel in its mouth and biting down with knife-like teeth. The soldier's cry of terror and pain was cut short by the bite, which severed his chest from the lower half of his body. The dragon dropped both pieces and turned to his next victim, slashing out with one of its front legs. Three deep rents opened in the man's chest, and he fell to the ground in a puddle of blood.

Some of the braver men attacked the beast. Arrows bounced off its scales like raindrops on the surface of a lake. Spears broke against its legs and chest. Men broke as well, falling like grass before a scythe to the dragon's claws. Those who avoided being sliced open were crushed against buildings by its tail, which was as thick around as Callan's torso.

"Dastynn. What can we do?"

Dastynn shook his head and shrugged his shoulders. Callan hadn't expected an answer. They couldn't kill this dragon. No man here was Ragnar the Slayer. Even if Callan really was descended from him, lineage meant less than nothing. He could not kill a dragon.

His eyes caught the bearded man on the dragon's back, waving his spears and shouting orders in a language that Callan had never heard before.

He could kill a man, though.

Callan's knuckles turned white on the hilt of his sword. "Can you distract it?"

Dastynn's eyes widened, questioning. Callan knew that what he asked was likely suicide. But he would ask the same of himself, and he wouldn't trust anyone but the paladin to do what needed to be done.

"I need you to make sure that it stays where it is. Can you do that?"

Dastynn set his mouth into a hard line. He hefted his hammer and nodded once to Callan, the veil of mist already reforming the blank mast in front of his face.

"Go!"

The two of them ran toward the dragon, Dastynn heading straight for it, Callan slightly to its left. The dragon's rider was protected by the monster's large body and canvas-like wings. Neither arrows nor swords could touch him. An attack from above, however…

Callan thought that he must have hit his head harder that he'd thought to even consider something like what he was thinking. The ground quaked around him as a ball of light struck the dragon in the chest. Dastynn's work. The area that was hit smoked, but looked no worse for wear. The serpent head snapped to the paladin and opened its maw in a roar that vibrated Callan's bones.

He darted into the shadow of the dragon's wings and into the nearest building. Immediately, he went to the stairs and started climbing. Once on the second floor, he found a window and glanced out. He could see only green scales. Higher, then. Again, Callan climbed. On the third floor, there were no windows. The entire building shook. Stone began to crumble from the walls and ceilings. Something *very* heavy had just hit the building.

One more floor, Callan thought.

He reached the fourth floor, the top. Again, the building shook. This floor had windows along the street-side wall. Callan ran to them and peered out.

The poisonous mist had dissipated, leaving the remaining cobblestones carpeted in bodies and discarded weapons. Groups of men still fired arrows and threw spears at the dragon. Futile. Dastynn was there, one arm hanging by his side and his hammer nowhere to be seen. He threw an almost constant stream of blue-white spheres at the beast's scaled face and chest. Its rider was focused on the paladin, oblivious to Callan, who was at least ten feet above him.

Callan whispered under his breath, "Mithaniel keep me safe," and turned his back on the window.

"Anashti keep my body safe. Jasko, god of fools, I need you now. Merrick, Eagle of Peace, help me to end this."

There were thirteen gods, but Callan was too shaken to remember all of them in his prayer. He could always apologize in the afterlife.

He breathed deeply and turned back the window at a sprint. His legs brought him across the room in what seemed like a heartbeat. He jumped out the window, soaring into open air. The jump was not a difficult one, once he'd made it. The dragon's back took up every bit of space beneath him. The bearded rider still had no idea that Callan was there.

He struck the man with his entire body, throwing him off the dragon's back. Callan went with him, tumbling through the air in a mess of arms and legs. The two of them hit the ground together, side-by-side.

Callan noticed the look of pure disbelief in the rider's face before his own head struck the ground, sending him into darkness.

Chapter 37

They came through the wall like phantoms, killing indiscriminately on the way. Most of the soldiers who had been near the wall when the missile hit were in no shape to get up and fight. The Visani executed them, putting them out of their misery before they had even regained their senses or their footing. Those who had kept their feet lived longer, but not much. They were pummeled, knocked over, or killed where they stood.

Gramm glanced back at Pyra. "Go! I'm right behind you," she said.

The two of them ran to the breach in the wall. Gramm dove right in to the fight, plunging his sword into the chest of the nearest Visani. Pyra searched within herself for the power that surged in her veins. She was getting better at accessing it. Still, even with years of training, the power would not always come immediately. She thought of the Visani mother that she had killed earlier. Pyra had been acting completely on instinct, then. Now, though, she had time to think and plan and worry. Calling the magic was more difficult.

One of the Visani crashed into her from the side, tackling her to the ground. The power came, then, almost as if it knew that she was in trouble. The Visani roared in her face, baring dagger-like teeth. Pyra turned her palms upward and released twin balls of fire into the feline's chest. The light of the blast nearly blinded her, but the Visani was launched into the air, nothing more than a smoldering corpse.

Fire had always been Pyra's most potent weapon, the easiest of the magics for her to control. Maybe it was luck that he father had named her for fire. Maybe the name was a small blessing from Gargrave himself. No matter the reason for her inherent ability, she meant to burn the attackers from her keep.

Another ball of fire from her hands smote a Visani as it crawled through the crater left by the catapult. A wave of her hand caused snow to drift up and around the ankles of another, where it solidified into icy shackles. The Visani was rooted in place until Pyra charred it to the bone.

There was another sound like thunder, and the ground trembled beneath Pyra's feet. Another boulder from the catapult, it must have been. She spun, catching a glimpse of smoke and dust rising from the newest wound in the wall, further to the east than the first had been. Pyra couldn't see them, but she could imagine the predators climbing through, into the yard of her keep, slaughtering her soldiers and those she had promised to protect.

Gramm dove past her, slamming his shield into the face of a man who had come up on her when she wasn't looking. The man's nose broke in a spray of blood. He had no time to recover before Gramm ran him through.

"Thank you."

"Don't thank me," he said. "We have to do something. There are too many of them."

"I know, I know!"

She waved her arms again, this time encasing an entire man in a drift of snow. It too, turned to crystalline ice, leaving him in a frozen tomb. They needed to be able to kill more of the attackers at once. *She* needed to be able to kill more of them at once. A sword or an arrow could only do so much. Magic, on the other hand…

Pyra left Gramm's side and ran the short distance to the boulder's impact zone. Neither the wall nor the boulder had survived the impact in one piece, but there were enormous bits of stone, nearly chin-high on Pyra, scattered around the area. She reached out with her mind and wrapped her consciousness around a large hunk of rock, then lifted.

Every muscle in her body strained with the effort. Her back bent, and her brain throbbed with the strain of hefting the huge weight into the air. But it moved. The boulder quivered and limped higher and higher until it floated a few feet above her head. Those who noticed what she was doing stared in open-mouthed wonder. Even the Visani and the humans who had attacked with them.

Then she *pushed* and threw the chuck of charred rock at a group of charging men. They saw it in time and dove to either side, dodging it completely. The rock bounced and rolled for a few meters, then stilled, having done no damage to the enemy at all.

Pyra's energy fled her body then, more quickly than it ever had when she had summoned fire or done any other kind of magic. She collapsed to the ground, legs too weak to support even her small frame.

Through blurred eyes, she saw Gramm rush to her side. He stood over her, swinging his sword and shield like an armored whirlwind. Men and Visani fell before him, most not even leaving a scratch on his silver armor before they fell to the ground in a bleeding pile. Others were more successful, though. Gramm was cut on his waist and at his shoulder by lucky strikes that found a way into the joints of his armor. Blood bloomed at the wounds and trickled down his body into the white powder on the ground.

Pyra had to get up and help him. She was so tired, though. So exhausted. She'd never tried to lift anything with magic before, and now she understood why Elder Moss had never taught her that it was possible. Every bit of energy that she had was drained from her and every limb shook like she'd just run up and down the mountains that surrounded Graveholm.

Gramm took another cut, this time to his elbow. His shield dipped as the strength began to flee his powerful arms. He kicked out at his attacker, breaking the man's shin, and then stabbed him through the thin armor on his chest. He was slowing. Pyra *had* to get up. Had to help him.

"I'm coming. I'm coming, Gramm."

She spoke so quietly that she could barely hear herself. Still, Pyra rolled onto her stomach and pushed herself to her hands and knees. Her vision dimmed with the effort, but she couldn't stop. She had to get up. She forced herself to her knees. She swayed in place, but found that she was stable if she didn't move too much. With a growl, she waved her arm and threw a ball of fire at one of Gramm's assailants. The magic was weak. Much weaker than it had been earlier. Even so, the fire seared the Visani across the back and sent him rolling to the ground, howling in pain. Gramm finished him there.

He turned to her, eyes wild. "Get inside! Go!"

Pyra shook her head. Even if she wanted to run away, she couldn't. He nodded, understanding the kind of shape that she was in then. He seemed nearly there himself. A Visani jumped onto his back and wrapped its claws around Gramm's chest. He staggered and dropped his sword to the ground. Rather than drop his shield, too, he moved it from his injured arm to his other, where he tried to defend from the men who still attacked his front.

The Visani's claws left deep rents in Gramm's armor. Pyra could only watch. She couldn't risk hurting Gramm if she threw fire at the Visani. One wrong move by either of them, and he would end up dead. But if she didn't act…

She screamed in frustration.

Gramm drove his elbow into the side of the Visani on his back. He couldn't quite dislodge it so he hit it again and again and again until it let go of him and took a step back, snarling. Gramm spun and delivered a backhanded blow to the Visani's face with his shield, shattering teeth and bones. It reeled back momentarily, and then slashed out, catching Gramm full in the cheek. He fell to the ground, deep rivets forming from jaw to forehead. He didn't move.

"No!" Pyra flung a fireball at the Visani and engulfed the creature in searing flames. It fell to the snow, screaming as it burned alive.

Pyra dragged herself through the snow toward Gramm. She couldn't yell for him, she didn't have the voice left, but she could crawl. He stirred on his own before she got there. His eyes flickered in her direction. He rolled slowly and stood, facing his opponents. They were circling, eyeing the two of them cautiously. None of the others were keen on getting set alight or being clubbed to death, it seemed. One of the humans stopped completely and raised his arm. Surrender?

No. An arrow whistled by Pyra's head and punched a hole in Gramm's armor, just above his knee. Gramm's eyes fell to the shaft that jutted out of his thigh. In a daze, he tried to put weight on it, but fell to the ground with a pained yell. The invaders advanced, closing in on their fallen opponent. Only then did Pyra realize how many of them he had been fighting. There were at least a dozen left, with seven or eight dead on the ground. She had caused this. It was her fault. She should have known better than to try being a hero. To try being a leader. She should have known her limits.

"That's enough," said a voice behind Pyra. It was firm. Commanding. Very human.

"Leave him be." Pyra couldn't see who was speaking, but the others listened to him. "Rale," the voice said, "get the battering ram and bring those doors down. Don't kill anyone else unless you have to."

Someone scurried off. Strong hands gripped Pyra by the shoulders and hauled her to her feet. The hands spun her around until she was face to face with an older man, his face scarred and weathered.

He smelled as if he hadn't bathed in days or weeks. He probably hadn't. He had a beard, but it also looked as if he wasn't accustomed to it.

He looked familiar.

"I know you," Pyra breathed.

He nodded. "You do."

Then he drove a knife into her chest. Once. Twice. Three times. Four times.

He let her fall to the ground and walked away.

She was warm. And more tired than before. Something knelt by her face. She couldn't move. All she could see was white fur. She smelled stinking breath.

"*Ro vamir no rokhar.*"

She couldn't talk. Couldn't move. Her shirt was wet. Why was her shirt wet?

"*Ro vamir no rokhar.*"

What? She couldn't understand. Couldn't speak. So tired. So warm. She wanted to sleep.

"You killed my mother."

She wanted to apologize. Couldn't. Couldn't move. So tired.

She slept.

Epilogue

"Your people have worshipped thirteen gods for centuries. Telaran, the Lord of the Sky. Gargrave, the Dragon's Fire. Karana, the Sea Maiden. Chytae, Caretaker of the Wilds. Dorian and Vala, the Sun and Moon. Tersis, War-Crazed and his brother, Merrick the Peacebringer. Vega, Protector of the Witless. Cassaundra, the Waykeeper. Mithaniel, the Warrior's Heart. Anashti, the Woundbinder. Sabriel, the Black Wings of Death."

Callan stirred and looked around. He could see nothing. The voice that spoke to him had no form. It came from above, below, all around. But it was familiar. He knew this voice.

"Why are you telling me this? I know my own people's religion," Callan said.

"There was another. A fourteenth god, bound in eternal chains by the others," the voice continued. "More destructive than fire, more wild than the most violent of wars, he was locked away for the safety of the world."

"Why are you telling me?"

"Babylon, Harbinger of Darkness. Bringer of End Times. He has broken free of his bonds. He is coming."

Callan screamed into the blackness, "Why me? What can I do?"

"Protect them."

"Who? How?"

"Babylon comes."

Callan's eyes flickered open. General Morningblade stood above him, a smile on his normally placid face. Callan was in a bed. Warm, comfortable. In pain, but comfortable. Sun shone through a window to his left.

"Well, well," he said, "you made it after all."

"What happened?" Callan croaked out. His voice was weak and it hurt to talk. Everything hurt, his head especially.

"You dove out of a fourth story window and tackled a man off the back of a dragon. You killed him, by the way."

"The dragon. What happened to the dragon?"

Arian shrugged. "Once you killed its rider, it flew away. North, toward the mountains. When it left, the royals lost all willingness to fight. They either ran away or surrendered." He paused, looking thoughtfully at Callan. "That was incredibly stupid, you know."

"I know." Callan nodded. "It had to be done, though. What happened to Dastynn? He was distracting it for me."

"He'll be alright. Broken arm. Inhaled some of that gas, but he'll be just fine. All of your friends are fine. The Firebrands are, for the most part, fine. I can't say the same for the people of Oakheart, though. Most of the ones who fought died."

Callan's heart sank. He had done everything in his power to make sure they fought for the rebels. Now they were dead. Dead defending their own city from an enemy that Callan's father had helped to create. Guilt tightened around his stomach like a fist.

"I might as well have killed them myself."

The general laid a hand on Callan's shoulder. "You can't let yourself think like that. They died defending their homes. If they hadn't given their lives, the royals might have overrun Oakheart and killed them anyway, along with their families."

Callan looked down at his bedsheets.

"You can't protect everyone, Callan. No one man can."

I have to though, Callan thought. *I have to protect them all from him.*

"That isn't going to stop me from trying," he said.

Arian nodded and removed his hand from Callan's arm. He looked unconvinced. "That," he said, "is what separates good leaders from great ones. A sense of morality. The ideal that you can save everyone from every danger. You can't save them all, no matter how badly you want to. Understand that. Those who do, will live longer."

"Understand this, General, as long as I'm able, I'm going to keep as many of my people alive as I possibly can."

"You can't protect them from everything," he said and walked from Callan's room.

To his back, Callan said, "I have to. I have to protect them."

Babylon comes.

Acknowledgments

There are so many people to thank for making this book a possibility. I'll do my best to include everyone.

Firstly, I can't thank my parents enough for everything they've done for me. Besides feeding me and keeping a roof over my head for my entire life, nobody has supported my writing more than my mom and dad. Dad was the first person to read Sentinel, and he finished it in three days. The first draft was a gift to Mom for her birthday. Words cannot express what your support has meant to me. Thank you so much.

Dr. Maria Moore...what can I say? Without you, Sentinel doesn't exist. Without you, I probably still haven't graduated from ISU. I am so unbelievably grateful that I took your classes and that you had my back during my senior year. Rest assured that I will pass on the kindness that you showed me.

My beautiful girlfriend, Jessica. You've dragged me up from some rough times and made me write when I didn't think that I was writing anything worth reading. You're my rock and I love you so much.

Jordan. We've been spitballing ideas for stories since we were in seventh grade. The friendship and inspiration you've given me are completely invaluable. Thank you.

Mike, at some points I wasn't sure I would get this book finished. You told me at one point, "You're a writer. Sit your ass down and write. That's all you can do." I remember that every time I need a boost.

Kossie, Toff, Indy, Manda, Rocket, Tris, Jazz, Alex, Monty, Fels, Koko, Chuck, Chris, Remy, Moonie, Andy, Thom, Clover, and anyone else who has ever been involved in SS. You guys got me through a lot of hard times and got me started taking my writing seriously. I love you all and want nothing but the best for all of you.

Charlie and Hayley, the advice and friendship that you've both given me from day one has meant more to me than you can know. I can only hope that both of you enjoy much success and take all the enjoyment in the world from the road that we're all on.

Tim Marquitz, my awesome editor. This book wouldn't be what it is without you and all the help you've given me.

Finally, I would be remiss to not thank anyone who is reading Sentinel. I can only hope that something about my story sticks with you. Because, as much as I love to write, telling a story is pretty pointless without someone to tell it to. By reading this, you have supported me and I cannot thank you enough for that.

May your swords stay sharp and your eyes on the horizon.

-Chad Ballard

About the Author

Chad Ballard is 26 years old and lives just outside of Peoria, IL with his girlfriend. He's a graduate of Illinois State University with a degree in broadcast journalism and a minor in creative writing. He has 3 cats: Stark, Oliver, and Izzy. His debut novel, Sentinel, was released on December 8th, 2015. When not working or writing, he spends his free time with a good book or a good game.